ONE HUNDRED
GIRLS'
MOTHER

ONE HUNDRED
GIRLS'
MOTHER

Lenore Carroll

A Tom Doherty Associates Book
New York

This is a work of fiction. All the characters and events
portrayed in this novel are either fictitious or are
used fictitiously.

ONE HUNDRED GIRLS' MOTHER

Copyright © 1998 by Lenore Carroll

This book is printed on acid-free paper.

A Forge Book
Published by Tom Doherty Associates, Inc.
175 Fifth Avenue
New York, NY 10010

Forge® is a registered trademark of Tom Doherty
Associates, Inc.

Design by Lynn Newmark

Library of Congress Cataloging-in-Publication Data

Carroll, Lenore.
One hundred girls' mother / Lenore Carroll. — 1st ed.
       p.   cm.
"A Tom Doherty Associates book."
ISBN 0-312-85994-5
I. Title.
PS3553.A7648054   1998
813'.54—dc21   98-23497
                CIP

First Edition: September 1998

Printed in the United States of America

0 9 8 7 6 5 4 3 2 1

To John William Carroll and Michael Leaton Carroll

The character of Thomasina McIntyre was inspired by the life of Donaldina Cameron, but is a work of fiction and imagination and should not be confused with the historical person.

Acknowledgments and thanks:

To Natalia Aponte, for the original suggestion.

To S. Gail Miller and Cassandra Leoncini, for practical help and advice.

To Amy Leimkuhler, reference librarian, University of Missouri–Kansas City Miller Nichols Library and to the Inter-Library Loan Department.

To Tim Richards, Modern Language Department, UMKC.

To Shu Chen, international student, UMKC.

To Nancy Erlich, of the Covenant Presbyterian Church, Kansas City.

To Charles Hammer and John Mort, fine writers themselves, who read the manuscript and made valuable suggestions, most of which I followed.

To Max Evans, a generous writer and friend, for his kind words.

Note: Chinese names are given family name first, then given name. Many of the girls were orphans and had no family name. Christian Chinese names are given Western-style—given name first, then family name.

ONE HUNDRED
GIRLS'
MOTHER

INITIATION

 1895

1

Miss Margaret Culbertson hurried through rainy midnight Chinatown streets, leading tiny Chun Mei, her translator, and two policemen down the San Francisco hills. Thomasina McIntyre, her twenty-six-year-old assistant, followed—breathless with fear.

Every movement startled Thomasina and the sound of their breathing and the scuffle of their shoes on the wet pavement tightened her nerves. If she stopped walking, her knees would shake. She wanted to turn around, but Miss Culbertson led and Thomasina followed.

Miss Culbertson coughed. The elderly woman looked too frail to lead them, but as the director of the Presbyterian Occidental Mission in San Francisco her duties included this errand—raiding a Chinese bordello to rescue a prostitute. She had the strength of a giant for her unfortunates.

Thomasina was scared to death to be out after midnight in Chinatown's alleys, even with two six-foot-tall policemen with billy sticks. Chun Mei, as fearless as Miss Culbertson, followed one half step behind, watching Miss Culbertson intently.

"This one, John Francis," said Miss Culbertson, directing the policeman. The five of them hurried down Spofford Alley.

So far, no one had shouted or given an alarm. The element of surprise was still theirs. Thomasina had never been on a raid before. She didn't know what would happen, and she was too frightened to think.

Miss Culbertson stood at the door and nodded at the policeman on her left. Thomasina jumped when the policeman pounded on the door. Water dripping off Chinatown eaves and awnings sounded like a running creek, some sinister waterway in the midnight city. Her nerves coiled ready to snap.

Miss Culbertson stood straight, waiting, then she spoke to the policeman and he pounded again. The second policeman watched the alley entrance. They were below Stockton, a few blocks from the square, in the heart of Chinatown.

Thomasina could see the beads of rain on the shoulders of Miss Culbertson's coat. Miss Culbertson, a proper Presbyterian lady wearing a serviceable coat and a styleless hat and sturdy boots, looked an unlikely angel. Even less likely was Chun Mei, Miss Culbertson's shadow—so tiny, so unobtrusive, Thomasina forgot she was there, but essential when needed. Thomasina suspected Chun Mei made clear in her translations what Miss Culbertson really meant, rather than what she said.

The five of them impatiently waited for the door—recessed and decorated with a curved, painted lintel—to open. Only muffled sounds of distant traffic and the bell of a cable car reached them through the fog. Respectable women weren't out on Chinatown streets at this hour.

Chun Mei shouted a command in Chinese, then repeated it. In this year of our Lord 1895 Miss Culbertson had managed to find two honest policemen in San Francisco's corrupt force. The fog grew in the alley, then the spy hole in the door slid open.

"We have a warrant for a woman, Wong Liu," said Miss Culbertson. Chun Mei spoke in Chinese, in an assertive tone. Miss

Culbertson's voice seemed reedy and thin but her determination was audible. She radiated righteous energy.

"Nobody here that name," came a man's voice. Thomasina couldn't see a face from where she stood. The thick, painted door looked solid. How would they get inside? Her knees weakened.

"We have a warrant," growled John Francis. The second policeman stood watching the street, his hands clasped behind him. "Open up," demanded John Francis. Miss Culbertson pulled a legal document from her pocket and flourished it.

Thomasina heard the bolt slide, John Francis shouldered the door open, then the five of them rushed inside. Miss Culbertson brushed past the objecting Chinese man and charged down the hall. Chun Mei followed half a step behind. The man, who wore a long dark gown and slippers, called an alarm, shouted in Chinese, and waved his arms, but didn't lay hands on them.

From nowhere, two burly Chinese men appeared, one wiping his mouth with a napkin. They wore workmen's clothes and were obviously there to defend the house. They shouted threats. Miss Culbertson rushed toward them, forcing them back into the main parlor.

Thomasina couldn't breathe as she stumbled after the others. She was inside a house of prostitution!

The bouncers shouted, the policemen brandished their clubs. The bouncers advanced a step and the policemen bristled. Thomasina thought a fistfight would erupt any second. Miss Culbertson stepped forward and the bouncers stopped, cowed. They knew a Caucasian woman was inviolable.

John Francis stood on one side of Miss Culbertson gripping his nightstick and his partner stood on the other. The bouncers could take on the policemen, but what about three resolute women? Thomasina shook. It was a standoff.

Silk tassels hung from carved wooden chandeliers. Incense thickly scented the room. The lacquered tables held lamps and carved jade figures. Brocade couches lined the walls. Rugs covered the floors. Somewhere a chime tinkled.

"Where are your girls?" demanded Miss Culbertson.

"Upstairs," said the doorman. The bouncers shouted at him, but the doorman didn't answer. He seemed resigned to whatever came next.

"Show me!" Miss Culbertson stood erect, never raising her voice, a small dark presence in the opulent room. "I want Wong Liu."

The bouncers looked at each other and the one with the napkin disappeared upstairs.

"Not here," protested the doorman.

"Show me the rooms, and open the doors or we'll break them down." Where did Miss Culbertson find the courage for such demands? John Francis shook his nightstick.

The doorman hurried away on slippered feet and the searchers trailed him up a flight of stairs. Thomasina caught the faint smell of food, which reminded her of the kitchen at the Mission. Upstairs they found a poor tenement hallway, with no carpets, no paintings on the walls. Somewhere a baby wailed.

A huge cream-cake of a silk-swathed middle-aged woman came at them screaming. The doorman cringed, but Miss Culbertson stood straight and motionless and the madam came to a quivering stop. Thomasina could smell garlic.

"Tell them to open up," Miss Culbertson ordered. Chun Mei translated.

The Chinese man called out something, the virago objected. Spit flew from her mouth with the shouts. The heads of curious young women emerged from doorways, one and two at a time, some obviously just awakened. These were the fallen women!

"Wong Liu," said Miss Culbertson. "We are looking for Wong Liu."

Musky, heavy scent issued from the rooms, along with disinfectant. Crumpled silken nightclothes in brilliant colors shimmered in the light. Shadows threw the women's faces into harsh lines of fatigue.

"Wong Liu not here," said the doorman again. His queue swung as he gestured down the hall. The huge woman began a harangue, but Miss Culbertson ignored her. Miss Culbertson searched each room in turn. Thomasina shrank back, unable to follow, until curiosity impelled her. The rooms each featured a bed, a chair, a dresser, a few personal decorations, and little else. She trailed Miss Culbertson into a room, startling a couple. The man leapt naked from the bed. He was Caucasian, with dark curly hair and long, well-formed limbs. In the shadow light she saw his muscular buttocks and back. He turned and stared at her and she stared back. Then Miss Culbertson brushed by her and she noticed the whore in bed, her hair disarrayed, the sheets drawn up over her small breasts. The man slid behind a screen and pulled his shirt over his head.

At the end of the hall Miss Culbertson stopped. "Are there more girls?"

"No mo," said the doorman.

The Chinese man barked something at the young women who stood sleepy and silent or whispered in twos and threes. John Francis stood near the fat Chinese woman. Was this the woman who ran this place? Standing alone, the madam seemed formidable, but she did not reach the policeman's shoulder.

Thomasina felt superfluous. She hadn't done anything to help the raid and had probably been in the way. She tried not to gawk at what she was seeing. She shuffled her feet nervously, felt gritty dirt under her feet, and looked down. This end of the hall hadn't been swept lately. She scuffed her boots and wondered what came next. Miss Culbertson noticed her, noticed the dirt, and stood motionless for a moment. Then she threw her head back and looked straight up. Was Miss Culbertson having a seizure?

"That's it," said Miss Culbertson.

John Francis followed Miss Culbertson's gaze to the skylight. He searched the hallway, looked around the corner, and found a ladder, much too handily. He leaned it against the wall and climbed up to the gray window. His feet looked huge on the rungs and the ladder shook with each step, but he kept going. At the top he pushed the skylight open with little resistance, then clambered through and missed a foothold. Thomasina gasped. He recovered. The other policeman, she noticed, watched the hall, not his partner.

She heard a woman's cry from above. Then John Francis shouted, "I've got her."

"Praise God," whispered Miss Culbertson. "Bring her down," she called.

A thin, shivering Chinese woman felt for the ladder with a wet, slippered foot. Her bright silk gown, rain-soaked, clung to her back. The night's rain plastered her hair to her head. Her face was delicate and pretty, but her lips looked blue. How long had she been out there? Had they hurried her up to the roof when the policeman pounded on the door?

The madam shouted, the Chinese man shouted. Thomasina quailed but Miss Culbertson stood her ground. She waved the warrant at them and moved her group, with the prostitute in the center, down the hall and toward the stairs. The sodden Chinese woman drooped, her neck bowed as though broken. The abuse from the madam wilted her. Miss Culbertson pushed the warrant into Thomasina's hands, then she slid out of her coat and draped it over the shivering woman's shoulders. She murmured, "It's all right, my dear. You are safe." The woman might not understand the words, but the coat and the sound of Miss Culbertson's voice, echoed by Chun Mei's, reassured. "Tell her her sister sent us," Miss Culbertson said to Chun Mei.

The fat madam unleashed one last threatening stream of Chinese, like an out-of-tune hurdy-gurdy, and then they were in the alley. Thomasina wanted to catch her breath, to lean against the building until her knees felt firmer, but Miss Culbertson hurried them down the alley and onto the main street. Fog dimmed the streetlamps and muffled their hurrying footsteps. Steady rain fell. They were the only people abroad, thank God.

The six of them hurried uphill, almost running. Thomasina couldn't catch her breath. The policemen supported the drooping Wong Liu. Within minutes they were all inside the Mission.

Miss Culbertson turned the near-fainting Wong Liu over to several older Chinese women, whose soft voices murmured familiar, calming words and whose hands comforted. The dark shirts, smell of sandalwood soap, and black hair pulled back from round Cantonese faces calmed her. Then Wong Lan Yu appeared and the sisters greeted each other, embraced and wept.

"I didn't know Lan Yu had a sister," Thomasina said. Lan Yu was a long-time resident of the Mission, a "Bible woman" who visited Chinese families and read Scripture to the women in their homes.

Miss Culbertson thanked the policemen. She offered them hot tea, but they refused. Perhaps they wanted something stronger. San Francisco policemen had a reputation for toughness, but these men seemed utterly intimidated by Miss Culbertson.

"I will talk to Amos, our lawyer, and get this regularized tomorrow. Thank you so much for your help," Miss Culbertson told them. Thomasina gave her the warrant. Miss Culbertson's dress was wet and she shivered. "The Mission needs its friends and you've proved your commitment, John Francis, and you, officer." She nodded at the second man. "I cannot thank you enough."

The men left and Miss Culbertson visibly wilted. Sheer determination had kept her going, but now she could slacken the self-discipline that had carried her through the night's events. Thomasina wondered what came next. Then Miss Culbertson took a deep breath and straightened. She took Chun Mei's hand and Thomasina's and they formed a circle.

"Let us give thanks," she said. She hummed a note and Thomasina waited.

"Praise God from whom all blessings flow."

The spontaneous song startled Thomasina. She gripped hands. Miss Culbertson's reedy voice took strength. Her face shone. Chun Mei's nasal tone and Thomasina's own husky voice joined in. Never had she sung the familiar song more fervently.

> "Praise Him, all creatures here below;
> Praise Him above, ye heave'nly hosts;
> Praise Father, Son, and Holy Ghost."

Thomasina felt the goose bumps rise on her arms. Miss Culbertson, exhausted and drooping a moment ago, looked transfigured. Miss Culbertson's voice became surer and purer, as though it took strength when she turned to God. They sang through the simple song again.

Tears ran down Thomasina's face. Miss Culbertson embraced both of them and kissed their cheeks and smiled. "Let's go to bed," she whispered.

The three women trudged up the stairs. Thomasina thought the evening's excitement would keep her awake, and her mind tumbled over what she had seen and heard as she put on her nightgown.

"O Lord, thank You for letting us deliver Liu from her dreadful circumstances. Thank You that we all are safe. Bless Miss Culbertson for her intrepid spirit. And thank You for not letting me disgrace myself."

She would record this in her journal tomorrow. She slept as soon as her head touched the pillow.

2

The next morning Thomasina could scarcely drag herself out of bed. It was almost time for her monthly and she always felt sluggish and dull then. She had been up too late last night and she felt as though she were catching cold. She hadn't heard the bell that began the day, but now she heard girls' voices, high-pitched as birds, coming from the washroom, heard doors closing. A soft knock, then one of the big girls came in with her tea.

The Chinese girl placed the cup and saucer on her dresser carefully. She had carried it a long way from the kitchen and she didn't want to spill any now. She smiled at Thomasina, ducked her head, and hurried out.

Thomasina's room at the Presbyterian Occidental Mission at 920 Sacramento Street in San Francisco's Chinatown looked down the hill and across the bay to Berkeley. Her room was as simple as a nun's cell—whitewashed, with plain white curtains, a bed, dresser, wardrobe, and chair. A deal table held her lamp, Bible, journal, and books. It was hard to keep it from getting cluttered with her current sewing project and boxes of books and all the things that seemed so easy to acquire, then tiresome to find room for.

She climbed out of bed, sipped her tea, and padded to the washroom. When she returned, she dressed in a fresh shirtwaist and skirt and made her bed. Her spread, which relieved the austerity of the room, was a double wedding ring quilt pieced in shades of blue from her own dresses and waists. She went late to breakfast. A McIntyre doesn't shirk just because she's tired.

Just outside her room, a little girl who hadn't been at the Mission long watched her with big almond eyes. Thomasina raised her hand to stroke the girl's hair and the girl jerked back with fear, drawing in breath with a hiss. Without a word, Thomasina stooped and embraced the child, who looked to be about eight years old. The child stiffened, then struggled and cried out, but Thomasina held her and murmured softly, "No need to worry. Nobody will hurt you." The sound more than the words calmed the girl and Thomasina smoothed her inky hair off her round cheeks and released her.

Thomasina had ducked obstacles and responsibilities when she was a child, but she couldn't remember cringing. What a privileged childhood she had had! She hoped this girl would live at the Mission long enough so that she could grow up without cringing. Thomasina was glad she had come down when she saw Miss Culbertson already at work in her office.

"Miss Culbertson will see you after breakfast," said Miss Alverson, one of the housekeepers. Mercy! What had she done? Was she in trouble? Thomasina always felt rushed, hurrying to class and meals at the bell's summons. In the dining room fifty girls and women, seated at long tables, chattered, waiting for grace. Thomasina smelled this morning's rice, and the oatmeal and bread and coffee. Miss Culbertson wasn't there, so Miss Alverson led prayers and afterward the voices surged again. Miss Culbertson often ate in her office, simply to savor a few minutes of quiet. Thomasina considered meals another teaching opportunity—for etiquette, to answer questions, to help the new girls learn how the

Mission worked, and to teach things not included in their school lessons.

Thomasina felt uneasy as she finished eating. Had she done something wrong last night? Did she need to do better in the classroom? Was it about the new girls who were creating such a stir? Thomasina took a deep breath and tried to calm herself.

Then she heard a shriek from the front door. Thomasina dropped her napkin and hurried to the front of the building. Miss Alverson, one hand to her mouth, pointed out the door. Miss Culbertson came from her office, picked up an umbrella from the stand near the door, and walked boldly outside. Thomasina followed her.

Six sticks of dynamite, tied together with crude twine, lay against the foundation of the mission building with a note. Thomasina's heart was in her throat.

Miss Culbertson told Miss Alverson, "Be quiet. It hasn't gone off." She turned to Thomasina. "Go find a policeman." Miss Culbertson carefully pushed the bundle of dynamite away from the building and into the street with the tip of the umbrella.

Thomasina hurried to the police station, and halfway there realized she had forgotten her coat. Shivering, she told her story and two policemen wearing sack coats and derbies accompanied her back to the Mission. She arrived chilled and breathless. One policeman examined the dynamite without touching it and said there was no fuse. He pulled the piece of paper from under the twine, instructed the other policeman to take the explosives back to the station, then went inside to talk to Miss Culbertson.

After the policeman departed, Miss Culbertson motioned Thomasina inside her office. In her hand was the crudely lettered message.

"White devil, *fahn quai.*" Miss Culbertson snorted. "I've been called that name before. The worst insult is to say you are a ghost, a dead person. They call us 'barbarians.' "

Miss Culbertson read her the note: " 'Your religion is vain; it costs too much money. By what authority do you rescue girls? If there is any more of this work, there will be a contest and blood may flow, then we will see who is the strongest. We send you this warning. To All Christian Teachers.' "

Thomasina sat awed, staring at the older woman. Any other gently bred woman of her age and station would have gotten upset or angry or had hysterics, but Miss Margaret Culbertson was simply exasperated.

"Aren't you afraid?" Thomasina whispered.

"It didn't go off. I'm sure it wasn't meant to go off. It's supposed to scare me. It was probably the owner of that newest girl. He's angry at losing his chattel." Miss Culbertson smoothed the paper. "But this won't stop me."

Thomasina looked at the frail woman across the cluttered desk. She must be sixty, at least, thought Thomasina. Old enough to slow down. Old enough to need an assistant. She reminded Thomasina of rich ladies at her church, with finely etched features and good posture, and a firm grasp of Presbyterian principles. Gray light filtering through the morning fog found its way in the windows, but the gas lamp was needed just the same. Her office was furnished with inexpensive cupboards finished with dark stain and comfortable horsehair chairs. Miss Culbertson's desk was large, heavily carved, with a thick glass covering the top. It was almost out of place in its opulence—the gift of a donor, Thomasina had been told.

Miss Culbertson had just gotten out of bed after a bout of the grippe. She looked pale and her hands shook, but Thomasina didn't think they shook from fear. Miss Culbertson's hands showed her age with delicate blue veins and brown spots. Then Miss Culbertson pounded the desk with one fragile fist, startling Thomasina.

"A child is not property!" she shouted. "This is the United States and we fought a war so people would not be slaves." Rage made her voice strong. Her eyes flashed with determination. "I will never stop."

She studied Thomasina. "I hope this holy anger infects you." Then she asked, "What do you want, my dear?"

"You said to come in after breakfast. Have I done anything wrong?"

"No, no, my dear. You're doing a good job with the middle girls. I wanted to talk to you about what happened last night. I didn't tell you much in advance because I didn't want to frighten you. What did you think?"

Thomasina didn't want to sound cowardly. "I was frightened, but I suppose we weren't in real danger."

"That is right," said Miss Culbertson. "The Chinese know that if any harm came to us both Chinese and Americans would take notice."

"But is it legal to force our way in like that?"

"We have Jane Doe warrants for the prostitutes. With the little girls, we break the *letter* but not the *spirit* of the law. There is no written law to uphold us in entering a house and carrying off a girl. Often the owners use a writ of habeas corpus to get the girl back before we can complete guardianship proceedings. We are working on an amendment to the existing law which will deliver the girl into our custody until a hearing can be held." Miss Culbertson looked at the legal paper on her desk. "Whether last night's rescue is legal will have to be decided by a judge. Our work is to free girls who want to be freed and this is the only way we've devised to accomplish this."

"I understand," said Thomasina.

"In the old days, Chinese women came off the boats near the old Oriental Warehouse on First Street near the Embarcadero. When we first opened the Mission, the secretary at the Society for Prevention of Cruelty to Children brought us children, but I soon cooperated with him on rescues. At one point, in 1882, public opinion was very strong against the Chinese, and people stopped giving to the Mission. One day we were down to one sack of rice for sixteen people. When we prayed, 'Give us this day our daily bread,' we truly meant it. A few days later, to celebrate the Chinese New Year, someone left some money on the entry table. I remember my first report to the board—I confessed to some heart-sinking at being left alone with people who could not comprehend our language, nor we theirs. I summoned my latent courage and went forth to do the work as bravely as possible, and found that once we began, difficulties began to vanish; and so we have gone on from day to day, led by the hand of our dear Father above."

"You are so brave," Thomasina murmured. And I'm so spineless, she thought. Latent courage. She hoped she had some.

"God helps me to be as brave as I need to be." Miss Culbertson seemed to refocus her thoughts. "Now, it is important that you know about this small but essential thing we do because people talk about our rescues. The glamour that is attached to the dramatic stories of the rescues is very exciting. The raids have established our reputation, and white people and Chinese alike know what we stand for. We must have our proper warrant and everything must be prepared for, and we must be both resourceful and strong." Miss Culbertson paused again to gather her thoughts. "The stories of the rescues often obscure the other aspects of our work."

Thomasina sensed that this was an important lesson.

"These raids are only an occasional thing. We do them always with policemen, always with a Jane Doe warrant. It isn't really dangerous, but naturally people resist. They call you names, slam the door in your face, but you can't let that stop you. You must be ready to go into some unsavory places. You mustn't get excited."

Thomasina nodded.

"You will see things you don't yet know the words for, my dear. Take heart and call on the Lord. We are doing valuable work. The board started the Mission over twenty years ago because the need was so strong. When I see a girl abused, treated like property, forced into that depraved occupation—" She paused until the anger passed. She took a deep breath. "We cannot stop all the prostitution in Chinatown. A large portion of the girls and women who come here are domestic drudges, abused children, orphans, mistreated wives, and immigration detainees."

Thomasina had a sinking feeling, the kind that made her feel weak, as the realization slowly dawned: Miss Culbertson didn't think the raids were really dangerous. But Miss Culbertson didn't think dynamite against the foundation to bomb the Mission was dangerous, either.

3

Later that morning Thomasina carried a handful of homework papers to her classroom. She wished the schoolrooms were upstairs instead of in the basement. Heavy burglar screens blocked the light and it was impossible to keep the barred and screened window clean.

Thomasina had earned her teaching certificate at Normal School in Los Angeles. Her brother, only a few years older and starting a family, couldn't afford to send her to school for a four-year degree. She had taught at an elementary school in San Jose and worked with a youth group in the Presbyterian congregation. When the missionary board began looking for an assistant for Miss Culbertson, Mrs. Olivia Brown, whom she knew from the time they lived in Oakland, visited the Puente Ranch where her father was manager. Mrs. Brown painted a thrilling picture of the work of the Mission, and of the Young Women's Christian Association, which she had just helped establish. Miss Culbertson was getting old and her last assistant had just left. Why didn't Thomasina come and work for the Mission, just for a year?

When she was a little girl, she had had romantic ideas of being a missionary, going to China or India and saving the heathens. She never thought of San Francisco as missionary territory, but you could say Chinatown *was* a little bit of China. It was not as romantic as traveling overseas, but last night was excitement enough. Despite fear and jelly knees, she was glad she had been included.

The girls were giggling in a cluster when Thomasina arrived in the classroom. The cluster broke apart, and Ah Hsiang stood at the center.

"Open your books, girls," Thomasina said, "to page fourteen." She distributed their graded homework sheets. Dark heads bent over their books.

If sometimes she hated to come downstairs to the dark classroom, the girls didn't seem to mind. They were used to being sequestered in their homes and to them the close, dark halls meant security. The classroom was a utilitarian room with tongue-in-groove wainscoting varnished a shiny brown and painted plaster decorated with religious art and the girls' own artwork. A blackboard covered one wall. She had learned not to lean against the chalk trough—she'd come away streaked with white across her backside.

She waited for the rustle of desks and papers to stop. Giggles escaped and whispers continued.

"Begin reading at the top of page fourteen," she instructed. Once they settled down to work, they would be quiet.

She nodded at a girl in the first row. The accented English came slowly. Fluency depended on how long the girl had been in classes and exposed to English, not how old she was. When Thomasina first arrived at the Mission, all the girls had looked alike—almond-eyes, peachy skin, black hair. Now she saw them as individuals, distinctive in looks and personality. Some wore their shiny hair in a Dutch boy bob and some in a braid or pinned up in a knot. All wore simple cotton overblouses called sams that buttoned diagonally from the stand-up collar. Thomasina could never get used to girls wearing loose trousers, but they were practical and comfortable and the girls were accustomed to them.

Thomasina knew of ranch wives who wore their husbands' denim trousers during branding and hoped no neighbors caught them without their stays. The girls wore soft slippers in the house, but each had proper leather shoes to wear when she went out.

Each girl read in turn. When she got to Ah Hsiang, the girl impudently read her paragraph in Chinese, translating from the English.

"Try again. In English this time," said Thomasina.

Hsiang made a face that sent several girls into giggles. Hsiang was perhaps thirteen, still childlike in her sam and trousers, her hair cut in a bob. Her angular face would look elegant when she grew older with its prominent cheekbones and pouty lips. For the second time Hsiang read the paragraph in Chinese.

Thomasina sighed and called on the next girl. Hsiang needed more challenge. Most of the time the girls were docile and well behaved, but Hsiang was a mischief-maker.

Just before lunch, Miss Culbertson arrived. All the girls scrambled to their feet when she entered. Miss Culbertson let the silence build. She looked at each girl.

"Our friends in Saratoga sent us four bushels of apples. This is a special treat, as you know. Now, some are missing. I must discover who is responsible."

Thomasina wondered that something so simple as an apple was a "treat." She remembered orchards of apples growing in the valley where she grew up. She used green apples for missiles in games with Al and her sisters. Here each one was precious.

Hsiang stepped forward. "I took apples," she said. Her chin was up and she stared brazenly at Miss Culbertson.

"Oh, Hsiang, how could you?" Miss Culbertson cried.

"Big girls upstairs said if I took apples, they would say they did it."

"Well, they didn't," said Miss Culbertson. "They were very wrong to put you up to it. And you were wrong to do it. You must be punished."

"That's not fair!" Hsiang exclaimed.

"Will you name the big girls?"

Hsiang hung her head.

Thomasina noticed that when her pert face was not creased in a grin, there were fine scars on Hsiang's cheeks. More scars streaked her arms white. Hsiang was braver than the big girls to have confessed.

"Back to washing dishes," Miss Culbertson decreed. "One week, after breakfast."

Hsiang groaned. After breakfast was when the girls competed for washbasins and hot water for themselves, to wash clothes that weren't done with the mission laundry.

During the midday break, Thomasina consulted Miss Culbertson's record book. Hsiang had been sold by her father in Canton, brought to San Francisco to be a *mooie jai*—a household slave. At age eight, she did the cleaning and laundry for her mistress with the woman's youngest child strapped to her back. When her work didn't meet the mistress's standards, she was punished with hot candle wax thrown on her face and arms. She came to the Mission begging to learn English. When Miss Culbertson saw the scars and fresh burns, she investigated. Miss Culbertson persuaded a generous Philadelphia businessman, Robert Merkin, who wanted to help the Mission, to support Hsiang. Miss Culbertson arranged guardianship. He agreed to pay Hsiang's expenses, including college when the time came if it was appropriate.

The Mission could scarcely abandon Hsiang after bringing her in under those circumstances, but more than once Thomasina wished she could send the impish girl back to her owner. Then she would vow to be nicer to Hsiang and treat her with consideration and love. That usually brought youngsters around, but Hsiang resisted.

That afternoon Thomasina opened the religion class with a brief prayer and let the girls sing for the whole period. The girls loved to sing and their clear, high voices raised her spirits. Sometimes, she went away, somewhere inside the music. She soared on pure sound and that was when she felt closest to God. The girls' chorus could sing dozens of hymns a cappella for celebrations. Their sweet, high voices must reach straight to God.

Thomasina realized that not all of the girls were innocent in the sense most people would accept. Some of the big girls, ones scarcely older than Hsiang, had been prostitutes, or worked in bordellos where they saw more sin than Thomasina could imagine. Yet, when they sat at meals in their simple blouses, with neat hair and shining faces, or lined up to sing, with the tallest girl, usually Hsiang, standing in the middle and the shortest at each end of the row, a visitor could never have guessed which had been kitchen slaves or former prostitutes. After a while in the Mission, all of the girls looked equally blameless.

After all the lessons were over, and the day's pages were covered, one of the girls asked, "Please, Missee Mac, tell what you did last night."

Thomasina started to refuse, then realized these girls came from those narrow alleys and dark buildings and would have to accommodate the new arrival in their world.

"What would you like to know?" she asked.

"Were you frightened?"

Thomasina nodded. The girls giggled.

"Which house did you go to?"

"I don't know if it had a name." She described the doorway. The girls took it all in with great interest.

"Did the police chop the doors down with a hatchet?" one asked.

"No, the people opened the door. Chun Mei knew what to say. The policemen would have torn the doors off, I think, if they hadn't been opened."

"Did you see—" The girl used a Chinese term that Hsiang translated: hundred man's wives.

They meant the prostitutes.

"Yes. They were asleep and we woke them up."

"Did you see head woman?"

That must be the madam. "Yes, very fat lady, in pink kimono, very loud voice." Thomasina mimed her hand waving and the girls laughed.

"The reception room was very grand," she said. "Nice furniture, elegant rugs. Upstairs, not so grand."

"Tell how you found girl," Hsiang asked.

Thomasina recounted the grit on the floor, the ladder up to the skylight, and Liu coming down. And Miss Culbertson putting her own coat around the girl. The girls oohhed and aahhed.

"Missee always good, always take," said one of the schoolgirls. "Missee" was a term of respect, and also the mission girls' favorite name for Miss Culbertson.

"Did you smell opium?" asked one girl with stringy hair.

"Whatever does that smell like?" Thomasina asked. Several girls giggled.

"Sweet. Heavy."

Most of last night's smells had seemed sweet and heavy and altogether strange. Thomasina could not tell which one might have been opium. "Perhaps," she said. Two girls whispered in Chinese.

She would learn the names of all of the new things she was experiencing. She knew that the food that was served in the Mission was not exactly Chinese, but a compromise between what the girls were used to and what Miss Culbertson thought they needed to be healthy. She knew her room, the wooden floors and plaster walls of the Mission, its bricks and windows. But outside the walls, she was naive. She knew her way around San Francisco, but she didn't know Chinatown even though she lived at its edge. What were the strange-smelling spices and the vegetables in bins outside the stores? Why did Chinese women wear slippers instead of proper shoes? What is it like always to wear the same style? What did the motifs mean? Why dragons? Why lotus flowers and chrysanthemums? Thomasina knew the girls needed to learn American ways if they were going to stay in this country. They needed to know God's love, but that didn't mean they couldn't learn and enjoy their own heritage.

The bell brought Thomasina from her reverie. For once the girls hadn't taken advantage of her daydreaming to talk.

4

Thomasina was sorry that Hsiang got punished for stealing the apples after she had voluntarily confessed. She tried to show the girl extra attention during sewing class, but Hsiang misassembled a pair of trousers. The girls smothered giggles, but Thomasina said, "Pull out the basting and try again. Do it as you would do your own." And she went on to the next girl. Thomasina was too tired to confront Hsiang's misbehavior today.

The girls liked sewing class. They could create new embroidery for the annual crafts fair. These moneymaking projects received lavish attention. They produced table linens, blouses, quilted hot pads, rag rugs, and delicate embroidery. The sams and trousers they made for the littlest girls and boys were duty-work.

Chien Wei combined her duty-work with intricate embroidery, swiftly sketching a tiny pink rose on each side of the collar in shining silk thread. She was nearly mute, scarcely contributing to the incessant chatter, but she sang readily. Thomasina had to remind herself to talk to the girl, who usually vanished into the wallpaper. Sometimes Thomasina couldn't remember if Chien Wei had been in class or not without checking her roll book. She must look her up in Miss Culbertson's log and see if there was a reason for her silence.

Thomasina was grateful for one quiet girl, in contrast to Hsiang, who threatened to leave when crossed, saying she would tell her "American father" about alleged mistreatment. Fomenter of rebellion, player of pranks, jokester, star pupil when the spirit moved her—Hsiang was what Thomasina's father would have called a "stemwinder."

Thomasina thought of the girl Liu they had brought in last night—dressed in rich embroidered satin silk, with delicate slippers, her hair dressed in elaborate coils. She seemed too limp and dispirited to have made the effort to escape, but Chinese often seemed passive to Thomasina, especially the women who were accustomed to being mistreated. Miss Culbertson turned Liu over to Lan Yu, who could show her the routine of the Mission. Lan Yu would give her plain cotton clothes, introduce her to the dining room, and initiate her into her duties.

During sewing class, Thomasina heard screams filter down from the top floor where the older women's rooms were. The girls stopped work for a moment, then took it up again. Most of them had been at the Mission long enough to have heard this before, but Thomasina stiffened with each scream. Who was screaming? And why?

After class, Thomasina asked Alice, Miss Culbertson's niece, who was living at the Mission while she attended college, if they should call a doctor.

"Liu has been smoking opium since she was a child," said Alice. "She will need time."

Alice was a year younger than Thomasina and had grown up around the Mission. She taught the youngest girls their ABCs and she played the piano and led singing in the kindergarten room. Thomasina tried not to envy Alice's sophistication about things she was learning to accept as commonplace—things that most respectable women never learned about, or certainly never talked about.

"Why does she scream?" Thomasina asked.

"Now she has nothing to dull her pain," said Alice. "Her body is accustomed to the drug and it is very hard to go without it. Sometimes they go into convulsions and we do call the doctor. Sometimes the girls don't want to live without it and they leave."

"Oh, no," said Thomasina.

Alice shrugged. "It must be very hard. They suffer terribly."

Liu did not appear for several days. Miss Culbertson said she was still ill. The screams stopped after a day. Thomasina wondered if Liu was able to eat. A square meal and a good night's sleep was the McIntyre cure for most problems.

When Liu was calmer, Thomasina was invited to a meeting with Miss Culbertson, Liu, and her sister. That Chun Mei was there to translate went without saying. Miss Culbertson reiterated the rules, which Thomasina was sure the sister had explained. So far, Liu refused to take part in the mission routine, to her sister's frustration. She came to meals, but would not sew or take her turn at cleaning assignments. At first, Lan Yu tried to help her sister and show her how they did things at the Mission. But Liu refused to demean herself with manual work. She had never roughened her hands with cleaning soap. She had never handled a cleaver or learned to cook rice and had never washed a dish. She would wash and iron her own clothes, but she refused the plain mission garb and spent the day on her bed doing nothing.

Miss Culbertson called for suggestions. Lan Yu had run out of patience and suggested putting her out on the street. Miss Culbertson reminded Lan Yu that she, as mission director, was now the girl's guardian and couldn't allow that.

"Then let her return to the house," said Lan Yu. "That is the only life she is suited for!"

"Would you want to be sent back?" Miss Culbertson asked softly. Lan Yu said nothing.

Sometimes Thomasina thought Miss Culbertson acted like the head of a business or the principal of a strange school, or the president of a small kingdom—a firm administrator. Then in a flash, Miss Culbertson's humanity came through in a phrase, in a gesture.

Thomasina realized the responsibility that must fall on the frail woman's shoulders was overwhelming. When other women would have stopped, Miss Culbertson always found strength because it was "the Lord's work." Thomasina despaired, but Miss Culbertson had faith. She, Thomasina, needed to trust that the Lord would provide. Miss Culbertson teased her, calling her Doubting Thomasina. Miss Culbertson had seen enough twelfth-hour donations that her faith did not waver.

It was just that nobody had provided when Thomasina's father lost their ranch in the San Joaquin Valley, and she always felt she had to do everything herself.

Miss Culbertson and Lan Yu decided to continue to encourage Liu and hope that peer pressure would bring her around. The sullen young woman said little. She must be in terrible conflict, thought Thomasina—between gratitude to her sister and the Mission and frustration at being forced to live their way. Thomasina learned that the prostitutes worked during the day sewing piecework for their masters. They were indentured by means of a work contract, legal in China and the United States, to pay back the cost of their passage. They were penalized for every day they didn't work and their contracts were extended. Sometimes years were added. Most prostitutes did not survive their contracts, but made thousands of dollars for their masters in the meantime. The masters provided food, clothing, and shelter, something like the Mission, only the girls did the devil's work, not the Lord's, for their board.

* * *

The next Sunday, at services in the mission chapel, Hsiang sat next to Thomasina. She stared the girl down, and Hsiang's eyes faltered and turned away. Thomasina wondered what new mischief the girl was up to.

The chapel was a plain, utilitarian room, with benches and a few chairs, and a platform two feet up from floor level where the singers stood. The high windows had long, colorful curtains and on a bright day enough light entered so that they didn't need to light the gas. Two girls were in charge of the hymnals kept in cupboards built under the windows. If they had a minister in attendance, he led the service and they had Eucharist; otherwise, Miss Culbertson, as elder, read Scripture and led the service.

The following Sunday Hsiang sat next to her again. When the light shone on the girl's face, Thomasina noticed the slick, uneven texture of scarred skin on her cheeks and neck. She noticed damaged skin at Hsiang's wrists and wondered what further scars the girl's sam covered. She was learning the source of Miss Culbertson's continuing rage against the treatment of their girls.

The next Tuesday Hsiang was showing off. She gave a garbled version of the Constitutional Congress that had the other girls giggling. Thomasina stopped that and continued the lessons, calling on the other girls. When it was Hsiang's turn again, the girl spoke in a pompous tone, as though she were a white businessman, huffing and puffing with self-importance. Thomasina broke up laughing.

"You must stop," said Thomasina. If she laughed, she just encouraged Hsiang to misbehave, but she was helpless.

"But . . . but . . . ." Hsiang huffed, "this is (puff, puff) most important, most important." The girl's expression changed, her cheeks got fuller. She tilted back as though she had a huge potbelly to support.

"Stop it! This minute! I can't conduct class." Thomasina spoke sharply now, and looked Hsiang straight in the eye.

"I tell secret about you!" Hsiang flared.

What secret could this imp hold against her? She tried to do her duty, but she was only human. She didn't share a box of chocolates that came from her family in the valley. She preferred to run errands alone and she savored those brief, solitary times. She longed to meet a suitable young man. She would have been embarrassed if anyone actually knew how much time she spent daydreaming about the opposite sex. The pain of her broken engagement to George Sergent was fading and Thomasina was glad she had told him no. If she had not, she would never have had this interesting year in San Francisco.

"I'll treat you the same as I treat all the girls," Thomasina replied. "And devil take the hindmost with your blackmail!" Thomasina was flushed and felt her hair coming down from the emphatic shakes of her head.

Hsiang's face mottled red, her anger matching Thomasina's. She clenched her fists at her sides. "You don't sing in chapel!" she screamed. "You just pretend."

Thomasina flushed deeper, this time with embarrassment. She was ashamed that someone had caught her out; she had to purse her lips to keep from laughing. Then she did laugh, a high-pitched titter, half nervousness.

"That's not a deadly sin, Hsiang," she answered. She covered her mouth, but the smile wouldn't go away. The other girls had watched their exchange, holding their breaths and swiveling their heads from one to the other.

Hsiang looked puzzled. She had expected Thomasina to lose her temper, not giggle, at the accusation.

Thomasina explained: "I'm tone deaf." The girls looked puzzled. She elaborated: "I can't sing on-key. If the person next to me isn't a strong singer, I can't find the notes. I sing, Hsiang, but very softly. I don't want to ruin the music."

Conversation buzzed in the room. The girls all sang several times a day in class and at prayers and they knew dozens of the songs in the hymnal by heart. When visitors came, Miss Culbertson called an impromptu choir to entertain.

"Let's sing 'What a Friend,' " Thomasina suggested, "and when

I drop my hand, you stop and I'll keep going. Get us started, Chien Wei."

The class began:

> "What a Friend we have in Jesus,
> All our sins and griefs to bear—"

Then Thomasina dropped her hand and they fell silent. She sang "What a privilege to carry . . ." and went flat. She continued the line, then made a face and stopped and they all laughed.

"Softly. I sing very softly," she said. Even Hsiang seemed amazed at this inability. Thomasina said, "Oh, please, girls, wipe away that sour sound." She nodded and Chien Wei gave the note and they started again. Thomasina sang along word for word, but if they had fallen silent again, only God would have heard her voice.

Thomasina felt that the Mission came close to obeying Jesus' command, "Love one another." They fed the hungry, three times a day. They clothed the naked, if the women consented to simple cotton. They visited the imprisoned at the Immigration Shed and Miss Culbertson freed the enslaved women who had the courage to leave the bordellos. They nursed sick girls and women and helped the ones who were pregnant when they arrived. It didn't do any good to preach God's word, if faith wasn't supported with action. First they ministered to the body, then the newcomers could hear the Word. If they were ill, hurt, hungry, and mistreated, the Word was empty.

Sometimes the simplest things were the hardest. Miss Culbertson had to figure out how to stretch the mission budget to cover all the food they ate. When it looked as though the mission board's budget wouldn't stretch, she visited congregations in the city, begging for additional funds. Generous people gave enough to keep the Mission going, and a few wealthy donors filled the

gaps or supported a single girl like Hsiang. Some people had con-
nections to farming families in the Santa Clara Valley around San
Jose who sent produce.

Thomasina only vaguely understood the legal steps that Miss
Culbertson took to have herself declared the guardian of each
young woman and girl. The previous "owner" could not reclaim
the girl without going to court. Since most of the girls were here
illegally, the owners, who could go to jail, chose not to take this
route. But what about the adult women? Most did not speak English and couldn't negotiate their way through the immigration
details even if they could afford passage back to China. Miss Culbertson spent much time trying to get stranded women released.
Thomasina hated the rickety barracks, the reeking sanitation.
Women were sometimes forced to stay there for months, taking
care of children when they had only a bucket to wash themselves
and their clothes. Often they lost heart. A few attempted suicide.
Then there were the orphans and *mooie jais* who did not know
their original families. They had been kidnapped or bought so
young that they had few memories. The Mission was their home,
not a way station. They had to be taken care of, taught a trade,
taught English, and taught that somebody loved them, that God
loved them. Some of the young prostitutes could not read or write
and had no trade but the one they just left, although most of them
could sew. They kept the sewing machines busy as they earned
money to return to China or begin a different life in California.

How could she help the women and girls if she didn't even
know what opium smelled like? Sometimes she doubted that the
Mission made a difference in the face of so much need. She despaired that she could do more harm than good in this foreign
world, that she could learn enough fast enough to help Miss Culbertson.

5

Thomasina often took advantage of the lull between lessons and dinner to steal into the kitchen for a cup of tea. Today she stopped in the sewing room to jiggle a fussy baby while the mother pinned plackets to shirtfronts. Someday, Thomasina hoped to have babies of her own.

This institutional kitchen was cramped in the extreme, with utensils hanging from walls and ceilings and pots stacked under tables. Food was kept in the pantry in the basement and brought up as needed. Huge rice cookers and enormous skillets covered the black ranges. Sun Lee, the cook, filled the kettle and dumped the old tea leaves from the chipped pot when she saw Thomasina come in. Thomasina always felt a little guilty if she was idle when someone else was working, but Sun Lee would stop for a few moments and they could both relax. Thomasina smiled at the teenage girls whose duty it was today to chop vegetables and scrub pots.

"What does opium smell like?" Thomasina asked Sun Lee.

"Opium? To smoke?"

"The girls asked me if I smelled opium and I didn't know what to say."

"You smelled it. Maybe you didn't know you smelled it." Sun Lee's face was round as a moon, pink from the steam of the kitchen. Her hair was coming down from a plain bun. She was plump with hardly a waist where she tied the big apron and she wore boots instead of slippers.

"Does it smell good?" Thomasina asked.

"Not good-good, like a flower. If you want it, it smells like heaven."

"I need to learn about such things," Thomasina said. She liked the steamy room, filled with light from lamps and a high window. It didn't look or smell like her mother's kitchen, and Sun Lee looked nothing like her mother, but the atmosphere was warm and friendly, the way Thomasina remembered her mother's kitchen. Sun Lee was quick and sure as she moved from table to stove to pie safe. Thomasina watched her measure tea leaves into the pot and pour boiling water. Her sleeves were rolled up revealing sturdy, rounded arms. The bouquet of fresh tea, almost as invigorating as the drink, spread through the kitchen.

Thomasina always felt cold and hungry when she hadn't gotten enough sleep and the hot tea would fool her body into thinking it was warm. In gray, damp San Francisco Thomasina needed a lot of tea.

"What is going on with the new girl?" Thomasina asked.

Sun Lee sat down beside Thomasina to wait while the tea steeped. "I thought that was why you asked." Sun Lee's English was heavily accented and sometimes she had to repeat her words, but no matter the syntax or pronunciation, she managed to convey her ideas and opinions. The *R*s and *L*s got garbled and lots of words ended with "ee" but Thomasina loved the music of English spoken by someone not born here.

"Alice said she was accustomed to opium, but nobody has told me what that means," Thomasina explained.

"Liu smoked opium," Sun Lee began. She stopped, looked uncertain.

"If you don't help me, I'll be ignorant and make mistakes with the girls. Please," Thomasina begged.

"Opium is nice, makes you feel happy, calm. Most times men smoke, just sometimes, for a little holiday. If you smoke it more and more, maybe that's all you do. Masters give girls opium, make them quiet to do their work. Liu is used to many pipes a day. Suddenly, no pipes. She's sick without it."

"Like the DTs when someone has been a drinker?"

"Something like. You know drinkers?"

"I've heard people talking. So it makes her sick when they take it away. Like doing without tea when you're used to it. I always get headaches."

"She feels so bad she wants to throw herself out of the window. Bars on windows are to keep owners from stealing girls back, but it keeps girls from suicide until they get better. You always crave it, even if you don't smoke."

"How do you know?"

Sun Lee did not answer. In the background the steady rhythm of knives and cleavers beat a tattoo against the table. Chopped greens filled a huge enameled pan. One of the girls dragged a basket of onions over to her table. If Thomasina stayed, she knew her clothes would smell of onion until they had a chance to air. Sun Lee poured the brewed tea.

"I heard Liu cursing Miss Culbertson. I thought Liu wanted to come here. Now she wants to go back."

"She wants to be here. She had to want to come very much because if her owners knew she sent word to us and Miss Culbertson hadn't found her, they would have beaten her, maybe taken her out of San Francisco. They say she has a contract to work, but no girls read English to know what the contract says."

"But she's being awful."

"Opium talking."

The sharp smell of onions made Thomasina's eyes water. She

finished her tea. "Thanks, Sun Lee," she said. "May I come for another lesson soon?"

The older woman smiled and nodded. On an impulse Thomasina wrapped her arms around the woman from behind and gave her a hug. Sun Lee stiffened, but she did not pull away. Thomasina missed friendly hugs from her sisters.

If it was possible to buy and sell people, then the men who brought girls over from China would be entitled to their property. But just because it happened in China didn't mean it was allowed in California. Thomasina could understand why the owners would be unhappy, but that was the risk they took when they broke the law.

"In China, a girl counts for nothing," said Miss Culbertson the following day. "A boy child gets everything. A girl child is considered worthless. Poor people don't welcome another mouth to feed. If she's beautiful, she might become the second or third wife of a wealthy man. If her father can't feed her, he thinks if he sells her, her new owner will feed her to protect his investment. It sounds cruel, but the father thinks he is giving the girl a life."

Miss Culbertson rose and opened a cabinet and took down a document box. "Here's the paper," she said. "Listen.

"An agreement to assist the woman Hsiao Lui coming from China to San Francisco; she is indebted to her master for passage. Hsiao Lui asks Mr. Yee-Kwan to advance for her six hundred ten dollars, for which Hsiao Lui agrees to give her body to Mr. Yee for services as a prostitute for four years. There shall be no interest on the money. Hsiao Lui shall receive no wages. At the expiration of four years she shall be her own master. Mr. Yee-Kwan shall not hinder or trouble her. If Hsiao Lui runs away before her debt is paid her master shall find her and return her; whatever expense is incurred in finding and returning her Hsiao Lui shall pay. If Hsiao Lui is sick at any time for more than ten days she shall make up by an extra month of service for any days' sickness.

"Signed and so on." Miss Culbertson returned the paper to the box. "Some contracts say if she conceives, her time is extended one year. If the owner returns to China, her contract can be sold and she must still serve it out."

"Surely, our heavenly Father didn't mean for people to do that to each other." Thomasina was so angry at the situation her voice shook.

"The only way to stop this cruelty," said Miss Culbertson, "is Christianity, where each person is considered a child of God and worthy of love."

"But we have to stop this at the source!"

"Don't think you can change hundreds of years of Chinese customs." Miss Culbertson looked at her sharply. "You will wear yourself out with useless efforts that do no good."

"But what can we do? This is hopeless!"

"We continue. We rescue girls who want to be rescued. We get guardianship of little girls used as slaves. We go to court with lawyers. We negotiate with Immigration."

"This will take too long." Thomasina felt her face grow flushed and sweaty. She was still indignant.

"What else are we here for?" Miss Culbertson's face did not look resigned. She looked into Thomasina's eyes for a long time and Thomasina tried to guess what her mentor was thinking. Then Miss Culbertson said, "You can become a harpy—nagging and scattering your power and becoming disliked. Anger can do that. What I see as a better plan is to take this power that rises from a righteous heart and channel it into the few, simple, effective activities we have learned we can accomplish. It is modest. It takes a long time. The raids are easy; rearing an undernourished *mooie jai* for years is hard. Don't waste your energy."

"My problems with Hsiang seem small compared with Liu."

"Is that scalawag giving you trouble?" asked Miss Culbertson. "She had just come to us when a visitor from Philadelphia was sitting where you're sitting now. Hsiang's owner stormed in here and Robert Merkin sat there dumbfounded while the Chinese man screamed at me. Chun Mei translated, and Merkin learned that the man didn't want Ah Hsiang because she was a trouble-maker, but considered he was owed the cost of the girl. When Merkin learned it was only one hundred dollars, he offered to buy her. I took the easy way out and agreed. Merkin insisted on a bill of sale and the owner signed it with his seal."

"How dramatic!" said Thomasina.

" 'Now the Mission has another orphan,' I told Mr. Merkin. And he asked how much it cost to support a girl. I told him and he proposed that since he 'owned' her, he pay for her keep. He sends a generous donation each year and she writes to him. I write also, keeping him abreast of her development. I think she is col-lege material and he seems agreeable to that, too. But I don't think she would be accepted by any college in California. The young Chinese men are scarcely accepted. And she thinks she is better than the other girls and threatens to tell her 'American fa-ther' whenever things don't go her way."

"Yes, I've gotten that from her."

"Don't let her intimidate you. If she weren't a stubborn, intel-ligent, brave girl she wouldn't be here. We don't want to break her spirit, but give her enough discipline to survive."

"I may break first," said Thomasina. "Were all the younger girls *mooie jais*, like Hsiang?"

"Many were. Some were orphaned, with no family to take care of them. Some came into the Mission with mothers that died. Some were brought over as children, to be put to work in the bagnios when they were old enough. We rescued a few before they became prostitutes. But even young girls were expected to re-ceive men."

"Before I came here, I never used words like *prostitute,* and now it is common parlance."

"You knew what hunger and abuse meant, but you perhaps did not see the results before," said Miss Culbertson. Her seamed face was sad with the knowledge she bore.

"When my family lost the sheep ranch, I'm glad they didn't sell me." It was a weak joke, but it brought a smile to Miss Culbertson's face.

"We always struggled to stay together, even when we moved to town and all went to work," Thomasina continued.

"You earned your teaching certificate, did you not?"

"Four years was more than my brother could manage." She thought of George Sergent who studied agriculture and wondered if he were all she would have in the way of suitors.

"Hsiang needs steady discipline."

"I don't like to be gotten the better of," Thomasina replied. "Especially by Hsiang, who reminds me of myself when I was younger and spunkier."

6

⁂ After all that had been done for her, Liu would not co-operate. It had been several weeks since the raid and still she lay on her bed, weeping and wearing her ever more disheveled satin tunic. Her sister talked with her daily but couldn't get her to co-operate. Thomasina personally thought not working wearisome and would rather scrub pots and pans or file collection cards all day than sit idle.

That afternoon Thomasina complained to Sun Lee. She appreciated a cup of tea, freshly made, after classes. Late afternoon was a difficult time with the girls free to get into mischief; everyone was tired and hungry. It wasn't fair to the cooks to expect them to serve a snack while they were preparing supper, but Thomasina's energy flagged badly if she didn't stop sometime during the afternoon.

Sun Lee poured water from a steaming kettle into the pot. Thomasina liked its unfamiliar pastel flowers on a white background. The lid was chipped. The older woman sat heavily and stretched her feet in front of her. Thomasina thought her heavy boots would tire her, but Sun Lee said they supported her feet better than slippers.

"Liu lose her face if she wash clothes," said Sun Lee.

"We think a prostitute has already lost her face," said Thomasina tartly.

"Not that kind of face." Sun Lee thought for long moments. Then she poured the tea into their cups. Thomasina loved the delicate, steaming scent.

"Like honor, but not quite," said Sun Lee.

"Virtue, doing the right thing?"

Sun Lee shook her head. "Honor, like people honor her because she don't do low work."

"We'd say status or caste."

"Something like that. She was first-class whore."

Thomasina tried not to wince.

"First-class whore don't cook, don't wash, don't empty slops. They keep beautiful long time, keep hands nice. Owner give lots of opium, girls feel good, don't care."

"Liu isn't getting opium anymore. I'd think she'd be bored to death. She doesn't even read."

"Can't read, write. She don't know what to do. She won't listen to sister."

"She listens when we pray. She came to Sunday services."

"She there. If she listen—" Sun Lee shrugged.

"What would reach her? I wonder. You're really much happier if you are busy. Idle hands are the devil's playground. She embroiders. Maybe some sewing. That's what idle American women do."

Sun Lee sipped tea. "Maybe fancy work. Fancy lady."

"Are we going to have to buy her silk to get her out of that sam?"

Sun Lee chuckled. "Pour water over head, maybe."

Thomasina giggled, imagining the beautiful woman's long silky black hair wet and dripping onto the crimson sam. "The little girls usually think of everything. Why can't they do mischief on order? But of course, that wouldn't be right. Do you ever talk to her? Could you pass a hint?"

Sun Lee shook her head. "Not listen to cook, I don't think."

"I'm not too proud to listen to you."

Sun Lee ducked her head and looked away. But she smiled.

"At least she is out of that place where she had to do awful things."

"Not all of it was awful," Sun Lee said. She sipped her tea.

"But I thought you said you hated it."

"When I first start, in San Francisco, before we run away—" Sun Lee stopped and tears welled up in her eyes. She wiped them with her apron. "When I first start, I was singsong girl."

"I never heard of that," said Thomasina.

"It's part of one hundred man's wife work, but if she beautiful, she go dinners. She dress up and make herself look good, sit behind men and serve, laugh, make happy. Important to invite friends to dinner for special occasions, they come and bring presents. Special food, many courses. Sometimes ten or twenty men come."

"What did you do?"

"We just be there. We help serve, we make music, we make pretty. We laugh at jokes. Everything like family—no bedroom stuff. Everything according to custom, very nice."

"That sounds strange."

Sun Lee shrugged. She was plainly enjoying the memory of those times. "That's how I met husband, he come to party and see me, first time. He think I'm girl from his village, but I just look like her, then he pay attention to me. I notice him, very good-looking, very nice manners. He see me in night, tell me he love me. I love him." The corner of the apron came up to her eyes again. "We afraid my master find out, sell me in Queen's Room. Finally, he gets money so he send me word to be ready and he comes and we run away. He pay my master very much money and he gets the paper. We go to Corvallis and we happy for a little time."

"How did you end up here?" Thomasina asked. But Sun Lee said nothing and Thomasina knew she would hear no more this day. They finished their tea in silence.

Later Thomasina went to Miss Culbertson and asked to see the ledger about Sun Lee.

Miss Culbertson took the book down and leafed through it.

"This won't tell you what you want to know," she said.

Thomasina read the brief entry, which said that Sun Lee left the employ of a Chinese and came to the Mission of her own volition and asked for refuge from a master who had put her to prostitution.

"Can you tell me her story? Begin at the beginning."

"Is the beginning the floods in her province, or the history of her family, which she can trace back for seven hundred years?"

"That long!"

"In America, Gold Mountains the Chinese call it, we are all first generation. You are a first generation Californian. We are always redefining ourselves. But the Chinese depend on stability, on knowing who your family is and venerating your ancestors."

"Why do they worship their ancestors?" Thomasina asked.

"It isn't as simple as that. It has to do with continuity and how they perceive themselves. Americans are individuals, identified by personal characteristics. Chinese are always part of a family, a clan, a tribe. They are part of the stream that comes from the past and moves into the future. That is why they love and treasure their children so."

"Begin again."

"Sun Lee was the fifth daughter of a poor farmer. When a sojourner returned from Gold Mountains with lots of money and stories of how you could wash gold out of the mountain rivers, everyone was impressed. Especially Sun Lee, who was young and pretty. When the sojourner suggested to her father that he take her back with him, this would have been about 1885, the poor man agreed. Sun Lee went willingly. After all, she would be the bride of this wealthy sojourner and live in ease and comfort.

"This man told her what to say to the immigration officials. The new laws, passed after the railroads no longer needed Chinese labor, meant that only daughters or wives could enter legally. She did not speak English, did not know the new legislation, and did not know the sojourner, so she learned what to say and she passed the examination.

"At first her master kept her in an apartment on Jackson and treated her well. An older woman, whom he called his mother, taught her how to get around in Chinatown, do the marketing, that kind of thing. Sun Lee said he did not treat the woman as his mother, and later she discovered 'Ma' was the proprietor of a bordello.

"When Sun Lee learned what the true case was, she pleaded with her master, 'Please don't make me one hundred man's wife. I came from China to be respectable wife. You promised my father. I came because it was my duty.' She told me she fought like a tiger and the man whipped her and locked her in her room. She was still pretty, so he obliged her to serve parties. The madam taught her the drill. Those dinners that the organizations put on for each other were models of decorum and fine manners. She was dressed in the most elegant silks, with her hair elaborately arranged and her face powdered. Even tong men behaved like gentlemen. And that is how she met her husband."

"She told me about the parties," Thomasina said. "Who was her husband?"

"A minor hoodlum. But when he found Sun Lee, who was very young and pretty you must remember, he wanted to get out of San Francisco with her. He decided they would disappear into the mountains. He and Sun Lee eloped. Sun Lee's master immediately put out notice and offered a reward. The lovers escaped San Francisco, but word had already reached Sacramento by the time they got there.

"Sun Lee's husband had just received a large sum of money, so he bought the contract her father had signed, which indentured her to repay the cost of her passage plus expenses.

"Only because the husband claimed his tong's protection did they manage this. In the past, girls had been rekidnapped and lovers had been killed. Sometimes the girls were also killed, or beaten and disfigured so they could barely work.

"The two of them went to a small town in Oregon where they

farmed a little. They opened a laundry and because they were thrifty and hardworking they made a living doing what white people didn't want to do. They had two children in two years. Sun Lee was happy.

"Then the tong of her former owner came after her, saying the husband hadn't paid enough for her contract. He had the papers, but the men who threatened him said he must pay more or they would take Sun Lee back. They gave him a week. They couldn't borrow the money because the husband had betrayed his tong by leaving.

"At the end of a week the tong men returned and took her away. She screamed and tried to hold on to her babies. One was still nursing. Her husband was beaten when he tried to stop them. They beat Sun Lee, too, and took her to Sacramento and put her to work in a Chinese bordello. She tried to get word to her husband, but he had disappeared from the little town with the children, a boy and a girl, because the tongs might take them next.

"She told me she thought she would die, but instead she got fat. Her master eventually brought her back to San Francisco to be a cook. One day, she left to do the bordello's marketing and came here, with all her possessions in a canvas shopping bag. I was glad to have her since she knew how to cook for a large group of women."

"How long has she been here?" asked Thomasina.

"Almost two years."

"I thought she was much older."

"She never stops looking for her children. It wasn't safe for her to leave the Mission for many months, but she would send messages to friends in Chinatown asking if anyone had heard of her husband and children."

"How sad! She hasn't given up?"

"No. And every time I go to another city, I ask and put out feelers. Do you know a man about thirty years old, with a crescent scar under his right eye? I'd give his name, but of course, he would have changed it. The children would be four and five. I haven't had any luck so far, but stranger things have happened. He may have gone back to China. He may be in the Chicago or New York Chinatowns, invisible among all the other immigrants."

Miss Culbertson put the ledger back on the shelf. Thomasina thought that book held too much pain and cruelty. She didn't think she could ever read the whole of it without her heart breaking.

The next day Thomasina gave her lesson plans to a trusted older girl while she accompanied Miss Culbertson to Oakland where she was speaking to members of the Presbyterian Home Mission Society at the residence of Mrs. Brown, a wealthy board member.

Thomasina had been so absorbed in trying to do a good job at her own day-to-day activities that she hadn't realized how many different tasks Miss Culbertson accomplished. Cho Woo, one of the young women who had been rescued when she was a young teenager, helped Miss Culbertson with accounts, using an abacus. Thomasina loved the rhythmic click of the wooden beads sliding on the wires. She must learn how to use one. Thomasina had done some bookkeeping when she worked in an office in San Jose, so she could understand the system. She had begun making entries and checking Cho Woo, to see how things worked. Miss Culbertson was an offhand teacher, rarely giving direct instructions, but she continued to put Thomasina in situations where she learned how the Mission was run. Of course, Miss Culbertson's greatest teaching was by example. Thomasina was often ready to drop and would have stopped, postponed, or given up many times if not for Miss Culbertson's example. More and more Thomasina noticed that Miss Culbertson drove herself until she was ill. Thomasina didn't like feeling bad and privately vowed she would learn to say "enough."

Thirty women attended the Oakland meeting—one of the largest mission groups in the state. Mrs. Olivia Brown was a tireless organizer of beneficent organizations and lived in a big house in the hills. Thomasina and Miss Culbertson arrived early and Miss Culbertson left to parley with Mrs. Brown and another board member, so Thomasina wandered off for a quiet moment in the garden, breathing in the heady scent of Mrs. Brown's roses.

When she was at 920 Sacramento Street, Thomasina didn't miss the country. The life of the Mission was all-absorbing. If she looked down the steep hill, she could see the bay, the boats, and on clear days the hills beyond, on the Contra Costa.

When she got away—to visit her brother Al and his family or her sisters in San Jose—she drank in the earth, the grass, the flowers, the trees like a parched traveler. She stifled the desire to lie down on Mrs. Brown's carefully tended grass and roll in its green thickness. She buried her nose in the rambler roses and caught the rich scent of the earth. A gardener came out to see who trespassed his domain; he smiled when he saw Thomasina.

Thomasina had had a full childhood of playing outdoors, on grass hills, watching trees change, learning the cycle of planting, growth, and harvest, but today she realized for the first time that many of the little girls at the Mission never walked except on pavement, rarely saw more than potted plants growing. She must see that they got a chance to play in the real outdoors.

Later, the ladies ate lunch and afterward turned their chairs toward the end of the room where Miss Culbertson stood to talk. She told the women the money they had donated last year paid for room and board for three girls for one year.

"But much more needs to be done. Let me tell you about Ngun Ho. She was taken from her family in Canton by a trusted family friend who promised to bring her to California and marry her to a rich merchant. Once here, she was put to work. All day long she carried the heavy infant son of her mistress on her back as she swept and scrubbed. She ran errands with the infant tied to her, never allowed away from the house for more than a few minutes. Her mistress knew she was helpless without the family friend, and continued to mistreat her until they noticed her burgeoning young beauty. Then she was relieved of her housekeeping burdens and sold to the highest bidder. Soon she was a mother of a little son when she herself was but a child of thirteen."

Thomasina heard the women sigh and murmur at this news. She could scarcely imagine a schoolgirl, who should be giggling with her friends and practicing how to put her hair up, already a mother.

"Respectable Chinese were roused to indignation against her master and pity for the child and they prompted a friend to come to us, appealing for help. Ngun Ho and her little son were rescued and are safe beyond the reach of her former master.

"What is more important, she lives as a good Christian woman. We had to take her away from San Francisco and she was placed with a family in another part of the state. She is a servant again, but treated with dignity.

"How deep is the heart hunger and need of these friendless Chinese girls! I appeal to you to continue your generous work on their behalf. They turn to us in their hour of need for comfort and guidance. It is our joy and privilege to be able to help."

Miss Culbertson bowed her head. Even Thomasina, who knew these stories already, was moved by her presentation. The ladies applauded long and steadily. Mrs. Brown took Miss Culbertson's place and said, "I know you good women of Oakland will continue to make it possible for the Mission to save these poor Chinese girls. We will discuss the ways and means at our next business meeting. Thank you for coming."

The ladies rose and chatted among themselves. Thomasina watched Miss Culbertson mingle and answer questions.

She was introduced to a few women by Mrs. Brown and she answered questions about the Mission. She referred to it as an orphanage for all ages. The women loved children and could understand motherhood, even if they couldn't grasp the other details of the Chinese women's lives.

Later that afternoon, on the ferry coming back, Thomasina found refuge inside the lounge from a stiff breeze. Fishing boats with lateen sails tacked back to the wharves. A tug guided a steamer from

Hawaii to its berth. The bay, with sunlight streaking through openings in the clouds over San Francisco, looked like a lithograph of heavenly illumination shining on Jerusalem, except for the crane angling up where another skyscraper rose in the business district. Thomasina said to Miss Culbertson, "You only tell the horror stories. You never talk about the trouble we have getting guardianship. Or the women who are stranded in the Immigration Shed."

Miss Culbertson gave her a sharp look. Then she sighed. "We are preparing the field for later harvest. The legal details are tedious."

"They're interesting!" Thomasina blurted. "I mean, they are complex and sometimes trying to get things worked out in a hurry is exciting."

"I'm glad you find them interesting. The same with the day-to-day bills and ordering produce and meat and washing soap and muslin and percale by the bolt. These are necessary, but they aren't"—Miss Culbertson paused while she searched for the right word—"dramatic. When you appeal for funds, you must make it easy for the people to respond. You have to make it simple and understandable."

"Like telling them thirteen dollars will support a girl for a month. How do you arrive at those figures?"

"I took the total running expenses, subtracted salaries, and divided the amount by the number of inmates. Then I rounded it off. It is very rounded. That's a number they can easily grasp." She held her veil more snugly against the bay wind. "It is a figure they can understand. Then later, in meetings with the mission board and with the elders of the churches, you can go into the details. God always sends us more girls than money."

In the year since she had arrived in San Francisco, Thomasina had learned her way around. She could get almost anywhere on trolleys and cable cars. Telegraph Hill was filling up with little houses, more and more streets were paved with vitreous stones. She read the *Bulletin* and the *Examiner*, but not every day, to follow the politics. She always felt she was coming in in the middle, never quite knowing why things happened as they did. She never did sort out the war between China and Japan and why Port Arthur was important. It was common knowledge that San Francisco city government was corrupt, but things got done. Abe Reuf was pushing Eugene Schmitz for mayor. Fortunes were made as streetcars replaced cable cars. Businessmen vied to put in telephone lines and sewers. Opera stars visited the city. Five-cent theaters, nickelodeons, were a new novelty. Discussion of a war with Spain over Cuba came up more and more.

The city grew as frame houses went up in subdivisions to the west and south. They even had skyscrapers, like the Palace Hotel, with its elegant courtyard.

Thomasina now knew which French restaurants had rooms available for trysts on upper floors and she wasn't shocked at that knowledge anymore. She felt she had been a bumpkin when she arrived and now was more sophisticated, until she ran into still another aspect of directing the Mission she hadn't known about, such as today's revelation of Miss Culbertson's soliciting.

"You must do this all the time!"

"Continuously. It is what I must do to keep the Mission going. The Mission is my lifework. I did not know when I started, but this is what I was meant to do. Whatever I must do, I do—sometimes easily and gladly, sometimes with difficulty."

"I would think it very hard to get up in front of a group to speak."

"But you do it every day!" Miss Culbertson's merry laugh followed.

"What do you mean?"

"You stand in front of your classes and instruct the girls."

"That's different. They're younger and . . ."

"You're not impressed by them. Well, just think of your audience as made up of friends—which it is for the most part—and talk to them as though they were children. Don't be patronizing, but keep it simple, so you can teach them what you want them to know."

"But I would be asking them for money and support."

"You would be doing your job. Remember, most people *want* to do some good in the world and you are helping them do it. Giving alms is a holy act and you are providing a channel through which this money can be put to good use. Yes, it feels like begging and we are taught to be self-sufficient, but I think of what natural mothers do for their children: put up with men who treat them badly, give up food so their children can eat, follow their husbands wherever they must, work outside the home, then come home and work all night. Yes, it is hard, but for them I can do it. And for the Lord's work."

Thomasina considered this as the ferry docked. Miss Culbertson never lacked for things to do. Thomasina didn't realize she must like some things better than others. Or that some were harder than others. The rescues were dramatic. The girls' stories were dramatic. Scrubbed and shining little girls in spotless sams singing hymns for visitors on Sunday mornings were adorable. Women who returned to Canton to their families or who were married in the Mission were heartwarming success stories. These were the visible parts of the director's work. She wondered if Miss Culbertson missed her family. Most of the time Thomasina was too busy, but then in a quiet moment, she missed her sisters' teasing and comforting.

Thomasina was learning about keeping accounts, begging for funds, and working with Amos Cohn, their lawyer, on guardianship papers. She learned about persuading the wholesaler to keep delivering vegetables when they couldn't pay his bill. She could not pass a baby in a woman's arms at the Mission without touching the warm head or patting the fat cheek. She often carried a baby to relieve the mother while she checked accounts or supervised playtime. The part she did now—teaching, disciplining the girls, teaching them how to sew, leading prayers—was just a small part of the picture.

Presbyterians had a tradition of missionary work. The first white woman over the Oregon Trail in 1836 was a Presbyterian missionary named Narcissa Whitman who went with her husband, Marcus, to a mission at Waiilatpu in Oregon Territory. It was easy to overlook that she was a difficult and unpopular woman and non-Christian Indians murdered her eleven years later. But there was no tradition for an urban mission to Chinese women. How did Miss Culbertson learn everything?

The men training for pastorates could study theology and homiletics and moral philosophy at the seminary in San Anselmo, but she could recall no courses that taught you how to feed sixty women and girls a day, keep the housekeepers and cooks happy, maintain good liaison with the police force, and look presentable when you go begging for money.

Miss Culbertson might be overburdened, but certainly she never had to worry about being idle or bored.

Thomasina turned to Miss Culbertson as they walked to the streetcar stop. "How do you ever find the strength to do all this?"

Miss Culbertson looked at her with a strange, almost pitying expression. Thomasina realized that Miss Culbertson never patronized her, although she certainly was ignorant.

"I pray," said Miss Culbertson.

"That's all?"

" 'Ask and it shall be given; seek and ye shall find.' Love and help are always here, if you remember to ask."

7

Liu finally accepted occupation. Lan Yu brought her a length of silk and a handful of embroidery floss. After one of the older women had sewn the long seams on a machine, Liu condescended to sew the rest of the garment by hand. She sketched an elaborate flower, transferred it to the sam, and began stitching in the design.

Thomasina watched the little girls in the play yard behind the Mission. They often skinned their knees and tore their trousers on the hard bricks. Scarcely a blade of grass grew in Chinatown, although pots of greenery and flowers stood on every balcony. At the top of Nob Hill, a few blocks away, fenced-off grass around rich people's houses grew for viewing, but not for playing on. The Chinese had taken land nobody else wanted in the old days and had been confined to "their" part of town. They had dug basements and subbasements and maybe sub-subbasements to find enough room to live. A labyrinth of alleys and streets and interconnected buildings resulted. They extended their living space with awnings over sidewalks. Thomasina knew she would get lost if she were to venture there alone. Thomasina had to leave behind her normal trepidations and shed her usual expectations if she were to go on a raid again. At least the San Francisco police were willing to accompany the women.

Miss Culbertson never lost her way.

Thomasina was called out of classes again and again. She designated a cadre of substitutes from among the "big girls." These normally giggly teenagers were the brightest and most responsible and considered their duty an honor. Some of the girls seemed to be so damaged by their pasts that they were slow. Others clung to Chinese and struggled with English. Most of the girls hesitated, then embraced American ways when they had a chance, but some became more traditional—from fear or longing, Thomasina guessed.

The classroom in the basement had only one window, covered with bars, and the ceiling lights burned constantly. The girls put up pictures cut from magazines and drawings they did themselves to brighten up the room. Thomasina considered herself practical and never cared much for decorating. At holidays and special occasions her big sisters, especially Annie, would get carried away with flowers and draped fabric and fancy food. She recognized the girls' need for some touch of beauty, some reminder of nature. She must find a way to do something about that.

Miss Culbertson sat behind her desk.

"I must take some time off and rest. The doctor says I've let myself get run-down."

"But I can't do what you do! I don't know how to go to court with Mr. Cohn. I don't know how to do a rescue by myself."

"Take heart and call on the Lord."

The sun came out—a watery, foggy sun, brilliant and evanescent—and poured through the window of Miss Culbertson's tidy office. The lamp on its tatted doily was not needed momentarily. Miss Culbertson's silver hair and glasses caught the light. For a moment she was radiant, like a painted saint. For just a moment, Thomasina saw her soul. It was tough and energetic and glowed with love of God and the work of the Mission. Thomasina was filled with love for her mentor. Perhaps if she'd had her mother longer, this woman's affection and trust and her good opinion wouldn't be so important. Then the light faded and the lamp on the desk cast its yellow circle again.

"Where you going, Missee Mac?" asked the thin little girl with straggly hair. Thomasina thought the girl hadn't been fed properly for a long time before she came to the Mission. She was undersized and her teeth were bad.

"Going to buy some things downtown for the women who sew," Thomasina replied.

"Can I go with you?" the girl begged.

"Tell me your name," said Thomasina.

"Ho Gop," it sounded like.

"You came here last month, didn't you?"

"Not long."

"Have you been out?"

"No. Who take me? Where we go?"

Thomasina thought about that. She left the Mission frequently to run errands, or visit a friend, or see an exhibition, but the girls and women were almost prisoners. They weren't held against their will, but they stayed within the walls for safety. They couldn't leave without permission. And they never left Chinatown.

Then she remembered herself in Mrs. Brown's Oakland garden: grass underfoot, roses blooming. Spring renewal, God's promise.

That day she left Ho Gop behind, but the next day she asked: "May I take one or two girls with me when I run errands? It will give them an outing and they can learn how to behave in public."

Miss Culbertson hesitated, but agreed. The next problem was which one to take. The oldest? The one who had been at the

Mission the longest? The one who acted most pitiful? Thomasina decided she must take them all, one at a time. The great difficulty for her was that while she knew the girls as individuals, she treated them as a group—"the girls," "the big girls," "the little girls," "the new girls."

She remembered her mother wiping her hands so she could cut pieces of pie dough for her doll's tea parties. She remembered her soft lap as they rocked before bed. Her sisters had made her their project from the age of six. But who made each girl here special?

"Wash your hands and face and put on your Sunday sam," Thomasina told Ho Gop the next time she needed to run an errand. It was a streetcar ride down to a shop on Market, not much of an excursion, but they would have some time together coming and going.

She brushed Gop's hair and rebraided it. She wiped her dusty shoes. She put a touch of oil on the girl's chapped lips. Gop's nose always seemed to be running, so Thomasina stuck an extra handkerchief in her own pocket.

"You must stay with me and speak softly," she said. Gop nodded. Then Thomasina helped her into her coat and they left the mission building and walked down to Stockton. She needn't have warned the child. Gop never said a word. When she didn't hold Thomasina's hand, she clutched her coat sleeve. Thomasina noticed the girl was trembling.

"Are you frightened?"

The girl nodded.

"Why?"

"Too busy."

"You're right—very busy. Noisy, too. Lots of people. But you will be fine. We're going into a big store to buy bias binding and thread and things like that. Watch for the park."

A smile appeared on the girl's face when the streetcar reached Union Square. The little park was full of people, but still it was an open green space in the crowded city. On an impulse, Thomasina got off the streetcar and led Gop through the park. It wasn't actually raining at the moment and they had time to walk the rest of the way. Gop looked around at the people, the shops, the hotels. They walked down to Market and the child gazed wide-eyed at the merchandise displayed.

"Have you ever seen so many things in such a big store?" asked Thomasina.

Gop shook her head.

Thomasina bought the findings and some buttons and an early edition of the *Bulletin*. Gop looked around, disoriented and frightened because they left the store by a different door than they came in.

Thomasina patted her on the shoulder and said, "It's all right." They walked through the crowds to the corner where they waited for the next streetcar.

"When I was a little girl, I would go to town with my big sisters and I watched them get things for our house. I'd help them carry groceries home for dinner. They took me lots of places, but it wasn't busy like this." Gop remained silent, taking it all in.

When they got back to the Mission Thomasina bent to help Gop out of her coat and the little girl, her eyes shining, threw her arms around Thomasina's neck. "Thankee, thankee," she whispered and ran off to her room. The story spread and all the little girls wanted to go out with Thomasina. She promised that each one would have her turn. And she began a list so she wouldn't forget who had gone and who had not.

8

Thomasina made her way through the crowded streets of Chinatown. Once she ventured off the main streets she always felt closed in, especially on a day of alternating fog and rain. The buildings were too close together. The street was too narrow. The awnings and balconies shut out the light. Vertical stacks of Chinese characters on posted notices peeled off the walls. Tattered banners hung in front of shops. On an overcast day like this there was no sky.

She dodged men in black unshaped hats, some with braids tucked up inside, who stood reading notices on the gritty walls. Men in skirts, men in pillbox hats. Their faces even more than their clothes seemed ineffably foreign. She learned never to assume they had just arrived; men here for forty years still wore quilted frog-fastened cotton jackets and flat-heeled slippers.

Her heart went out to a little girl who carried an infant on her back. Another *mooie jai* or just a big sister? A pipe bowl mender sat on the sidewalk with his tools beside him. She dodged a vegetable peddler's shoulder pole baskets as he hurried down the street. Pots of cut flowers lined the curb in front of the groceries. The bootblack plied his trade on a busy corner. Her life, she realized, was as restricted as a nun's; she saw few men of any race except when she was out on errands. She must ask Dr. Robert Marrs, the minister, about the young men in the congregation of the First Presbyterian Church on Van Ness.

She looked at the address on the card she carried. She knew she was on the right street, but most of the buildings lacked street numbers. She was looking for an herb shop. Mrs. Gladys Cross, a member of the mission board, advised Miss Culbertson to try an infusion of a root called *dong quai*. Miss Culbertson seemed frailer than ever to Thomasina in spite of her rest. Her bronchitis seemed chronic now and she coughed often. Thomasina wondered if it could be TB, but Miss Culbertson had been to the brilliant diagnostician Dr. Albert Abrams, who prescribed a medicine she would not take: rest. Thomasina always felt a tremor of panic when Miss Culbertson was sick. She thought of her mother and wondered if she had been ill like this before she died. Thomasina couldn't remember much, mostly impressions that had been overlaid with her sisters' stories.

Thomasina turned a corner, looked for someone who might give her directions. Then she heard men shouting. A woman's shrieks rang out. A young Chinese woman, her vermilion silk dress ripped half off her shoulders, bolted out of an invisible alley a hundred yards in front of Thomasina and raced toward her, screaming. Thomasina stood frozen. Then three men, thick-muscled and coarse-featured, came after the woman. They shouted what surely were curses. Thomasina was stunned. She wanted to escape; she wanted to help the woman. She couldn't move and she didn't know what to do.

The woman sprinted toward Thomasina, her mouth open to gulp air, her eyes blank with terror. She ran toward Thomasina with her hands stretched out for help. Thomasina stepped forward without thinking, reaching for the woman. Their hands briefly touched. Blood oozed through torn silk on the woman's back. Then the men caught her and roughly hauled her back. She kicked and shrieked as they carried her away. Thomasina heard the sound of silk tearing. She started after them and reached the alley in time to see the men disappear with the girl through a carved door flanked by ornate lanterns.

Thomasina stood motionless, her heart pounding. She could not draw a deep breath. This was the kind of woman she never saw on the streets. This was the kind of woman Liu had been. This was the kind of woman she was supposed to help. The woman's fear made her want to help, but how could she find out which house and whether the woman really wanted to escape? How could she demand release?

She shuddered. How could she forget that face, those piercing shrieks? She must learn how Miss Culbertson arranged the raids, how she got the warrants, how she lined up the policemen who accompanied her, how she could do it without getting arrested herself. The ex-prostitutes at the Mission had found a way to get word out to Miss Culbertson, but how many more women who were prisoners wanted to leave and couldn't find an outside ally who could speak English and persuade Miss Culbertson?

Thomasina turned a corner and suddenly, framed in the narrow opening between buildings on either side of the street, she could see for miles—to the gray water of the bay and to Oakland floating in the silver fog beyond. How beautiful the world was beyond the limits of Chinatown! What was her role in this small, exotic patch of the world?

When she found the herb shop at last, Thomasina hesitated at the threshold. For a moment the smells addled her—the heady mix of sharp, sweet, organic, chemical aromas. At her entrance, business paused imperceptibly, then resumed, as singing voices discussed purchases. A smiling clerk bowed and she walked up to the counter. Boxes and bottles on shelves lined one wall to the ceiling. Drawers labeled with pasteboard cards of calligraphy lined another. The glass counter held boxes of substances Thomasina could only guess at. Were they for cooking? For medicine?

She smiled uncertainly and handed the man a slip of paper with the words *dong quai* and equivalent Chinese characters. The man was short, compact, and neatly dressed in a dark gown, with his queue hanging down his back. Incongruously, a pencil was stuck on his ear. He nodded and smiled and pulled a stool over so he could reach a drawer high on the wall. He brought the entire drawer down to the counter.

He asked Thomasina something, but she shrugged. The man consulted with the other clerk, who was perhaps the owner—an older, thinner man with gold spectacles.

"Missee, power or lut?"

"What?" Thomasina recognized English, but what was "power"?

"Power or lut?" he repeated.

Thomasina looked around in panic. What was she supposed to do? She looked at the plump clerk, then looked into the drawer. He picked up a jar and opened it. A funny bacon smell reached Thomasina. The clerk dipped fingers into the porcelain jar and sifted a yellow-brown powder between his fingers. "Power," he repeated and drifted another pinch of the stuff between his fingers.

"Powder!" Thomasina exclaimed. The man nodded and smiled and said, "Power."

Thomasina looked again into the drawer, hoping for inspiration for "lut." She saw pieces of dried vegetable matter, like mushrooms. The clerk picked up a piece and said, "Lut. Lut." He turned to his compatriot and she heard a string of Chinese words with "lut" repeated. She heard the liquid sounds and remembered the usual substitute and said, "Rut." The little man turned and she repeated, "Rut."

He smiled and nodded vigorously. "Lut, yes."

"Is it hard to make into a powder?" she asked. The little man reached for a mortar and pestle and added a small flake of the root and turned the pestle swiftly. In a few seconds, the flake was powdered. But Thomasina knew Miss Culbertson would need more than one flake and that she might not feel like powdering it herself each time.

"Thumbnail piece," said the clerk. And mimed putting a piece of the root into his mouth and chewing.

Thomasina didn't know if Miss Culbertson would chew it. "How many times a day?" Thomasina asked.

"One time, two time." The man shrugged.

"Prices?"

The clerk wrote one price and pointed to the jar, another price, much cheaper, and picked up a piece of root. Thomasina had been told to buy two ounces and had enough money for powdered *dong quai,* so she pointed to the jar. "Two ounces."

The clerk measured carefully, tapping the powder from the end of a blunt spatula onto a paper on one side of the scales, then he twisted the paper into a cornucopia and folded the end over. Thomasina placed it carefully in her case and gave the clerk the money.

He smiled, a sunny face that had more than just commercial warmth in it, and she smiled back. "Powder or root," she said and giggled. He laughed and nodded.

When Thomasina returned from her errand, the Mission was in an uproar. Miss Culbertson stood at the door of her office, giving orders to search places in the mission building.

"Basement storerooms," she said and two pairs of older women scurried off. She pointed to four teenage girls. "Start at the top floor and check everything, every room and every closet, too." The girls nodded and with serious expressions took the stairs two at a time.

Liu's sister, Lan Yu, stood wringing her hands nearby.

Thomasina tried to ask Miss Culbertson what was going on, but the older woman waved her away with a peremptory, "Later."

Thomasina went to her room and took off her hat, then made her way against a surging tide of searchers to the kitchen to Sun Lee.

"Liu run away," said the cook. She filled a kettle and put it on the stove.

"Why did she do that? We treated her well." The search continued in the other rooms, but footsteps were slower. Only braver, older girls would go to the subbasement and then only in pairs because devils might lurk in the dark.

"You treat her like 'Melican girl. She used to Chinee whore."

"But . . . but . . ." Thomasina rejected the idea. "Surely she didn't want to go back to that, that *place* where we found her?"

Sun Lee shrugged. "Why not? Plenty opium, plenty men, plenty silk sam. Not have to sew or sing English songs."

"But that isn't hard, is it?"

"Too hard for Liu."

Thomasina watched the cook's stately movements as she made the tea.

"Today I saw a woman try to run away in Chinatown. She would gladly trade places with Liu."

"Today, maybe." Sun Lee poured steaming water over the tea leaves in the pot and stirred.

"Why do some women want to stay here and some change their minds?"

Sun Lee settled down on her stool. She looked hard at Thomasina and Thomasina wondered what she was thinking. Then the older woman cleared her throat, her signal she was lining up the English words so they would mean what she wanted them to mean.

"I know a woman who ran away, came here, begged Missee to take her in. She stay here, never went outside because old master might grab her. She good worker, sew clothes, cook. Then sister send word she want out, too. First girl go to Missee and ask, can we go get sister? She wants sister to have a chance even if it means no silk, no lotus, no men."

"Tell me," Thomasina said.

"Don't know all the words," Sun Lee began. "Hard to tell. You maybe don't want to know."

"Go slow. I need to know so I can make good judgments, so I can understand."

Sun Lee hesitated, searching for the right English words. At first Thomasina offered words, then she sat in silence.

"In China, woman is nothing. In China, woman belong to father, husband. If people starving, father sell daughters."

She noticed Thomasina's look of sadness. "Better than die. Sell daughters to men who put them in—places." Thomasina nodded. She knew Sun Lee meant brothels.

"If man buy girl, he can do anything. Make her wife, make her second wife, anything. He can sell her, make her hundred man's wife, take her money. She do what he says. She must show respect. It is her destiny. How she live? He has money. She can't talk English."

"Can't she leave, get a divorce?"

Sun Lee shook her head. "No. All Chinese men same. Take her back or use her same way. Sometimes grab women off the streets, take them. So this woman stay inside house all time. Too many men come Californee, leave wives behind. Women can't come unless wife or daughter, so men need whores. Buy baby girls and raise them for houses."

Thomasina's mouth dropped. "They raise them, like cattle, to do this?"

Sun Lee nodded.

"Could they take you!?"

"No. They know Missee go to law, but I don't leave much. Good woman no go out on streets."

"It must be awful to do that work," said Thomasina.

"You work, alla time, anyway. But Chinese not like 'Melican— they think okay for hundred man's wife because that human nature."

"You mean it's not looked down on as morally wrong?"

Sun Lee's face revealed her struggle with the words. "Human nature to want sex, so why make whore bad person? She just filling her place, someone has to do. Sometimes they go back and marry, if they don't get sick. They send money to families in China. Sometimes even families tell them to go because they want money. Father tell girl who to marry, so why not tell her to be whore?"

"That's awful!" exclaimed Thomasina.

"That's 'Melican," said Sun Lee. "Chinee say it just is." Sun Lee picked up the thread of her story. "One mission girl stay here, get her sister out. She know her sister is treated bad. Sister sick, and fall behind when she don't work. Both women afraid of sister's master, he lose money, he beat sister, call her names, say she's worthless. She have no face.

"One night Missee go to get her. Girl wait and wait, seems like all night. Missee say later sister put in secret hole in wall, but they find. Missee know how to look.

"Sister come to Mission and girl and sister together. Girl take care of sister, but she too sick. She die soon."

Sun Lee wiped tears. She could weep without her voice changing, without her expression changing, as though she had learned not to reveal herself. But her tears betrayed her. "Missee didn't put her in street to die, but let her die in house. Then she not understand we need scare away spirits with noise and prayers. 'Melican believe different. When somebody die, they talk over her, Dr. Marrs talk over sister. Nobody afraid of her spirit. Nobody care for her grave Chinee way, so her spirit wanders for ten thousand years."

"How sad," said Thomasina. "I didn't know that's what you believed. We must step on Chinese beliefs all the time because we don't recognize them."

Sun Lee gave her a hard look. And Thomasina knew she had guessed the truth.

"You never complain," said Thomasina. "Very few of the women complain to me or Missee. We have roll call in the morning and everyone has to have permission to leave the house—that's not like living in an ordinary way."

"That way Missee know no girl stole back or run away. We know she try to keep us safe even if rules funny."

"What's funny?" asked Thomasina.

"Singing alla time English. Why not some Chinee song?" And Sun Lee began a nasal whining melody, a mischievous expression on her face. Thomasina needed to learn Chinese beliefs so that she didn't violate what they cherished, no matter how foreign or heathen. And she must try to make sure everyone knew the reasons for the rules.

Thomasina sipped her tea. The hubbub had died as they talked and she should take Miss Culbertson's *dong quai* to her. Miss Culbertson would fill her in on what had happened.

"Thank you," said Thomasina. "I must learn more about your culture."

Later, with Miss Culbertson, she related what Sun Lee had told her about the woman and the sister who died.

"Sun Lee's sister," said Miss Culbertson. "Liu and Lan Yu remind her of her own efforts."

"Sun Lee's sister?!" exclaimed Thomasina. "I should have guessed."

"Some of what we learn about the women is sordid," said Miss Culbertson. "I have tried to accustom you to it in stages. Sun Lee has introduced you to another stage. The women are degraded. We must not only feed and clothe and protect them, we must always treat them with respect, even the ceremonial Chinese style of respect that often seems absurd to us."

"Sun Lee said she had lost her face."

"When you curse a Chinese or treat them badly, it isn't just a sign of disrespect. You can destroy their spirit. Did you notice how abject Liu was when we found her, her head down and her shoulders, her whole body drooping and cowering, her whole spirit servile? Restore their spirit and they are a light in the world for good. Their souls shine through because they know God loves them and we love them. It's not the same as the love of their natural family, or a beloved husband, but it is respectable and they have dignity. Do you understand, my dear?"

"I am beginning to. I thought I had learned everything I needed to know the first six months. But the longer I stay the more there is to learn."

"You are a most apt student," said Miss Culbertson. She smiled at Thomasina. Miss Culbertson treated everyone with dignity—Officer John Francis and Dr. Robert Marrs and Liu and Amos Cohn. And herself. At that moment Thomasina realized that Miss Culbertson now treated her as an equal. The older woman gave Thomasina dignity, too.

9

"Ladies do not shriek and babble," said Thomasina irritably. Today she was in no mood for the noise. "You must control yourselves. Well-behaved girls learn to stop giggling and be quiet." The clamor of the smaller children in the morning energized Thomasina. They climbed all over her and hugged her and she laughed as she taught them. But after lunch these older girls—twelve, thirteen, and fourteen—drained her.

"Chinese women not quiet," retorted Hsiang. If all giggles stopped, Hsiang's audience would disappear.

Thomasina nodded. She knew this went against their cultural tradition. She had heard women in Chinatown speaking loudly at the markets, almost barking at each other. The language seemed harsh at high volume, not musical.

"You teach us we equal, then tell us to shut up," Hsiang continued.

"Hsiang!"

The girl fell silent, pouting. Thomasina knew that, as usual, there was some truth in what she said. The more irritating Hsiang was, the more Thomasina knew she had to address the issue.

"I was reared with the saying, 'Children should be seen and not heard.' Respect for your elders is always necessary," Thomasina began. She put her pointer down. "Children don't know the wisest way to behave and they need the guidance of older people, who have lived longer and learned more." Thomasina was feeling her way into this subject. "Children cannot run the world and when they don't listen, they can't learn from adults around them."

The girls looked subdued. They were really good girls, eager to please. She continued: "So we make you learn how to control your tongues so you will be considered courteous and well mannered by American people. Sometimes just keeping still will allow people to accept you. If you are rowdy and noisy, they will say the Mission isn't doing a good job. It will reflect badly on all of us. This is hard to explain. If you are dirty or noisy, white people will think you are low class. But you aren't. You are smart and pretty." The giggles started again and every girl but Hsiang at least smiled. "You look neat and you sing like angels." More giggles because they knew Thomasina couldn't sing. "People will be prejudiced because you aren't just like them. I don't want you to be just like American girls, but I want you to make a good impression. Not just to make me proud, but because in the long run it will allow people to appreciate you. You will find husbands." The last was always the girls' wish. An unmarried Chinese woman was considered unfortunate.

Hsiang still glowered. "If quiet and well mannered is important, why you never get married?"

"That's impertinent!" Thomasina exclaimed, louder than she wanted to. "Go sit outside Miss Culbertson's office and if she asks, tell her what you said. Tell her I sent you out. Go!"

The thin girl, still glowering, walked out of the room, looking daggers at Thomasina. Hsiang's eyes were small and she was one of the few girls on whom the shingle cut was not becoming. Hsiang was the only girl who could easily provoke her.

Thomasina finished the lesson and went with the girls to the sewing room and got them started. Then she called on one of the older women to oversee them. She went to her room and closed the door. She had said she had a headache, which was true, but mostly she felt too miserable to keep going. Augustus Booker and his daughters and a missionary from Calcutta were coming to stay at the Mission. Her sisters Annie and Helen were coming for Christmas and she was thinking of home in the valley and all the people she knew there—the Ducik family with two attractive brothers, Ben and Charlie, and two homely sisters, and of George Sergent, who had been her fiancé. In the valley, everyone called her Tamsen, her family nickname.

Back in her room, she took up her journal and her pen, but did not write. She lifted a photograph from her dresser and looked at the two teenage boys in it. One of the boys was her brother Al and the other was George Sergent. They sat on the ground with their hands clasped in front of their knees. They wore boots and broad-brimmed hats and Al had a pipe in his mouth. They were on their way to the mountains for a hunting trip and they were smiling.

Truth be told, Al was the better-looking of the two. George had a receding chin and pale eyes.

Thomasina remembered them coming back with a deer, which meant plenty of fresh meat and sausage for the table. They had a great time and regaled the girls with stories of their adventures and all the deer they didn't get. Thomasina remembered envying their freedom to go off that way, without a care about whether they could find a place to relieve themselves, or if they would start their monthly flow.

They hadn't worried about washing, or what they'd eat. They came back when they were ready.

Thomasina was still angry at George. And hurt. If she weren't so tired today she wouldn't be weeping in her room. She pulled a handkerchief out of her pocket. Hsiang had reminded her that she wasn't married.

At twenty-six it wasn't too late, but she didn't meet many single men working here, surrounded by women. She stretched out on her narrow bed and closed her eyes; memories came unbidden.

George was one of the boys from San Jose—they had been in Sunday school together and their families knew each other. George was a year ahead of her in grammar school. She had been gone from San Jose for her teacher's training, when she ran into George at a church gathering that spring while she was still in school. He was at Davis, studying scientific agriculture.

She had been glad to see him, a familiar face at the big meeting. They ate together and talked about people they knew. George looked at her affectionately and she felt herself hoping he liked her. He grinned and told her jokes and they sat together at the picnic lunch in the church yard. A small apricot orchard stood behind the church building. The congregation had grown in just the few years since the McIntyres had moved to the area and already they were talking about selling the orchard. What would the valley be without crop farms and vineyards and orchards?

"What do you want to do when you finish school, Tamsen?" George had asked. He lay on the grass, staring up through the branches of the tree. Tamsen leaned against the trunk, watching him. The sunlight, bright and hot once the fog burnt off, caught the gold in his hair.

"Teach somewhere." Tamsen wondered what it would feel like to put her hand in his. She longed to touch him and feel his skin on hers.

"Little children?"

"Of course. I love children. And when I'm around them, my enthusiasm makes them want to learn. I always teach Sunday school. I have such a good time."

"I don't have the patience for that," he answered.

"You have the patience to handle cattle—and they don't ever get any smarter." Tamsen wondered if she should have just agreed with him. No, if she had to pretend it wouldn't work.

"That's different. If you shout or take a prod to them, they don't cry. Might try to get you, but you don't have to worry about the future."

"What do you plan, George?" Tamsen asked, caring what he said.

"I want to raise sheep. We've done better with sheep than Herefords, over the long run. A dry year and there's no pasture and we have to cull the herd and then when prices go back up, we don't have as many to sell."

"Sheep need pasture, too."

"Yes, but they can get along better than cattle. If I could get on as manager at a big ranch, I could live there and work with the sheep and manage the rest of the operation."

"Nobody's going to give you a big ranch to manage."

"Well, maybe I'll have to start with a small place, but that's how I want to live—in the country, raising livestock. Where do you want to live?"

Tamsen wasn't ready for that. She had to think. "I'm used to living with my sisters. I guess I think we'll be together forever. A ranch would be nice, with fresh air and lots of room for children to run and play. I lived on a ranch when I was little," Tamsen said. "I loved it. You could see the mountains."

"That's what I like—you can live in the valley and still have mountains nearby."

Tamsen wondered if he would laugh if she told him about God-the-Mountain she believed in when she was little.

"That sounds perfect," she agreed. They were talking about some misty future, but they both knew they were talking about themselves.

"I wish I could kiss you," George said.

Tamsen was so embarrassed she didn't know what to say. She was eighteen years old and she had only been kissed a few times. "I'd like that, too," she whispered.

"We can't do that in front of everybody," he said. "I wouldn't want anybody to think anything."

"Of course not," she agreed.

The bell rang for the next session and Tamsen gathered up their plates and napkins.

"May I call on you, when I can get away from school?" It sounded formal and stiff, but she knew he was being proper.

"Certainly. My family knows you and I'd be happy to see you." Tamsen's heart raced.

That was how it had started.

Tamsen worked hard to make good grades. She knew her sisters and brother were making sacrifices to send her to school. She hungered for all the knowledge in all the books in the library, and was impatient with the limits of her assignments, but knew that the price of being able to do what she wanted later—teaching—hinged on doing what the school wanted now. Once she learned how to learn, she could keep going the rest of her life.

And George started coming around on weekends when she was home. They went for walks, they bicycled, they attended church services, they went on family picnics, they visited friends for musical evenings—things all young people did. George and Al were old buddies and it was no trouble for them to share Al's room overnight. That fall, the boys went hunting together, as the photo recorded.

George brought up marriage early, and he and Tamsen talked in tentative ways about getting engaged. They seemed in perfect accord about how they wanted to live: on a ranch, raising livestock, having a family. She felt comfortable with George—they both had the same background. They went to the same church, prayed the same prayers. Al and her sisters admitted him to the family with no probation.

On Christmas Eve the year Tamsen was eighteen, George said he had a surprise. This trip he stayed with the Bogardus family and visited the McIntyres in the evening. Tamsen assumed he was talking about a Christmas present. She had sewed him two new flannel shirts, to keep him warm outdoors. They were wrapped and under the tree. Annie, who loved nothing better than a party, had decorated the living room with evergreen boughs tied with ribbons and made a special dessert, a flaming plum pudding instead of one of her decorated cakes.

After dinner, Jessie led the singing and Annie made fudge. They strung popcorn for the tree, mostly for nostalgia since they had already hung their ornaments. Then they lit the candles and the piney smell of the warmed boughs spread through the house. George took Tamsen aside.

"I have a special present for you," he said. He looked excited, as though he had a great secret.

"Where is it?" Tamsen hadn't seen any wrapped gift in his hands.

George reached in his coat pocket and pulled out a tiny jeweler's box. Tamsen gasped. George shyly held it out to her. She opened the stiff box. Inside was a sparkly brooch with tiny diamond chips, in the shape of a heart. Tears sprang to her eyes.

"Oh, George," was all she could say.

He put his arm around her. "I want us to get married. I want to set the date."

"But how can we afford—"

"I have a position as manager of a ranch after this semester. I'll be working near Santa Barbara. It's not much, but it includes a house."

Tamsen's heart was pulled two ways: she wanted to be with George but she also wanted to teach and use what she was learning this year.

"We must talk it over with the family."

"Of course," George answered. He ducked and kissed her, barely brushing her lips. She was startled and pulled back. Then she leaned forward and kissed him tenderly on the cheek.

Tamsen felt George's warm hand search above her stockings. Her thighs felt warm, too, and she didn't know what to do. She had let George go this far, encouraged it even, and now she knew it was time to stop.

She pulled away from him and sat up a little. She felt hot and flustered. He scrambled after her, grabbed her, and kissed her again. To her shock, he tried to stick his tongue in her mouth. When she jerked back, he refused to release her. He held her tightly and pushed his face against hers, his body against hers.

"This is not what I thought you wanted to do!" She was angry that he had stepped over a line she had drawn. But then she hadn't drawn it very clearly. She was torn between what she wanted and what she thought she was supposed to say.

Tamsen pushed herself out of his grasp and got to her feet. George didn't say anything. She could hear the creek trickling nearby and birds singing in the dusty trees. It was deserted up here in the park on a weekday. She walked back over to where their bicycles leaned against a manzanita tree. She had left her stylish puffed-sleeve shirtwaists at home and wore one of Allan's old shirts with the sleeves cut off at the elbow. She and George had pedaled up to the foothills of the mountains near Saratoga where the landscape tilted steeply, a barrier between the ocean and the valley.

"I would expect you would want to find out," George said. He sounded sulky.

"Why would I want to do something that's against the way we've been raised and against decency?" Tamsen felt guilty, as though she had done something to provoke George. She could feel his hand yet, warm on the bare skin between her bloomers and the top of her stocking.

"I thought you loved me," he accused.

"If you loved me, you wouldn't try to do anything like this," she countered.

"You know that animals that can't breed are useless on a farm."

"I thought you wanted me for more than breeding!"

"You know what I mean. Besides, nobody will know. We're up here alone. How will we know that we're, uh, compatible if we don't try?"

"I'm ashamed of you. I thought I knew you better. I didn't think you were so low-minded." Tamsen wouldn't have been so righteous if she hadn't felt guilty, if she hadn't wanted to do it. She had to leave, she couldn't stay here without succumbing to George, but she wanted to calm down before she got on her bike. The road was rough and twisty and she didn't want to fall.

"I think you're being overly particular," George said. "Al and Maggie have probably done it a dozen times."

"I don't care what anybody else has done. Shame on you for saying that about Al. I intend to save myself until my wedding night. And I don't think it's going to be with you!" Tamsen mounted her bicycle and pedaled to the road. She had grass stains on her skirt and her shirttail was out, but she wasn't going to argue with George. He could apologize later. She hoped she remembered the way back. It would be a long way home across the flat valley without him.

He caught up with her on the main road into San Jose. He didn't say anything, but adjusted his speed to hers. She didn't say anything. She wasn't going to mention this to Al or her sisters. She didn't want them to know she had even come this close to doing something she would be ashamed of. She was still too angry to talk to George; she felt too guilty. He followed her home.

She turned on him in the drive up to the house.

"What do you want?" she demanded.

"You know what I want," he said boldly.

"And that will not happen! I'm not a woman who lives one way in public and another way in secret. If you don't know me well enough to know that, then you haven't been paying attention. I suggest you find another girl who doesn't mind finding out if you're *compatible.*"

She stormed into the house and returned with the small jeweler's box. She felt like flinging it at him but presented it politely, turned on her heel and went back inside.

She had cried a long time that night. She didn't tell Annie what was the matter. George must have said something to Al because the next day her sisters stopped asking her what was wrong.

She had done what she thought was right. You were supposed

to feel righteous and elevated, but she felt miserable. One minute she wanted George to come knocking at the door to give her back her brooch. The next minute she wanted to be back up under the manzanita tree with her skirt up. The next minute she wanted never to see him again. That turned out to be the painful part. She saw him at church events when he was home from school and by the next summer he had found a buxom girl from a Bohemian family who looked like a good breeder. Tamsen prayed that her bitterness would pass. When she had come to the Mission, she hadn't had time to think about George and she thought she had gotten over him, but now and again the memories rose up and surprised her and she would find tears in her eyes. She regretted nothing, but she was sad that she had lost a friend and gained a bit of cynicism.

What she had taken so seriously with George she now considered commonplace, at least for the girls at the Mission. She wondered if it had been very hard the first time. Most of them had been forced to do what she had been privileged to refuse.

How had they been able to face the loss of their dignity? If Tamsen had felt guilty for leading George on, how much more degraded these women must feel who had done nothing? It would have destroyed her, she thought now, to have succumbed to George's pleas. When you learn what is right, and you don't live by those principles, your conscience destroys you, she thought.

A knock startled her. "Yes?"

"Missee sick. You come."

Oh, dear Lord! Thomasina hurried to Miss Culbertson's room. Sun Lee bent over the bed. Miss Culbertson looked like a shadow. Her face was gray and her lips colorless. Thomasina's heart tightened. This looked very serious.

"You must keep things going while Miss Culbertson is on leave," said Mrs. Brown. The Occidental Mission board met hurriedly the next day; the women with veiled hats and impeccable gloves sat around the table in the conference room. There had been no time to arrange for flowers, although cookies and tea appeared immediately from the kitchen. Miss Culbertson was going to stay with a friend in Berkeley until she recovered. She couldn't wait; she must stop working.

"I don't think I can do what she has done." Thomasina was not being modest; she knew her limitations. "I've only been here one year."

"This is too big a burden to put on you alone. But there is no one else who has your knowledge of Miss Culbertson's work," said Mrs. Brown. "Miss Alverson, the housekeeper, has no knowledge of what Miss Culbertson did outside of the Mission. You were learning, and you must keep things going. Alice and my daughter, Evelyn, can help fill the gaps."

Thomasina nodded. "I can perhaps keep things from stopping, but I don't even know some of the people Miss Culbertson works with."

"We will help you and you can go through Miss Culbertson's files and records."

Thomasina felt the blood drain out of her face. Drawers and drawers of papers, ledgers, and logs. She would never get through all of it! She felt buried under responsibility.

"We realize that we are asking a great deal," said Mrs. Brown. "But you are the only one we can call upon. We don't expect miracles."

"I will stay here until Miss Culbertson recovers. I will do my best. I won't be able to do everything Miss Culbertson did. I will try to do my duty and pray for her recovery. I hope I may call upon you for help."

"By all means," said Mrs. Brown, relief coloring her voice. The other women murmured their thanks. The women rose and began to make their way out of the meeting room. Thomasina always wished the furniture was better. These were wealthy women and only the big conference table, a gift from a benefactor, was at all imposing.

Before she could sink into depression over the size of the job she had taken on, Thomasina was called to the kitchen to deal with a missing delivery. After dinner, she went to Miss Culbertson's office and pulled open the first drawer. She read through half of its contents before she stumbled up to bed, her eyes burning. She would never be able to do this. The Mission would have to close. She could never manage.

"Oh, dear God," she prayed, "how can I do Miss Culbertson's work? Help me! I can't think my way through. How can I manage the cooks and housekeepers and teachers? How can I rescue anybody? How can I take up the burden of fifty girls and women?"

Thomasina gave in and cried, stifling sobs in her pillow. She was so frightened!

After a bit she calmed down and thought of Miss Culbertson's indomitable figure marching into a Chinatown tenement armed only with a writ and her faith. Thomasina could hear her say, "Take heart and call on the Lord."

Why must she hit bottom and feel utterly defeated before she remembered?

"O Lord," she prayed more tranquilly, "give me the strength I need to do Your work. Help me because I can't do it alone. Bear us up on eagle's wings till Miss Culbertson returns."

10

Her first official act as Miss Culbertson's temporary replacement was to host a board meeting. One of the board members quoted a stanza from Kipling's "The White Man's Burden," referring to "Your new-caught sullen peoples / Half-devil and half-child." Thomasina listened as the well-dressed woman dwelt upon the vulgar habits of some of the rescued girls and low-grade Mongolian women who were conscienceless, fiery and voluble, and utterly bereft of reason—truly half devil and half child.

Thomasina disagreed but did not openly confront her. She felt cowardly, for she knew she had thought these things and worse when a girl was giving her trouble. And she tried not to. She looked at Mrs. Brown, whose lips pressed into a disapproving line. She would let Mrs. Brown deal with board members. Miss Culbertson would return soon—she accepted every person without judging and Thomasina thought this a good policy, since it was easy to be wrong when you didn't understand why a woman behaved as she did.

Thomasina arranged for the big girls to sing at this board

meeting. They lined up at the end of the meeting room, dressed in their best sams, trousers, and shiny patent leather shoes. Most of the girls had their hair cut in a Dutch boy bob, which made them irresistibly cute. Then one of the youngest girls, Ah Dong, a bright and precocious child, read from Scripture. She had been shampooed and bathed and her clothes washed and ironed until she gleamed. When she had arrived, she told Miss Culbertson she thought she was about ten years old, but she was small and impish and looked younger. Thomasina wished all the girls could look so cared-for every day but they played and ate and worked and studied and usually looked like "real kids"—not quite so starched and clean. Ah Dong had been coached and last night she had practiced reading in front of Thomasina, who praised her and made hot chocolate in the staff kitchen as a reward for her hard work.

Today the women of the board noticed that the girls smiled more and ascribed it to Thomasina's buoyancy. Then Ah Dong read. She stumbled only once. When Ah Dong finished, she looked at Thomasina. Thomasina was so proud tears had come to her eyes. She nodded and the little girl ran to her, and climbed into her lap. Thomasina whispered what a good job Ah Dong had done and the little girl buried her face in Thomasina's bosom.

"What is she saying?" asked Mrs. White. "What did she call you?"

"Lo Mo," answered Thomasina. "When she first came she attached herself to me. She spoke no English. She used to rub my back with her little hands. They said she had done that for her former mistress and it was her way of saying thank you. The older girls told her 'Lo Mo' wasn't respectful, it was like 'little old mama' instead of 'respected elder mother.' But it's easy to say and easy for me to understand."

"You seem to know what the girls need. Do you think you can find the energy to mother so many?" Mrs. Brown wasn't questioning Thomasina's sincerity, but sounded truly concerned that Thomasina could provide so much affection.

"I was going to stand up and present a proper speech, but I

can do it with Ah Dong here." Thomasina turned in her chair to face the women, still holding the girl in her lap. "Ah Dong arrived one Sabbath morning with only a few dirty clothes, a comb, and her chopsticks. She had a scrap of paper with her name written in Chinese characters. She had enough spirit to get here, then she put her fingers in her mouth and couldn't speak. We welcomed her as the father welcomed the Prodigal Son. She marched up to me, put her bundle aside, and prostrated herself before me. I was embarrassed to death, naturally. I picked her up. She was stiff with fear, but she didn't back away. When I kissed her, she began to cry and so did I. We held each other for quite a while, then I turned her over to one of the older women who began the long process of teaching her by love instead of with blows and curses. That was right after I came. You can see what a bright girl she is. The girls and women always called Miss Culbertson 'Missee,' and I was 'Missee Mac.' Then Ah Dong called me 'Lo Mo' and that kept everyone from being confused."

She paused and Ah Dong slid from her lap and ran upstairs, overcome with pride and embarrassment.

Thomasina knew she must choose her words carefully, not because Mrs. Brown wished to put her on the spot, but because she needed to clarify for herself what she could do.

"I lost my own mother when I was six years old," Thomasina continued. "I wish I had more memories of her. My sisters and brother became my family. I received so much love from them that I have a well that never runs dry. I may be tired or distracted or worried, but I can raise my eyes to the mountain and find strength. The girls nurture me with their affection. I don't feel adequate to fill Miss Culbertson's shoes, but I want to do this needed work. Miss Culbertson accomplished more than any other person could have done. But even she didn't do it alone. She has the wonderful knack of getting people to work with her. I hope I have a little of that ability. Did I answer your question?"

Thomasina looked at her hands. She had been twisting a handkerchief as she talked. She had spoken well, but her nervousness was obvious. So be it. It hadn't seemed to put them off. The women rose now and congratulated her. They went to the meeting room for tea, then settled down to work out the year's budget.

Miss McIntyre was also invited to address the Presbyterian Home Mission Society at a new congregation in Berkeley. Ah Dong and Suey Lee stood in silent fascination at her doorway. The girls' rule was: no entry without an invitation. Everything Lo Mo wore or used was interesting to the girls, who had grown up among traditional Chinese women.

They watched in silence as she pinned a fresh collar to her best blue suit, which was now four years old. Her salary of twenty-four dollars a month didn't stretch very far. She put a fresh handkerchief in the pocket of her skirt. She brushed her hair again and twisted it up and began pinning it on top of her head. It was thick, sandy, and never looked completely smooth—the San Francisco humidity made it want to curl. Already she found too many silver hairs to count. The two girls chattered, then Ah Dong said, "You go out, come back today?"

"Yes. I must talk to some nice women. I wish I knew the exact words that would move their hearts, so they will send us money to care for more girls."

"I talk to them," said Ah Dong. "I tell them." Suey Lee giggled at the boast.

"I sing songs and tell stories and you won't have to work hard," the girl offered.

Thomasina walked over and hugged both girls. "You are a big help," she said.

The girls watched wistfully as Thomasina finished pinning her hat in place.

"When I'm a big girl, I'll go out, wear hat and gloves," said Ah Dong.

"How long since you've been outside the Mission?" asked Thomasina.

"Not since never. Old master might take Ah Dong back. I'm not afraid," she said with bravado. "Other girls not have master maybe waiting."

Thomasina knew that Ah Dong arrived at the Mission about the same time she had. And she had not been out since! She knew that many of the wives of Chinatown labored inside their homes and were never seen on the busy sidewalks except during the Moon Festival. All outside business was transacted by their husbands. But for a child never to go farther than the fenced play yard in back of the Mission!

"Get dressed," said Thomasina. "Hurry! Sunday clothes. Both of you. Tell Ho Gop, Elizabeth, and Yeen to get dressed, too. Wash your face and hands, don't forget."

The girls raced upstairs to find the others. Miss McIntyre needed help to keep five little girls in line, translate for her, and watch them on the excursion. She thought of the big girls she could call on. Most of them were obedient and helpful, but she needed someone who could be resourceful if necessary. She found Hsiang in the sewing room and explained she was needed. In twenty minutes six girls, five little ones and Hsiang, stood in their best sams, with polished shoes and combed hair, ready to go. Ah Dong had to borrow a coat.

"You must stay with me all the time," said Thomasina. "We will take the streetcar, then the ferry, and you mustn't wander off or get lost. No noisy talking or games. You must be very quiet. Hsiang will be my second. If Hsiang tells you to do something, you mind her. I must talk to the ladies while we're there. Has everybody been to the necessary? Does everybody have a handkerchief?" She watched nods all around. She checked to make sure she had enough street carfare for everyone and a bit more. Her notes were in her bag. With some trepidation, she said, "Then let us go."

The girls were silent and big-eyed as they traveled to Berkeley. On the ferry they clung to the rail. One girl had been born in San Francisco, but the others had come from China and remembered, at least faintly, the sea journey. Thomasina watched the fishing boats and the freighters, always amazed at how big the bay was. Thomasina felt like a mother goose with her charges clustered around her. When they got to the church, the little girls drew much comment. She knew they looked presentable. More than that, they looked happy and well taken care of. If they continued their good behavior, they would make a good impression.

"Are we going to sing?" Hsiang asked. She had been a good lieutenant, watchful but not too bossy.

"Why, that's a good idea. Which songs?" They hadn't practiced, but all the girls sang every Sunday. "You choose."

Hsiang spoke to the girls. Suey Lee put her hands in her mouth, but Hsiang had them sing one song under their breath and that centered their attention. When the meeting was called to order Miss McIntyre introduced her charges. They joined her at the front of the room and stood in a row. Hsiang gave the note and they sang "From Greenland's Icy Mountains."

Their singing surprised and pleased the women. Applause was immediate and warm. Hsiang began a second song and the girls' voices rose in the air, pure and lovely.

When they finished, the ladies enthusiastically applauded again. The girls looked proud as they marched back to their chairs.

"My good friends," Miss McIntyre began. "Today you see the results of your generous contributions. You should be proud that because of your efforts, girls like these now have a safe and loving home. They have learned that our Father loves all peoples and that they are cherished.

"Our last little girl was brought to the Mission by her brother. He had labored long to get her out of the loathsome Immigration Shed. Older women, some of them incarcerated without good cause for months, took care of her.

"Ah Lin was terrified of the 'white devils,' but our housekeeper and several of the girls calmed her down and began the process of absorbing her into our family. The brother had discovered his sister was trapped until he could bribe the right official. The Chinese are used to this and consider it part of the cost of emigrating.

"The patterns that are legal and accepted in China are against our laws, but the old ways die hard. Many of the girls and women are helpless because they know no other way of life. All we can do is try to give a home to the girls and women who find their way to 920 Sacramento Street.

"That is where your charity is most valuable. Without the money you so selflessly raise over the year, we could not open our doors to new girls. Who knows what cruelty they endure? When you are in Chinatown and see a picturesque child in Oriental dress, with an infant strapped to her back, you are seeing slavery, as surely as if the girl were a black child picking cotton fifty years ago in the South." She heard a few gasps in the audience. She mustn't be too graphic. She didn't want to disgust the women.

"It costs thirteen dollars a month to feed, clothe, and educate each girl. Many of them have no more than one change of clothing when they arrive. They do not speak English and cannot function outside a protected environment. They do not know the ways of Americans or why they were brought to San Francisco—the Gold Mountains. Thanks to your good work, they learn of their heavenly Father's love. They learn they are valuable children of God, not unworthy girls lucky not to have starved on a Toinsin hillside."

Bring it home, she reminded herself. She was imitating all the charity appeals she had heard in Presbyterian churches all her life, but she wanted to make this real for the women who sat attentive to her message.

"We don't always succeed. Sometimes the owners hear of our coming and hide the girls or take them away. Sometimes the girls lose heart, or they buckle under aggressive questioning by the lawyer at their hearing and are returned to their owner. Sometimes illness claims them in spite of our efforts. But even if we only save one girl, we have told the Chinese community we are on the side of the angels." Thomasina walked over to where the girls sat.

"Here is the proof that what you do is not only worthwhile, but delightful and joyous."

Ah Dong buried her face in Thomasina's skirt and the other girls scurried around her. Her arms embraced all of them. "Thank you," she whispered.

The room was silent for long moments, then the hubbub of talk and applause erupted, along with the snap of handbags as handkerchiefs came out.

The president thanked Miss McIntyre and the little girls were led away for cake and punch. Miss McIntyre talked individually to all the women who came up afterward. She answered questions until they were satisfied. The president promised her they would raise their pledge and thanked her for the entertainment.

On the way back to 920, she felt let down from the nervousness and anxiety of speaking, but relaxed and tired. On the ferry, the girls drew her over to a bench and insisted that she sit down. They stood nearby, resisting the urge to scamper around the deck.

"Hsiang, you are a smart girl," Thomasina said. "I must give you credit. Singing was a good idea."

The girl blushed and said nothing, but her smile was full of pride.

"We must do this every time. If the people can see what their money does, they can't help but be generous. You girls are our best advertisement." She squeezed Hsiang's hand. "I couldn't have done it without you. You are my voice in Chinese. Next time we will get the girls ready in time." Then she paused. "I should ask you if you *want* to do this for me?"

"Yes," said Hsiang. "I am happy to do this. Besides"—and she grinned—"you can't manage without someone to translate."

"Or someone to keep the singing on-key." Thomasina smiled and hugged Hsiang to her. Hsiang hugged her in return, then walked to where two of the little girls were chattering and herded them back toward Thomasina.

A woman dressed in stylish clothes watched the brood of girls. She heard Ah Dong call Thomasina "ma" and got a startled look on her face.

"Are you really their mother?" she asked in a southern drawl that revealed her as a tourist to San Francisco.

Thomasina paused, thought of the guardianship papers with her name on them. And said, "Yes I am." She smiled innocently.

The tourist looked at the six girls ranging in age from eight to fourteen. "But you look so young," she murmured.

Thomasina repressed a smile.

Hsiang waited till the woman was out of earshot. "You're mother to more than us, even. You're one hundred girls' mother," she said.

Thomasina nodded. "That's right. Better than one hundred man's wife."

Hsiang laughed behind her hand.

They stopped for cream puffs at the bakery before they returned to 920.

While Miss Culbertson was gone, Thomasina had trouble finding time to pray. The days were too busy and she never knew when she would be interrupted. Early in the morning and late at night were good times, but she often fell asleep with her Bible in her hand.

She thought if she could stay focused and pray faster, she would keep alert, but that didn't work any better. She was always so sleepy—early or late—that she couldn't concentrate. She thought of priests reading their breviaries as they paced, but her room was too small and in the evening her feet hurt.

One night she gave up.

"O Lord," she began, exasperated. "You know I love You and strive to do Your will. I've tried hard to read my daily portion, but nothing I do is effective. If I can't stay awake and pray, it must be Your will that I sleep.

"Help me tomorrow to know Thy will and do Thy work. May I be a force for good in the lives I touch. Grant this in Jesus' name."

She had stayed focused for the moment. Because she was fed up? Because she had given up? Because she spoke from her heart?

After that, she made her own prayers. Sometimes she asked for help with particular problems or people, but most usually, she gave thanks for the day that was ending and asked for strength for the day that was coming.

11

Amos Cohn had offered his services to Miss Culbertson when he first passed the bar in 1887. He had time, few clients, and a natural inclination for public service. Miss Culbertson and Amos obtained Jane Doe warrants so that when Miss Culbertson raided a dwelling, she had the word of the law and the force of the policemen with her. Later, if the owner objected, Amos defended Miss Culbertson's actions in court. Owners would try for a writ of habeas corpus. Few attorneys would accept work from the Chinese community. Over the years, his practice increased and it became more difficult for him to find time for Miss Culbertson, but their friendship was a warm working partnership forged over time.

When Miss Culbertson returned from her short leave, they rescued a young girl who called herself Choie Ngoh. Miss Culbertson faced curses from the owner the night of the raid. Thomasina did not know what was said that night, but she recoiled at the harsh shouts. Then Miss Culbertson had been notified she was accused of theft and that the owner intended to reclaim his property. That had gotten Miss Culbertson's dander up and she'd sent word to Amos. Most of the routine running of the Mission remained Thomasina's duty; Miss Culbertson handled the legal matters.

The rain began softly blotting the afternoon sun, and continued, a steady, light fall all evening. Thomasina thought her room was chilly. She had gotten used to the unheated rooms, just a little cooler than was comfortable, but this night there was a fire brightening and warming Miss Culbertson's office for dinner with Amos Cohn. Sun Lee and the housekeeper had planned an especially delicious Western dinner—beefsteak, potatoes, green beans, rice custard. (They had plenty of rice.) It was served in Miss Culbertson's office, her desk having been transformed into a buffet with linen cloth, sparkling glasses, and the only bone china they had. A low bowl of hothouse roses, deep bloodred, decorated the center of the buffet. Thomasina was invited and she recognized the importance of this evening: she would learn the legal aspects of the rescues. Miss Culbertson had warned her that the raids themselves were dramatic and easy to understand. Everyone knew about them. Keeping the girls was a matter of using the law to their advantage. Miss Culbertson spoke of "losing some" and Thomasina didn't even want to think about what that meant.

She had washed and changed into a fresh shirtwaist and twisted her hair up more securely. It rarely stayed neat a whole day and this evening she wanted to look especially businesslike and tidy.

She had seen Amos at the house several times in passing, but had never talked to him. He had lively dark eyes and a generous mouth. He smiled easily. He and Miss Culbertson kept business out of the conversation during dinner.

"How long have you been here, Miss McIntyre?" he asked. She answered that it had been nearly a year and he nodded, as if filing this valuable information away. She asked about his connection to the Mission and learned it stretched back nearly ten years.

"Oh, but you don't look . . ." she blurted out.

"I was just a tad when I started," he said. "Miss Culbertson lured me from my office before the paint dried on my shingle."

"Now, Amos, Thomasina won't know when you are teasing and when you are telling the truth." Miss Culbertson smiled easily with his conversation.

Amos told stories suitable for mixed company about happenings at court. He had an interesting case involving two businesses, each accusing the other of unfair practices. Thomasina saw how his incisive mind worked its way through the intricacies of the problem.

"Whoever wins will appeal this case," he predicted, "and I'm looking forward to facing the higher court."

"It won't hurt your reputation if you win," said Miss Culbertson. She went to the door and called two girls who quickly cleared away the dishes.

Amos and Miss Culbertson reminisced about victories and trips to Portland and Los Angeles, and one close call when Amos hid a girl in a taxi. He knew Abe Reuf, who was an up-and-coming politician, and told about his wheeling and dealing. Permission for saloons and railroad spurs and rights of way were up for grabs from the city commissioners. San Francisco still had some frontier spirit. Thomasina thought city politics endlessly fascinating, with bribes and influence and lots of money changing hands. She thought of it as a huge Dickensian story unfolding in installments in Fremont Older's *Bulletin* and in the *Examiner* day by day.

When he paused, Thomasina didn't know how to fill the silence. This wasn't exactly social small talk—Miss Culbertson had little patience for that—and it wasn't exactly business.

"Without you, we would never be able to keep the girls safe," Thomasina blurted. Amos looked at her, appreciative of her awkward recognition. Thomasina blushed at his smile. She started to apologize, but he waved her to silence. Then the papers came out. Miss Culbertson produced her fountain pen and Amos pulled his briefcase from under his chair. Thomasina read each paper, trying to divine its meaning, as they went through them all. Thomasina listened intently as they outlined their strategy.

"The weak point, as always, will be the girl. Do you think she can stand up to questioning? According to the plaintiff, she is his wife and answered the questions the immigration officials posed. What does she say?"

"My translator, Chun Mei, says Choie Ngoh was coached by Ah Toy before the boat docked in San Francisco. She doesn't think the girl will hold up."

"What do you think? Habeas corpus is straightforward."

"I think it's worth the effort, especially as the girl insists. But you are the one who must face the judge. I hate for you to pursue this when there's a chance we might lose her."

"Do you want to give up?" he asked.

"Never!" answered Miss Culbertson.

"Well, then we must coach her, too," said Amos.

Miss Culbertson asked Chun Mei to call Choie Ngoh. While they were waiting Miss Culbertson gave him all the information she had gleaned.

"Choie Ngoh was brought in as the legal wife of her owner, who made yearly trips to Canton. But he made a mistake with Choie Ngoh and didn't learn that she had relatives in San Francisco until their boat was under way. When the relatives learned of her situation, they came to me and we planned a raid. They did not know how to fight the wealthy master and our mission was the only place that had the resources to go to court.

"The testimony of a Chinese person is, as you know, not accepted in court and no one would have believed their word out of general prejudice."

Thomasina thought Chinese people as truthful as anybody, and their business dealings were generally scrupulously honest, but people confused their refusal to swear with dishonesty. The Chinese, on the other hand, thought swearing was foolish. A person who would lie, they thought, would lie under oath.

Amos questioned Choie Ngoh for half an hour. Thomasina almost fell asleep after the heavy meal, but she needed to follow his reasoning. Choie Ngoh looked plumper and prettier than the girls usually rescued. Her face was an almost perfect circle-moon and her eyes were full of anger.

Thomasina learned that she was a fourth daughter of a Canton businessman. He had no sons and thought if she became a second wife to a Gold Mountains businessman, she could move up in the world. Choie Ngoh had memorized the right answers to the immigration official's questions, saying she was the wife of her master. He provided a photograph of himself and another round-faced woman for identification. When Choie Ngoh learned that the business was boardinghouses for men and a bagnio for women, she immediately wanted out of the arrangement. Relatives, who had been glad to see her, came to the Mission begging for help.

After he had finished questioning Choie Ngoh and making notes, Amos gave Miss Culbertson a look. Choie Ngoh left and Amos said, "I don't think this one will stand up to cross-examination."

"I respect your hunch, Amos," said Miss Culbertson. She looked worried. "We will coach her and show her she has nothing to fear."

Miss Culbertson had gone through trials and survived, but most women in the world had not had that tempering. The rest of us aren't so sure of ourselves, Thomasina thought.

Amos outlined his defense, Miss Culbertson and Chun Mei agreed, and the meeting drew to a close. Then, to Thomasina's surprise, Amos lingered, making small talk. He said nothing that could not have been said in the starchiest drawing room on Nob Hill, but everything he said seemed to have a second meaning, if she cared to take it. Miss Culbertson left to see to another unexpected visitor, but Amos showed no sign of leaving.

"Do you plan a life of service, Miss McIntyre?" he asked.

"I don't know what the Lord has in store for me. Originally, this position was for one year, but Miss Culbertson needs me. How often do you do this for her?"

"I've done dozens of cases over the years. Once I understand the owner's argument, I can find a way to attack it. Most attorneys don't bother with domestic matters like guardianship unless someone adopts a child. It had always been available as a legal move, but today only the Celestials use it so liberally for adults, and especially for women."

"I don't understand how there can be slavery in this day and age. It's against the Fourteenth Amendment."

"It isn't slavery in the old sense. It is a form of indentured servitude."

Thomasina listened wide-eyed as he explained. "Because of conditions in the western areas of China men indenture themselves to organizers who pay their passage to California. The workers then have to repay the organizer, make enough money to live, and save money to send back to China. It began with the railroad workers and miners, so it's been part of California history almost from the beginning."

"Thank you," said Thomasina, "for explaining." She remained thoughtful, then said, "Miss Culbertson showed me a contract. We don't know if the girls might really owe their masters money."

"Yes. Sometimes they become concubines—second wives— and are treated well. But the women who come to the Mission are not. They have rights, but don't know it because they don't understand English. So they never learn."

"Some American girls don't exercise their right to say no," said Thomasina. She was thinking of George Sergent and how she had said no.

"American girls exercise charm instead," said Amos. Thomasina had been listening closely; she noticed his voice became playful and his eyes danced.

"Some American girls use their good looks as well," she bantered. "I am too forthright. Subtlety and charm were not gifts that I received at birth. My sister Annie has tried to teach me otherwise, but I seem to blurt out the bald truth without thought to whether the person wants to hear it or not." She gave him a hard look.

"You blurted out a great compliment this evening," he murmured. "It was appreciated."

"I'm afraid I'm as likely to say something brash. I never mean to be hurtful. I'm trying to guard my tongue better."

"I think you should let your tongue find its own truth," said Amos. His voice, cultivated and trained to be heard in a courtroom, had dropped to a husky murmur. Its low register soothed Thomasina. If she closed her eyes, each word vibrated. She must keep her eyes open. His formidable energy, which he had turned toward Choie Ngoh's case, now focused on her. She felt herself blushing and her eyes slid away from his. She was deeply flattered and a bit uncomfortable. No man had paid her attention in a long time.

"You're too flattering by half," she said. She felt light and playful and wished she had the art of flirty conversation.

"If I don't tell you, how are you to know? You and Miss Culbertson are known and recognized by everyone in Chinatown. Hated by some—"

"*Fahn quai,* white devil," she quoted.

"Loved by many." Suddenly that phrase had a special meaning. Then Amos took a deep breath and continued. "Most Chinese are decent, moral, law-abiding people. They brought China to San Francisco because they think we are barbarians and because originally most of them planned to return. They are prisoners of their culture, as much as the girls are prisoners of the brothels."

"What are you a prisoner of?" Thomasina asked.

Amos started and paused in his smooth flow of talk. "You mean we are prisoners, too?"

"We are considered normal for San Francisco, but our way of doing things would be 'foreign' in their country. We have our own constraints."

"You do blurt out the truth, Miss McIntyre," Amos admitted. "Yes, we have our own ways of doing things. Have you studied other cultures to learn the contrasts?"

"No. I am not well educated, but I've read a lot. Jews face prejudice as strong, although more subtle, than that against the Chinese, do they not?"

"Yes, in many ways," admitted Amos. The playful note died. "San Francisco is more open than cities in the East. People think Abe Reuf and a few others run this town from behind the scenes."

"Do Jews marry outside their faith?"

"Not if their family has anything to say about it." Amos's humor was returning.

"If some nice Jewish boy liked me, his mother would stop it, would she not?"

Amos's expression changed. He nodded. Thomasina didn't like reminding him that he was a Jew. Her "forthrightness" had ruined their tête-à-tête.

She sat helpless to undo what she'd said as he gathered his papers and stood. Why bring that up? He was being pleasant, not asking to marry her. She fetched his coat and helped him put it on. She caught a scent of bay rum and leather and clean linen. She rested her hand on his shoulder longer than necessary. He was very attractive. She was glad she stood behind him so he couldn't see her expression—she was sure it revealed her feelings. He was the first man in a long time that set her imagination flying. She envied some lucky Jewish girl.

"You cut right through to the core, Miss McIntyre," he said. He spoke lightly, but it was that false lightness that covers bitterness. "We face a different kind of 'exclusion.' "

"How does it touch you?" Thomasina asked. This was yet another thing she was ignorant of.

"Some companies prefer not to have us represent them. We do not receive domestic cases from the old families. We are valued by businesses, but rarely invited to social events. We cannot join some clubs."

"How unfair! You are smarter than any of them!"

Amos smiled. His eyes were so full of sorrow that Thomasina's heart opened to him. He started to say something, then swallowed. He was obviously touched. Most of the time when Thomasina blurted out something, it got her in trouble or was rude, but Amos was right—sometimes truth escaped. Amos picked up her hand and kissed it lightly. Thomasina felt guilty; she was no better than the merchants who exploited his talents. He had charmed her all evening. First she hadn't noticed, then she was embarrassed. Now she was afraid she had been prejudiced and cruel.

"Will you be in court, Miss McIntyre?" he asked.

"I am learning everything about the Mission. This is one of the most important things the Mission does, so certainly I must learn it."

"May I call on you?" He looked at her appealingly.

"I will consider it," she said. She truly didn't know what to say.

He nodded and bent to pick up his briefcase. They stood and Thomasina prepared to show him to the door. He was short, and they stood eyes even. She remembered that tipped-over feeling she had around George, that half-dizzy, losing-her-balance feeling. She didn't have that feeling about Amos. Feelings were too unreliable—having both feet on the ground was better. Making friends was better. She'd get over this breathless feeling.

She went back to Miss Culbertson's office to see if there were further duties tonight. She felt flushed and excited. She wondered if it showed.

Miss Culbertson returned. "You were quite a hit tonight," she said.

Thomasina blushed. "I didn't mean to be."

Miss Culbertson put a motherly arm around Thomasina's shoulders. "I know that. You are too naive. You must know that you are attractive."

"With my messy hair already turning gray? I haven't flirted with a man in months, not since I left home. I am awkward."

"That doesn't mean you aren't noticed. You behaved very well. I want you to come to court with me Thursday. I have a premonition that this time it won't go well."

"I hope you're wrong. You've worked so hard."

That night she tried to sort it all out in her journal, so she wouldn't forget what Amos and Miss Culbertson had said about the court case. In the brief moments between the time her head touched her pillow and sleep overcame her, Thomasina fell into a reverie about Amos. He was very good-looking. His large liquid eyes were expressive. She couldn't help but wonder how his mouth would feel kissing hers. What was she thinking of! He was Jewish and nothing would come of this.

"O Father, quiet my heart! I am foolish to desire what is not my lot. Please bless Amos for all the good work he does for the Mission. Please let me forget his warm looks and gentle voice. And thank You for his smart brain that does so much good in the world."

Thomasina's hand went to her mouth. They were losing! Miss Culbertson reached over and took her hand away and put it back in her lap. She shook her head sadly.

"But he is not my husband!" Choie Ngoh proclaimed. The Chinese woman leaned forward in the scarred wooden chair. She gripped the railing that separated her from the courtroom. She wore a plain gown of dark cotton, carved shoes, and white stockings. Tension lay thick in the courtroom. Across the room, the Chinese contingent watched closely.

"You swore to the immigration official when you left the boat that Ah Toy was your husband. Did you lie?"

Choie Ngoh hung her head.

"Answer!" demanded the lawyer.

On the other side of Miss Culbertson, Amos Cohn sat motionless, watching and listening.

"Yes. I did what he told me," Choie Ngoh answered.

Chun Mei, Miss Culbertson's right hand, translated. She stood beside Choie Ngoh and repeated each response. By now she was flushed with anger at what she saw the other lawyer doing, but she knew she must keep translating accurately. She had been sworn in, too. Her frail frame wavered, but her voice continued firmly. She was slightly cross-eyed and wore her hair pulled back from her round face. She wore her best silk sam and trousers, but practical American shoes.

"Why would he tell you to lie? Your husband must look after you." The opposition lawyer almost gloated. He was destroying

Choie Ngoh's credibility. He loomed over the stand where the Chinese woman cowered, enormous in his strength and size.

"He's not my husband! After that day I never see him again till now." Choie Ngoh's voice was becoming high and hysterical. "He sell me to Miss Wong to be one hundred man's wife!"

"Yet today, he claims you are his wife and you were abducted by the mission woman, taken without his permission. You have broken the American law!"

Choie Ngoh collapsed in tears under the browbeating. She bent almost double with shame and the pressure of the questioning. Miss Culbertson looked at Amos and Thomasina turned, too. His expression told her they had lost. Ah Toy had found a lawyer who also knew his way around the guardianship laws and knew that Chinese women could be broken with repeated questioning.

"And you say you know Ah Toy paid fifteen hundred dollars for you, but you can't remember the day and you didn't hear what he and Miss Wong were saying. How do you know they were discussing you?"

Choie Ngoh didn't answer.

"When did this exchange take place?"

Chun Mei had to repeat the question.

"In early part of June, two years ago," Choie Ngoh answered.

"What date?" pressed the lawyer.

Choie Ngoh didn't answer.

"You don't remember when this so-called conversation took place, a conversation that decided your fate and your duty to your husband?"

Choie Ngoh hung her head. She seemed to shrink back into the chair.

"Miss Wong says she and your husband were discussing his import business. Miss Wong has stated that at no time did she keep you against your will at her home on Jackson Street. What answer do you give to that?"

Choie Ngoh said nothing. Chun Mei prompted her in a whisper but Choie Ngoh shook her head.

"You say you know what they were discussing! This is another lie! Your legal husband was conducting business and you have no proof about the money involved or that it was even about you."

Choie Ngoh whimpered and shook her head.

"In addition, you have been discovered in perjury. Either you lied to the immigration officials or you are lying now. Which is it?"

The lawyer, sleek in a snowy collar, his watch chain across his waistcoat, loomed over the Chinese woman. His bullying had destroyed her testimony. Her owner would take her back, punish her, and she would return to her previous work. Thomasina looked at Ah Toy. He was heavyset and prosperous-looking, with traditional robes, a queue and pillbox hat, but several Chinese men with him wore American clothes. Miss Wong sat impassive and calm in embroidered satin. She looked old in the harsh light of the courtroom, her unpainted face slack and her hair simply dressed.

Thomasina wanted to shout in frustration, "This isn't justice!" The hangers-on in the courtroom seemed to view the hearing as entertainment. They stood or sat in an attitude of people with nothing else to fill their time.

"In conclusion, Your Honor, I propose this woman, an admitted liar, ran away from her legal husband, a merchant who conducts business in this city importing food from his native country to be sold in his grocery store in Walnut Grove. This woman connived with Miss Margaret Culbertson who abducted her from the domicile of Miss Wong on the night of September 17. He accuses the American woman of unlawfully harboring his wife. Under Chinese custom, a wife is subject to her husband. This woman you see here on the stand has violated that custom, broken her marriage contract, and defied her lawful husband. We ask the court to return her to him."

The opposition lawyer's voice had risen until the last sentence rang out like a call to arms. Thomasina looked over at the "husband." The procuress sat with a blank expression. Thomasina wondered what threat they held to compel her statement. The judge looked over toward Amos.

"Any comment, counselor?"

Amos shook his head. The judge said he would take the matter under advisement and issue a ruling within a few days. The hangers-on, the Chinese contingent with its triumphant attorney, the sergeant-at-arms, and the policemen who had accompanied Miss Culbertson on the raid all filed out of the room. Thomasina felt exhausted. Chun Mei led Choie Ngoh to Miss Culbertson, who helped her with her coat.

"That's all right, my dear," said Miss Culbertson. "You did the best you could." The missionary could not keep the disappointment from her voice.

"Oh, Amos," Thomasina said, "you worked so hard!"

"We all did," he said. He was quiet in defeat. He was a chameleon who could charm, instruct, and mesmerize the court. Now he was invisible. Thomasina felt miserable. Miss Culbertson seemed not to be affected. Her expression was bland, her posture upright. She spoke briefly to Amos, then marched out of the courtroom, followed by Choie Ngoh and Chun Mei. Thomasina took a deep breath and followed her.

When she returned, Lo Mo was called to settle a dispute between two teenage girls, who fought over a new sam. The woman who conducted the little girls' class had questions about the lessons. Thomasina slipped back into her role at the Mission without a ripple. That evening, before bed, she sought Miss Culbertson.

"Why did we lose? How can that man lie and say she was his wife?"

"He was losing money," Miss Culbertson said with some cynicism. "He paid for Choie Ngoh's passage and she had to work for Miss Wong to pay her debt. He probably has a signed agreement with her mark."

"I don't understand this," said Thomasina.

"Amos says he thinks the man has a wife in California. The man went back to China, found a woman who looked like his real wife—that was Choie Ngoh—and brought her here. The immigration officials say all Chinese look alike, so Choie Ngoh was coached to lie, and she passed as his wife. She looked enough like the wife's photograph to fool Immigration. She had been promised a new life, so she willingly did what she was told. How could she know better? In China, women are chattel, and Chinatown *is* China."

"Amos was wonderful. He presented our side so well." Thomasina remembered his mobile features, the slight flush that came to his cheeks in the heat of the hearing.

"Amos is unsuitable," said Miss Culbertson.

Thomasina blushed. "I didn't mean—"

"You wear your heart on your sleeve," said Miss Culbertson. She smiled tightly. "Certainly he is an admirable person and a staunch friend. But a Jew—" She didn't finish the sentence.

Two church women, poor as mice, living in a mission that was half orphanage and they considered *him* unsuitable!

A scratching at the door revealed Choie Ngoh. Chun Mei followed her into Miss Culbertson's office.

"Choie Ngoh tell you she sorry. She ready to leave," said the translator.

"When will they come for her?" Thomasina asked.

"In a few days," Miss Culbertson answered.

Choie Ngoh sat down. She still looked dejected. Her eyes were red and swollen. She had been happy at the Mission, and she didn't want to leave.

Miss Culbertson took Choie Ngoh's hands. "Tell her we are sorry she is leaving."

Choie Ngoh responded hesitantly, waiting for Chun Mei, but as she spoke the words came faster and faster.

"Choie Ngoh say she come to Gold Mountains because her father send. When Ah Toy come with lots of money, she's happy because she will go to America and her family will be safe. He tell them he make her second wife, honored and rich."

Choie Ngoh hurried on, taking this last chance to tell her story.

"He sell her to Miss Wong and disappear. Every time she ask,

Miss Wong have her beaten until she do what Miss Wong say. It is worse than village—she never see the sunshine. Today when she sees Ah Toy in courtroom, she remembers he bring her to San Francisco, give money to her father. She owes him loyalty. He reminds her of her father and she feel shame that she is prostitute. Ah Toy will pay priest who will call up demons."

Chun Mei murmured several words in Chinese to herself, then said, "Curse her. Priest will curse her and all bad things will happen to her. Choie Ngoh sorry she cannot stay now. She make thanks to you. She thanks you."

All the women were silent for a long moment. Then Miss Culbertson embraced Choie Ngoh. She held the Chinese woman and Thomasina watched her lips move. She must be praying for Choie Ngoh. Thomasina would have been angry and she thought Miss Culbertson had a right to be angry—she and Amos had tried, she had made arrangements and gone to the trouble of raiding Miss Wong's. They had kept Choie Ngoh here at the Mission. Yet Miss Culbertson treated her as a beloved daughter. She did not berate Choie Ngoh or blame her for collapsing on the stand. Forgiveness was another of Miss Culbertson's virtues. Thomasina wished forgiveness sprang to her heart instead of the resentment she felt. And doubt—maybe they weren't meant to take these women after all. She thought it was terrible that a woman could be made a prostitute against her will, but the Chinese way had lasted for centuries and their culture thrived. Then she remembered the woman in the vermilion dress in the street, trying to escape; her sympathy and anger swept away doubt, at least for now.

Tonight she would pray for Choie Ngoh and pray that she could grow to be as generous as Miss Culbertson. She would not think about Amos Cohn.

Her natural ebullience rode like a sailboat on hope's sea, her great curiosity for what came next unquenched.

12

Thomasina had become Lo Mo, a role she treasured. She was treated with deference and respect, like the venerable aunties of Chinatown families. She was a member of her own tong, the Women's Board of the Occidental Mission, San Francisco, Presbyterian Church U.S.A.

The Chinese tongs were powerful organizers of Chinatown life. They took in immigrants from their home area in the Pearl River Delta, lent money, made sure the sojourners found work. They decreed debts would be settled before a man could return to China; these benevolent organizations granted the travel permits. A man could live at the headquarters of one of the Six Companies between jobs. American police and immigration officials allowed the tongs their power because it saved them trouble and kept the peace. Only lately had feuding broken out. White San Franciscans read about it in one of the newspapers and dismissed the murders as "just Chinese trouble—let them settle it among themselves."

Thomasina turned over the metaphor in her mind. The

Presbyterian Church U.S.A. was her tong. It protected her, gave the Mission its base, and gave her a pattern for living her life. All this aside, of course, from the Christian, civilizing, moral, and *religious* teachings. Before she was part of the organization, she thought of the Presbyterian Church as a religious organization with social fellowship and missionary outreach. Now she had learned how it operated—how pastorates were offered, how the money flowed, who was actually in power. She still loved it and adhered to its beliefs, but she had lost some of her girlish idealism.

She wondered if she had lost her moral idealism, too. She had turned down George Sergent's crude suggestion at nineteen. (If it were offered again today, she would probably turn it down because it was crude, not because it was sexual.)

The prostitutes who came to the Mission, the girls living with families and in bordellos, the women who arrived pregnant or with infants, had all experienced more sexuality than she had. Instead of keeping prostitution secret and subsequently shameful, the Chinese were much more open and matter-of-fact. At first Thomasina had thought it was disgusting that such things could be talked about openly and she wondered if she were becoming vulgar now that she was able to accommodate the ideas without wincing. By now she had seen through Americans' hypocrisy about sexuality.

So many single Chinese men had come to Gold Mountains, beginning in the gold rush, and during the building of the railroads, that prostitution was thought a necessary evil. If they lived here for years, working to send money to families they never saw, then the men needed the outlet of Chinatown joss houses, bordellos, fantan games, and opium parlors. Not that she approved of any of those things, but they did seem to be part of Chinese life.

Thomasina didn't borrow money from the Presbyterian tong, but it did provide her a place to live and work. The Presbyterian Church was a gentle tong. It did not decree death for people who crossed it. It kept no hired assassins, no hatchet men. It sheltered the less fortunate. It served a community purpose by organizing services. But few of the saved were baptized. Thomasina couldn't let herself speculate about the women. Would they have gone elsewhere if places existed to shelter and feed them? The Chinese system was based on family. If the woman had no family of her own or if she turned her back on her husband's family, she had no one to take care of her or give her instruction or use the fruit of her labors. The Methodists ran a mission, too, along the same lines. The Baptists kept their house busy with classes, mostly at night. The Catholics were beginning an effort. Each denomination was like one of the benevolent organizations, the Six Companies— offering similar services, and expecting faith and loyalty to its beliefs in return.

Thomasina wished her tong sent women to its seminary in Marin County. She had heard Dr. Marrs and some of the board women talk about it. If she went, she could learn the ideas that underlay their practices, have a time of retreat to examine her life and beliefs, and be more on a par with the ministers whose congregations helped support the Mission. Of course that would be impossible. She was one of the young, active workers, like the highbinders who executed the tong's decisions. She saw those men—usually young and tough-looking—swaggering around Chinatown, very well dressed in Western clothes. She enforced the board's will to succor Chinese women damaged by the yellow slave trade; they enforced the head man's orders. It pleased her to think of herself as a tough—somebody strong enough and adaptable enough to do a hard job, somebody smart enough to understand most of what was going on but not so smart she would question policy or rebel.

Even though she was learning about the denomination without idealism, she knew it was good because it was for life. Women rescued, girls released, infants given a chance to live. As assistant director, she was in charge of their necessities for life—not just food and shelter and something to wear, but the greater necessity for respect, for spiritual sustenance, for love (however institutional).

She could never manage it alone. She was not strong enough or smart enough. She would never be capable of sufficient bravery and industry to do the work Miss Culbertson did. Once having admitted that, she relaxed. Since it was impossible, she would have to rely on God to help her help Miss Culbertson. And the board and the women and girls and the employees. She would organize everyone, but she would ask for help and love.

Sometimes when she wished she could have a new dress or more money so she could send presents home to her sisters, she would remember she was a secret highbinder in a tong for God.

Once Thomasina realized that the little girls ordinarily never left the Mission, she rarely went anywhere alone. People became accustomed to doing business with her with a silent child nearby. Her trips away from the Mission were now shared with one of the little ones if it wasn't a difficult errand, or one of the older girls if it was. Hsiang always wanted to come, and Lo Mo usually included her if the trip was to Chinatown, since, as Hsiang delighted in pointing out, Lo Mo's Chinese was so rudimentary that only she, Hsiang, could understand it.

She knew that each girl needed to feel loved and that it was easy to treat them as a group not as individuals. But she remembered her big sisters taking her everywhere. It was their way of saying they valued her—she wasn't just a nuisance. If the girls knew that Lo Mo had a chart and a list of when each girl had gone where with her, they might not have felt loved or valued as individuals; but Lo Mo needed to keep records so that bright girls like Hsiang didn't go every time and quiet girls like Chien Wei didn't get overlooked. It was her chance to talk to them and find out what they felt and wanted and liked. It gave her another perspective on how to help Miss Culbertson run the Mission. When she heard their hopes and delights, she learned how much she was constrained by custom, lack of money, and her ideas of what was good for them. She learned to listen and not censor their childish wishes. When she asked them about how things should be run, she was surprised that they, with their immature minds, could think through the morality of things that happened. At the Mission it seemed the girls' voices were in constant clamor—fighting, teasing, joking, studying, talking for its own sake, getting to know each other, confirming their identity.

Lo Mo learned they could do moral theology of a subtle order. They had absorbed the Presbyterian lessons, understood the basic tenets of Christianity, and could apply them to the situations that arose at the Mission. In fact, when she considered some of the compromises she had to make to keep things running—nothing very bad—white lies to the food merchants or the dry goods dealer about late payment, she realized that they were better people than she was in many ways. She had wondered if all the Christian moral teachings were wasted since some of the women returned to their former profession and many of them returned to China if they could manage to earn their passage. Very few converted to Christianity.

Then she saw the pure love the girls expressed when they considered what was fair or decent—how do you treat another girl who wears your sam and gets it dirty? What is the difference between pushing ahead in line and lying? And she was heartened that her work was worthwhile.

Besides, she was afraid of losing her lighthearted attitude as she got older and the girls kept her young.

She had a cot, a sort of trundle bed, put in her room for girls who needed a little extra attention. She remembered her sisters comforting her as a child. Her girls needed to know she loved them.

She thought she was used to traveling with little girls, but when she took them in a group, it was a different story.

The day began with rain and heavy fog, but the weather could be bad in one part of the bay while the sun shone in another, so Lo

Mo decided to carry on. The girls—all eight of them—had yellow slickers, thanks to a contribution from a shopkeeper. They ranged from six years old to twelve, but did not include the big girls. Lo Mo wished they all had better boots, but at least they were wearing leather shoes, not slippers. They had been primed by older girls, Miss Alverson, and herself to be quiet on the streetcar and to stay together. The most timid, Mei Fa, clutched Lo Mo's skirt and wouldn't release her. Lo Mo felt like the Queen of England with a train. Every time she moved, Mei Fa moved with her. The girl seemed younger than she was because she had a habit of sucking her thumb and because she was shy. The little girls who came to the Mission as infants did not have to overcome years of abusive treatment as house slaves. Mei Fa seemed mentally slow as well as physically undeveloped. Emotionally, she seemed to have frozen with fear and never recovered. She was not an attractive child— maltreatment seemed to have distorted her and made her not just plain, but malformed, although she had no obvious defects. She rarely spoke, and then usually in a whisper. The more outgoing girls rode right over her and she never exercised her right to have her own way about anything.

Each girl carried something on that trip. When she scanned and counted each head, Lo Mo also checked for bags and blankets and three carryalls of food for a picnic. Lo Mo hoped Miss Alverson had written down everything so they could do this again without so much planning. They had rice and cold noodles and cooked vegetables and oranges. Once they left the streetcar, they made their way on the path into Golden Gate Park. She had to caution them not to run, they were so eager. They walked quickly away from the buildings and streets, through the landscaped gardens and the wooded areas. They walked beside huge fields of grass, found a picnic area with lots of room, and dropped their burdens on picnic blankets.

The rain had stopped and Lo Mo could hear drops falling from leaves. It was damp, but that wasn't going to ruin their fun.

Several of the little girls stood motionless, taking in the long grassy field, the tall trees, the damp air. This wasn't real country, but Lo Mo felt it would do even if concrete and brick were only a few hundred yards away.

She had forgotten the smell of damp earth and decaying leaves in the woods. She longed to take her shoes off and run barefoot in the grass, as she had as a child. If she did, the little girls would mimic her. Well, as long as they didn't lose track of their shoes.

But first she organized circle games and the one ball they had brought got steady use. Around noon, energies began to flag and she gathered them around for grace. They didn't look like China dolls anymore. Their trousers had grass stains and their sams showed they had been playing. They cleaned up a little and spread the blankets and ate their picnic. Lo Mo wished for a hot cup of tea, but bringing wood for a fire was more than she could manage today.

After lunch, she stretched out on a blanket. The most timid one had forgotten her during the games, but now Mei Fa crept back beside her and held a fold of her skirt. Lo Mo lay back on the scratchy blanket and the timid one nestled in her arms. Another girl, feeling left out, insinuated herself between them. The others seemed content to nap or rest, as instructed. She might not be their biological mother, but she had developed a way of scanning them every few minutes to make sure every girl was there. Real mothers must check their children constantly. They could so easily hurt themselves or get lost.

"Why don't we come every day?" asked the one who had squeezed in.

"When would you do your lessons?"

"Bring lessons out here."

"What would we do when it rained?"

"Stay under trees."

"Would we eat a picnic every day?"

"Yes! Only bring cookies next time."

"That's a good idea, Chen Lee. Remind Miss Alverson."

Chen Lee smiled, happy that her ideas had been heard. Lo Mo knew it was important to listen. Sometimes that was all she did. It was the one way a girl could learn she mattered—when someone paid attention to her. Lo Mo hoped that she was doing the right thing. She tried to give the girls, especially the little ones, what she had gotten when she was a child. Her sisters talked to her, scolded, instructed, dressed, taught, punished her—but always with love and always listening to her to see if she was getting what she needed.

She thought what children needed was love. That was simple, but also difficult. When she was preoccupied with the Mission's business, or tired from the many duties or nervous because she had guests or board meetings, she had no time and little energy for loving. She did her best and forgave herself when she fell short.

Perhaps she wasn't doing them a favor. She was treating them like American girls. They seemed to thrive on the treatment—most were boisterous, noisy, and energetic inside the Mission, not like the restrained and suppressed slave girls she saw carrying infants on their backs on the streets. She wasn't socializing them to be proper Chinese girls. Would they be able to fit back into their own culture when they were grown?

She had watched several of the women return to China, never learning more than a few words of English, never changing their ways. Chinatown was China for most of them. But as the big girls reached marriageable age, they had to find a bridge from the old ways to American ways. It was hard enough to learn how to behave as an American girl, but they had to learn how to be Chinese-American and they didn't have big sisters to show them how.

Stretched out in the shade, with a damp breeze shaking the leaves a little, Lo Mo didn't sleep, but she felt herself relax with the warmth of the two girls. She brushed their hair back from their flushed faces with her fingers. She checked to see if everyone was accounted for, and then despite herself, she dozed. When one of the little girls asked about going to the necessary, she was disoriented until she remembered where they were. She organized a trip to a rest room, then they lined up their shoes and stockings beside the picnic bags and played in the grass. The sun had come out and the rain stayed away. When the last game of Keep Away disintegrated into a wild melee of tag, Lo Mo began to think of leaving.

"Are we going to see the water?" the timid one asked.

"You mean the ocean?" Lo Mo asked.

"Yes, big water," said Mei Fa.

Lo Mo was inclined to refuse, thinking this was too much for the first outing. Then she realized that the timid one had asked for something. The shadow had come out with a request instead of silently accepting whatever happened to her.

"The big girls said you could see all the way to China."

"No, no. Not that far, Mei Fa, but a long, long way." Lo Mo considered. It would be a long walk, but she would like to see the water, too. They had plenty of time. She helped them clean up and get their shoes back on, then they began walking west with their almost-empty carryalls, the ball, and the blankets.

Lo Mo was afraid she had pushed them beyond their strength. They walked for most of an hour and still hadn't reached the beach. Then she could smell the sea in the air and see gulls wheeling in the salt gray mist and the open place between the trees widened to become the beach. Wind whirled the pale sand, neither brown nor yellow, into drifts and waves. The little girls ran down to the edge of the water, then scampered back out of the reach of the waves. Windblown sand got in her teeth.

"Girls, you must stay back on the dry part of the sand," Lo Mo called. She hadn't prepared them. They shrieked, in a new wave of energy, and ran wildly after the long-legged seabirds. One girl picked up sea grape and draped it over herself like a green boa. Another began throwing rocks into the foam. The lulling rhythm of the pounding surf was hypnotic and soon the girls called and Lo Mo led them down the shore. She was half-asleep, tired, and relaxed when a surprise wave caught them. They ran, but the wave sprang farther up onto the sand than they expected and knocked two little girls over and soaked Lo Mo to the knees. The others got their feet wet.

Several girls sobbed, afraid they would be scolded for ruining their clothes and shoes. The two who were knocked over cried, shivering and frightened. Two more were shocked to immobility. And two older ones tried to comfort the ones who sobbed.

Mei Fa stood frozen, wet to her knees. She wasn't frightened or weeping. Lo Mo wondered if she was remembering.

The troops were utterly disorganized. Lo Mo felt awful! She hadn't been prepared for this. She had heard of these errant waves, but hadn't been to the beach enough to experience them firsthand. She might have let the girls come to harm! Then she calmed down. She wrapped the two wettest girls in the picnic blankets and checked to make sure no girl was actually hurt. She felt chilled at first herself, then her body warmed her wet shoes and stockings. The girls' smaller bodies shivered longer. They hurried down the beach to the edge of the park to the streetcar stop.

Once on the streetcar, out of the wind, they were a little warmer. Lo Mo hoped none of them would catch cold.

The timid one again attached herself to Lo Mo's skirt. They leaned against each other to keep warm and said little.

Lo Mo was afraid this would make them dislike what was supposed to be a treat, but once back at the Mission, after they got dry and warmed up, she heard them boasting to the older girls how exciting and dangerous the beach had been.

They became the Girls Caught by the Wave. What had been a cold, frightening experience improved with the telling until it became a great adventure and the envy of the girls who hadn't been there.

That night Thomasina took off wet shoes and tipped sand out. Her hems were still damp. She would have to get everything laundered. Her face felt taut from sun and wind on her skin. Her mind's eye saw the remembered line of waves flinging themselves on the beach's breast.

"O gracious Lord, thank You for days like this. Thank You for Your sun, the grass and trees of the park, and the high spirits of the girls. Thank You for our games and our trek and our adventure. Most of all, thank You that we are all safe and unhurt.

"When all the ordinary days run together and are forgotten, please let me remember this shining day."

13

Miss Culbertson had become transparent. If she stood with the sun behind her, Thomasina was sure she could see through that frail body. Thomasina's joy at Miss Culbertson's return to full duty was tempered with perplexity because she didn't know which duties she should turn back to Miss Culbertson and which she should keep doing.

"Miss Culbertson, shall I go back to the classroom?" she asked after the third day of feeling uncomfortable. She didn't want to make Miss Culbertson feel as though she were being pushed aside. On the other hand, she didn't want the director to overburden herself with duties Thomasina could as easily do for her.

"No, no, my dear. I need you."

"What do you want me to do? I feel as though I'm usurping your place. I'm neither here nor there."

"You're used to being in this chair, after all these months," said Miss Culbertson.

"I never thought I could take your place," Thomasina hurried to say. "I have been doing my share to keep things going."

"I am sorry. I know it was difficult."

"You were ill, you couldn't shoulder the duties required. Nobody expected you to—" Thomasina didn't know how to put it. "You tried to prepare me, but I haven't learned enough."

"Well, we can go back to that, but you will have to do more, I'm afraid."

"Did you know Amos was getting married? The announcement was in the *Bulletin* last week."

Miss Culbertson looked closely at her. "We must plan a gift."

"Of course." Fierce envy flashed through Thomasina, then she buried it.

Miss Culbertson pulled a black ledger across her desk, disturbing one of the orderly stacks of letters. "Let's see how much money we have on hand."

"That hasn't changed," Thomasina said.

Thomasina still handled most of the routine day-to-day work of running the Mission, but she tried to be deferential to Miss Culbertson. While Miss Culbertson had been gone and she knew everything depended on her, Thomasina had found the strength to carry on and even bring about some changes, to enjoy the girls and add new experiences to their lives. Suddenly, she had to rein herself in and get used to the older woman's ways all over again. The effort to behave one way while thinking another was more exhausting than the long days and increased duties had been. At least now she could let go mentally from time to time knowing every burden was no longer on her shoulders.

Just when Thomasina thought things were getting back to normal, Sun Lee woke her up early one morning.

"Lo Mo, you come see Missee," said the older woman. Sun Lee's face was still creased from sleep and her unbrushed hair hung down her back.

"What is it?" Thomasina struggled to consciousness. She pulled on a wrapper and padded down the dark hall.

Sun Lee walked over to Miss Culbertson's bed. Miss Culbertson was dead. Thomasina touched her cold hand. "Bear down and trust the Lord."

"She wake up, start to get out of bed, maybe. I find on floor."

"Let's straighten her out."

Tears rolled down the women's faces. They settled the body in a peaceful attitude and smoothed the bedclothes.

Thomasina was surprised at how young Miss Culbertson looked now that pain no longer twisted her features into a strained mask. She seemed smaller and slighter and Thomasina was shocked that this thin husk had held such a great soul.

The first wave of grief subsided and confusion rushed in. Thomasina thought of all the duties she must reassume. She went to the office and began making lists for the housekeeper and teachers. She would notify the mortuary, but the cooks would have to prepare food for mourners; Miss Alverson would have to keep things running; the teachers could write notes and inform friends. Letters would have to be written to newspapers, and especially to church officials. Chun Mei could inform the Chinese newspapers and a few key people in the benevolent organizations.

The day that started so early seemed interminable. The girls and women tried to comfort each other, but tears and wails broke out repeatedly. At prayers that night, reminders that Miss Culbertson had joined her heavenly Father offered some solace.

The next few days were a blur of work and grief. Thomasina was never able to recall how it all came together.

The memorial service was attended by many people Thomasina didn't know. Originally she planned to have it in the mission chapel, but it became necessary to move it to the First Presbyterian Church on Van Ness, to accommodate all the people. Dr. and Mrs. Marrs helped her greet visitors. Miss Culbertson's family took over as chief mourners. Thomasina was heartened that so many people felt warmly toward Miss Culbertson. Their kindness would help her in the days ahead. Amos paid his respects to the family and noticed that she stood alone. He came over and took her elbow.

"You need to sit down," he whispered. "Let me get you some water."

"I'm fine, really—" she began, but her knees buckled when

she took a step; Amos caught her and helped her to a pew. He disappeared and returned with a glass of water. How he found it, she never learned.

"This is a great blow to your cause," he said. "Will you continue in her footsteps?"

"I can never be as smart and brave as she was," said Thomasina. Tears she didn't want began. "But I will do my best. I will need you more than ever."

"I am at your service."

He sat with her through the long service and accompanied her to the cemetery where Miss Culbertson's earthly remains joined the earth. Thomasina was glad for his support, glad for an arm to lean on, glad for his deep voice and male presence. She wished she could hold his hand, but that would not be proper. They had tea when she returned to the Mission. All spare beds were occupied with friends who had come for the funeral, and she let the activity swirl around her. She thanked Amos and wished he could stay and be in charge of all the papers and bills and people for a while.

Take heart and trust the Lord, Miss Culbertson had said.

After the funeral, after the worst of the tears, Thomasina tried to return the Mission to its usual routine. When she lifted her head from the papers on Miss Culbertson's desk, her desk, someone was there with a cup of tea or her jacket or just to see if she needed help.

Thomasina drove herself. All the things she had postponed until she could consult Miss Culbertson had to be handled now. She finally called on Dr. Marrs and the Women's Board of the Mission for a meeting to set policy so she could make decisions she had deferred.

Their response lifted some of the weight, but more and more administrative details avalanched upon her. She would have to find an assistant to help her or she could never continue. Miss

Culbertson's niece Alice consented, until her wedding the next summer.

All the details of running the Mission, including a raid that Miss Culbertson had planned, fell to Thomasina. She was Lo Mo to a huge family of loving but demanding people. During the days that seemed always to be filled with work, she found she could cope very well. After the first overwhelming days, her confidence returned. After all, she had been doing this for a year, however well or poorly, and the Mission kept going.

But at night, alone in her room, the sorrow crashed in upon her. She took off her shoes and brushed her unruly hair, now more gray than brown, put on her nightgown and wrapper and took up her Bible. Sitting there beside the window that looked out over the brick buildings of Chinatown, she wept. It was as though she bunged a cask of sorrow and every night despite herself, the spigot opened and sorrow cascaded. It filled her chest and stopped her heart from beating. She had thought Miss Culbertson was her superior, the head woman of her tong. Miss Culbertson had been her model as an administrator and her inspiration as a Christian woman. She had shown Thomasina how to be strong and effective although female, showed her how to get things done, how to organize people, how to administer the business of the Mission.

What Thomasina hadn't realized was that Miss Culbertson loved her. She could carry on all the time Miss Culbertson was gone because she knew that Miss Culbertson would come back. She hadn't realized until Miss Culbertson was gone, really gone, that she had put Miss Culbertson in the place of the mother she had lost as a child. Miss Culbertson became the woman to look up to, the one to go to for help, for advice, for information. For love.

Miss Culbertson had given her the attention she tried to give the little girls, but with immensely more subtlety. She had listened to Thomasina and gently shaped her as lovingly as a mother prepares a daughter for marriage. Thomasina hadn't realized it at the time.

When Miss Culbertson died, it was as though she were six years old again. She was bereft, dismayed, and utterly alone. Where were Annie and her other sisters? If they were here they would help. She could tell herself, sensibly, that she had employees, friends, and people who could help her run the Mission. She could congratulate herself on how much she was able to do. She even began to find odd moments during the day to talk to a girl or drink a cup of tea with Sun Lee.

She could tell herself the evening collapse was to be expected, that she was being emotional and making herself unhappy. She could tell herself that this grief would pass. She could tell herself that Miss Culbertson wasn't her mother and it was unseemly for her to grieve so fiercely for this demanding woman. She could tell herself to stop feeling sorry for herself and pull herself together.

But she couldn't believe what she told herself. Every night she cried with the corner of the pillow stuffed in her mouth so no one would hear. She didn't want to disturb the little ones or upset the teachers or housekeepers.

She understood now why men drank. Or perhaps why the Chinese brought opium with them to San Francisco. The sorrow was unbearable. If she could have done something to lessen its weight, she would have—no matter how damaging or bizarre. She had read about Plains Indian women cutting joints from their fingers or cutting themselves until they bled. No funeral exercises would seem too extreme. She wished she could have sent Miss Culbertson's body out onto the bay in a flaming Viking farewell.

And while she wept, the rest of the world rushed on. The war with Spain got closer, with Hearst's papers hammering on America's involvement. The city boiled with frontier energy that still fueled California's politics. New fashions appeared in the stores, and new books in the stalls, but she couldn't take in any more information.

All she could do was weep. She tried to find solace in the Bible, but it failed her. She couldn't concentrate and the words blurred as tears welled. What good is religion if it doesn't help when you need it! Then she was ashamed of herself for having so little faith. Her detailed prayers shrank to a plea: "Help me. Have mercy. Help me. Have mercy. Help me. Have mercy. Help . . ."

She stopped. How could she pray? She was frozen. She begged for help but there was no answer. Her grief bubbled up, inexhaustible as hot springs, as bitter as her salt tears. Why had the Father forsaken her? Would she stay mired in this anguish always?

She had lost her center. What would get it back? She wished she could sit mindlessly with her rosary, telling her beads like some monk until she died. The sun had gone out and she plodded through gray days, sorrow covering her like fog coming through the Golden Gate, impenetrable and opaque. She dropped things, spilled food, cut herself with her penknife. She stumbled on the stairs—her balance off in some inexplicable way.

"Help me. Have mercy."

Instead of recovering from the strain of Miss Culbertson's death, each day she felt weaker and less able to cope.

The little girl creeps through the woods. The rocks beside the path sparkle where the sun hits them through the leaves. The leaves gleam and wave overhead. A blade of grass is a shining spear pointing to the white sky. Her bare feet pad silently along the path. Dew diamonds catch the light.

Birds watch her silently, blinking jeweled eyes. Their feathers glisten silver and jet. The wood is a huge monster, making sounds, growing animals as plants grow flowers, shimmering and vibrating in the first sun. The trees signal that she is there and the animals are hiding.

Tamsen escapes the woods, and lets out the breath she is holding. She wades through tickly golden weeds in the grass that catches her pinafore. She jumps when a meadowlark whirrs out of the blue wildflowers, the sun behind his wings. The valley wind blows grass-smelling waves of heat and her sandy hair gets in her eyes.

She leans on the splintery rail of the fence. The brown and gold mountains hold her safe in the valley. The snow tops shine like ice diamonds.

Sometimes clouds hide the tops but not today. The valley breathes in sun all day and breathes out green breath at night. Grass grows like Papa's whiskers. The valley is alive and the mountains are God. His hair and face are snow. His eyes gleam when the sun shines. The brown-green trees and earth cover His body.

When God is angry, the mountain moves, the earth shifts. Dishes rattle in the cupboard and Mama holds her. Cracks run up the plaster of the back wall. Dust stirs.

Animals live on the mountain, but people live here in the valley.

Tamsen turns around. She hums to herself and spins until she's dizzy and cool. She turns and turns, then like a flower when it's picked, she's flying. She rises in the sky and looks down on the waves of grass, the scary woods, and she flies, but not too far from home. Then she comes back and she's still spinning in the meadow. She falls into the grass and watches the clouds turn around the sky, slower, slower, until they are still again.

Mama is calling, "Tamsen, Tamsen! Breakfast is ready." She will sit between Annie and Jessie, and Mama passes the food to them and Papa and Al. They talk about everything and tease her because she's the youngest, but Mama won't let them be mean. Mama buttons her pinafore in the morning and washes her face and brushes her hair.

She stands. The valley wind says, "Hurry home."

Mama is calling.

Mama is calling.

Mrs. Brown noticed Thomasina's strain at the annual board meeting in April. Thomasina brought the meeting to order and the women began working their way down the agenda when she stopped. Mrs. Brown noticed that Thomasina had lost the train of thought.

"Shall we continue?" asked Mrs. Brown.

"Where were we?" Thomasina lifted the paper in front of her. The elegant perfume each woman wore was suffocating her.

"Accounts," said Mrs. Brown. The woman next to her said something Thomasina couldn't hear.

"Shall we stop? Are you well?"

Thomasina looked at the sheet of paper shaking in her hand. She slowly placed it back on the polished table. "I'm sorry. I should concentrate better. We need to discuss . . ." Her voice dried up and nothing came out. She must stop this and carry on! These were busy women, and she mustn't waste their time. But tears began rolling down her cheeks. She tried not to make a noise, but a sob escaped her, then another. She could hear the women murmuring.

"I don't think I can—" she said. Then she shook her head.

"But who will?" asked Mrs. Brown.

The tears poured. Thomasina shook her head. She got up from the table and turned away. She blew her nose, but the tears wouldn't stop.

"This isn't just a onetime thing, is it?" Mrs. Brown rose and placed a motherly arm around Thomasina's shoulders. "We must realize that you are only human."

Miss Culbertson had been more than human, but Thomasina was not.

"You need a vacation," said Mrs. Brown. "This has been entirely too much responsibility for a woman of twenty-seven."

Thomasina sat helpless with her head bowed and listened to the board members as they took over. She would go away for at least a month and they would petition the congregations for a woman to stand in for her.

She felt a pang of jealousy and possessiveness. Nobody could understand what was needed as well as she! Then she gave up. She couldn't keep going. Her heart speeded up, frightening her as always, but she said nothing.

She wasn't sleeping and she had a sore throat that wouldn't go away. She inexplicably wept at odd times during the day. She clamped down on inexplicable rages, holding them inside, then exploding. The girls were surprised and the housekeepers dismayed.

Mrs. Brown sent her upstairs to rest. Miss Alverson sent word to Thomasina's family and Terry Bailey, sister Jessie's husband, came to fetch her.

She was torn between loyalty to the Mission and a simple desire to lay down her burdens.

"Oh, Annie, it's good to be home!"

"Tamsen! You look a fright! Here, let me get you a cup of tea." Her sister embraced her and led her into the warm kitchen. "I'm making Parker House rolls for dinner. Sit down and talk to me."

"No, you talk. I want to hear all about Terry and Jessie and Al's wife and his baby." She didn't want to admit she had trouble putting thoughts and sentences together.

Annie looked over at her. The teacup was actually not shaking very badly when she put it on the saucer, but her sister said, "Why don't you lie down till dinner? There's an afghan on the foot of the spare bed. Put your suitcase on the old toy box."

Tamsen hugged her sister, who smelled like rose water and yeast dough, and did as she suggested.

That evening after a big family dinner, she and Annie sat on the porch with Helen. The evening had cooled and their rocking chairs creaked sociably.

"I'm so glad you're here, I don't want to ask what's wrong," said Annie. The family all spoke with a Scots burr, but Annie's was strongest since she had lived longest in Scotland before the family emigrated.

"I can't seem to get over Miss Culbertson's death," Tamsen said. And the inconvenient tears began.

"One death reminds us of all the others," said Annie.

"Is that it? I don't really remember Mama and Papa's was almost a blessing, he was suffering so."

"I only know it gets harder, not easier, as you get older."

"What happened when Mama died? I only remember feeling confused and everything was upset. Then you and Jessie and Nursey were my mothers."

"You took it well, we thought. Mama had been sick and we had taken care of you for a year, at least. You were a wee, sober little thing. Papa took it hardest, of course. And the ranch was going downhill because of the dry years."

"I remember telling God that I would be a good girl always if Mama could get well."

"You *were* a good girl," said Annie.

"But not good enough." Tamsen felt a cold hand grip her chest. "I tried so hard! I worked, really I worked, more than I would have thought I could. I was a good teacher to the girls and I worked with Hsiang and I tried to understand the older women, who still seem as strange as people from another world. I did everything I was supposed to—ran errands and ordered supplies and used every speck of charm I could muster with the tradesmen, who had to be paid, somehow, somehow. Oh, Annie, I wasn't good enough for the Mission!" She stopped when she couldn't talk through the tears any longer.

Her sisters said comforting things and led her inside and talked while she got ready for bed. Annie all but tucked her in, and still the tears came.

The days went by fast. Annie pushed her into the spare bedroom for a nap after a country dinner each afternoon. They bought vegetables from a farmers' market and put them up in steaming Mason jars on a hot afternoon. They got Al to drive them to church for services. They went into town for shopping. Out of curiosity, Tamsen looked for her old bicycle. She found it hanging in the barn, dusty but still working. She cleaned and oiled it and got new tires, then she took long rides into San Jose or out into the surrounding orchards and farms in the Santa Clara Valley. She would pedal to Los Gatos or Saratoga. There the mountains rose, protecting the flat valley, separating it from the sea. She became reacquainted with the Duciks, a Bohemian family whom she had known for years. The youngest son, Charlie, was in San Jose visiting a college chum. Annie invited them to dinner and filled them with dumplings and chicken. They entertained the women with stories and jokes from Occidental College in Los Angeles. Charlie was pale blond, and had a limp from a childhood bout of infantile paralysis, but he had compensated with exercise to strengthen his legs.

For two weeks Tamsen lived in the cocoon of protected family life. She ate, slept, went out, and refused to think about the Mission. She took up her journal and wrote long entries, sifting and sorting through the last two years.

One evening as she sat again on the porch with Annie and Helen, known as Nursey, she said, "I don't deserve to be in charge of the Mission. I don't know enough."

Her sisters pooh-poohed that.

"I can't keep it running the way Miss Culbertson did," Tamsen continued.

"But who else would do it? The board chose you," said Helen, ever practical. "They offered to make you director and you refused."

"Superintendent is title enough," Tamsen said.

Sitting at ease like this—outdoors, with her sisters, the people who knew her best—was something she never got to do in San Francisco. It was quiet, with no traffic sounds, only night noises of small animals, chirring insects, and wind in the apricot trees. Sweet smells reigned instead of the smell of motors and horses and the scorched wood smell of cable car brakes. No bells rang out. A passing wagon's wheels seemed loud. She had eaten well—Annie's meat and potatoes, fresh vegetables, homemade sweets—all food prepared in small quantities, not the institutional meals of the Mission. When the day was over Nursey and Annie rested. No little girls squabbled in the halls, no woman vented her fears and frustrations in dissonant shouts. She knew what to expect from her sisters. The air was cooling now, but it had been warm this afternoon after the fog burned off. Every sight and sound that came to her seemed gentler, softer, less of a strain. And most of all, nobody wanted anything from her here.

"When are you going to take credit for what you do?" asked Helen. "They had other assistants and volunteers, and none of them could do it. Don't give yourself any airs, but don't pretend you aren't competent."

"You mean it's false modesty?" Tamsen should have known her sisters wouldn't treat her with kid gloves indefinitely.

"It's like saying it was nothing when sister Jessie went to teach in Hawaii. Yes, she had a good time and saw a bit of the world, but not just any teacher could have done what she did. Just because she decided to get married and have a family doesn't mean that she wasn't a crackerjack teacher."

"Of course," murmured Tamsen.

"You did all any woman could do. You are serving the Lord when you serve His creatures."

"But Miss Culbertson—" Tamsen's thoughts whirled.

"Miss Culbertson was flesh and bone," said Helen. "She wasn't a saint. She ate and peed and put her drawers on like any other woman."

"If I try to take Miss Culbertson's place, I'll fail."

"Then don't try," said Helen. "Don't think of being her. You can't, for one thing. And you shouldn't, for another." Nursey was always bossy and tonight Tamsen was grateful.

"I don't deserve—" The sentence stopped. What did she feel unworthy about? Tamsen rocked and from the dark silence of the yard and orchards, from the fecund garden, from the whispering trees, came the thought: I am afraid.

"I can't go back and face all that work. I want to meet a good man and have a family," said Tamsen. "I am with girls and women all day and only meet businessmen and pastors. I don't want to give myself to a place."

"I don't know as you have a choice," said Helen. "Where else would you go?"

"I could teach."

"Have you kept your certification current?" Helen sniffed. She taught at the high school in town. "What I meant was: where else could you do such interesting things? Meeting people, running about canvassing for money, doing public speaking? It sounds like great fun! And you learn about new people all the time. True, most of them are Chinese. I know it's not the same, but you have a big, loving family, not that it takes our place, I should hope."

Tamsen wanted to giggle. A giggle? This was the first time since Miss Culbertson died that she felt like laughing.

"False modesty—the worst kind." Helen pontificated beautifully: "It should be a great waste for you *not* to go back."

"Besides, you can't stay here," said Annie softly.

"I can't?" Tamsen feigned disappointment.

"Not if half your heart is at the Mission."

"I hadn't really thought of doing anything else, only that I didn't want to go back."

"Don't go yet," Annie said.

A week later a noisy farm cart rolled by outside her window. In the early morning light, which barely outlined the trees and houses, she remembered the dream. She was walking with her mother in a field with blue flowers. Only she was grown-up, not a little girl. Mama took the flowers she picked and wove the blossoms into a crown for her hair. The flowers smelled sweet, sweeter than any perfume. The grass smelled like sunshine. Then Mama walked away and Tamsen ran after her. Mama got farther and farther away; Tamsen stumbled, got up, and kept running, struggling to follow. Her arms and legs were too heavy and she couldn't make them move. She stumbled again, falling and rolling over and over. When she stood up Mama was gone. She couldn't fly with Mama, she had to stay behind.

It seemed a different version of Thomasina and Miss Culbertson. She had tried to keep up. Then she remembered last Sunday's service, about the Prodigal Son. The minister had pointed out that everyone realizes the father forgave the son. But he also had to forgive himself before he could accept the son back—forgive himself for being human.

Tamsen would have said she had too much good sense to believe in such fanciful things, but in some way she must forgive herself for losing Miss Culbertson. She knew in her head that she could have done nothing, but in her heart she wanted to heal Miss Culbertson, cure her, and keep her alive.

She dozed again and woke up later. She continued to gain weight and her color improved. She walked and bicycled and worked in the garden. She thought more and more about what she would do when she went back. She became bored with so little distraction. She made plans to return to San Francisco.

"I didn't think you would stay here long," Nursey said when she set a date to return. She had been in San Jose a month.

"What else would I do?" Tamsen said.

"That's not just the reason," Annie said. She brought freshly ironed shirtwaists to be packed. "You need something that needs you."

"I can give it a fancy name, like duty or service to the Lord, or that I am needed, but if truth be told, I have gotten used to being in charge."

Nursey laughed boisterously. "Now that's hardly noble, but it's understandable."

Annie said, "I think it's good you try to see your motives clearly. Don't give yourself airs about the why of it. The merit is in the doing."

"I still feel guilty for Miss Culbertson. I know it is foolish."

"Then foolishly think of returning as a way of getting rid of it. She taught you how to do what you so much want to do. You can give back to the Mission for her sake."

Tamsen didn't know if that was true or if she could think in those terms. She should sort out Mama and Miss Culbertson and not confuse them, but perhaps that wasn't necessary.

When the fog and rain and damp chilled her bones, she would remember the steep brown hills. She would remember the orchards in the flat valley and the vineyards in the hills. The sun would be shining in the valley and her sisters would welcome her.

14

In 1898, after a decision by the U.S. attorney general, new classes of Chinese were excluded from immigration. Previous interpretation that allowed officials, teachers, students, merchants, or travelers was reversed. All who were not technically laborers were excluded, so many were classified as laborers whether they belonged to that class or not. The 1891 law had excluded idiots, paupers, convicts, and diseased persons, and it had been upheld in court. Thomasina could understand why few people wanted these categories as immigrants, but "diseased" was arbitrarily interpreted by immigration inspectors.

America was mobilizing for war in Cuba, but that seemed remote from the Mission's battle with exclusion laws.

Merchants, wives and daughters of merchants, students, travelers, and government officials had always been allowed entrance previously. Originally, the exclusion laws were passed to keep laborers from competing with native-born and white workers; agitation by labor unions kept anti-Chinese sentiment high and politicians responded. Thomasina became cynical when she realized that it was easier and safer for a man running for office in California to fight the Chinese than to make war upon the great monopolies, the true cause of labor problems. It became the policy of politicians to divert and pacify discontented workingmen with anti-Chinese measures.

The situation was made worse by the Six Companies, the benevolent organizations that helped immigrants. They were informed by the collector of Internal Revenue at San Francisco that if they had directed their members not to register, their people would be subject to fine and imprisonment. The laws of the 1880s were so extreme that they were declared unconstitutional and the Six Companies had advised their members not to comply since they considered the law in violation of every principle of justice, equity, and fair dealing between friendly powers. While diplomats and lawmakers slowly worked out the justice of the earlier laws in Washington, Chinese could be arrested and deported for almost any reason. The Six Companies lost face because their advice resulted in hardship and deportation for their members.

Immigration inspectors, such as James R. Dunn, wielded much power because they were allowed to exercise extreme anti-Chinese prejudice. In a later report to the Senate Immigration Committee, many instances of arbitrary, discourteous, and unscrupulous conduct and rulings came to light. Thomasina thought Dunn's irascible personality, compounded by his profound deafness and his disregard for ordinary rights not only of Chinese but of attorneys, witnesses, and friends, such as Thomasina McIntyre, should have made him unfit for public office. His superior, Commissioner Powderly, evidently gave Dunn permission to exercise his authority to its limits. His license extended to misrepresenting testimony in cases appealed to the department.

Thomasina prayed for James Dunn daily. She prayed that he would become reasonable and, barring that, that he would be removed. His deafness was a metaphor—he couldn't hear the cries of the Chinese people he hurt. He was a continuing obstacle that Thomasina and Amos Cohn had to work around.

Dunn seized papers from Chinese immigrants and did not return them. He detained members of exempt classes for months in the Immigration Shed on technicalities and ordered deportation even though a case was being appealed within the legal period allowed.

Thomasina visited the shed many times over the years. At first, as Miss Culbertson's assistant, she went to give comfort and take supplies to the detained women. They were always unhappy and often downcast. Some became so despondent they tried to commit suicide.

Now she went to remove women when she and Amos could get them out. The women were segregated from the men and forced to live in a cheap, two-story wooden building at the end of a wharf, built out over the water where they suffered the odors of sewage and bilge. The place was unclean in spite of the inmates' efforts, at times overrun with vermin and always inadequate to the numbers detained. The food provided was poor and the conditions worse than city jail.

Salesmen, clerks, buyers, bookkeepers, accountants, managers, storekeepers, apprentices, agents, cashiers, physicians, and proprietors of restaurants, among others, were refused permission to immigrate. Public sentiment began to turn and citizens in Portland and San Francisco protested the treatment of Chinese at the hands of immigration officials. Besides, instead of protecting American jobs, it was beginning to affect trade. People needed the Chinese to do work at wages American workers disdained.

Thomasina and Amos Cohn spent hours talking to immigration inspectors, judges, and city officials, trying to get Chinese women released. All classes were detained arbitrarily. A well-known merchant from Macao, who came to San Francisco in 1899, was detained even though all of his papers were legal and visaed. He became ill, Inspector Dunn refused to allow him to have medical care, and it was two months before he was released on a writ of habeas corpus. He was removed to the county jail and died there a few days afterward.

"Is there nothing we can do?" Thomasina asked Amos Cohn. They sat in his office after a morning spent obtaining writs of habeas corpus to oblige immigration inspectors to release two women. The windows were opened and the day was unusually oppressive and sultry. The winds blowing through the Gate failed. The smoke of thousands of cooking fires lingered in the air. The layers of clothing that usually kept her from feeling the city's chill clung to her damp skin.

"We do what we can do," he said.

Amos's office was on the sixth floor of one of the new skyscrapers. The view of San Francisco's hills was spectacular. The din of traffic hummed far below.

They stared out the window in silence. Thomasina couldn't make her brain work in the heat.

"What we do never changes the overall situation," Amos said. "We deal with one case at a time. We do the same thing over and over. We are fighting laws going back to the 1870s, layers of laws, building up like sediment in a river until we're snagged on a bar."

"We are fighting James R. Dunn," commented Thomasina.

"He couldn't run roughshod the way he does without the laws behind him. We get one slave girl out, we rescue one high-born, small-footed first wife, and more arrive."

"And the high-class women I bring to the Mission are deeply offended at their treatment. At the Mission, we cannot offer them the luxurious accommodations they expect."

"I must admit, the Chinese are very clever about coaching the ones who are illegal, but that means legal immigrants are held incommunicado so they can't be drilled in what to say. Papers are sold to be used by new Chinese coming in. The right answers and a well-placed bribe and anybody can get a certificate."

"Well, you can scarcely blame them, Amos. Families want to be together. Men want to see their wives. But the unscrupulous ones use it to the detriment of the innocent."

"I feel depleted after one of these sessions with Immigration." He rubbed his eyes and yawned.

"Praying isn't accomplishing enough—not yet, not quickly. And we're not able to get beyond the day-to-day details."

"You think praying will accomplish anything?" he teased.

"In God's good time. I don't think we should stop working on each case as we are asked to help, but I think we should take a longer look. We need a broader perspective. Can we do anything that would effect a long-run, long-term change?"

"Let me think about this," said Amos. The light was back in his eyes. "I have done work for Jewish organizations."

"I'm sure you'll find a way, Amos." Once the wheels in Amos's brain began turning, he would come up with something. "You Jews are used to fighting prejudice, unfortunately." Amos stiffened. Had she offended him? Her efforts to help the Chinese sometimes blinded her to others' problems. "In the meantime, the problem of the boy Lew seems impossible—too complicated, too distant, too sad."

"How is that coming along?" asked Amos.

"I don't think it is."

Thomasina took her leave and decided to walk back to the Mission in spite of the heat. It was a long walk from the business district on a sticky day but she needed to clear her head. She would bathe when she got back. Today, she had no little girl with her, so she could do as she liked. She almost felt guilty spending time this way instead of hurrying back in the streetcar. She wanted to avoid thinking over the problem of baby Lew Lin Gin, whom Dunn had deported. If she walked briskly, she could put it right out of her mind. She loved the distractions of the city streets—messenger boys darting between pedestrians intent on their own business, clanging streetcars, hucksters shouting their wares. Bicyclers weaving in and out of traffic. Huge delivery wagons pulled by ponderous Percherons. More and more motor cars every day, it seemed. She would let the commotion, along with the rhythm of walking, clear her mind. If she neglected to walk the city hills for a while, she felt it in her legs. She smelled onions and meat cooking as she passed restaurants. Carriage wheels and horses' shoes on paving stones made their own rough music. Streetcar rails gleamed like silver in the stones of the street. When she had worked her way uphill, she looked behind her at the cubes and blocks of the buildings with the bay behind them. The hills might be hard to climb, but the views from the top lightened her heart.

She was sweaty when she got back to the Mission. She indulged in a bath, ate a cold lunch, then went to her office. She picked up the sheaf of papers and read again about Lew Lin Gin, a chubby, quick-witted boy of five, still a baby, that the collector of the port had allowed to be placed at 920 Sacramento.

The father of Lew was a merchant in Sacramento, a native Californian, and thus a U.S. citizen. While on a visit to China, he had a son born to his legally wedded Chinese wife. The child was, therefore, a citizen of the U.S. also. The mother died in China, the father married again and left Lew with his stepmother. When the boy was five years old, the father sent for them both and when they arrived in San Francisco a few weeks ago, the stepmother was allowed entry, but the boy was refused on the ground that he was born in China.

The father immediately sent to China for documents to fix the boy's status and his own, and meanwhile the boy lived at the Mission. He was bewildered and unhappy, but the older women fussed over him and spoiled him. At first, the stepmother was not allowed to see the child, but Thomasina was able to obtain a permit from the chief inspector.

She had no sooner sat down at her desk than Chun Mei brought in the stepmother who carried a soft parcel, obviously clothes for Lew.

"The stepmother of Lew Lin Gin is here to see him," said Chun Mei.

"Why didn't you take her to him?" asked Thomasina.

"The chief inspector came and got him just an hour ago. We tried to stop him. He said the steamer leaves in two hours for Shanghai."

"But we can't let them take the child!" said Thomasina. "Find a messenger to take this note to Amos. We must get a writ immediately."

Thomasina pulled a piece of paper out of a drawer and uncapped her pen. The stepmother questioned Chun Mei, who evidently explained. The woman cried out. She clutched her bundle and tears ran down her face. Thomasina wrote a note to Amos, then she, Chun Mei, and the stepmother raced down to the wharf. Amos arrived minutes after they did and presented the writ to the U.S. marshal. The passenger agent was cooperative, and he and the marshal searched the Chinese section of the boat. While they searched, Thomasina prayed. The father of Lew arrived, and he and his wife waited in silence. Thomasina watched gulls searching for food in the debris floating near the wharf. Tension pounded at her head and she felt sick with anxiety.

The marshal and the agent returned without the boy. The steamer lifted anchor and the tug pulled it out into the bay on schedule.

The father of Lew did not weep publicly, but he said, "I will find my son. I will never abandon my search." His anger would be channeled into the effort.

Thomasina's heart ached for the couple. She was exhausted. She had met failure too many times today. Her walk had raised her spirits, but now she was cast down again. She wept for the family's loss and she wept because she had failed them. Her best efforts and Amos's best efforts hadn't been enough.

Amos shook his head and held her hand for a moment, then he turned abruptly and found a hack to take him back to his office.

That night her heart overflowed with compassion for the parents of Lew Lin Gin.

"Blessed Lord, please help that child! He must be terrified and confused. He doesn't know why he is separated from his mother. He has been cast into the dark well like Joseph. Please help him back into the light. Comfort his parents and give them the strength to carry on."

She thought of the heartbroken parents clasping each other on the wharf and she recalled the dejected slant of Amos's shoulders. It's easy to love your friends, but she must find a bit of charity to love her enemies.

"And Lord, please help James Dunn. Any man that evil must be unhappy. Give him joy to brighten his heart. Let him see the glory of Thy love. Show him mercy that he may show it to others. Shine Your light and love on him. Whether he deserves it or not."

A few months later, she received a letter from Presbyterian missionaries who had sailed on the same ship. The letter said a Chinese child, dressed in Western clothes, had been hidden in a stateroom in the part of the ship reserved for Caucasians. After the ship was under way, he was taken to steerage and later taken ashore by other Chinese at Shanghai.

The father continued to try to trace him.

Who wanted a Chinese boy enough to steal him? Did someone on the steamship sell him? Why would anybody be so wicked?

Meanwhile, Thomasina followed reports of the Senate committee that held hearings to discuss a new exclusion law. A meeting in San Francisco had resulted in a delegation made up mostly of union men and politicians who demanded yet sterner controls; but a treaty with China was pending and senators from eastern states endeavored to soften the majority bill, known as the Mitchell Bill. The Senate committee heard the labor representatives and politicians, but for almost the first time, another group gave testimony. This group of notable men represented the claims not of California or trade labor alone, but of the entire country and of a broader viewpoint. John W. Foster, an ex-Secretary of State and diplomat, showed how existing legislation violated treaties and operated as both insult and injustice to the Chinese people. The representative of a group of New Englanders protested against discrimination against a single race. But the most outstanding argument was made by Simon Wolf, chairman of the civil and religious rights committee of the Hebrew Congregations. Wolf and Amos had worked together for Jewish rights in the past; Amos had prepared a statement that would speak to the legalistic minds of the congressmen. Wolf's convincing testimony declared the exclusion laws discriminatory and objectionable because the general immigration law did not apply to the Chinese precisely as to other nationalities. They were unnecessary for the protection of labor because most of the evils complained of were purely imaginary. And further because the economic conditions both in the U.S. and in China had wholly changed—gold fever had passed, while the rapid development of China herself tended to keep her laboring population at home. The exclusion laws, Wolf continued, threatened peaceful relations between the two countries, handicapped the American missionary and the American merchant, and limited trade and commerce. The time of exclusiveness was past.

The committee also heard James R. Dunn of the Chinese Bureau and Edward J. Livernash of the *Examiner.* The committee, Thomasina was glad to learn, apparently saw through their falsity and recognized the venomous prejudice of their statements.

Eventually, because other interests were represented beside Californian politics and labor, the Mitchell Bill was postponed; a less stringent bill was proposed that was not inconsistent with treaty obligations; an amended bill was passed and signed by the president.

None of this helped Lew Lin Gin.

15

When Thomasina returned to the Mission, she told the board that she would work for two years, at the end of which she would decide whether she would take a permanent contract. She would be superintendent, not director, until that time. She would continue as Miss Culbertson had, with a policy of providing a refuge for house slaves and prostitutes and women who needed protection.

More than ever, she became Lo Mo to the women and girls in her charge and to the people of Chinatown. People she didn't know greeted her as Lo Mo; she was treated with respect by decent Chinese.

While she never knew when she would get a message from a bagnio, or receive another threat from some slave's master, life fell into a pattern that could be anticipated.

Problems continued: there was no provision for infants, but Lo Mo could not refuse to allow a woman to keep a baby with her, and especially, she couldn't ask women who were pregnant when they were rescued to abandon the infants they delivered. She couldn't resist the babies and often stopped as she moved through the building to hold one or kiss a round cheek.

Her first annual report recorded the death of Margaret Ng, ten-month-old daughter of Ng Sing, named for Miss Culbertson.

"She was a beautiful and wonderfully winning child who drew to herself hosts of friends," Thomasina wrote. "None who were present will forget the beautiful funeral of this Christian Chinese child—the small snow-white casket covered with exquisite flowers—her own picture laid at the end, and a lovely engraving of the Madonna and Child, which she loved, placed at the head by her father. The sweet singing by the children from the home who were present made the occasion more touching."

The Mission became a peculiar kind of tourist's attraction. Notable Presbyterian laypersons, such as Augustus Booker from Camden, N.J., who gave generously to missions, visited when he was traveling through California with his daughters. Sun Lee hinted broadly that Thomasina should make herself agreeable to the widower.

"Good man," said Sun Lee. "Lots of money, lots of churchee."

"I know, but he's too old. I'm just a few years older than his daughters. He should meet my sister Annie."

"Be nice and he remember you."

The Bookers were en route to Calcutta where one son was a missionary.

Friends from San Jose, including irrepressible Charlie Ducik, stayed at the Mission. She looked forward to these visitors who took her away from her daily concerns for a while. She entertained people from the East Coast who wanted to learn about settlement houses. The benevolence movement, spearheaded by women, was gaining momentum. Jane Addams and her friends had begun Hull House in Chicago. The Mission did not serve white, European immigrants, but it had been operating for over twenty years and people wanted to learn about how it was run. Thomasina hoped they wouldn't repeat its mistakes. Thomasina, in turn, learned what was happening in the growing social welfare movement in other large cities. Of course, foreign missions were a continuing interest and she cherished every opportunity to talk with visiting missionaries and interested officials from the Philadelphia headquarters of the Presbyterian Church. The cooks would provide tea, she found beds for everybody, and she brought out her girls to sing and recite for the visitors.

Every raid was different, but there were certain elements that didn't change—the excitement, her determination and moral righteousness, and the feeling that she had to save the women to keep them from harm. Kum Kui's rescue resulted in public notice, which Thomasina hated, but which gained attention for the Mission and helped later, she thought, when she solicited for funds.

This time the owners of a valuable prostitute devised an elaborate plan to recapture their property. She would always remember this rescue; it happened the week before Thanksgiving the first year of the new century.

Since the men who could afford to bring a wife to America tended to be middle-aged, and the women tended to be between eighteen and thirty, every liaison was looked on with suspicion by immigration inspectors. When a young woman made her way to the Mission, her owner could claim she was his "wife," and arrive in court with friends paid to testify falsely. If Thomasina could learn the girl's family, frequently the girl was returned to China. Otherwise, she was taught domestic skills at the Mission. Some women earned passage back doing piecework for clothing manufacturers. The girls who grew up in the Mission were introduced to Christian Chinese men who were closely examined by Lo Mo to be sure her charges wouldn't return to the life she had rescued them from.

Lo Mo knew well the hatred directed at the Chinese in California. She knew, too, that they could be as cruel to each other as whites were to them. She tried to understand a culture that made women less than dust under a man's feet. She very well understood the economics of the situation—girls could cost thousands of dollars, plus their passage. A businessman tried to make a profit. When she interfered, she aroused hatred that went beyond mere money because she had attacked the system that kept the Chinese community intact. If women were valued as much as men, then men felt their power threatened. If she could use the law, and those laws were enforced evenly, their money gave them no advantage. All the brilliance and subtlety of thwarted masculinity was brought to bear to outwit her. Money was spent on bribes and lawyers.

If the men were unscrupulous, the women were submissive. Lo Mo often wished Chinese women weren't so acquiescent and trusting. Their betrayers knew how to take advantage of the women's lifelong indoctrination in filial piety and respect for men, which made them pliant and easy to debauch.

After several years, Lo Mo should have known not to unlock the door without checking, but she was not expecting a particular problem that morning. Usually friends in Chinatown warned her when an owner or tong planned action and she refused them entrance to the Mission. If they had a writ of habeas corpus, the woman was hidden. That morning she did not think to connect Kum Kui, most recently arrived, with the hearty uniformed American constable from Palo Alto and she opened the door. He had a photograph of the woman and he insisted on searching 920. He had a warrant for Kum Kui's arrest on a charge of larceny for stealing a valuable string of pearls. Several Chinese Lo Mo hadn't noticed when she opened the door entered and waited for him.

As always, the gong sounded, calling everyone to the chapel. All lessons and work stopped. Sewing was left in machines, brooms were propped in corners, and dusters dropped. Dishwater cooled. Usually a girl who had recently escaped her master was hidden between folding doors, or under rice sacks behind the gas meter in the sub-subbasement, but today everyone gathered as usual in the chapel. Lo Mo didn't understand what was happening until she saw Kum Kui. The woman filed into the large room with a group of women and saw her former owner. The blood drained from her face. Kum Kui visibly shrank at the sight of her owner, then cringed when he glared at her. She looked guilty. She had come to America to be a good daughter and earn money. Her owner stood in place of her family and was owed obedience. She had been unfilial when she ran away.

The constable arrested her on a charge of stealing jewelry. Lo Mo felt caught in a nightmare. The huge policeman reeked of cheap cigars. His uniform needed brushing and his boots carried mud. But he was the law and Kum Kui's owner had sworn she was a thief.

"Come along," demanded the policeman, "we must be off."

"You can't take her! She has stolen nothing!" Lo Mo couldn't explain the complicated situation in a few words. This country constable wasn't an immigration official. She was enraged at what the men were doing. She was also irritated at Kum Kui, who wilted into submission, with her head hanging as though her neck were broken. The more irritated Lo Mo felt, the more she knew she must stand by this woman because Kum Kui wouldn't stand up for herself.

The constable announced: "I have this warrant. This is the woman charged. I am doing my duty and no female is going to stop me." He took Kum Kui's thin arm in his beefy hand and led her out the door.

Lo Mo wanted to scream and claw the girl out of the constable's hands. She couldn't let them take her!

One Chinese man in a quilted jacket, bareheaded, with his queue hanging down his back, waited just inside the door. Another, an older man, evidently the owner, wore a pillbox hat squarely on his head and stood with his feet planted.

Lo Mo had no memory later of thinking things out. "Wait!" she called and dashed out the door, without hat or coat.

"I'm going with her," she announced to the surprised men.

16

Chun Mei ran after Lo Mo with coats.

"You can't understand her," said the translator as she helped Lo Mo on with her coat. "Do you want me to come with you?"

Lo Mo looked at the young woman. Chun Mei worked beyond her strength daily. She knew the frail translator was too ill to leave the Mission. Lo Mo herself didn't know what would happen. "I want you with me always," said Lo Mo, "but I don't know what will happen. I can talk to the policeman and maybe that will be enough."

"This girl was told she could return to Canton," said Chun Mei.

"And she shall." Lo Mo kissed Chun Mei and hurried after the party.

She sat beside the downcast woman all the way to Palo Alto on the train. Neither could speak the other's language, but comfort didn't need words. Kum Kui shrank when her eyes met her master's. Lo Mo feared for the treatment she would receive later from his hands.

"This is the end of the line," announced the constable. He

transferred everyone from the train to a buggy and they drove to a shack on the main road of Palo Alto. The town was growing now that the university was established, but the streets were mostly unpaved with weeds growing beside them. She saw people sitting on their porches, working in their yards, and men returning home at the end of the day. Late roses climbed wood fences and vegetable gardens gave the last of their bounty.

"You can go back, now. She ain't going nowhere," the constable told Lo Mo.

"I'm staying with her." Lo Mo didn't know why she insisted, but her instinct for foul play had been alerted and she would make things as difficult as possible for the men.

"Are you cold?" she asked. Kum Kui curled up on a packing box in their cell. She looked miserable but resigned. Lo Mo wished Chinese women had more American spunk and less sense of fatality. Lo Mo lay a protecting hand on her shoulder. "Sleep, if you can."

Lo Mo could not sleep. What had she gotten herself into? Once the constable entered the Mission, Kum Kui was as good as lost. Lo Mo didn't know enough yet to anticipate what the owners would do and she didn't know enough law to think her way through the problems. She hoped someone got word to Amos. A writ of habeas corpus, the usual attempt by an owner to get back a girl, could demand the girl be released to her owner, but a charge of larceny for stealing a string of pearls? The owner must have something more up his sleeve. He didn't go to all the trouble of getting Kum Kui out of San Francisco to leave her in this wretched jail.

Lo Mo was cold. She rewrapped a knitted scarf around her neck. She tucked her hands in her armpits. She was too cold to sleep and too tired to think. She hadn't eaten since breakfast. She lay in a half daze and wished for morning.

Around midnight, she heard voices outside the cell. She barricaded the door with a plank from the cell.

"Good news," called the constable. "Your friends have posted bail."

Lo Mo remembered Miss Culbertson's stories of girls jailed, then bailed out. They disappeared and if they were ever found, it was in horrible circumstances.

The constable tried to push the door open, but Lo Mo had barricaded it with scrap lumber she found stacked beside the packing boxes. Palo Alto mustn't get many miscreants, since the jail "cell" looked like a storage room.

"What's going on?" the constable shouted. The boards gave a little under his pushing.

"You can't take her!" Lo Mo said.

"Like hell I can't!" Footsteps told her the constable left, then she heard him return. He broke in with a fire ax. The now-angry policeman pulled Kum Kui to her feet and marched her out of the jail. Lo Mo followed, protesting.

The owner, smiling with satisfaction, waited in the buggy. Lo Mo forced her way into the buggy as the driver geed the horses, but the owner shoved her out into the tarweed beside the road.

Lo Mo hit the ground hip first, got the wind knocked out of her, slid on gravel, then rolled into the dusty weeds. The buggy had barely been moving, but she hit the ground with enough force to shock her. She sat up, heart pounding, her hair coming down, tears streaming down her gritty face. She couldn't catch her breath. She sat there for long moments, trying not to cry, trying to think her way out of this. She slowly got to her feet. Nothing seemed to be broken. Her knees shook and she couldn't stop crying. She wasn't crying for the bruises, but from sheer frustration.

She was stranded in a strange town where she knew no one and could not call on the police for help. Where could she go? She thought there was a Presbyterian church here. She didn't know this part of the Bay Area.

She got to her feet and brushed herself off, to gird her spirits as much as anything. Without a mirror, she couldn't do anything with her hair, but she wiped her face carefully with her handkerchief. She began walking toward the center of town. She saw a light in a building from blocks away and headed toward it, wondering which business was open at this time of night, thinking that whoever was there might help her.

The beacon shone in a drugstore, where the druggist worked at this late hour. She tapped on the window, introduced herself, and Dr. Chambers led her to the lobby of Larkin's Hotel where the night clerk gave her a blanket and let her rest on a couch in the lobby until morning. Drummers' cigars had scented the upholstery and every time she moved the wicker creaked, but she was warm and safe and she slept.

Lo Mo's grasp of the fine points of law was shaky, but she knew what happened at the jail was highly irregular. Why the hurry to remove the girl? Why had the owner been present at every step? She learned the next day that the buggy with the owner, his friends, Kum Kui, and the driver had met, surely by prearrangement, the local justice of the peace on a country road. The judge consented to hold court then and there. The interpreter said Kum Kui pleaded guilty and the justice fined Kum Kui five dollars for her alleged theft. The owner paid the fine, got a receipt, and departed.

The next morning Lo Mo tidied herself up as best she could and found the local newspaper where she told her story to the editor. Word spread quickly to the university students and townspeople, and stories appeared in the local and San Francisco papers.

From there, it turned into a circus.

The editor guided her to the Stanford University chaplain, D. Charles Gardner, and that evening she stayed with his family. He was an elderly man, a retired pastor, and he and his wife lived in a big old house, letting rooms to students. She talked to Reverend Gardner and his wife, and explained what had happened. They both had heard of the Mission. She sent word to the Mission and Mrs. Brown, and rested at the Gardners'. By nightfall the university students had denounced the public officials involved. Handbills urged people to attend a rally at eight P.M. and "Bring your own rope."

Thomasina McIntyre had grown up thinking that a woman's name only appears in the newspaper three times: when she's born, when she marries, and when she dies. Now she was the subject of notoriety, a public person, scorned for stepping out of her place and hailed as a deliverer of Chinese women. Neither charge was deserved. She had foolishly followed her instincts with Kum Kui and she had failed.

She overcame her aversion to publicity. If the story became public, maybe justice would prevail after all. She tried not to admit she liked being the center of attention, at least for a while. Her board did not object. People didn't know that the yellow slave trade, rampant in the 1870s, still existed and had taken new variations. If they knew, it would be easier for her mission to help the women.

Thomasina felt as though she had stirred up a whirlwind and was being carried in its force willy-nilly. She tried to calm the student leaders, explaining that courts don't respond to public demonstrations, but the youngsters' energy overrode her pleas.

No officials appeared at the rally. Dr. Gardner had drafted resolutions condemning the affair, and sober members of the faculty and incensed citizens signed it.

Instead of calming the throng of students, the resolution, when read, heightened their excitement. Shouting "Let's burn the jail!" leaders began a torchlight march to the building. They contented themselves with ripping boards off the decrepit structure and carrying off the boards, boxes, and blankets from Lo Mo's cell. Dr. Gardner went along, pleading for calm, and told her later that the items were burned outside the jail amid much shouting.

Thomasina returned to San Francisco the next day, but was invited to a meeting a few days later at Turn Verein Hall in San Francisco. The son of friends in the valley, a student at Stanford, heard that the defense attorney planned to pack the meeting with unsympathetic witnesses. Paul Jensen raised five hundred dollars by subscription from other students to charter a train from Palo

Alto to carry enough Stanford students and townspeople to pack the reserved center section of the great hall.

It all happened with so much tumult and was out of her control so quickly that Thomasina wondered if she were even needed at all. She decided it was all a great tempest in a teapot. Saving Kum Kui was important even if this hullabaloo was not. She mustn't get caught up in it. She reminded herself she mustn't put on airs just because she was in the public eye. She refused an interview with a San Francisco reporter and told the women at the Mission to speak to no one.

She dressed carefully that evening. She wore her best blue suit, a soft wool crepe, with full leg-o'-mutton sleeves and a spotless white shirtwaist with a lacy jabot. It seemed very important to look as respectable as possible. She must not appear to be a flibbertigibbet. She twisted her hair up a third time before she decided it was as tidy as it was going to get. When she put her hat on, the gray was covered, but that made her look too young. Her sandy hair was half gray. She took off the hat. Better to have her white hair visible—for maturity and authority.

She sat on the dais and listened to Colonel Archer denounce the perpetrators of the foul outrage. Such action besmirched the fair name of Palo Alto. Santa Clara County would never again be brought to shame in the name of the law.

The college delegation interrupted Archer's tirade with frequent applause. Like youngsters anywhere, the boys treated this as a lark.

When the time came for her to speak, she was petrified. She was afraid she would faint. She had spotted Amos in the audience near the front of the hall. He watched her dispassionately, but when she caught his eye, he smiled. That warmed her and encouraged her. She would pretend she was just talking to Amos, bringing him up-to-date on what had happened. She would have to be thorough, remember all the important points, and keep it in chronological order. Amos would expect that much of her.

The chairman of the meeting wound up his denunciation of

the police officials of Santa Clara County to storms of applause. She listened, trying to concentrate on what was being said. You are just an instrument, she reminded herself. God speaks through you. You are nothing in yourself without grace.

When the chairman finished, he introduced her. She walked to the podium and thanked them all. That was only good manners. It also served to calm the crowd. Her schoolmarmish manner served her well.

She could make herself heard, but just barely. She wasn't used to addressing such a large crowd, but if she could make herself heard in a large Presbyterian church, she could make herself heard in this hall.

"My good friends," she began, "I thank you heartily for your support tonight. Don't forget, amid this excitement, that somewhere in California a lonely and abandoned girl waits in fear for the next step in this sordid story."

Keep it simple, she reminded herself.

"I have had more adventures recently than I would like. I was not heroic, but stupid. If I had been alert to what these evil men would do, I might have prevented it. But if I had, we wouldn't be here tonight and I wouldn't have this chance to tell you what we are trying to do.

"Kum Kui was recruited from her family in Canton to be the second wife of her abductor. She was subject to the first wife's authority and lived a miserable existence as a housekeeper, cook, and caretaker of the husband's children by the first wife. After living almost two years in this situation, her master put her on the block at the barracoon. She was publicly humiliated and sold for three thousand dollars. Every promise her husband made to her family was violated. She had lost her face. She was made a hundred man's wife."

Thomasina looked in the front rows and found Amos again. He looked serious, but interested, as he always did when she explained a case to him. She took a deep breath and continued.

"Kum Kui escaped from a Chinatown bordello and found her

way to our mission at 920 Sacramento. We took her in and began legal procedures so she could return to her family."

Thomasina's mouth was so dry her upper lip stuck to her teeth. Her hands shook, so she pressed them against the podium. She was sweating into her shirtwaist, but at least her jacket covered that.

"Then came a knock at the mission door—" From there she gave a simple narrative of what had happened. She didn't think it was much. It was more stupidity than heroics, but the audience cheered when she dashed out of the Mission, and gasped when she described being pushed from the buggy into the Palo Alto road. The druggist was cheered, as was the hotel clerk and Dr. Gardner.

The San Francisco Chronicle reported she proved by her beauty and modest manner that she was a refined and cultured woman (as opposed to some crank feminist, she thought). She tried not to let it turn her head. Amos hadn't sought her out. She saw his head disappear as other people clustered around her afterward.

The next day she read the newspaper and felt deflated. One news story said she had brought upon herself the "vile indignities" in the Palo Alto jail, but the *Chronicle* was kind enough not to mention that. She was sorry, but not surprised, to read that Kum Kui had been married the previous Saturday afternoon. A Justice Johnson had been visited by two Chinese men and the clerk of an attorney who arrived in his office with a license late Saturday afternoon and asked him to perform a marriage ceremony.

They led him to a building on the north side of Pacific Street, between Kearny and Dupont, and took him up three flights of stairs, through a long passageway to another building, and finally to a room bare of all but a few chairs. Two Chinese women were present.

Justice Johnson thought this a little irregular, but the license seemed in order. He questioned Kum Kui through an interpreter and she said she was entering into the marriage willingly, so the justice quickly performed the ceremony that made her the wife of a Chinese man presenting himself as her fiancé, a mining man from Trinity, according to the attorney's clerk, Horace Gutzman. And Thomasina's heart stopped. That was Amos's clerk! Amos was working for Kum Kui's owner! He was working against the Mission!

She put the newspaper down. Her hands shook with rage and she couldn't read for tears. Why had Amos abandoned them? Had she done something that turned him against her? She needed him. What would she do?

She wept because she wanted him, with his charm and sensuous good looks, for his incisive brain and keen legal instincts. And she knew she was a hypocrite. He wasn't good enough to be a suitor—he was Jewish. He could be an employee or someone who volunteered to help the Mission, but he couldn't get too close. He was Not Suitable.

And now he was gone. Not just gone, but working for the enemy. All the brains and talent and legal knowledge he had brought to bear on the Mission's behalf would now be working against them.

Don't let hurt stop you, she warned herself. Think your way out. You will have to beat him at this game. She knew Kum Kui had come into the United States on her husband's papers. Thomasina wondered if Kum Kui had her individual permit. Kum Kui had been hazy on that topic. The next morning Lo Mo went to Colonel Jackson, the Immigration Commissioner for San Francisco. He kept her waiting for half an hour before his secretary ushered her into his impressive office.

"What do I owe the honor of your visit?" asked Jackson. "I read about your meeting in the papers."

"I have not given up," she said. "Kum Kui will not be made a hundred man's wife!" She explained she needed his cooperation.

Several weeks later, Lo Mo got word Kum Kui's master was traveling through San Francisco. She took a policeman to the train station. She recognized him immediately and a cold fire burned in her heart. She had him arrested and he was quickly tried for abduction, since he had taken her from her husband after the hurried ceremony. Thomasina was present during the entire trial, which took place in the country town of Mayfield. She had brought about this trial, but she still didn't have Kum Kui. Kum Kui had sworn she entered the marriage willingly, but Lo Mo couldn't believe this.

Amos appeared in court. His dark eyes sought hers, and he nodded. She returned the cold courtesy. She felt hurt and betrayed, but she wasn't going to let that stop her. She accomplished many of the things she did, her board had told her, because she didn't know she couldn't do them.

The testimony continued. If Kum Kui was married to the abductor, then she could be kept in this country. Several witnesses testified, then in the late afternoon, when everyone glanced repeatedly at the big clock in the back of the courtroom, the late sun slanting through the dusty windows, Amos called Kum Kui. Lo Mo woke up. The woman was led, wearing Western clothes, to the witness stand by an American woman.

Then the judge recognized John Endicott, sent by Jackson, the San Francisco Immigration Commissioner. He asked Endicott to act as interpreter. This was their chance!

"May I ask the girl a question?" Endicott asked the judge.

The judge nodded. In Cantonese dialect, Endicott asked the girl if she had a registration card. She shook her head.

Then Endicott said, "I place you under arrest in the name of the government of the United States."

Amos started, realizing what was happening. Endicott explained to the judge that Kum Kui was illegally in the country and must be deported. She must be returned to her family in China. Lo Mo hoped Kum Kui understood what was happening. She was heavily veiled and Lo Mo couldn't see her expression.

Amos asked the judge if Kum Kui could remain with the woman who accompanied her. Lo Mo thought it was Amos's secretary, but had only seen the woman once. The two women went to the buggy they arrived in and sat in the backseat until the explanations and legalities were reviewed by the judge.

Lo Mo saw Amos's clerk slip away and a moment later heard

shouts from the men on guard watching the women. The clerk untied the horses and leapt into the carriage. He whipped the horses before anyone nearby could act. Endicott hurried from the courtroom, and with the sergeant at arms, drove his rented sulky after them.

Only an unexpected locked gate on a farm road stopped the clerk from again abducting Kum Kui. They returned to the courtroom and that day Kum Kui was given to Thomasina for safekeeping until passage to Canton could be arranged.

Later, Lo Mo asked Kum Kui about entering into the marriage willingly. The girl said they had told her they would kill her before they let her get away. She knew the tongs had men who enforced their rulings and she was afraid to tell the truth. Lo Mo wanted to ask her about Amos, but she refrained.

"I hope you forgive me for arranging for your arrest," Lo Mo said. "It was the only way we could get you out of their hands."

Kum Kui said at the time she thought she had gone from a bad situation to a worse one, but she trusted Lo Mo. She stayed at the Mission several weeks until she could be deported.

Lo Mo reported to her board her gratitude to the people of Palo Alto who rallied to her cause. Her Chinese daughters in the Mission sent this message to the Stanford students: "In all thy ways acknowledge Him and He shall direct thy paths."

TRANSITION

 1902

17

After that first vacation, when she had gone back to San Jose broken and weary, Tamsen made regular trips to the sunny valley to visit Annie and Helen who now lived with brother Al and his growing family. Sometimes she made the longer trip down the coast to Alhambra, near Pasadena, to visit sister Jessie, her husband Terry Bailey, and their little daughter, Clara.

Tamsen doted on her only niece, talked long hours with her, and helped brush her curly hair and tie it up with ribbons. One Easter Tamsen helped dress Clara in a new white dress with ruffles and petticoats. When everyone was ready, they walked to Easter services through the blooming spring town to the solid square church. Birds sang in the sunshine. Tamsen listened closely to Ben Ducik's sermon. He stood in a black frock coat and high, stiff collar and lifted her mind and soul to God. She saw his brother, Charlie, his sisters, his widowed mother who kept house in the parsonage for them. During the service Clara was quiet and she told Tamsen later that she had been studying the details of all the ladies' Easter dresses.

Whenever the fog and rain and chill damp of her good gray city lodged in her bones, Tamsen would remind herself the sun was shining down the coast. She and Jessie laughed endlessly and she enjoyed a few days of a "normal" family life. Jessie's family lived in a modest house on the outskirts where the small town blended into countryside. She had furnished it with plain, craftsman-style furniture, no-nonsense, plain upholstery—a typical McIntyre house. Tamsen liked the way Jessie softened the decor with lace curtains and rag rugs and colorful throws and afghans.

The Duciks were old friends of the McIntyre family. Ben and Tamsen rode horses into the hills and had long talks when she visited. She told Jessie she thought he was "homely and attractive and had a glorious baritone voice." When Jessie asked how he could be both attractive and homely, Tamsen just smiled.

Jessie arranged for Ben and Tamsen to be together. All the matchmakers in the congregation were sure they would make a perfect pair. The Duciks shared the same values—family solidarity, love of the out-of-doors, and an abiding faith.

Ben's younger brother, Charlie, visited the same summer weekend as Tamsen. He was a student at Occidental College in Los Angeles and full of high spirits and college humor. Tamsen worked with the women in the kitchen preparing huge dinners for both families. Sister Jessie and Ben's sisters, Aggie and Louise, her name Americanized from Alosia, watched Tamsen and Ben closely.

"You never talk about anything but religion," Aggie complained at dinner that evening.

"Yes, and you never agree on anything. You must be Presbyterians," Charlie commented. Tamsen smiled.

"We didn't put on this dinner to listen to a dispute on salvation," sister Jessie said and started a bowl of stewed tomatoes around the table. Jessie's husband Terry shook his head. He let the women talk and refused to comment on the activities. Before the food arrived, sister Annie had decorated a holiday table. Cut-work linen cloth and napkins set off old Haviland with a dark blue rim. Condiments in crystal bottles sparkled from the gleaming footed holder. Around it Annie had arranged low cut-glass bowls of jonquils and daffodils, with trailing ivy dark against the white ground. Annie had a flair for decoration and Tamsen always thought it was a shame she hadn't married a millionaire with huge houses to furnish and decorate.

The women wore thin summer waists of batiste or silk in pastel colors and the younger women wore gored skirts that flared from small waists contained in stays. Tamsen always wore blue, a shade more intense than pastel, lighter than royal blue. Her eyes were dark hazel—brown and green flecked—but her coloring responded to blue. The women's color was high from the heat of the cookstove by the time they sat down to eat.

Mrs. Ducik was a pretty woman, plump and energetic, who spoke little. She was self-conscious about the accent she still had after forty years in California. The girls were homely and dark-haired, like Ben. It was beginning to look as though they would never marry. They both taught school in Alhambra.

"Is this ham saved?" joked Charlie, spearing a chunk. He held it aloft. "Yes, the apotheosis of this ham will take place—in my stomach."

Clara listened to the grown-ups. Sometimes she laughed with the women, but mostly she watched the faces and puzzled at the words. She told Aunt Tamsen that Charlie was the most fun and Daddy was serious. Most of the time Ben was serious, too, but he smiled at Aunt Tamsen.

Besides the ham, the women had prepared creamed new potatoes and peas, creamed cauliflower and steamed asparagus with hollandaise sauce, and strawberry tarts for dessert. The Ducliks brought braided and glazed holiday sweet bread, pickles and marinated artichokes they had put up last summer, and sweet potato pie, which was so good Tamsen thought it should be dessert. A southern parishioner had given Mrs. Ducik the recipe.

After the spartan fare at the Mission, Tamsen found this holiday meal almost too rich. She still could not enjoy the strangely seasoned vegetable dishes the Chinese cooks made, but she ate her cutlet with rice instead of potatoes and she and the other Caucasian women were served plain steamed vegetables, which were good for them.

Jessie pointedly asked Tamsen if she was going with Ben's youth group on an overnight trip up Mt. Wilson the next day. Yellow poppies carpeted open fields outside of town. Tamsen knew the Chinese name came from the gold in the ground, but when the poppies bloomed, the whole country looked like Gold Mountains.

"You still treat me like the baby of the family," Tamsen commented. Jessie's eyebrows went up. "Yes, yes, of course I am," she continued, "if you'll lend me a bedroll. I planned to stay on another day and go back Tuesday."

"Mohammed goes to the mountain," cracked Charlie. "Saves the mountain a lot of trouble this way." Charlie refused to be serious about anything. He was a few years older than most college students, but not as old as Ben and Tamsen. He bubbled over with high spirits, freed from school for a holiday, home with his family where he was coddled by his sisters and mother. He resembled Mrs. Ducik—fair, with finely etched features and pink-gold skin. He always had a half smile and his blue eyes were lively with humor. His nose had been broken playing football, which saved him from looking pretty.

"I haven't stopped laughing all night," said Tamsen as she finished drying dishes with Jessie.

"Charlie was always a charmer," said Jessie. She rubbed glycerin and rose water into her hands. "And good-looking to boot."

Tamsen looked at her hair in the mirror over the sink. It had curled in the humidity from washing dishes. Her pompadour was half gray and the silver hair was wispy and harder to keep neat. She smoothed it down and shook her head. She thought she looked rested. Thank God for family and small towns. She and Terry took Clara for a ride in Terry's rig, to Pasadena, where Gail Borden, a prominent Presbyterian layman, lived in a spacious house with his wife and daughters surrounded by dozens of flowers blooming in the mild sunlight. When they returned she went to sit on the porch with Terry, Ben, and Charlie and the other women.

Tamsen was drawn to Charlie, and she found it embarrassing. She shouldn't be this foolish at her age—thirty. But there was something she responded to—his vitality, his ebullience. True, he was not very mature, but that was part of his charm. She sat next to him on the big swing on Jessie's front porch. Mrs. Ducik rocked slowly nearby.

Morning glory vines climbed up twine stretched in front of the porch to create a bit of privacy from the street. It was too early for blossoms. Conversation rose and died. Even Charlie, sitting on the swing, was subdued.

"What time do we leave tomorrow?" Tamsen asked Ben.

"We'll assemble at Grogan's farm at ten and leave as soon as the gear is packed," Ben answered.

"He always has to pack it himself," Charlie said.

"Is it a terrific job to remember everything?" she asked. It seemed difficult enough to prepare for special occasions at the Mission, and there everything was at hand.

"Him big white hunter," said Charlie. "Make many trips to the interior. Capture elephants and tigers and native maidens."

"Oh, Charlie!" Tamsen giggled. She was acting silly, but her heart was light when she was around Charlie and it was easy to laugh.

"After a few trips when you forget the can opener or you can't start a fire, you remember," Ben said.

"It sounds like fun," she answered.

"It'll be more fun since you're coming," Ben said. "It's a big excursion—lots of youngsters from the church go along. We laugh all night."

"That I can believe," she said. "I like being outdoors, but I haven't had many chances since I moved to San Francisco."

"How long?"

She thought a moment. "Why, it's been six years already!"

"That's too long between camping trips. We'll have to get you out more," Ben promised.

"I feel like a kid again. This reminds me of my San Jose youth group when I was a youngster," she said.

Charlie reached over and grabbed her hand. She started at his touch. "I'm glad you're coming. You laugh at all my jokes," he said. He squeezed her hand gently, but Tamsen felt as though he were branding it. She flushed and hoped he couldn't see her face in the dark.

Charlie's blond hair was parted in the middle and wings fell over his eyes. She wanted to brush them back from his forehead and feel the softness. She wanted to keep laughing at his nonsense. She wanted the warmth of his grin and his big, strong hand in hers. She shook her head. This would never do. She had too many responsibilities.

Charlie's sister called from inside: "I need you to lift this bucket, Charlie. I want it out of the kitchen for the night."

He pulled his hand away and suddenly hers felt empty. "Excuse me. They're calling for the garbageman."

Her heart pounded and her hands were hot. She liked the Duciks—they were warm and outgoing. Charlie, Ben, Aggie, and Louise sang as a quartet for public occasions. Ben was serious about his religion, but ready for fun, leading the young people on this excursion. His mother was gracious and his sisters were like her own.

Charlie made her hot and nervous. She was glad he was coming on the trip. She wanted more time around him, but not alone with him.

That was at Easter, and Tamsen returned to Alhambra at Pentecost and Midsummer—more times during the summer when Charlie was home from college than she had since she moved to the Mission. Jessie noticed and teased, made one last plea for Ben, then subsided.

Beneath his charm and good humor, Charlie was serious about his studies. His family sacrificed so he could be in school and he repaid them with excellent grades.

"But you must at least think about the ministry," Tamsen said. They bicycled into the country for some private time together late that first summer. It was hot pumping up the hills through the farms and ranches, but cool coasting downhill. She liked to feel the muscles in her legs flex and stretch. She liked the sun on her back and the bumpy road under the tires. She'd left her corset off and felt girlish and free. And a little wicked. They found a huge black oak tree near the road and spread a picnic on one of Jessie's old tablecloths on the dry summer ground. Nearby a grove of eucalyptus rattled and scented the breeze.

They drank lots of water, then ate the lunch Jessie prepared. Afterward, they sprawled on the old tablecloth. Charlie kicked off his heavy shoes and socks and pulled his shirttail out. He stretched out his bad leg, which was a little shorter than the other. He had compensated for childhood polio by exercising all through high school, to make his legs symmetrical again. He played football, ran track, and played baseball. He was both taller and more muscular than Ben. Tamsen kicked off her shoes and eased her stockings down. She stared idly at Charlie's feet, flawless as a child's with smooth toes, and a well-formed arch. Polio hadn't distorted his feet. She wanted to squeeze them, as she did her little niece's. He lay on one side, his head propped on one hand.

"How can your feet look like that when you wear those brogans?" she asked.

Charlie shrugged.

In contrast, her feet looked misshapen with calluses and knobs on the toes and the beginning of a bunion. She blamed it on walking in French heels on hard San Francisco pavement. She pulled her feet up under her skirt.

She chewed on wood sorrel, enjoying the sour taste of the leaves, a memory from childhood. She listened to the short-beaked birds nattering in the trees.

"We've already got Ben in the church. I can't be a minister, too, Tommy. I'd better make some money," he said. "To take care of Ma and the girls. A minister's stipend doesn't go very far. Only about halfway to March."

"Be serious." But Tamsen laughed. She always laughed with Charlie. She loved him and she couldn't say it, couldn't admit it. After all, what was "being in love"? It wasn't anything tangible. You couldn't build a life on a feeling so brief and intense. When she was away from Charlie, it faded until she didn't think of him more than a dozen times a day. Love was God in the world—respectful love for her parents, or family affection for her sisters, or maternal love for the girls in the Mission. This was eros, which she considered lust. It was as impermanent as the breeze that shook the oak leaves overhead. Who could see it? Who made the breeze, where did it go? Wind could blow oak trees down, whip the ocean to froth, but it couldn't be held or seen and it came and went as it willed.

"Penny for your thoughts," Charlie said.

"Can't tell you," she said.

"You looked so serious."

"I was thinking about how I feel about you." This was so terribly hard.

Charlie ducked his head. Maybe she should say nothing. If she told him how she felt, she might humiliate herself. Maybe he didn't feel the same way. At last she managed a whisper: "I like the way I feel when I'm around you."

Charlie looked at her. He didn't move. His eyes, serious for once, held hers. "I love you, Tommy," he said. He had no trouble saying it. He looked straight into her eyes and said again, "I love you. I want to marry you."

It took her breath. She could say nothing. Tears came to her eyes. She tried to speak and instead lifted his tanned hand and kissed the palm.

"Is that yes?" He looked closely at her. "Nod for yes, shake your head for no. Nod twice if you want me to keep going." He took her hands.

Tamsen smiled and nodded twice.

"You feel at least a little like I do," he continued, "but it makes you feel funny. Besides, you're years and years older, so you feel guilty."

She reluctantly nodded again.

"Oh, it's true. You're what? Five years older? A dried-up old spinster." She pulled her hands away and sulked.

"The most beautiful spinster I ever met. Even though you have more gray hair than Mama. It's silver in the light. So you think you shouldn't feel this way—" He looked in her eyes again. She nodded and pursed her lips. He retrieved her hands.

"So you say I should be a minister to calm your conscience. Isn't that so?"

Tamsen didn't nod and she didn't shake her head. She thought about it.

"I'm going to graduate and find a job making a lot of money so we can get married."

Tamsen shook her head. "You're hopeless, Charlie."

He picked up her hands again and danced them back and forth. Then he straddled her legs and put heavy hands on her shoulders. His eyes were dark and intense and almost frightening. It had been a long time since a man had kissed her seriously. She lifted her chin and tilted her head and it was the wrong way, so she tried again and they bumped chins. Her neck stretched awkwardly. He shifted position, knocking over a basket of rolls that tumbled across the tablecloth.

He took her face in both hands and came straight in for a kiss, turning his head at the last minute.

Tamsen felt all warm and soft and she squeezed his hands. This would never do.

She loved him.

Charlie made one trip to San Francisco before he returned for the fall term. There was always room for visitors at the Mission and the women fussed over him. Tamsen turned over her mission duties to Wilhelmina Wheeler, her assistant, while he was there. She showed him the Mission, her girls, her life. He took her to lunch at a lovely restaurant near Union Square and for a lark, they watched a two-reeler at the Electric Theater. Charlie helped turn a cable car down at Market, where they window-shopped, but they preferred to stroll, not ride. Thomasina never strolled—she was always on an errand. What a treat simply to enjoy the surge of people, to hear the streetcar's clatter without thinking of where it was going. To be mindful of keeping her skirts clean, to gaze into shop windows. To study the other women's fashions, to wonder what was being served when they passed a restaurant. And all the while, holding Charlie's arm, feeling that sublime tension of touching him.

They ambled past shops and up the hill into Chinatown streets, with Charlie openly gawking at the balconies where potted plants grew in the damp city sunlight. He commented on the awnings, the notices on the fences in Chinese characters, the decorative lanterns and the obscure, narrow alleys. She heard the twitterings of birds in cages hanging over the balconies.

"I don't see any women," he said after a bit. "Just men and children all dressed up in fancy clothes." They had strolled through the small district and had come out the other side of Chinatown. They wandered up Columbus Avenue.

"The Chinese must think I am a terrible person," Tamsen said. "Their women live sequestered lives and only come out for the Moon Festival. There was one a couple of years ago to Quan Yin, a female goddess, a bodhisattva, and suddenly I saw all these beautiful women smiling and enjoying themselves. Mostly they stay home and work very hard."

"It must be terrible."

"For someone like you, yes. But that is their culture."

"Why do you excuse them?" Charlie asked.

"Their culture is so different, I don't try to understand. I accept that they have reasons for what they do, even if it makes no sense to me. They think much of what we do is incomprehensible.

And uncivilized, to boot. Like you." She paused. "I don't understand men and I never know what you're going to do."

Charlie put his arm around her to hold her at the curb while they waited for a huge beer wagon, pulled by enormous horses, to roll by. He gave her a squeeze. It felt funny to be acting like a kid, here in San Francisco where she had always striven to be mature and responsible.

"You respect them."

"I must. Even if I don't share their culture, I must allow them their beliefs."

"I thought you were supposed to convert those women," he blurted. Then he said, "I mean, it is a Christian mission." They continued down Columbus Avenue into North Beach. Now the Chinese shops gave way to Italian grocery stores with wrapped cheeses and sausages hanging over the meat counter and dark coffee smells escaping into the street. Sailors, unmistakable with their peculiar gait, headed for the Barbary Coast.

"That's our goal, but I can't force them. Many of them have been coerced all of their lives and we try to give them some freedom. Of course, we want them to use that freedom to embrace Jesus, but usually only the little girls absorb Christianity fully. We teach them to sing, we give them religion lessons, they study Scripture. We can put it out, but they have to catch it."

"You give them a place to stay and all that, not just the rescues."

"That's more important. If they aren't safe, fed, and protected, they can't look beyond those needs to God. Faith without works is empty." She glanced sideways at him. She had to hurry to keep up with his long strides. He had a peculiar gait, like a sailor with sea legs. She liked the way people looked at them—a handsome couple out for a stroll.

"It's hard to believe you're my Tommy, the girl who went on picnics and kissed me, when I think about the Mission. You're Madam Director." He ducked his head. "I'm a little awed about the rescues, to be honest."

"Is that why you're so serious today?"

"I'm just a country boy," he said. "I ain't used to this here big city, you bet."

They walked another block. Thomasina felt at home here in the bustle and traffic and noise and dirt, and hadn't thought that Charlie might not, even though he was used to the sleepy city of Los Angeles.

"How do you find the courage to go into those places, Tommy? Even in daylight, those alleys look sinister."

"I don't go until I know a girl wants me to come for her, then I make sure I know where she is. I take policemen and I have a warrant. But when the call comes, courage has nothing to do with it. If I thought about it—I'd be paralyzed. So I don't think. Well, actually, I think about Miss Culbertson. If she could do it, I can do it. Later, when I'm home safe I get scared and have to take a hot bath to calm down."

"You make it sound—possible."

"It must be. We do it." Tamsen turned and led Charlie into an Italian shop. Smells of pastry and coffee greeted them. Patrons at metal tables read the *Examiner* and *Chronicle*.

"Let's have some of their good coffee and a cannoli," she said. "Don't look so worried. It's just an Italian cream pastry."

They had another day of roaming the city and Charlie seemed more at ease. After an excursion to the park, they went to a concert and ate at a German restaurant. Tamsen went to the train station to see him off. After two days as Tommy, she was Thomasina again, and Lo Mo. They exchanged letters until Thanksgiving holiday when she hurried to Alhambra. As long as she knew when she could see him again, she could bear the absences. Her life at the Mission continued as usual.

She was called farther afield for rescues—to Sacramento and Spokane, Portland and Vancouver, usually accompanied by Chun Mei. Before she left, she always checked the ages of the children taken away from Sun Lee years before. She saw the pain in Sun Lee's eyes, but she wanted Sun Lee to know she kept trying.

When she arrived in a new city, she would send a message to a respected elder who acted as head man of the community, a person likely to know the history of everyone there. She looked into adoptions, but hadn't found Sun Lee's children after all these years.

She learned to pack for travel as carefully as Ben did for a camping trip. She met such wonderful people that she always felt it was worth the exhaustion that claimed her when she was back in her own room.

She still hired teachers and recruited volunteers. When Alice Culbertson got married, Mirian Olney, the daughter of the board member, came to the Mission after graduating from Mt. Holyoke where social work was beginning to be taught as a discipline. Serious young women were seeing the need to help the poor working classes. Mirian was anything but serious most of the time and her friends enlivened the Mission when they came in the evenings for conversation and music.

Thomasina corresponded with Jane Addams, who was starting a place for poor immigrants in Chicago. Other women in other cities were eager to learn how the Mission had started and how it sustained itself.

Thomasina still took little girls with her everywhere she could. Hsiang left for Philadelphia where she would live with her American family, spend a year in preparation, then attend Haverford College in a small town near Philadelphia. Thomasina thought she would rejoice in Hsiang's good fortune, but she could scarcely bear the thought of the girl leaving. She had been a reliable lieutenant, trusted translator, and like other difficult daughters, most loved.

Thomasina found Sidney Nussbaum, an attorney she could work with, and who was willing to handle the kinds of cases she would bring. She also became friends with Gerard Finley. He had worked the Chinatown beat as a patrolman and when the city fathers decided to clean up graft in the police department, they chose Finley as the first permanent sergeant for the area. He was straightforward, good-natured, almost without a sense of humor, but utterly honest. In the past, if a policeman needed money, he requested the Chinatown beat. The Chinese were used to bribing officials since it was a way of life in the Far East. Many of the evils Thomasina fought were protected by policemen on the take. Now, she had a cooperative sergeant who would provide help and perhaps things would change, little by little.

Every woman and girl pitched in for a major effort when they were told President Theodore Roosevelt wanted to see the Mission. Every little girl had a dust cloth or a mop and was directed by an older girl. No cobweb remained undisturbed. The meeting room was decorated with flowers and borrowed potted palms, but the president did not appear at the appointed time. Thomasina thought his secretaries were overly optimistic in scheduling. Given the president's enthusiastic interest in almost everything, she could imagine him delayed. She talked to the girls, told them how proud of them she was, and sent them to bed. It took a while to unwind, but she finally went to bed about midnight.

She had just begun to drift into sleep when a messenger pounded at the door. The president's party was arriving! The gas was turned on, the sleepy household was aroused, and all was in readiness when the guests arrived. Yawning little girls lined up and sang and several recited verses they had memorized. The older girls served refreshments with grace and efficiency.

The president looked both larger and smaller than Thomasina expected. Even at this late hour he exuded energy and a fierce interest in what was shown to him. On the other hand, he wasn't a tall man, or even very stout, and his spectacles gave him a slightly vulnerable appearance. He pronounced the little girls the most charming little people he had ever met.

About the same time, Mrs. Harbison, a board member, bought an entire houseful of new furniture when her husband sold his interest in the Clay Street railway at a huge profit. She persuaded her husband to hire a wagon to take all the old furniture to 920 Sacramento where it disappeared inside the Mission. The board had a new inlaid conference table with matching captain's chairs. Thomasina claimed another wardrobe and sections of glass-door bookcases that stacked to the ceiling of her room. They made her room crowded but tidier and she had shelves to display her framed photographs. While her room showed no consistency in its plan, its contents had a certain style that was hers. The blue dresser scarves and bedspread, the dark wooden frames on all the family photographs, and the sheer blue curtains that let in as much scarce San Francisco light as possible made it feel as though it were hers alone.

The Teamsters Union on the waterfront went out on strike that summer and the Employers Association fought them. The draymen were locked out in July. The conflict escalated and the men rioted September 29. Governor Henry T. Gage ended the strike October 2. The teamsters lost the closed shop. Thomasina was just glad to have things settled. The men's families suffered when they were not working. She could not have predicted that the unions would organize after that or that Abe Reuf and Eugene Schmitz would ride to power in city affairs with the Union Labor Party, with Schmitz becoming mayor after the next election. She saw Amos's name in the paper often and wished him well.

Evelyn Brown had come back from Europe a few months earlier and stopped at the Mission wearing a Paris traveling suit and ostrich plumes on her hat. Thomasina came downstairs after a particularly trying morning of peacemaking with the women, discipline with two new big girls, and a boisterous visit to the little ones' classroom. She knew she would lose her temper if she spent another minute with them. The most difficult part was that there was no malice—it was simple high spirits. And it was all her fault. Good little Chinese girls were beaten for disobedience, punished and shamed for breaking the rules. Since she would not allow herself or any of the women in the Mission to strike a girl, she had to find the patience to extract obedience without force. A little more filial piety would have been useful today.

"Why, Tam, you look so businesslike. Can't you smile?" The

stylish young woman's laughter rippled through the downstairs. "If I want people to think I'm a serious person, I'll have to get Mama to find me a job," said Evelyn.

"I can do that," said Thomasina. Evelyn's high spirits were contagious. She was feeling better already. "Come here and help teach. You can sing and play and you've studied music. The rest of us merely love it."

"And you can't carry a tune!"

Thomasina smiled ruefully and nodded. "But I can read music and play enough to lead the hymns."

"A joyful noise unto the Lord," said Evelyn and then she laughed again. Thomasina presumed Evelyn laughed from a memory of her attempts to stay on-key.

Evelyn moved into the Mission where she worked six days a week. Her lighthearted approach to life kept Thomasina from taking herself too seriously. Stir Evelyn into the flour and the bread was leavened.

Even more, when there were no meetings or duties in the evening, Evelyn invited her friends to the Mission. For a few hours Lo Mo, the burdened mother of fifty women, could become the Tamsen of old, able to laugh and enjoy a good time. She suspected Evelyn of matchmaking, but since nothing ever came of the young men who paraded through the Mission, she didn't worry about it. The wealthy young swells in their exquisite tailoring weren't looking for a church mouse to marry. But oh! what a joy to have them visit. What nonsense they talked, what jokes and stories!

The visits stopped during the scarlet fever epidemic. Thomasina stayed up nights nursing sick children, then worked all day at her desk. Ho Yuen broke the quarantine to bring her sister to the Mission. The young prostitute was dying and all Thomasina could do was make her comfortable. Ho Yuen was able to stay with her sister through her last days.

Months later, when Gail Borden visited San Francisco, Thomasina took Ho Gop and another little girl, Fu Kui, to visit the family at the hotel. To everyone's amazement, Borden's daughters, five and seven, made friends immediately with the mission girls and the four of them played happily with dolls and a tea set while Thomasina visited with the Bordens. She hated to bring up the subject, but this was her opportunity and she must take it. She apologized for bringing mission business into a social call, then explained how the Mission operated and how dependent it was on the generosity of people like the dairy magnate. Borden called his secretary into the room and whispered instructions. Mrs. Borden asked about the Duciks and they resumed their visit. Thomasina hadn't expected to stay more than half an hour, but when Gail Borden finally stood, she was surprised to see it had been two hours. The girls reluctantly said good-bye to their new friends and Mr. Borden pressed an envelope into her hand. It wasn't until she prepared a bank deposit two days later that she realized just how generous he had been.

Her birthday in the year 1901 held a surprise the girls had prepared while she was gone on a trip to Seattle, where she worked with Immigration to get a girl on a boat for Canton. She returned to discover that while she was gone the big girls had painted her room a soothing light blue and made new curtains and counterpane for a birthday present. Everything was back in place in the fresh, clean room.

"What a joy you are, my daughters," she exclaimed and hugged each girl in turn. The cooks had made cakes and they had a party that night. The women and girls had draped bunting and arranged flowers. Even the huge copper wok in the entryway was full of poppies and snapdragons held in place by round black pebbles from the Marin shore.

The little girls sang a song they had just learned and the big girls sang all her favorites, including "Just One Touch" and "That Man of Calvary."

They sang "Happy Birthday," of course, then demanded a speech.

"My good girls," she began, "I came here seven years ago to be Miss Culbertson's assistant. I didn't know how to do anything. I had never lived in a city, in a big building like this. Miss

Culbertson taught me how to manage this big family—and I became Lo Mo."

The girls murmured agreement.

"It is only when I take time to look back, as I have tonight, do I see how far I've traveled. I was so scared I couldn't talk the first time I went to rescue a girl. I didn't know what Missee did when she went to court or talked to immigration people or what the laws were. I didn't know how she asked good people in our churches for money, or how she solicited individual people. I didn't know how everybody was connected—Mrs. Brown and the women on our board, the policemen, the Bay Area ministers and especially Dr. Marrs, or the Chinese highbinders and masters, or the good people of Chinatown, or the women and girls here in the Mission.

"I've learned my way around. I've learned how things work. I've learned the laws and regulations and how to do many tasks.

"Two things I would never have guessed: I feel comfortable. I am Lo Mo—the one who gets things done. And also: we are all connected. Everyone—helpers, benefactors, workers, and enemies— we are all in this city, in this Chinatown, in this life together. We are all God's children, even if that's hard for me to remember sometimes. Love your enemies, Jesus said. Maybe he meant, love your enemies because we are partners on the same path to the kingdom.

"I can never thank everyone who has helped me. When I see all your faces, and feel your love, I realize *why* I am here. And I give thanks."

She was having trouble keeping her voice even as tears built. She hadn't known what she was going to say and was almost surprised to find out how she felt.

"Thank you, thank you. It is a privilege to know and serve you." She lifted her arms as though she would embrace all of them and they broke into applause.

The next day a book arrived as a birthday present from Charlie and her heart flew to him. Again, she was torn between Lo Mo and Tommy.

18

"Why do you want me to become a minister?" Charlie asked.

"If you studied at the seminary in San Anselmo you'd be closer to San Francisco. We could see each other oftener, without a long trip each time."

"But it'd be years before I finished, and then I wouldn't make much money."

"But look what you'd be." Tamsen and Charlie loaded a picnic lunch into the panniers of their bicycles. Sister Jessie brought an old tablecloth and a jar of coffee wrapped in newspaper.

"Are you sure you haven't forgotten anything?" Jessie asked. She looked doubtful. It was the second summer Tamsen and Charlie had been keeping company and sister Jessie seemed doubtful about that, too.

"Of course," Tamsen replied. Jessie went back inside. "She still treats me like a helpless six-year-old," she told Charlie.

"You are the least helpless woman I know." He checked their tires. "I think *you* want to be a minister, the Reverend Madam McIntyre," he teased.

"Yes, I would like to study divinity and theology and Old Testament history and everything! I can do it on my own a little at a time, but it's better if you have a teacher to guide you."

Charlie mock-groaned.

They closed the panniers and pushed their bicycles out to the road. Tamsen felt the effort in her calves and thighs as they began. She was used to walking San Francisco hills, not pedaling along country roads in southern California.

Winter rains hadn't started. It had been a dry autumn, like those years that broke her father's resolve, when the sheep ranch failed and the rustlers came. Life here breathed with the seasons while San Francisco was always cool, always damp. She loved it here where country sun burned away the dross in her soul, and left her clear, like a clean Mason jar, and Charlie filled her with joy.

She liked her life—she worked hard for little money, but she was not confined to hearth and home. She was truly a missionary as much as those Bible-bearing women who followed their husbands to China or Africa. Idealistic, of course, but what was life if she didn't aspire to be more than she was now? This didn't mean she had consecrated herself like a nun to a celibate life. She always thought she would marry and have her own family, as her brother and sister had done, and that they would all get together with their children for holidays. That dream had a chance, now, with Charlie.

It had rained a little at dawn, a promise of the rains to come. The earth gave back a damp breath of warming greenery, faint scent from wildflowers and tarweed, pungent bursts of rosemary and wild bay. Drops of water on grass and leaves reflected light. Wet stones with bits of mica or quartz sparkled. The day shimmered with promise. Dazzling light on washed leaves beside the road lifted her heart and mud puddles mirrored sunshine. Color sang from wildflowers nodding in the ditches. Dusty eucalyptus leaves rattled a welcome. The countryside sang with life and she was in tune with it all.

After an hour or so, they stopped when they found a shady place for lunch and propped their bicycles against one of the frowsy, peeling eucalyptus trunks. They spread the cloth in the deep shade of the trees. Sometime after they'd devoured the sandwiches and apples, they spoke of idle wishes and hopes. Tamsen lounged against a tree and Charlie sprawled on his back on the picnic cloth. The warmth of the day and their closeness melted self-consciousness. First they held hands, then Charlie gave her a quick cousinly kiss. She took him by the ears like a hound and pulled his face gently to hers for a real kiss. Then he sat beside her and put his arm around her. She nestled against his ribs. Every move seemed slow and clumsy and her breath came in ragged gasps.

She had wondered, did Charlie think she was pretty, did he like her hair, should she have put on some cologne? She wanted to touch his pale hair that took the sun's light and the warm pink of his cheek. She was used to enclosing her emotions in a cocoon of reserve and she could not say a word, but her feelings were so strong she thought he must feel the turmoil through her skin. She was thinking me, me, me and then Charlie kissed her again, and it lasted a long time. They pulled apart in mutual embarrassment. She looked into his eyes. He seemed as confused and eager as she.

They drew together again, awkward in their urgency. She tilted her head the other way, brushed his nose. He smiled, then she felt his hands around her. She ran her hands up his back. What a hard, warm body, so different from the soft women and girls she touched in a day's work. A fine oniony odor reached her as she moved nearer. Then their lips found each other again. This time it was firmer, experimental. She felt a ripple in her belly that she hadn't known.

That warm, softening feeling urged her on. She wanted pleasure increased, then released. She wanted to touch Charlie's strong body everywhere. She wanted to feel her skin come alive. She wanted to breathe him in—his essence, his spirit. She wanted to race to the finish.

Charlie glowed, lit from within, blood singing close under the skin. Skin degrees warmer than usual fevered hers with its touch.

She heard the wind singing in the trees, she felt its breath. She thought of the earth's fertile body, the mountains' glorious thrust. Each place Charlie touched seemed electrified. She must be sending out sparks of light. Her body hummed.

"Tommy," he whispered, "I don't want to do anything that would shame you."

"Charlie," she answered. "I'm proud you chose me."

"Anyone could come along and see us."

"But probably won't. This is too far into the country."

They sat on a soft mound of grass shaded from the valley sun. She smelled bruised grass, felt the soft warm breeze, felt warmer touches, heard his breath in and out with hers. Her blouse came off. His belt came undone.

Charlie stretched his bad leg out, then wrapped his arms around her and she was on the welcoming earth. Gently he lay her back until she felt her head in the grass. He stroked her face, then her lips. She cried out. She reached up to lay a finger on his cheek. She could no longer hold her feelings inside, and her hands seemed to move on their own.

Charlie cradled her shoulders in his arms and she felt muscles hard as bone through his shirt. He bent to kiss her again and she levitated to meet him. This kiss was wilder, and then she felt her belly throb again and her wayward hands pulled him on top of her. She wanted to be enclosed by his body, covered and subdued.

He chuckled and wrapped his arms around her. She ran her hands into his fine cornsilk hair and pulled his face back to kiss again. His eyes glistened and his teeth gleamed. He could tease or humiliate or rebuke her, but she knew he wouldn't. Just for this moment, this warm afternoon, this crushed grass, these dusty trees, this antic breeze, just for this time out of time, she would let go. And when she did, she rose up and flew over the trees, over the fields, she soared into the white summer sky.

She forgot herself, stopped caring what anybody thought.

More clothes came loose. She unbuttoned his shirt with shaking fingers. He eased up her skirt and petticoat, found the button of her drawers. She could not manage his trousers and he laughed, a soft, friendly sound, as he undid the buttons.

She was afraid to look, afraid that part of him would look too strange and frightening. He kissed her closed eyes. She tasted the sun on his neck, salt on fair skin. She wanted his body in contact with hers and moaned when he lifted himself and pushed up her skirts.

Urgent, aching, she clawed his back. He breathed into her hair. She flew again, into the white sky. She could top the brown-green mountains where God lived. She could race the red-tailed hawk. She soared and circled. They were one animal, breathing and gasping. They were one with the welcoming earth, the invisible air, the protecting mountains, the white midday sky.

Then he froze, gave a strangled cry, and shouted, "No, no." He threw himself away from her, covered his head with his arms, moaned, "No, no."

"What's wrong?" she gasped. "Don't stop."

"We can't. It's not right."

"I don't care!" she screamed, reaching for him.

"I can't."

Shot in midair, she plummeted. She died as she fell, wings trying one last lift, lead weighting her feet, one last cry a mutter of despair. She rolled over so Charlie could not see her face. Tears of frustration, anger, longing, hurt rolled down her cheeks and fell into the grass.

After a long time when she could hear Charlie gasping and feel her own embarrassment, she turned back to him.

"You're right," she said. Resignation and resentment tasted bitter in her mouth. Guilt began crowding in. She lifted a leaden arm and tipped the water bottle into her dry mouth.

"I couldn't do it," Charlie said in a choking voice. She rarely saw a man weep. She thought she should comfort him, but she was shaky and unsettled. She couldn't stand up the first time she tried, but when she was on her feet, she stood beside him and lay a calming hand on his shoulder.

"After we're married," she said.

That afternoon bonded them. Each learned something he hadn't known. Charlie learned he lacked nerve and he seemed deeply ashamed that she had seen him crying. Tamsen learned that she could succumb to temptation. She could no longer believe herself superior. Now she knew she was truly no different from any other woman, American or Chinese, who had been compromised by passion. She was the country girl sent away to relatives, the husbandless mother, the girl who ended up in the Chinatown crib. She could throw away all her indoctrination, her convictions, her ethics for this overpowering moment. Love's fury could destroy her. And for what? A feeling intangible as the breeze, invisible, ephemeral.

That night, in her room at Jessie's, shame and guilt caught up with her.

"O Lord, what has become of me? I nearly stumbled from the straight way. Forgive me! I wanted to stumble. This awakening is painful, but how do we know Your love except through others?

"Help me and protect me against my own inclinations. And bless Charlie always."

In every letter, Charlie repeated his proposal. Tamsen urged him to the seminary. They met in Alhambra several times during that second winter and through into spring. They wrote long letters. Then it was time to decide and Tamsen talked to Dr. Marrs. She told him about Charlie, and how she thought he would make a good minister, even as his brother had. Dr. Marrs listened and suggested other seminaries, but no other occupations. He took her word that this was the right thing for Charlie.

* * *

After talking to Dr. Marrs, the next time she visited Alhambra, she was ready to tell Charlie what to do, but she knew she couldn't force her wishes on him.

She didn't want to beg or plead. Sometimes she thought they argued over whether Charlie would continue his studies because they couldn't argue over the real situation: she was older and the director of the Mission; he was too young and too poor to marry. And he lacked nerve.

"You'll do well in seminary. You won a prize for your paper on world religions," she said. She would be forthright and use the facts.

"Other people's funny habits—that's how other religions look—as funny as sitting in a pew and singing on Sunday morning and initiating our young in youth bands and taking them camping."

"Oh, Charlie, you're never serious!" Tamsen said.

"It made me see that our way of doing things is not the only way."

"But it's the best way."

"You see the Buddhist and Confucian religion in Chinatown."

"It hardly seems like religion—more like superstition." Then Tamsen heard herself and realized how parochial she sounded. Perhaps if she learned more about other religions, she would respect them more.

They sat on the swing on Jessie's front porch. The family had gone to bed but she and Charlie lingered. Fireflies surprised the dark, floating higher and higher in the trees. Little Clara had collected a few in a jar and left them on the porch step. They blinked on and off like a faltering lamp, signaling the insects in the trees.

"Have you made up your mind about schooling?" Tamsen asked.

"I think about it all the time, but I don't know if it's the right thing for me."

"What would make it right?" Tamsen wondered. They sat side by side, but made no gesture to touch each other. She knew if they started, she wouldn't want to stop and neither of them could risk another painful encounter. Jessie wouldn't understand if she came downstairs and found them.

"Some sign."

"Apply for scholarships and stipends. If you get enough to live on, that would be a sign."

"But if I do, I should apply many places. Just to apply at San Anselmo, to be near you, doesn't seem right, Tommy."

"Oh, Charlie, apply wherever your heart leads! You'll be such a good preacher, such a good leader, better than Ben."

"Tommy, you want too much." Charlie didn't sound unhappy, merely making an observation.

"I want everything! I always have." She thought a moment. They told each other everything. She might as well tell him this. "I want the Mission to bring a woman from China, a woman who speaks Chinese, who can teach my girls about their own culture. I want all my girls to grow up and marry good Christian husbands. I want the women to find their families and be protected and taken care of and happy. I want the money to pour in so that I can rescue more girls and not worry about money. I want the high-binders to quit importing women and auctioning them off in the Queen's Room."

She heard Charlie chuckling.

"Is that too much? Most of all, I want you." She found his warm hand and held it between hers. She kissed it softly and put it in her lap.

"You are too intense. You scare me sometimes. You do so much. Sometimes you look thin and tired and I wonder what horrors you've seen. I live with young men wealthier than I am, without a worry in the world. Their families send them to college and expect them to go into the family business or become lawyers or stockbrokers. If they think about Chinese women at all, it's for their exotic promise. I think of you, going into those dark alleys with only your Scotch brass to carry you through."

"And it does!"

"Why would you want to give up being the director? Why should you want to be the unknown wife of a poor pastor?"

"Why should I want to live my life alone?"

"You're surrounded by women. You're never alone."

"I long for someone who cares for me. Someone special I can love and coddle and spoil. Children of my own. A life with you, full of joy and love. Public attention is no substitute for that."

Before she returned to San Francisco, Charlie agreed to apply several places and see if the response was encouraging. In the end he was accepted at Princeton Theological Seminary in New Jersey. It was prestigious, and thus endowed with scholarships. He would start with the fall term of 1902. Charlie would not only be educated, he might take on a little eastern polish.

Tamsen tried to hide her envy. She would have loved the chance to learn, to live somewhere else, to meet new people. But if she couldn't, she was glad for Charlie.

The family held a farewell dinner at the Presbyterian manse, a huge feast of summer harvest. Tamsen gave him a small hand grip that matched the bigger piece of luggage his family gave. She tucked a note inside, dozens of handkerchiefs her girls embroidered with his initial, extra handknit socks, and Chinese-style pajamas, with a card signed by each girl.

After dinner, Charlie covered his sadness with an exuberant show of nonsense. Clara was entranced when he picked up an old hat of her father's and strutted around the room roaring funny songs.

"Frog went a-courtin' and he did ride," sang Charlie. He picked Clara up and they "danced" while she sang along. Tamsen laughed until tears rolled down her face. Next Charlie grabbed her up, sang a popular song, and they did a cakewalk, with Charlie doing all the steps and Tamsen faking it, trying to keep up. His sisters made mock-solemn presentations of silly gifts and the Duciks and McIntyres sent him off with their best high spirits.

"What if you don't come back?" Tamsen asked. The next morning she stood with Charlie at the station waiting for the train that would take him to Los Angeles, then to the East.

"You'll have to come where I am," he said lightly.

"This feels so final."

"Maybe because we'll be apart longer that we've been together—three years."

"Sometimes I think you agreed so you can get away from me."

Charlie looked away, down the track. "Not you, Tommy."

"I want so much for us."

"That's what makes you who you are," said Charlie. He bent so he could peer under the brim of her hat. She was dressed to travel and would take the train in the opposite direction later that day. "If you weren't so serious, you wouldn't be you."

"If you weren't so funny, I'd sink with that seriousness."

"I am serious, too, but I don't show that side."

"I know. I should give you credit for your brains and hard work. You had to work your way through college and you still got good grades. And were funny." She didn't want his last image of her to be tears.

The train's whistle warned them and they turned to count Charlie's suitcases and boxes again. The station master came out with his pocket watch; the local slowed and stopped.

Charlie and Tamsen embraced one last time. She was crying and couldn't speak. He brushed away her tears, then knocked her hat askew, like a little boy teasing. She smiled and set it right, and by then he was aboard. She stood there, waved at him through the window, then watched the train till it disappeared in the distance.

19

The Presbyterian Church of America held its General Assembly in Los Angeles the summer of 1903. Thomasina attended with a dozen girls. It was more suburban, more spread out, slower, and sleepier than San Francisco. The meeting hall was huge and hot, and many delegates stayed with local church members, but Thomasina stayed in a hotel. She didn't want to waste any time traveling when she could be learning, meeting people, listening.

It was all very busy and exciting. Thomasina met women from all over the country who were there for the Presbyterian Women's Missionary Board meetings. She attended as many of the sessions as she could. She also met ministers' wives and young women training to be missionaries overseas.

She brought Hsiang, home from Philadelphia for the summer, two other big girls, and the best of the young singers. She had learned that "Chinese maidens" with Buster Brown haircuts, black patent-leather Mary Janes, and low-waisted middy blouses made a good impression wherever she took them. They were drilled on correct comportment. Her girls were as rowdy as any American girls at the Mission, but they loved to sing, so they stayed on their best behavior for the reward of going places with Lo Mo. She thought they were more afraid of Hsiang than of her. They stayed with Christian Chinese families in Los Angeles, who spoiled them. It was a strain to make sure each girl had the right color hair ribbon and had washed her hands, but Lo Mo was glad for a chance to show them off. She was never completely relaxed because there was always a chance a former master might try to steal a girl back, or a potential master might seize the opportunity to grab one. These girls no longer resembled the overworked *mooie jais* who arrived at her door, but she couldn't be too careful. Generous businessmen, like Augustus Booker whose son was a missionary, was especially interested in the Occidental Mission's work. Thomasina became better acquainted with him and his daughters Mary and Gertrude, and they spent several luncheons laughing and exchanging stories. Augustus was a type Thomasina knew—a sharp businessman, but a warm and generous person. She liked his kind eyes and the way he treated her mission girls—as though they were his favored nieces. He gave them silver dollars and patted their shiny heads and led the applause when they sang. Anybody who liked her girls immediately rose in her estimation. And Mary and Gertrude were like her sisters—a few years younger but lots of fun.

Then it was time for her presentation to the Women's Missionary Board, after a trying morning meeting and a hurried luncheon. She wished everyone could see her girls and hear her plea.

"Do you have handkerchiefs?" Lo Mo asked. Each girl patted her pocket. "Have you cleaned your fingernails?" Each little girl held her hands out proudly. "Hsiang, did everyone's hair get combed?"

Hsiang gave a mock salute and clicked her heels together. Lo Mo smiled and gave Hsiang a hug.

"I will talk for a few minutes about the Mission to these ladies, then I will introduce you," she explained. "Hsiang, you come out first onto the stage and the rest of you, line up in two rows. Do you remember your places?" One little girl looked doubtful, so Lo Mo said, "Let's practice." And she said to the little one, "Who are you standing next to? Can you stand beside her? That's how you remember."

She hoped she hadn't put too much responsibility on Hsiang. Hsiang seemed to thrive when she acted as lieutenant and Lo Mo desperately needed a translator. Chun Mei seemed frailer and thinner as time passed. She was willing, but Lo Mo saw how ill any exertion made her.

The women's meeting had a different atmosphere, different from the general meetings. The chatter seemed more relaxed. The agenda was fiercely battled over, but the presentations less formal. This year the women could congratulate themselves on the number of children's bands organized and increased members of mission circles.

The women sat, dressed in good waists and suits, fanning warm, dusty desert air that blew in the open windows. As always, Thomasina had a moment of terror as she stood to face this group. They looked pleasant, dressed in silk and cotton, their taffeta petticoats rustling as they moved, but they could be serious about their interest in missions. She was glad she had managed to find money for a new summer suit with lace insertions in the shirtwaist. The girls insisted she have sky blue broadcloth for the suit and good China silk and Belgium lace for the blouse. She avoided extreme styles because she knew she would wear the suit for years. New trim, new collars, and different blouses would keep it from looking too familiar. It fitted perfectly and she was confident she looked good.

Whenever she needed courage, she always called on her memory of Miss Culbertson, fearlessly entering some barracoon or bordello. Mission magazines recounted adventures and hardships of women overseas, but never gave her any model for Chinatown, or the poor neighborhoods of American cities. But she told herself, if Miss Culbertson could do it, she could do it. She took a sip of water and waited for the talk to die.

"My good friends," Thomasina began, "thank you for letting me come today. I know that you have worked hard this week, planning for the coming year. I know that your devotion to worldwide evangelism is bearing fruit. Without taking anything away from your work overseas, I would like to tell you what the Occidental Mission does in San Francisco's Chinatown.

"Many of you come from a background where the women of your church have gathered to pray and work for the foreign missions. My family adopted a child in India when I was a little girl and we wrote to her teacher for several years. We were taught as children to save our pennies and nickels for the missions.

"But most of all we were taught to pray. The power of women's prayer has never been measured. It accomplishes miracles every day. You have expanded your role from your own hearth to the whole world and the whole world is hearing the Word."

She described the Mission, hoping the speech she had given so many times sounded fresh to this new audience.

". . . but the orphanages for white children refuse these Chinese girls," she said. "They are as needy; they are as smart and eager to learn; but most of all they are also daughters of our Father.

"I am proud for them to be here today. You will see for yourself that with loving care they grow into normal, healthy children. And they are happy to sing for you."

Lo Mo looked into the wings and nodded to Hsiang, and the dozen "maidens" marched onto the platform and took their places. She was relieved that each remembered where to stand. Hsiang gave the downbeat and they began a spirited "Stand Up, Stand Up for Jesus." They sounded clear and pure in "Jesus Loves Even Me" and "Looking on the Bright Side" and "Little Blossoms."

When the girls sang, Lo Mo got chills. No matter that she heard them daily, sometimes she hid tears that came. Their voices were pure fountains of sound pouring their innocence and praise to God.

She remembered a teacher in the grammar school in the San Joaquin Valley telling her class there were bluebirds and marbles. Bluebirds sang and marbles were silent. She must have been very young, perhaps six or seven. She had a memory of a dotted swiss pinafore over her school dress. This was her first teacher in a classroom. The teacher said Tamsen and a boy with cowlicks would be marbles, who didn't make a sound. The marbles obediently put their fingers over their lips and listened while the other children sang "My Country 'Tis of Thee" and "Oh Susanna." Tamsen sometimes hummed under her breath very softly so the teacher couldn't hear, but she didn't ever think of singing out. Later, other teachers let her sing, but she always sang very softly, quiet as a marble, so that if she were off-key, nobody would notice and maybe she could find the note. Everyone in her family was tone deaf except Papa, who had sung when he was happy, before Mama died.

The girls sang for half an hour, mostly familiar hymns. The last high notes hung on the air, then the women applauded generously. The girls bowed, their silky hair falling forward over their cheeks. The women, some with tears in their eyes, clapped and clapped; Hsiang shooed the girls back onstage for another bow. Everyone here had heard and sung these songs many times, but today the songs sounded newly minted.

The girls sang again the next day to another group. Their performances went well and Thomasina had a break when their host families claimed them. She wished Charlie were here to meet all the people he would need to know in the years to come.

Dr. Henry Van Dyke, a professor from the seminary at Princeton, gave the keynote address on "Religion in Relation to Human Rights." Later she met Dr. Van Dyke and told him about the Mission and they spoke about the rights of the Chinese women she worked with. She found him more progressive than she had expected. The rank and file of church membership was more conservative than their leaders. She mentioned Charlie.

"Of course," said Dr. Van Dyke. "Ducik is a promising young man. And full of good humor." Dr. Van Dyke asked intelligent questions about her work, charming her with his interest. Later, she wrote Charlie that she thought Dr. Van Dyke was elegant in dress and manner and most distinguished, and that he was lucky to be learning under professors like Van Dyke.

She had a chance to talk to other people who had visited the Mission and Dr. Marrs helped with introductions to new people. He knew almost everyone there, it seemed. Whenever she could, she talked about the Mission. She could summon anecdotes about the girls to show how important it was. It seemed she was always begging for funds, and she never felt right. McIntyres learned to take care of themselves and not ask for charity, but when it was for her girls, she found the strength to ask.

Mission work overseas was gradually becoming more of a professional calling for young women. Once it was only the church mouse–poor wives who accompanied their husbands, but now girls prepared at Moody Bible Institute and other schools and went alone to labor in the vineyard.

The Presbyterian Women's Missionary Board heard reports and Thomasina was proud that the organization was large enough and healthy enough to support a separate Occidental Mission in San Francisco. Mrs. Brown was there, of course, and made her committee's report. Evelyn and Thomasina took a few hours off for luncheon and a taxi ride to enjoy Los Angeles. Orange groves still grew in town.

Too soon it was over and she was herding her tired, overexcited girls aboard the train for San Francisco. This was when she prayed for patience.

Once the girls settled down, Thomasina could stare out the window at the changing landscape and think about her situation. She had met many important people who might help support the Mission either with influence or money. She and her girls had impressed people favorably, she thought. She had found a special present for Hsiang—a painting of flowers and birds from China, different from any she had seen in San Francisco. She tried to be forceful, but not doctrinaire. She had no liking for feminist rant and knew it put most people off. Again, Miss Culbertson had showed her how to be strong without losing her ladylike demeanor. Secretly she admired militant women who led the march toward women's suffrage and improved conditions for the poor, of whatever race, in the crowded cities.

She seemed to be able to touch people's hearts with a combination of brass and charm. No thanks to herself, but rather her Scotch family that knew how to be tough and knew how to laugh just the same.

When she thought of Charlie she wondered how life with him would compare to her life now. They wrote less often than they had at first. They both were very busy. She suffered so after he left, it was a relief not to have him constantly on her mind.

They kept their courtship alive with letters. She would see him this summer.

20

When Charlie came home from Princeton Seminary, something had subtly altered. He seemed more pensive and everyone commented on his new gravity. He was still affectionate and attentive to Tamsen, but he looked preoccupied, then he would remember where he was and be more like his old self.

Tamsen wasn't sure she liked this new Charlie. The old one made her laugh. They got into a heated discussion over covenant churches and black ministers—something she and Ben had talked about many times, but a new topic for her and Charlie. Before, he would have slid out of the argument and made a joke. This time he defended his position. Had she lost a playmate and gained a debate opponent?

"You're looking mighty serious, Charlie," sister Jessie noted.

The Duciks and Jessie's family and Tamsen sat around Jessie's big oak table on a cloudy Sunday afternoon early in summer. The usual bounty from the combined kitchens covered the sideboard and the table. Little Clara was still all ears and eyes, but she was taller and plumper than the six-year-old who studied the ladies' dresses at that Easter service two years before.

"I'm serious thinking about next term's board and fees. I can always shovel coal and tend boilers in those big houses, or wait tables at one of the college eating clubs."

"You afraid of a little hard work?" Jessie teased.

"Not that—I just hate to do something that takes so much time from my studies."

"Shoveling coal will keep you from getting round-shouldered," she said.

"I'll be working for my cousin in Watsonville this summer. That should keep me hale," he answered. "I'll come back brown as a Mexican and speaking Spanish."

"Your blond hair will give you away."

"I'll grow a big mustache and wear a sombrero," Charlie said. "And carry a machete."

"Maybe you can take the machete to Princeton and use it to persuade the seminary to give you more scholarship money," Tamsen added.

"Now that's an idea," Charlie answered. "If it doesn't work on the hard-nosed registrar, I can use it to cut wood to sell."

"See, good Presbyterian thinking—make the best use of what you have," Tamsen said.

"That's the Bohemian in me—you're the Scotsman."

"You mean the stingy one," Tamsen said.

"Well, you did save the string from the butcher's parcel."

"Waste not, want not," she answered primly. "It has to do with the economics of survival. You've studied economics."

"Philosophy, economics—all the reasons men give for what they do. Got good grades, too."

"I'm proud of you, Charlie," said Tamsen, seriously.

"That and a nickel will get me a cup of coffee," he said, trying to stay in this light mode. "Well, it's good I'm working on a farm this summer. My classmates all think I'm a country bumpkin anyway since I grew up on a farm. I'm the only one from California. They think I'm fooling them when I say we have our own orange trees. The city boys are soft, but smart. They're the ones who are already jockeying for the big-city congregations."

"Do you want a city congregation?" Ben looked serious. "Mother and the girls were hoping you'd settle in some little town around here so we could see you once in a while."

Charlie's mother nodded. She said little, but her eyes followed his every move.

"I don't know yet. Maybe I'll stay back East."

Tamsen saw him take in the crestfallen expression of his mother's face.

"I'll have to find as good a situation as I can. Ben can't support all of us forever." Tamsen knew the light tone in his voice was thoroughly counterfeit. How to provide for his mother and sisters was a constant concern. Ben could barely support them now and he planned to marry a local girl soon. How would he provide for his own children? Charlie was expected to take over the support of his mother and sisters. It didn't look as though Aggie and Louise Ducik would ever marry—they were already in their thirties, homely as Ben.

Tamsen felt her heart take on lead weight. How could she and Charlie get married? By the time they could afford it, she would be too old to have children. He was working his way through seminary now and as soon as he could earn a living, he'd take on more responsibility. If she could keep working, Tamsen could at least support herself, but it was unheard of for a married women to do what she did, except as a volunteer.

"When is Marilee Mackenzie leaving for Chicago?" asked Aggie, and the conversation veered into local gossip.

Later that evening, after everyone had gone to bed, Charlie and Tamsen sat on the swing in the summer night. Birds were silent, a mild wind blew. Dogs barked at nothing in the distance. Stars sang bright notes against the black sky.

"You're different," said Tamsen. "I don't know what it is exactly."

"Everybody says I'm more serious," Charlie offered. He had taken off his collar and opened the neck of his striped shirt.

She loved the clean line from ear to collarbone, the swell of his chest.

"No, it's more than that. Some part of you has changed in a way that I can't grasp." What was she trying to articulate?

He picked up her hand. "This hand can grasp any part of me it wishes."

Tamsen giggled. "That's more like the old Charlie." She kissed the palm of his hand.

"I think I was living a sheltered life," he said, "and now I've gotten out into the world a little bit and I see what it's like. I'll have to be responsible. I can do it as a minister, but I do have to do it."

"I wish I were as rich as Evelyn Brown."

"You make it harder, because I want to be with you." He warmed her hand between both of his.

"I'll be a helpmate. I'll support what you do. I'll be a model wife, give teas and teach Sunday school. Maybe I'll start a missionary circle."

"You'll have to give up a lot to be with me," he said.

She couldn't read his expression in the dark.

"Yes, but I'll be happy."

"You'll give up being the center of activity."

"As long as I'm the center of your attention." Tamsen had been attracted to men before. George had been just a boy. She thought Amos, unsuitable as he was, was fascinating. She had met Evelyn's bachelor friends who excited her. She thought she had been in love, but only Charlie had ever excited her mind and her body. Her heart didn't know how to beat—whether to speed up or stop altogether. She forgot to breathe, then with Charlie's help, she could take in enough air to live an hour. Only Charlie could make her belly ache. It was almost like cramps, pain-pleasure, low and deep. She had no doubt she was in love now. It was hard to sit through dinner with his family and not be able to touch him. She couldn't lean close and inhale him, couldn't lick his neck or stroke his hand.

"Charlie, I want to marry you more than anything. More than saving Chinese girls, God forgive me, more than changing laws, more than being in charge, more than having people look up to me. I want it more than morality, more than practicality. I am not a frivolous woman. When I say this, I mean it. I will bend all my will toward working out a way for us to be together."

"Tommy, I want this, too."

"I didn't think I could take over for Miss Culbertson. I didn't know enough. But somehow I managed. It must have been God because I couldn't have done it alone. If I could do that, I can find a way for us to be together."

Charlie took her in his arms and kissed her. She dissolved into his kiss, as though surrender would seal the promise.

Charlie and she shifted together and the swing rocked as they embraced. He buried his face in her neck, and she could feel his warm breath in her hair. Then he kissed her ear, her cheek, her lips. They kissed as though starved.

She held back, feeling tight and nervous. He touched her breast through the cambric of her bosom. She stifled a moan.

He pressed against her and she wished he could enter her through the pores of her electrified skin. If she could possess him, breathe him in, hear his voice, taste him, contact as much of his body as she could, then maybe she could slake this hunger. She pressed herself against him, hip to hip, breast to breast. She feasted on his lips.

Then abruptly, cruelly, he pulled away and left her gasping for air, her lips softened, her belly aching, her craving unquenched.

They both knew they could never take the last step—their training was indelible, their misgivings too strong. She wished Charlie were as weak as she. Curiosity alone would have pushed her over the invisible line that girdled her virginity, desire for Charlie made it easy, her body demanded it. But Charlie was strong enough for both of them. Why couldn't she honor that? Why did she secretly think he was afraid to take the last step? And a thought she could not bear to entertain but once, briefly—he did not love her as much as she loved him.

While she sat there her emotions stormed like a ship in a hurricane. Charlie reached again for her hand. She almost withheld it, but that was the only contact she was allowed and she craved his touch so intensely she couldn't deny herself.

Then Charlie put one arm around her and comforted her. "Tommy, Tommy, it's best this way," he whispered, circling her in his arm. She leaned her head on his shoulder. Silent tears soaked into the striped fabric of his shirt.

"We'll find a way," he promised. "I know we can. I love you too much."

Charlie left for Watsonville to spend the summer where artichokes grew in snarly clumps right up to the edge of the beach. She returned to San Francisco to find Chun Mei very ill. They had realized the little translator had tuberculosis all along, and Thomasina knew it was contagious, but Chun Mei refused to go away for a rest cure. Women at the Mission tried every remedy known, and refused to acknowledge that the illness could win. Thomasina had to make a trip to Sacramento to rescue a girl from a house of ill repute; the Sacramento police were unfamiliar with her way of doing things and set barriers to the raid. She had to find a woman in Sacramento to translate, and there were none, so she settled for the bilingual owner of the largest Chinese shop.

The usual problems awaited her when she returned, in neat piles of paper stacked on her desk.

Her monthly was late that month. If she and Charlie had made love that night on the porch, she would have had cause for worry. How would her life change if she *were* pregnant? Charlie would have to marry her. She wanted that, but not under those circumstances. She would let people down—her family, all the people associated with the Mission, all the people who had put her on a pedestal. She would have to leave town and never show her face again. Her musings were painful.

Sun Lee noticed she looked unwell and asked her point-blank

what was wrong. When Thomasina said she was late, the older woman's eyebrows went up.

"No, no. I almost wish I were pregnant," Thomasina confided. "It must be overwork or I'm just getting old."

Sun Lee made an herbal tea and insisted Thomasina drink the foul brew. It was dark brown and tasted like cut alfalfa and rotten mushrooms. She sat in her room and stared out the window at the roofs of Chinatown, the gray sky, boats far away in the bay. She was weary to the bone. She waited till the tea was almost cool, then drank it straight down without smelling it.

If she were pregnant, she would have to work even though she might feel tired and unwell. But at the end she would have a beautiful baby! Charlie's blond baby, smart and happy. Child of her flesh, not someone else's daughter.

Each time she left her office, paper seemed to multiply in her absence. One day during that interminable week of herb tea, she pushed a stack of papers onto the floor so she would have to sort through it. A few items on the bottom had taken care of themselves.

"Lord, please heal my body. I know that I would have broken Your commandments, but forgive me and look kindly upon me. If I am to do Your work here at the Mission, give me the strength to carry on. And bless Charlie always."

Since she knew she wasn't pregnant, her next thought was female problems. She dreaded going to doctors almost as much as she dreaded learning what might be wrong. It could be simple or serious. She knew of too many women who died in their thirties with cancer. She was paralyzed to think she might have some secret disease gnawing inside.

Then she woke up one morning and the blessed thing had arrived two weeks late. She was so relieved to see the stain on her nightgown that she wept. The weight on her mind gradually lifted like a hot-air balloon. She had severe cramps that month and drank another of Sun Lee's concoctions for that, but everything was regular and unexceptional for years afterward.

*   *   *

As the weeks of summer passed, Chun Mei grew worse. Hsiang sat beside the older girl's bed whenever she could, and fetched water or medicine. She took food, mostly broth and crackers, and begged Chun Mei to eat.

Thomasina knew that Chun Mei had been badly treated before she found her way to the Mission. Miss Culbertson discovered the girl knew English and trained her to be her translator. Chun Mei was so effacing that sometimes Thomasina forgot she was the go-between. Miss Culbertson said, "Chun Mei survived by being inconspicuous. She is wracked with passions that have no outlet, but she knows no other way to live."

Tuberculosis was an infection, with a bacillus that you could see under a microscope. No microscope existed that could look at the effects of passion thwarted, but Thomasina thought it made it easier for germs to flourish. The doctor who visited weekly just shook his head. Thomasina checked Chun Mei's condition each day, speaking a few words. Hsiang was always there.

"I see Missee," Chun Mei said one evening.

"No, this is Lo Mo," Hsiang corrected.

"Go where Missee," Chun Mei whispered. Her voice had faded to a raspy whisper.

Thomasina wept. Chun Mei was saying she would go to heaven, like Miss Culbertson. Thomasina looked at the sunken eyes and pale lips. Chun Mei was a ghost already. Thomasina wiped her face and blew her nose, and sat down beside the bed. She took the girl's wasted hand.

"You have been the greatest help to Missee and me. You have done what no other girl could have done—you bridged Chinatown and the Mission. Your gift of words helped us save other girls. Most people only help a few other people, but since you came here you have made life better for hundreds of girls."

Chun Mei looked at Lo Mo, trying to grasp what she was saying. Lo Mo felt as though she were pronouncing Chun Mei's eulogy while she still lived, but her conscience goaded her into honoring this reticent, quiet, nearly invisible woman who had worked so hard for the Mission.

Lo Mo leaned over and kissed Chun Mei's forehead. She brushed the fine hair back and tugged the blanket straight. Then she left and Hsiang crept back on the chair for her vigil.

Early the next morning, Hsiang knocked on her door.

"Lo Mo, come quick!"

"What is it?"

"Chun Mei."

On the way upstairs, Hsiang, shivering with fear or cold, told her, "Chun Mei's face changed."

Lo Mo knew the Chinese were superstitious about the spirits of dead people, but she couldn't deal with that now. She was shaking when she entered Chun Mei's room. She wasn't afraid of her spirit, but of the fact of death. She touched the cold face and knew that Chun Mei was dead. She couldn't bear it! She fell across the bed sobbing. Too many girls left, too many died. Human beings all sailed on an ocean of pain and some went under. Why couldn't praying save anyone? Why did they die anyway? What good was praying?

She heard herself keening—a high-pitched sound that seemed to come from someone else, not her. It came from a woman who was helpless and weak, who could not function without Chun Mei—her bridge, her voice.

Then she felt Hsiang's hand on her shoulder.

"Don't cry, Lo Mo. I help you."

Hsiang's tears rolled down her face. They held each other and wept.

Dr. Marrs conducted the funeral service in the mission chapel. He brought gravity to the occasion and the tears and cries of the women quieted. Tien had taken several girls to the wholesale flower market that morning and they returned with armfuls of flowers. The fragrant vases of gladioli and lilies and carnations surrounded the coffin and filled the huge copper wok in the entryway.

Hsiang offered to drop out of school to become Thomasina's translator, but Thomasina wouldn't hear of it. She would manage. She told Hsiang she could understand most of what she heard in Chinese, and could say a few words in an emergency or to be polite. She could manage with help from other girls. More and more, girls were coming who could at least speak some English. "Besides," she said, "I'm counting on you to be our first girl to finish college."

The older women acted uneasy about the dead body inside the Mission, and Hsiang scoffed at their fears about spirits. Even in Chinatown the days of abandoning dying people in the streets were passing. A few people from the neighborhood, who had gotten to know Chun Mei, sat in front seats. She had no family in California.

Thomasina had one black dress which she donned for the service. The alpaca was rusty and it was years out of style, with oversize sleeves. She had to relace her corset before she could fasten the waist. But she thought Chun Mei deserved her most dignified mourning.

She hoped she could speak without tears sabotaging her.

"My good friends," she began, "we all have had our share of lights and shades in our lives, but the darkest shadow in many years fell over our home when dear Chun Mei became ill. This lovely, wise, and capable young interpreter of our mission began to fail in health. Suddenly and relentlessly did this shadow deepen and darken until it became to us the darkness of death.

"The loss of Chun Mei is irreparable. We feel that no other will ever be quite what she was, and what shall we say of the deep personal loss to us, of one whose every thought and act seemed to be for our help and comfort? Her life among us was a blessing to all and her memory will be a constant benediction. Her sun went down while it was yet day, it went not down behind a cloud, but into the pure light of heaven."

Thomasina had meant to ask for prayers for Chun Mei, but she couldn't continue. Dr. Marrs finished the service.

21

⚜ Life went on as it always did. Each morning Thomasina forced herself to get up. She was ready to give up and retreat again to the valley, but instead, she made a commitment—again—to do her best. The news in the papers—of events in China, of building the Panama Canal, of wars in Europe, of Roosevelt's reelection— seemed remote. The labor unions were gaining members as businesses took more drastic action to keep them in line. Fortunes were still made and lost overnight, a reminder of the gold rush boom and bust days.

The happiest event that year was a wedding.

Tamsen wrote to sister Annie:

> I know that nothing delights you as much as a party and I want you to come and help me organize this wedding. You will know all the California things to do to make it proper and the Chinese women will make sure I don't shame myself before their countrymen.
>
> Lue came to us as a *mooie jai* five years ago. At first I

thought she was slow, but she had been so mistreated, she was afraid to speak. I put her to work in the kitchen and she was so bright that eventually she did all the ordering from the Chinese merchants for the kitchen. She also grew to be very attractive.

She went out in domestic service and was commended by her American family for her willing effort. Her English improved. I did not send her to a family with grown sons because I didn't want to put temptation in the path of some older boy who might take advantage of a beautiful servant girl.

Mr. Toy, a Christian Chinese of Los Angeles, sent his emissaries to the Mission in search of a bride. He is the owner of a prosperous hardware store in Los Angeles's Chinatown. He is about forty, but Chinese girls are used to arranged marriages and prefer a secure match. I planned for them to have time together at the Mission and they carried on a chaperoned courtship. She will be his first and only wife.

I hate that I have become suspicious of Chinese men, even supposedly Christian men, but I cannot tell you what ruses and subterfuges the highbinders have used to get their girls back. Besides the open, legal ways, they have resorted to trickery, lying, and outright kidnapping. I asked friends in Los Angeles to check on his background. After coming to love and care for Lue, I did not want to cast her into misfortune.

Mr. Toy passed all tests. In addition, Lue said she was fond of him. This might seem essential for an ordinary American match, but is not considered necessary in Chinese marriages. If everything else is auspicious, affection will follow. Continuing the family line is the prime concern.

We have invited about one hundred people from Chinatown, and he has invited his friends, so we will have about two hundred people. I don't expect all the members of the board to attend, but some of the people I'm inviting as a matter of etiquette may accept.

Mr. Toy is paying all expenses and told me he wants everyone to celebrate his good fortune. He wants to thank me for the treasure I am losing.

If you could work with the cooks and manage a wedding cake, I would be extremely grateful. The girls can go to the flower market at Fifth and Harrison for roses, dahlias, chrysanthemums—whatever is available. John McLaren, a true Scot and a friend, who is the superintendent of Golden Gate Park, has promised me his gardeners will prune greenery and save me the cuttings, so you will have a lovely, immense amount of greenery to work with. I had thought to fill the wok in the entry with white dahlias, and put white roses at the head table, then my invention flagged. I suppose you can think of something to do to make the plain meeting room festive, a bower perhaps. The girls love weddings and will follow your instructions gladly.

I even have a new dress for the occasion. If only fabric weren't so dear, I could be the best-dressed woman in town. The women here are expert seamstresses and make sure I don't shame them. They insisted on a silk dress, a princess style this time in a sober navy, but with a wide white piqué collar. Do you think I should wear a hat? I always look as though I'm balancing some strange growth in my hair, which, by the way, is almost all white. At least it still curls in the San Francisco humidity so that I don't look too drawn.

I wonder, too, if I should give away the bride. The American custom is for a male relative to do it, but I have been the only father, uncle, or brother Lue has had in this country. Perhaps I am a glory hound, but I want to rejoice in this holy occasion, and I think it is my right to give the bride away.

I'm so glad we got Lue before she had been sold into prostitution. Most American men would demand a virgin, but Chinese men are more realistic. It doesn't have the same bad connotation as it does for Americans, but still, Mr. Toy has proved to be a good and generous man and I am glad he is getting an unsullied girl.

Chinese brides wear red for luck, but my girls wear white. Sometimes they object, but I am sending a symbolic message to the community: even girls who have been prostitutes have been purified by their virtuous lives here. The sin and contamination of the past has fallen away like dead skin from a snake. No one could imagine their histories from looking at their clear, shining faces.

Please tell me yes and I will have the girls prepare a room for you. What fun we will have, talking together and laughing while you are here! The wedding is a month from today. Tell me when you'll arrive!

Love,

—Tamsen

On the day of the wedding the fragrance of baking and perfume of flowers filled the air. The excited chatter of dozens of girls in their best sams competed with the steady ringing of the doorbell. Honored guests were shown to their seats; girls and women from the Mission filled the big meeting room. The bride, in a huge illusion veil and a lace and pearl-encrusted dress, descended the stairs on Lo Mo's arm. The girls oohhed and aahhed as the piano struck up the joyful Mendelssohn march. A very nervous Mr. Toy, resplendent in cutaway and boiled shirt and highly polished dress shoes, stood beside Dr. Marrs. Lo Mo kissed Lue good-bye and the couple exchanged their vows.

Lo Mo reminded herself not to get puffed up. She hadn't done any of the work alone. But still, a secret voice inside said, "You can be proud of what you have accomplished."

When sister Annie came for the wedding, she had warned Tamsen she was working too hard. Tamsen knew she felt tired all the time, and her back hurt constantly, but a McIntyre doesn't shirk. She caught bronchitis, then pneumonia, and Wilhelmina Wheeler, her housekeeper, kept the Mission running. Thomasina worked through the shadow of Chun Mei's death and the sunlight of Lue's wedding.

But it wasn't only the strain of work that defeated her. Sometimes, she felt Charlie slipping away like sand through her fingers. She asked him outright if his feelings for her had changed. Better the painful truth than the uncertainty. His answer: "I love you more than ever. Absence makes the heart grow fonder and the resolve firmer. You are the polestar for my life."

Thomasina, his Tommy, needed reassuring because she had known from the moment they first touched that emotions were evanescent and transitory, but more powerful than logic and practical knowledge. Their love was a reflection of God's love, the most powerful thing in the universe, and they were willing to build their life together on it. Love was as invisible as the wind and as hard to hold. Her thoughts were confused and contradictory. She didn't know whether to believe Charlie, or believe her intuition, or doubt both.

Miss Wheeler organized the cleanup for the annual board meeting in April. A general with an unwilling army, she organized the cleaning supplies, divided the tasks, decided the strategy, and managed the personnel. The Mission was gleaming by the time the out-of-town members arrived the night before. Thomasina was grateful and told Wilhelmina, "Without you, the Mission would not run. You are the active, strong arm that makes things happen."

Wilhelmina, a woman Thomasina's age, blushed. She was fair and stout, with a strong voice and a passion for details. She stayed at the Mission and kept everything there on an even keel while Thomasina traveled to Los Angeles or Bakersfield or Portland to rescue a girl. That year Thomasina made almost weekly trips to Sacramento to lobby on behalf of a law that would regularize what she had been doing for the last eight years. She was able to include in her annual report of 1904 progress regarding the law.

Thomasina felt increasingly weary. She sometimes had trouble keeping her mind focused and she cried easily. She privately told herself it was the beginning of the change and to get a grip on herself. Before the board meeting, she took an afternoon to rest, read, do her nails, and get ready for the events. She felt a little refreshed when she presented her report.

"In years past," she confessed, "it was necessary to break the letter though not the spirit of the law when we rescued a Chinese child. A writ of habeas corpus would deliver the child back into the custody of the Chinese until the matter could be settled in Superior Court. We seldom or never won such cases. Our attorney, Sidney Nussbaum, saw what must be done and he proposed an amendment to the state law in the matter of guardianship of minor children, which would give power to a presiding judge to sign an order to the sheriff commanding him immediately to take into custody the child whose name appeared on the warrant and place her in the care of those applying for guardianship, until such time as the hearing could be held.

"Our board here and representatives of our work in Sacramento took up the matter last spring. Those who had friends in the Senate or Legislature used all their influence to have the bill passed and it went through with flying colors. It had gotten that far in previous years, but the governor vetoed it. A member of the board is acquainted with the state controller, who brings the documents to the governor for his signature. The controller was asked to lay the matter before Governor Pardee personally. Many letters, telegrams, and telephone messages passed back and forth between the Mission and the capital. I made many trips, as did Mr. Nussbaum, in this effort.

"When our friend, the controller, appeared before the governor and prepared to use his influence to get the bill signed, he was too late. Governor Pardee had already signed the bill! Now it is the law of the state and we can go fearlessly into any house where we believe a slave child is and take her away."

The rest of the meeting went uneventfully. Thomasina had trouble concentrating, but she had prepared well and got through the meetings. The budget for the coming year was set and matters of policy were decided.

*   *   *

Thirty Chinese women were brought into the U.S. to appear at the Chinese pavilion at the Omaha International Exhibition in 1902 by means of a special Act of Congress that said they must return to China within six months after the exposition's close. Instead, most were spirited into San Francisco where they were put to work as prostitutes, some by choice. When Immigration found them, they were brought to the Mission till they could be deported. They disrupted the mission routine and demanded treatment that Thomasina could not provide. She was relieved when the last one left.

Then one morning Thomasina got out of bed and collapsed on the floor of her room. One of the big girls heard her fall, and when she found her, called for help. Wilhelmina sent for the doctor who examined Thomasina, diagnosed exhaustion, and prescribed rest, but warned her that if she continued, she would have worse health problems in the future.

She had felt increasingly foggy the last few months, as though distant from everything that happened. It took great effort to concentrate and think through problems. She cried easily. She tried to delegate more routine work, but there was always more work than workers, and as soon as she gave away one task, another arrived. She missed opportunities to speak to groups and she didn't meet boats from China to get the women through Immigration and out of the Immigration Shed. She was failing to do her duty. Increasingly, she felt as though she were playing a part in a play where she didn't know the lines.

Then when she got a call for a rescue, she felt so ill and weary she didn't think she could manage. But if she didn't do it, who would? She contacted Sergeant Gerard Finley who always cooperated and girded herself for the ordeal.

This bagnio featured porcelain lions of stylized ferocity at the door and carved, gilded dragons on the walls of the entryway. Usually, the thick scents of spicy cooking, sandalwood, musk and opium, and the smell of bodies overwhelmed her, but this time they didn't reach her. She felt muffled and numb, and watched herself from far away.

Without Sergeant Finley's presence she would have lost heart. His honest face reassured her. He was a huge protecting bear—inches over six feet, commensurately broad and terribly solid.

Inside the bordello, the atmosphere of decadent desires seemed palpable, as though it sent waves of sound, crickets swooning in dusky light. She thought she might faint, but her hands were steady. She marched through the parlors, over blue and rose carpets, under painted, tasseled chandeliers. She could sense waves of anger, passion, disgust. The very walls seemed to sweat with fear and desire. Thomasina felt all the sinister emanations of the house through her skin. Never had evil seemed so real.

Once Sergeant Finley led the way in, she waved the warrant at the madam, whose screamed Chinese curses seemed muted and indistinct. She searched the girl's room, then the entire house, without finding the girl. She went back to the girl's room, with its photographs stuck in the dresser mirror, face powder spilled in the crocheted dresser cloth, a blackened incense holder. She caught a glimpse of herself in the shadowy mirror—a white-faced woman in drab black, her mouth a grim, determined line.

She knew the girl wanted out. She had a letter begging for help and a photograph to identify her.

She sat on the neatly made bed and said, "What do you make of this, Sergeant Finley?"

"She's here," he said. "Her bag's here." He gestured toward a canvas carryall on the floor.

The sins of the house called out to her from the floor, from the walls, from the ceiling. She could almost feel the girl's fear. In a daze, without conscious thought, she said, "Sergeant Finley, will you help me move this bed?"

The two of them pushed the bed aside, pulled a rug away, and found a trapdoor.

"Let me down there," said Finley.

"No, you'd never fit," said Thomasina. She stepped down a

ladder and lowered herself into a passageway. "Hand me a lamp, please," she asked. Then she crept down the passageway on her hands and knees, pushing the lamp before her. She turned a corner and there was the terrified girl, weeping silently. She touched the cowering girl's knee. Thomasina had seen that look of fear too many times. "Come, my dear," she said. "You'll be safe now." And crouching, she raised one arm, as though to welcome the girl. The girl moved toward her.

Thomasina couldn't get turned around so she had to back out of the passage. If this were a play, she would find this part comical, utterly without dignity or grace. Both women were dirty when they emerged, with cobwebs in their hair. The madam shouted from the hallway.

Thomasina led the girl out of that evil place. She felt as though she were watching someone else go through the motions. Sergeant Finley hurried them to 920 and at length the girl was settled with the women on the top floor, provided with tea, and comforted in her own dialect. Thomasina fell asleep in her overcoat, her boots soiling the counterpane. The next morning one of the big girls found her propped there, still dressed, with cobwebs in her hair, and tears rolling down her cheeks.

"Don't cry, Lo Mo." The girl brought Miss Wheeler, who helped Thomasina undress and get under the quilts. Then Miss Wheeler sent word to the board that "Miss McIntyre is having a breakdown."

Mrs. Brown was well aware of how much Thomasina did. She had watched Miss Culbertson's regime and hoped that Thomasina could manage the demanding work. Her daughter Evelyn had told her how hard Thomasina worked and, of course, everyone knew she had been ill. First, they assured themselves she did not have tuberculosis, or any other physical problem beyond bronchitis and pneumonia. At first the members of the board wanted to give Thomasina a vacation and send her to her family to recover, as they had when she collapsed before. But Mrs. Brown pointed out that Thomasina was thirty-six years old, and had been serving the Mission for ten years. She needed more than a few weeks' rest. And she deserved better. In the end, the board voted for a year's sabbatical, to begin immediately. Thomasina's income would continue and her place as director would be held for her. Mrs. Brown activated her network of donors and got a fund together. At Evelyn's suggestion, she made travel arrangements for Thomasina to take a round-the-world passage, on modest but comfortable ships. Thomasina would meet Isabella, her oldest sister, left behind in Scotland with Carmack relations when her family emigrated. She would sail to India where she would stay with a cousin in New Delhi, then meet another relation in Shanghai and finally go to Canton, her goal, where she would stay with Presbyterian missionaries.

But first, she would meet Charlie for a week in Philadelphia.

22

She bought trinkets to console the littlest girls because their Lo Mo was leaving. She had to see about her passport and have a photograph taken. She had to explain everything she took years to learn to Wilhelmina Wheeler, who would be acting superintendent of the Mission. She planned to visit a "daughter" in Minneapolis, and Hsiang in Philadelphia, and stay with Hsiang's American family. Even Augustus Booker's daughters in Newark insisted she stay with them. James Harrow, the passenger traffic manager for the Southern Pacific, provided a train pass. Mrs. Lyman Kelley, an Occidental board member, arranged for passage on a freighter that carried live beef cattle to Liverpool. She would be among the few passengers and planned long days of reading and writing without the luxury and formality of more expensive accommodations. Of course, she would see Charlie in Philadelphia, then spend a week in New York. The sailing date depended on when the cargo could be loaded in Philadelphia. All the foreign currency had to be arranged for. People helped, of course, but she had to make decisions.

The Chinese women who sewed on the top floor of the Mission had insisted on outfitting her from the skin out. They shook their heads when they took her measurements. She was thin and they left fabric for ease in her dresses because they told her she was going to eat more and fill out. Most of her dresses were the shade of blue named for Alice Roosevelt, the president's daughter. It was the color Thomasina looked best in, although she lacked her usual high coloring these days. If she had worn gray, she would have disappeared completely. She wanted to look her best when she saw Charlie.

Even her delight at a rendezvous with him seemed dimmed by the weight of fatigue. She thought she had been tired forever and forever would be thus.

Blowing cinders and smoke meant the windows of the Pullman car stayed closed and the heat was stifling. The gritty plush passenger seat was her torture. She couldn't wash properly in the little sink and after a day felt sticky and stale. She retreated into a dull stupor, watching the landscape change as the miles rolled past. Her book lay closed in her lap. She yielded to the heat. The harsh desert landscape seemed featureless at first, with trees only occasionally, then she caught the rhythm of the grass, the sage, the great curving shapes of the hills, the brusque upthrust of mountains. What a great, beautiful country the train rolled through! How could anything, even gray grass, survive? She saw few cattle, an occasional horseman. It needed water.

She felt kinship with the desert. She was burnt dry by the demands of the Mission. She felt she lived in an airless cell, separated from other people by her great weariness. She blocked out the other people in the car—the women with children, the traveling salesmen—and sat without a thought, watching the miles roll past.

Through the hot night, hypnotized by the clack of the train wheels on the rails, she gazed out the window that became a mirror reflecting the occupants in the car against the curve of sage-covered hills, or an occasional light from a farmhouse. She prayed in a passion of anticipation: "O Lord, help us find a way to be together."

She was met in Minneapolis by Mrs. Ng-Lin Hsi formerly of 920 Sacramento Street. This delightful daughter poured her troubled thoughts to Lo Mo who tried to counsel her in the ways of a Chinese wife in the midlands. She felt inadequate in the extreme, but she told Hsi how lucky she was to be safely ransomed from the tong by her hardworking and loving spouse. Hsi's husband treated Lo Mo like his own mother, which is to say, with the greatest honor and deference, in the Chinese custom. She hoped the couple would work out ways to be happy together. To be a Chinese in Minneapolis was to be both conspicuous and without the comfort of a large Chinese community.

Miss Emma Page, a prominent Presbyterian woman active in benevolent causes, had expressed interest in Miss McIntyre's work with the Chinese. When they met, Miss Page took one look at Thomasina and insisted on a week's rest at her Lake Minnetonka lodge. Instead of the bustle of New York, Thomasina chose a week beside the peaceful lake. After a few days she got out her journal and brought it up-to-date. She confided to it her fears and hopes about meeting Charlie after all these months.

The last leg of her train travels seemed interminable. She knew when the train curved around the Johnstown horseshoe she was nearly there. She was a little better rested when she arrived in Philadelphia. Her feelings for Charlie confused her. She loved him and wanted to be with him more than anything, but she had responsibilities that couldn't be ignored. Had he changed? Was his work in the seminary making him different, more serious? Had absence made his heart grow cooler? She felt very shy and uneasy until she spotted him striding toward her on the train platform at the downtown station, then she thought her heart would burst with joy. He was handsomer than ever and smiling like the sun coming out. They embraced awkwardly.

First, they went to see about getting her trunk moved to the boat. She learned that her freighter would leave in just twenty hours. She and Charlie had less than a day together!

She wanted to rant and scream at the agent, but she only wept in feminine frustration. "I have no choice but to accept this," she told Charlie. "The board bought all my accommodations and tickets. This is my schedule. How I hate being a charity case!"

Charlie shrugged. He put his arm around her shoulders and said, "You're lucky to go at all. We'll make the most of today, Tommy." Before they left the station, she phoned a message to Hsiang's family, who had arranged to meet her for dinner that evening at Bookbinders.

"I am free of the Mission's routine, but constrained by time tables and schedules," she told Charlie.

Charlie led her out of the freight shed and remarked, "You loom so large in my thoughts, I forget that really, you are a small person. I'm afraid I'll crush you with my big arms."

"Crush away," she said. Already she felt her heart lighten. She put her hand in his and they stood looking at each other without talking. Then he did crush her in front of everybody and she rejoiced.

Then Charlie said, "I bet you'd like some Philadelphia clam chowder for lunch." And he led her to a Child's restaurant redolent with seafood and good cooking. Tamsen liked the thick soup with tomatoes, but could only eat about half the bowl. Charlie, who had gotten up early to catch a train from Princeton, put away a plate of baked fish and potatoes, too. They had no place to stay, so they lingered long over lunch.

She studied Charlie's face across the table. He looked more mature—his hair was thinning, the bones of his face were more defined, the shape more pronounced, with the last of the youthful softness burnt away. His voice was deeper and slower and its natural resonance had become more polished. He sounded somehow less sincere when he said he loved her. She missed the spontaneity of his husky, boyish voice. He moved less impulsively; his tread was heavier. He seemed ten years older than the playmate of that first carefree summer three years ago.

Later, she would remember that they walked and talked all of that long day. They talked without pause, stepping on each other's sentences in a rush to tell everything.

"Why do you talk with a Scots burr when you've never lived in Scotland?" Charlie asked.

"From Mama, I suppose. All my family spoke this way." She watched Charlie pay the restaurant bill. "For two people working for God, mammon looms large in our lives," she said. "The work is satisfying but unremunerative."

"I suppose we might as well talk about that," Charlie said.

"Money, you mean?"

"Of course."

But they didn't. They talked about people in their lives and things they did and what they had left out of their letters.

When they left the restaurant, Charlie led Thomasina in a long, meandering tour through the city. They strolled past the refurbished Wanamaker's Department Store with its huge signs, then walked blocks to Rittenhouse Square, past the mansions, then under trees with dusty summer leaves. Charlie led her through narrow alleys of two-story colonial row houses where laundry hung overhead and children played beneath.

They emerged onto busy streets where she enjoyed the familiar city rhythm of foot traffic, horse carts, trolleys, and a few automobiles. Mounted policemen watched. In San Francisco's climate, flowers grew from every window box, barrel, and patch of garden, but here all was paved and greenery was confined to the squares, each of which seemed to have at least one church with an impressive spire.

They stopped for lemonade at a street stall, then Charlie said, "You showed me around San Francisco through Chinatown, so I'll show you some picturesque neighborhoods."

"You mean slums?"

"They're so quaint."

"I hope you know your way," Thomasina commented. The day was hot and her underwear stuck to her, but she was supremely happy just to walk with Charlie.

"I know my way a little, but we're between the rivers. The number streets go north and south and the name streets east and west, so we can always get our bearings."

In Little Italy she smelled familiar cooking—North Beach without the sea. A goat tied to his cart followed a huckster selling vegetables. Ragged children who didn't know they were poor played happily on the trash heaps beside the shops. An outhouse drained into an open gutter. She had heard of the Octavia Hill Association, which bought houses and renovated them. These laughing children died too readily from tuberculosis and meningitis. As in her Chinatown, the street life was messy, but full of vitality.

They walked through streets that seemed more foreign than her Chinatown. On one block she saw Kosher butcher shops where housewives bargained. Pushcarts sold everything from clothes to pots and pans. Orthodox men in gabardines and beards filed into a temple. The people spoke a language she didn't understand. San Francisco Jews were more American; these seemed still European.

"They don't separate businesses from residences here," Thomasina observed. "A factory or an art school might be across from row houses." Later, she would remember her feet on the hot pavement, the strange accents she heard, and the heated, humid summer air.

After an hour, Charlie showed her into a tea and confectionery shop. Fans turned overhead and the sweet smell of ice cream greeted them. Thomasina noticed elaborate chandeliers and polished marble tables with wire chairs and girls in starched white uniforms. They ate strawberry ice cream, then ordered tea, which was served in thick white china. She was glad to sit under the overhead fans and cool off a little.

Late in the afternoon they reached Bookbinders. Ah Hsiang was the first mission girl to attend college, but not the last, if she had anything to say about it. The family assembled—the father from his office, the mother from the Main Line, and Hsiang from Haverford College—and they had a joyful supper. Hsiang's American father recalled how he "bought" her and they all laughed at the story about Hsiang discovering that Lo Mo sang off-key. Hsiang bubbled over with enthusiasm about her studies and her college life of football games and dances.

"And I'm coming back to the Mission when I graduate," said Hsiang.

"Oh, Hsiang, I'd like nothing better," Thomasina said, "but you have a chance to do things most Chinese-American girls can't. You can become a professional woman—teach or study medicine or law or go into business. I don't want to tie you to the Mission and keep you from a better life."

"It's a life good enough for you," replied Hsiang.

"Tell the truth and shame the devil," said Thomasina. She and Hsiang were alone in the ladies' room after dinner.

"I'm good with all languages, it turns out," said Hsiang. She looked proud, but didn't want to boast. "I'm doing French this term and Spanish next year. Maybe Portuguese, if they can find an instructor. I can help the Mission with all kinds of people."

"Hsiang, you have made me very happy," said Thomasina. Tears began, but Hsiang had seen her in tears, in rages, in every emotion a daughter could observe. She couldn't hide her true self from Hsiang. "I wondered if we were doing the right thing at the Mission. No, even I have doubts. We were turning you girls into Chinese-Americans and you had to find your own way."

"A guidebook would have helped," said Hsiang with an ironic smile.

"Perhaps we did the right thing or something close to it. Your first thought was to help someone else. That is the highest Christian, highest *human* value there is."

They embraced, then Thomasina said, "I always hope my girls turn out to be good people and I never should have had a doubt about you. You are the best reward."

Both women were weeping now.

"I'm glad I make you happy," said Hsiang.

After they said good-bye to Hsiang and her family, Thomasina and Charlie followed directions that took them closer to the river. Thomasina barely felt the street underfoot, barely breathed. Her head felt light and only Charlie's warm hand anchored her. They had run out of news and the important thing, the subject they had avoided, loomed.

"Are you getting along okay at school?" she began.

"I'm stoking furnaces and grading papers next term. I'm close to graduating, so the seminary is helping me finish."

"It could be that you're very promising and they want to help you along."

Charlie grinned. "Could be."

"What will you do when you graduate?" Tamsen asked but was afraid of the answer.

"I must find a congregation and bring Mama and Aggie and Louise to live with me. Then Ben can get married."

"Ben deserves his own life, I suppose."

"He's done his share all these years. Now it's my turn."

They found the Swede's church, Gloria Dei, and wandered through the graveyard in the fading light. The dates were all older than any cemetery in San Francisco.

"I have to think about my sisters, too," Tamsen said. "Al's family is growing. Helen and Annie are getting older and they can't work forever. The McIntyre sisters help their fellow man, but they don't have much money put back for their old age. I assume I will help them as long as I work."

"What will you do, Tommy? Must you provide for them all?"

"I'll do the best I can and hope that among us, we can get along."

"Must it all fall on your shoulders?" Charlie squeezed her hand.

"No, but I'm the one who knows how to get things done. Annie's almost fifteen years older, but they look to me."

"You're their Lo Mo, too."

"No, they raised me. I *want* to be able to help them. But if I'm working and you're taking care of your family, how do we get married?"

"Perhaps I could take on additional work, besides a congregation."

Charlie limped a little by now—he was tired, too, from their long walk.

At home she saw sea or sky at the ends of the streets, but not until they approached the waterfront did Thomasina get a sense that this was a port. She kept sniffing for the river, the wharf, the familiar water smell she associated with boats. She saw gulls; where was the water? Then, between the sheds, she could see the river stretching gray and flat. The slanting sun caught the haze on the water and it shimmered with invisible light. Tugs eased big freighters into their berths.

They dodged drays carrying away bananas unloaded at Pier 9. Thomasina recognized tea boxes coming off a clipper. Sailors patronized the ale houses that looked as though they had been pumping beer since colonial times. They found the wharf where her cattle boat was being loaded. Brick factories faced the docks across broad Delaware Avenue. Later she would remember rows of federal-style houses and shops, lively citizens dodging wagons, mail trolleys, bright-eyed children (none Chinese), and over all, the coal-fire haze of a big city. The clean lines of the buildings seemed austere compared to San Francisco's exuberant Victorian architecture. The rest of her life, she could recall the names of all the ships anchored along the wharfs.

The captain confirmed that the boat would leave at midnight. Her trunk was in her tiny cabin and there was nothing she could do.

By then the sun was gone and the heat lifted a little. She and Charlie found some deck chairs out of the way and sat in the shadows. Stevedores loaded feed for the cattle. She could hear the animals complain and she smelled fresh dung. The dock workers loaded barrels of water, canned goods, and boxes of fresh produce. She felt as though she would remember the span and temperature of Charlie's hand always—could almost feel the whorls and bumps of his palm print, the lines of Heart and Head and Life, the knuckles, and the pad of the palm. She wanted to hold on for strength and reassurance, to know she was loved and protected, and she knew it was a fantasy. He loved her, but he couldn't protect her and she couldn't call on his strength for her problems. But she was grateful for his hand today, to hold and feel close to him, to touch him perhaps for the last time.

"You can't take on extra work. You may be serving more than one congregation anyway, especially at first. How could you do more?"

"I don't know. If it was in San Francisco, we could be together, but I'm not sure where I'll be going, but it looks like Redding, and maybe another congregation up north."

Charlie wiped sweat from inside his collar with his handkerchief. They both were weary, but she couldn't be tired! Today was all they had.

Tamsen tried to look inside Charlie's eyes. Why could they not come up with any solution? They were both smart people, but their path was blocked in every direction.

"If you could live at the Mission and I could continue, it would be easy, but I am an inmate there as surely as the girls. A man couldn't live on the premises, and I'm not sure you would like fifty women and girls around." She thought of the shrieking children, the conversation of the older women, the bells, their monthlies that all seemed to come at the same time and the subsequent grouchiness and competition for sinks. "I'm not sure my board would agree to a married director. They would think my place was by your side. We would always be struggling to find time together, and when we did we would be weary."

She couldn't concentrate on one thing and their conversation shifted from the trifling to the most important. She wanted to tell him some of the things she'd done, but it sounded as though she were boasting when she mentioned the president's visit.

"We aren't used to talking," she said. "I feel as though we're skimming the situation. This issue is real and insurmountable, but we aren't speaking our hearts—what brought us to this point."

Charlie looked at her and seemed embarrassed. Had she touched a nerve? They talked about getting married like business partners, not ardent lovers. Had they lost their feelings for each other? She studied his face.

"I can't resign myself. Why can't we do what we want!" Charlie said. "I was hoping that when we put our heads together we could come up with a solution. But we have walked and talked for hours and we're no closer."

"I don't think there is any solution. Let us accept that we cannot marry in the foreseeable future."

They held hands; he turned hers and rubbed the palm with his thumb. A memory flickered of how her body responded to him, that sweet tension. They had been together all of today scarcely touching. Two summers ago they would have found a way to be alone. She ignored the other passengers who were boarding.

"I am too old and too bossy, besides," she said jokingly.

"You are too powerful," he said soberly.

This shocked her. She expected banter and some attempt to be lighthearted. "What do you mean?"

"You don't need a husband—you are enough unto yourself."

"Why would you say such an awful thing?" She could hear the tears in her voice.

"I don't mean to hurt your feelings," he said. He looked at her with such tenderness her heart melted. "You are Madam Director, the head of the Presbyterian Mission, rescuer of Chinese girls. Everyone in San Francisco knows who you are and respects you. Marriage would take that away from you and take you away from work that is necessary and important."

"But matrimony is holy. I never planned to stay at the Mission, it just happened." And somewhere in her heart she knew what Charlie was saying. "You've had to compete for my attention," Tamsen said and felt the words bitter on her tongue.

"I would just be some pipsqueak assistant pastor, starting out."

"Your ego would have to grow a thick skin."

"I could, if I thought we could work everything out. But it would be too big a burden to put on a frail, new marriage. My family, your family, your fame, your work abandoned, my work distracting me. I couldn't take the place of all you'd lose."

"So that's how you feel," she murmured. She felt like crying, but the tears didn't come. A headache started instead.

"You are the only woman I have ever wanted to marry," Charlie said. "I was a spoiled boy, always getting what I wanted—a new bicycle, a college education. Now it's my turn to give back to my family."

Now Charlie looked unhappy. She had seen him cry once and he looked close to tears again. She didn't want the burden of his embarrassment, so she changed the subject.

"I was sick last winter," she said. "They called it a breakdown. I thought I was just tired. Maybe I knew then that we couldn't make our lives together and I couldn't accept it."

"Aggie wrote you were ill, but you didn't say very much. You look flushed from the heat, but it's put a little color in your cheeks."

Tamsen touched her face. "I didn't put much on paper because I was afraid I'd sound self-pitying."

"McIntyres never sound self-pitying. It's against the family code," he said, smiling.

"Tough Scots never complain." She managed a smile, but couldn't hold it in place.

"Maybe I was lovesick," she said. "Not like a girl over a beau, but sick because I loved you and I loved Chun Mei and I loved the possibilities of people. I was a juggler with plates on the end of sticks, and the plates were dropping and breaking. I learned a hard lesson: I'm not indispensable. When I gave up my duties, others carried on. I thought the board would throw me out for incompetence, but they were very kind." The sailors called directions to each other. Their strong bodies bent to their tasks.

"I didn't realize—"

"I didn't admit to myself how tired and ill I was until I couldn't move."

"Nobody would ever say you're stubborn."

"Not me." Their teasing felt strained, but at least they were trying to be easy with each other.

"So what happened?" he asked.

"I stayed in bed for a while, and they gave me a furlough, this sabbatical year, ten months actually, and I made preparations and turned everything over to Wilhelmina, the housekeeper. I don't like to think the Mission can run without me, but I know it can and will. I must take care of myself or I won't be able to continue, years down the line. In the future—" Sudden tears overwhelmed her factual little recital and she covered her face with her hands. "Years and years! Without you! I can't bear it!" She tried to stop, but couldn't. Charlie squeezed into her chair and took her in his arms. She cried into his soft shirtfront, the sobs shaking her, his arms holding her.

"Will you be all right?" he asked when she stopped. Charlie looked uncomfortable. "You'll be all alone for days at sea to brood about this."

"I'll be able to weep in peace. After years of thinking in one path, it's hard to change everything in my mind all at once."

They sat sideways, feet outstretched on the wooden chair, as close to each other as they could get. They didn't try to talk for that last hour. Tamsen breathed in his oniony smell, the laundry soap of his shirt, his hair tonic. She felt the muscle and bone through his clothes, his warmth on this warm night. She brushed his hair with her hand and traced his cheek, his jawline, the clean line of his neck. She squeezed his hand, memorized now. She lay her head on his chest, felt the ridge of his clavicle, heard his heart pumping, and imagined the lungs' exchange, the blood's visit, all the organs silently making him whole. She remembered his flawless feet inside his heavy shoes, as smooth as a child's, straight and perfect.

They heard the captain give notice that visitors must leave.

"I wish I were a larger person," he admitted, talking rapidly. "I wish I didn't care that you were important. I wish I didn't have any egotism. But I do."

Tamsen waited, wondering what he was working up to.

"I hurt you when I said you didn't need a husband. What I meant is that you are strong and smart and know how to get things done. You have great executive abilities. You could probably run the whole Presbyterian Church, U.S.A. And you have a heart big enough for a hundred 'daughters' at a time. You are feminine and dainty and your fine sensibilities are evident in all you do. You don't need a husband to make you whole—you are whole."

"Then why do I feel as though something is missing?" She heard the cattle lowing and the shouts of the sailors. The fecund smell of decay rose from the water. The boat's lights gently illuminated the planes of Charlie's face—his fine cheekbones, the full lips, the pale hair.

"We grow up expecting to marry and we think that it's necessary. Maybe it is. Maybe some year I'll take a wife. She won't be you and she'll suffer in comparison. No woman will ever be so complete."

"This sounds like my epitaph."

"I didn't mean to be so solemn, but I wanted to tell you how I love you even if we never get married, or even see each other again."

"You are as dear to me as the blood that runs in my veins." Words couldn't carry all the emotion in her heart and now there was no time. "You made me laugh, you taught me to love my earthy self. You are all the man I ever wanted." Tears blurred Charlie's face.

They embraced, one last imprint of each other's body. Charlie kissed her one last time, hurried down the gangplank, and turned to watch from the wharf as the lines were cast off. The boat began moving, slowly, slowly down the river to the sea.

23

At first Tamsen spent a lot of time at the rail. As long as she could see the horizon, she was all right, but shut up in her cabin, she was queasy. The captain gave her soda crackers and seltzer and after a day, she felt perfectly fine. Thank heavens the weather was fair.

At first she wondered how she would fill this span of empty days. She hadn't been this idle since she was a child. She had books, her journal, and prayer, but hours vanished and all she had done was think of Charlie and cry. She pretended the wind and sun made her eyes red. The other passengers included Rose Ottinger, a social worker on her way to Europe for a vacation, and an elderly gentleman from Fresno, who accompanied them as they walked on deck. A pair of businessmen appeared at meals and exchanged information about cattle markets in Britain.

Tamsen and Rose got on famously. Rose was the daughter of immigrants, she had studied at the University of Chicago and worked at Hull House as a student. They discussed Jane Addams's work and her writing, with which they were both familiar, and they talked for hours about issues they had in common. Tamsen was glad Miss Addams didn't condemn the girls involved in the social evil, but had learned the reasons they entered the life. She wondered if the vote for women would accomplish everything that Miss Addams thought it would—that suffrage could get laws passed that would outlaw a red-light district and eliminate child labor.

"You seem sad, Miss McIntyre," said the captain, who had followed her out after an evening meal. He was a roly-poly man of middle years who kept photographs of his wife and six children on the bridge. They stood at the rail and Tamsen wondered at the stars. More shone over the sea than in cities, and they looked brighter.

"I am sad, Captain Bloemink. When sad things happen, I respond. But give me more of this fresh air and good food and I'll recover, I'm sure."

"You are connected with the Presbyterian Church, in San Francisco, I believe."

"I direct the Mission in Chinatown."

"A lady like you in Chinatown?!" Then he recovered. "I mean, that can be a very dangerous part of town, or it was when I was a young man on shore leave."

"Most of the people who would like to get rid of me know that my dear friend, Sergeant Finley, would never stop until he arrested them."

"How do you know policemen by name?" asked the captain. He puffed on a pipe filled with tobacco that smelled like cherries. Here in the open air it was pleasant.

"I always take at least two policemen when I rescue a girl."

"Rescue?"

Rose joined them and Tamsen described a typical raid in Chinatown. This was something other social workers never did. She got absorbed telling of the time they rescued Liu from the bordello and she even got a little breathless recounting what it was like. The captain seemed entertained and Rose was fascinated. Maybe she could stop weeping if she told more stories.

She tried to hold the memory of Charlie—the exact blue of his eyes, the weight and texture of his hair. She listened to the timbre of his voice in her mind's ear; she ached for its resonance and intonations. She could scarcely bear to think of his body, the muscle and bone under the fair skin, but she fed upon those images, the music of his voice, the remembered touch. And even as she tried to burn him into her memory, he was gone, like a candle flickering out. All that was left was the absence of his warm hand, the silence where his voice had been, the silhouette outlining his shadow face.

She woke up one morning to a rough sea feeling seasick. She had been dreaming of a Chinese toddler crying on the landing to the second floor of the Mission. She bent and lifted the child who buried her face in Lo Mo's bosom. The child was crying for something she didn't need—a rag doll perhaps or a sweet. And Wilhelmina was calling Thomasina and the bell for classes was ringing. Before she could take care of this distraction, she awoke feeling she had put in a day's labor already. Since unfinished business always nags, she felt all day that some task was left undone. She stayed on deck, with Rose, and they spent hours in the peak of the bow sheltered from the wind, talking. If she could watch the horizon, she was a little better.

The next night, the same little girl appeared in her dream, blocking her way. The girl didn't cry this time, but chattered at her in high-pitched Chinese that sounded like an annoying piece of squealing machinery. Lo Mo hated herself for judging the Chinese language. After all, she could barely follow the simplest conversation and she could never reproduce the sounds herself. Many people described it as "singsong"—true enough because words had to be sounded on the right tone. Spoken by mothers to infants, it sounded soft and loving. She had gone once to a Chinese opera, one of the few places proper Chinese wives could appear in public. The story was easy enough to understand and about as simple as an Italian opera, but the singing sounded so discordant she could scarcely listen to it. Like lychee fruit and the strange root vegetables she saw displayed on Chinatown sidewalks, it must be an acquired taste.

So why did she find the child's chatter so perturbing?

The next day she stayed in her cabin and wrote in her journal recording what Rose said about teaching English to immigrants. She also drafted letters to everyone in California to be mailed when she landed. She rarely recopied letters since she rarely had the time, but she didn't want to appear self-pitying about Charlie. The reasons that compelled them apart were difficult to articulate.

She wrote to Ben about Charlie's seriousness and resolve and her fear that she would lose this close connection to the Ducik family. She explained that Ben could feel relieved of some of the family responsibilities. In a similar letter, she wrote to Mrs. Ducik, Louise, and Aggie. She already thought of them as her sisters and she had to rewrite that letter twice.

Writing the letters helped her order her thoughts and grapple with what had happened. This was God's will for her. If it had been His will for her and Charlie to get married, they would have found a way.

But if marriage was not the Lord's will, then what was? And the answer came: the work at hand—the Mission, lobbying for social legislation, caring for her daughters, public speaking, court appearances. It should be obvious that her life's direction was already set.

The wave isn't separate from the ocean, it surrenders.

The next night she dreamed of the same little Chinese girl, who was dragging Lo Mo down the second-floor hallway toward something she didn't understand. The next day was bright and the wind brisk and she didn't want to stay in her cabin, but she knew this discipline of writing about dreams and fantasies in her journal was important.

She wrote to brother Al and explained in logical sequence what had happened, how she and Charlie had come to their decisions. She declared her willingness to relieve Al of some of his burdens regarding their sisters. She had no confidence that she could provide for their old age or hers—but she would do what she always did: pray for answers.

These letters, written with such effort and such care, full of logic and reasonable explanation, seemed a simplified version of her thoughts, something written for Sunday school children, not the deep version of the books on moral theology. She returned to her journal to explore her dreams of the little Chinese girl. She knew the girl's name meant some precious thing, like Pearl Treasure, Chu Pao. She knew the mother was dead and the girl was a ward of the Mission without family in California. She knew the girl was unhappy—sometimes with cause, sometimes not.

Tamsen awoke sweating and out of breath after the fourth or fifth dream. Little Chu Pao had wandered out the front door of 920. Tamsen saw the paving stones, the trolley lines overhead, the curb, and the child, toddling into the street. She rushed out of the Mission when she heard Chu Pao cry out. Three girls who were coming in just then blocked the front door and Tamsen tangled with them in a comic exchange. "Let me out!" A deliveryman carrying a large package blocked the steps. In the meantime she heard Chu Pao's cries and a streetcar's bell. Chu Pao hadn't been taught it was dangerous to go into the street.

She finally forced her way through the doorway and down the steps. Out of breath and frightened, she scooped Chu Pao out of the path of a downhill delivery wagon with straining brakes. This time the dream didn't end there. She sat on the stoop of 920 and held the child. She needed to hold on to something because she was shaking.

Tamsen began crying as she recorded the dream. She didn't know why, only that she felt profoundly sad. The child might have been hurt. She was wrong not to teach the little girls about going outside as soon as they could walk. In her imagination she sat for a long time in cool San Francisco sunshine, holding the child.

At first, her journal and her thoughts were simple. She loved Charlie and when they couldn't make their lives together, naturally she was unhappy. Then she had to admit that she was physically frustrated because she could no longer anticipate that sweet guilty release of sex. But that wasn't all of it, either. She missed Charlie's lighthearted energy. With him, she became a different person—gay and optimistic and carefree. He brought out some part of her that her strict upbringing had squelched but not killed.

She wrote herself a lecture on taking herself too seriously. She reminded herself that Jesus was invited to parties, so he must have been good company. Dr. Marrs was a warm and cheerful servant of God. She had been very serious because she had started out as the insecure and very young successor in a role that society hadn't yet defined.

As she sat with a pen in her hand, an image came to her of how she would look as a man—a little like Al, she thought—slight but wiry, with sandy hair already white. She, too, would have a heavy beard, which Al complained about having to shave. She imagined working beside him in the fields, bucking hundred-pound hay bales, carrying sacks of feed into the barn. She liked feeling strong and physical and competent. Her egotism was masculine, when she faced a donor or planned some public presentation.

The freighter continued an uneventful journey. They didn't have any violent weather, although a few squalls came up and blew themselves out. She spent those hours in a limbo of nausea, waiting for the relief of throwing up, then wishing she couldn't.

Her face took on color and her baggy dresses fit a little better. She certainly felt stronger and more rested in spite of nights spent with frustrating dreams.

The next dream of Chu Pao was a rescue from the roof of the Mission. How had the child managed to find a door to open and climb out? Tamsen found the child fearlessly walking in the gutter at the roof's very edge. After that, she kept the child with her all day. Chu Pao played at her feet while she worked at her desk, accompanied her on errands, and even went with her when she spoke to a group of businessmen at a luncheon downtown. Chu

Pao held her hand when she led the Sunday service. Chu Pao cried less.

The ocean view was featureless. With no trees or buildings to help her judge, she had no idea how far she could see. She needed streets and trees and hills to give perspective. She wished she had perspective for her life. She had read about Hull House and rejoiced at the work they accomplished, but they dealt with a European immigrant population, and what worked for them wasn't practical for Chinatown. Her church encouraged the work, and the Baptists and Methodists also had missions in Chinatown. The Episcopalians supported the Y.M.C.A., but she and other women were making the guidelines as they went along, and they made mistakes. When people praised her for doing good works, she remembered the girl who disappeared the night before the raid that had been planned to rescue her. She was found months later, in a warehouse in the delta, starving and ill. She died soon after she arrived at the Mission. Some of the babies of the prostitutes were sickly and too small to survive. The women's work exposed them to diseases that killed some of them within a few years. This made her angry and kept her motivated.

But in this journal, never to be shown to another soul, she confided her notions, whatever they were. The act of writing, the effort and work of it, calmed her spirit.

"Sometimes I think I lived previous lives, as the Buddhists say," she wrote in her journal. "I think I lived in times and places in the past and I was a man as well as a woman. I feel great affinity for Old Testament stories of the Babylon Captivity. I feel as though I know the Scottish Highlands I will in actuality be visiting the first time. I meet people and I feel I know them already.

"If I had been a Chinese man, a bandit outside the Great Wall, would that explain my affinity to the girls I work with? Perhaps I lived in the time of Calvin, or some other church father, and that is why I'm now involved with religion.

"What occurs to me most is that I am a woman in this life because I wanted to have children. That is why I am so dejected at the turn of events. I had expected to bear children, rear them as my own, and learn the rigors and delights of maternity. Instead I am parent to dozens of children, but unable to claim any single one as my own."

She didn't believe in reincarnation, except as an idle fancy. She didn't really think she appeared masculine in any way. Charlie had planted a wicked thought when he said she was male and female both.

The next day, when she reread what she had written, she wept because she truly wanted children. She wanted to be some tow-headed child's mama, not Lo Mo to Chinese girls. She didn't know what that desire would have meant or how her life would have been if that wish were lived out. She saw what happened to women who had families—they died in childbirth, lost their looks and figures, became careworn, and aged early.

Even more than losing Charlie, she lamented the loss of these imaginary children. She craved that personal, distinctive relationship to one man, to her own children. She wanted to be all-important to them. She wanted to be someone who couldn't be replaced.

That night she lay in the hot darkness waiting for sleep. Stifling late summer heat in her cabin made her feel as if she were standing too close to a fire. She imagined herself stepping into the fire, her feet on the burning logs. She stood on the burning logs and the fire consumed her with physical pain. This pain was different from punishing hellfire. She felt she was altering shape and substance—first she was heated, then dried, then charred, and she glowed with fire, like one of the logs. The fire burned away all the leaves and twigs, then the bark, then penetrated to her core. And the smoke blew away and she waited for the next step and it happened: she became the fire. She consumed herself, became pure energy, and rose into the air.

She lay there transfigured. She was aware that she was sweating in her nightgown, that her hair stuck to her neck, that the air was stuffy in her cabin, and that the boat rocked as it sailed forward.

But she was not there, not in this time or place, but beyond, beyond, where tears never flowed. She was larger than the sky and higher; she was beyond her body's demands and the demands of people or responsibilities or livelihood. She was beyond desire, not fettered to the earth or people or her own limitations.

She must have slept toward morning because she dreamed that she carried Chu Pao everywhere now. The child clung to her and she felt the warm arms around her neck. Chu Pao was not a burden but a part of her life, a part of her. She could not imagine living without Chu Pao.

She felt she could never tell anyone the strange dreams and fancies of that voyage. She didn't understand the images herself, only that they were more important than the "logical" things she wrote for other people. She was more at peace now than when she left Philadelphia.

And finally, when she knew they would dock in Liverpool the next day, she remembered to write to Charlie.

She wrote:

> You are my best part, the part that makes my heart sing. You made me know more of myself and the world because I could see through your eyes how glorious it is, how much fun, how delightful.
>
> I have always gotten what I wanted, in the largest sense. I lost my mother, but I had the love of my sisters and brother and I was reared with much care and attention. I got to go to college long enough to qualify for teaching. I found an interesting position and while I was afraid I wouldn't be equal to it, I still wanted to become director, and at least I had a little time to learn what to do before Miss Culbertson died.
>
> I wanted you to want to marry me, but I must acknowledge I have been given something else I also want. I think you were right—I like being Madam Director, maybe more

than I admitted. You presented hard truths so gently and lovingly I could have asked for no better teacher.

I am sad that this time I won't get precisely what I thought I wanted. Now that the pain is not so fresh, I remember that I have received a full cup, running over, of love and good treatment from all the people in my life, and that I can pass it on to the girls in my care.

When much has been given, much is expected. Times when I feel empty and dry, I need to remember that the cup always overflows, if I will let it.

You have made my life richer. Nobody ever sang to me alone. Nobody ever let me know my body. I never have relaxed with any man but you and that was worth the world. I never felt so understood, and with all my faults and seriousness, so accepted.

Thank you for that, and for all the things I can't put into words. I wish I could write a great poem that would match my feelings, but this prose is the best I can do and I offer it, with my love, always my love.

—Tommy

24

In Scotland, Thomasina hiked over soft Scottish hills with her sister, Isabella, known as Bee, to tiny kirks where her ancestors had worn hollows in the stones. She could almost hear the centuries of hymns and psalms sung by McIntyres and Carmacks, hear the murmur of praise. From there she went to London for a few weeks, then boarded a boat for the Far East.

The captain of the *Mombasa* woke her one morning in the Mediterranean and said, "Sometimes we can see Mt. Sinai, if the day is clear." At dawn, she stood at the rail as the mountain emerged from the dark, loomed in the distance, then disappeared in fog.

She stepped ashore in Shanghai with great anticipation. At long last, she was in China, the country her daughters came from.

"Finding the same hymnals here that we use at the Mission makes me feel at home." Thomasina sat over tea after supper with

Evelyn Burlingame, a former teacher of Chinese from San Francisco, Lucy Durham, and Dr. Mary Niles of Canton Christian Hospital, cofounder with Lucy Durham of work with blind Chinese. Miss Durham, a plain-spoken and attractive spinster, had furnished the money to open and maintain the station until the Presbyterians took it over. They were handsome women, a few years older than Thomasina, practical and hardworking as good Presbyterian women should be. She had stayed in bed for a day sleeping 'round the clock, then her hosts took her through the busy streets to Evelyn's school nearby, then they had returned for supper.

"I worked to support foreign missions when I was a child, and now I've actually seen one. I keep finding parallels to my mission. We both try to provide physical help and a moral environment."

"The Chinese lack knowledge of Western medicine, especially about blindness and how to educate blind people," said Dr. Niles. They sat at a rattan table under a rickety pergola in the courtyard at the compound where a leafy vine made speckled shade. Thomasina was getting a hint of the origin of the awnings and balconies of Chinatown. She enjoyed the strange vegetables served on familiar blue and white plates. She felt at home with the laughter and shouts of children nearby.

"We need missionaries who have other talents, like Mary," said Lucy Durham. Miss Durham's considerable executive talents had found an outlet rescuing orphans and giving refuge to unwed mothers.

"It is interesting," observed Thomasina, "that we, all single women, agree that the unwed mothers need to be cared for, so that they can care for their children. Married women condemn them because it threatens their sphere. Our attitude has nothing to do with moral uplift."

"No," said Evelyn, "the men who fathered the children and abandoned the mothers are never found or punished." Evelyn's fair complexion was high in the hot afternoon and she fanned herself.

The tea grew cold in the porcelain pot. Cries of babies reached them from the mothers' dormitory. The courtyard and the low buildings with tile roofs reminded Thomasina of old Spanish houses in California. Shouts and laughter came from the kitchen and reminded her of the women's voices she heard at the Mission. The sun sank behind the impossibly steep hills. The doorkeeper came in to light the lamps. This compound was outside of Canton proper and away from areas where Western businessmen and diplomats built homes that reproduced a bit of Britain or Holland.

"Miss Jane Addams writes about the attitudes of the givers toward the poor. She says we think that poverty exists because of moral failings," said Thomasina.

"If that were true, the situation would be reversed and people with money would be poor and the poor would be raised," said Mary. "I don't think Miss Jane Addams understands the true needs. She organizes classes to uplift the ignorant immigrants, but they need better wages, not classes in medieval stained glass or modern poetry."

"She did make me examine my own attitudes," confessed Thomasina. "I've even been criticized for calling the adults 'girls' instead of 'women.' It is difficult when everyone looks to me as director."

"We probably look as crudely unaware to the Chinese as they do to us," Mary said. "We don't understand their culture, although I'm learning."

Their conversation had that relaxed, disjointed quality of friends who shared the same background. Thomasina felt comfortable, as though she had known them for years.

"We think as Americans we treat our girls better because we value them, but boys get the best chance at education; girls will end up in the home and their education will be 'wasted.' " Thomasina heard a bitter tone in her voice.

"If you take the long view," said Lucy, fanning herself with her handkerchief, "Chinese attitudes have kept their culture stable through upheavals. Family is the rock they build their lives on."

Thomasina thought a moment and admitted, "I know I am sometimes patronizing, but the girls—and yes, they are *girls* because they are so young and immature—are passive. They simply give up and wait for fate to happen to them. Perhaps in China this is a good attitude, but I want to wake them up."

"I could say, 'Oh, no, you're fine,' and comfort you," said Lucy. Her face became animated as she took up the subject. "But I'm afraid I am guilty, too. When we give help, we make them mind our rules. They must listen to Bible readings and not leave without telling us. They do that with passive grace, too. Some of them convert, but we are always being questioned about the low figures. We are more interested in providing help and dealing with the blind than counting numbers."

"Alas," said Mary, "many of the givers are great number counters."

"My board trusts me," Thomasina said.

"The poorest of the poor are the most generous," Lucy said. "They share their meager belongings with those worse off. They send money back to their villages when they barely have enough to survive. They become prostitutes at their family's insistence, then end up here, with child, and afraid to go home. We seem stingy to them because they give with a free hand while we ask for something in return."

"It's a complicated situation and I keep praying for strength to act for the girls—women!" Thomasina laughed. "I think, of course, that I am morally superior, but then something happens and I compromise my conscience and I know I'm just as human as they are."

"You certainly have taken Miss Jane Addams's ideas to heart." Evelyn drank cold tea and stretched her feet.

"She is becoming the public conscience for wrongs that need righting. Her settlement house in Chicago works with a different kind of immigrant, so much of what she has learned doesn't apply to what we are doing in San Francisco. When I started, it wasn't called 'social work.' Miss Culbertson and the board simply saw a need and responded. Now academic studies are being offered and soon credentials will be required. We get idealistic college graduates as volunteers."

"It's the same," said Mary Niles, "for missionaries. Once wives accompanied husbands, now girls are taking a one-year course and going on their own. I was allowed into medical school to train as a doctor so I could become a missionary."

Thomasina stifled a yawn. The busy compound had grown quiet as the light faded. The yellow glow of lamps cast circles of light on the pounded dirt of the courtyard. The talk died and Lucy said at last, "Tomorrow awaits. We have found a translator and guide who will help you interview. Edgar Cheng is a friend of the Mission. He's easygoing, but don't let that fool you. He's very smart. And well connected, a Christian Chinese, very old family, and he attended Princeton University, not the seminary. He knows both cultures and we read him your letter about finding a teacher."

"I think I can raise enough money beyond mission expenses to pay for a teacher to come to San Francisco who can teach my girls about their own culture. That's one place the Mission fails."

The women said good night.

Edgar Cheng arrived midmorning wearing a Western suit, a shirt with a stiff collar and a tie. He alighted from a ricksha, then sat with Thomasina in the arbor while she explained what she was looking for.

"Besides just the information, the *facts*, about China, I want her to be able to teach geography, history, and Cantonese dialect. My girls are American girls, but people take one look, see their faces, and assume they are Chinese. I don't want them to lose the best of their culture."

"That is asking a lot," said Edgar. "Very few educated women know English, but I'll see what I can find."

"I'm only here for a few weeks," said Thomasina. She liked

the way Edgar's eyes disappeared in the creases of his cheeks when he smiled. She felt as though she had known him always.

"You must take a trip up the river," said Mary. "Edgar has found a place on a family boat going up the Pearl River. If you can stand it, you'll see a part of China most travelers never find."

"That sounds fascinating," said Thomasina.

Edgar explained she could take only a handbag and that quarters would be crowded, but interesting. Edgar took her shopping for presents to take home. He led her to Stationery Street, which was so narrow she could almost touch merchandise displayed on both sides. The streets that seemed crowded in Chinatown would seem wide in Canton. She thought she could understand a little Cantonese, but the locals spoke too fast and she and Edgar laughed at her mistakes.

"I'm keeping you from your regular work," Thomasina said.

"It'll keep," said Edgar. His eyes sparkled with humor. What a lovely man, she thought. What a necessary guide!

In the ricksha on the way back to the mission, she said she wasn't used to having a human being doing the horses' job.

"It bothers Westerners," Edgar said, "but he makes a living and survives this way."

"All the contrasts." Thomasina looked around the streets where rickshas and bicycles and horses swarmed.

"Yes," said Edgar. "Squalor and decadence, opulence and beauty all mix in China."

"Less poverty, more democracy," suggested Thomasina.

Food vendors pushed carts and a street barber shaved around the queue of his customer seated on a stool on the sidewalk. Thomasina saw no Western faces outside the European section, and wondered if she was safe, then she remembered Edgar was Chinese.

"I don't question that you do good work, but after living in the States, I notice that places like your mission keep immigrants in an inferior status."

Thomasina's back went up and she tried to rein in her defensiveness long enough to hear what he was telling her.

"You have a common bond with the Jesuits in Peru, believe it or not," Edgar said. "I have read an account of their proselytizing among the Indian tribes in the mountains. There primitive hut-dwellers perform some surgical abuse on their girls so horrible the reports gave no details. Then they—the girls—are sold to the highest bidder among the settlers for sexual purposes, or if too damaged, for fieldwork. This usually kills them in a few years while they bear the half-breed children of their masters."

Thomasina liked listening to his accented English, liked the lively spark in his eyes.

"The priests have been taking the girls from the tribes, promis-ing to educate them," he said. "The families see this as gaining power vis-à-vis the white man, so they allow the girls to go to a school in Lima. Is this starting to sound familiar?"

Thomasina admitted it did. But what was he getting at?

"Once in the city, the girls are taught to wear dresses and bathe, and they are given basic schooling and a heavy course of Catholicism. Then they are put to work as servants in the houses of Spanish aristocrats. The Jesuits save their souls, and give them a European existence, but the girls can never return to their vil-lages. They grow too far away from their roots. In Lima, they are at the bottom of the social ladder, providing a steady source of labor for the homes of the rich. The girls lose their native culture but never fully enter the other."

"But it is almost impossible for a Chinese woman to do any other work outside of her home!"

"I know that. But you must see how an economist might look at their role in the labor pool."

"Of course, I see them as more than workers." Thomasina mulled over what Edgar had said. "If they were considered human beings with all the rights of other American citizens, they could do anything."

"Nobody but you sees them as equals," said Edgar. "So it is up to you to prepare them for other roles. You already have several girls who chose to live at the Mission rather than with their fami-lies so they can learn English and go to school. You must turn your efforts to these ambitious girls because they will be the future."

"Oh, they are. I must tell you about Ah Hsiang."

"I never knew how to tell this story without worrying that the church person would take offense. You seem open to ideas and the parallels of the stories struck me. I think if I give you a problem, you will chew on it until you find some answers. This isn't something that will happen in a month or a year, but you have a lifetime to work on it and it is a task worthy of your steel."

"I need to have my prejudices challenged. Perhaps that is the true reason for this trip—not to rest or meet my family, but to learn what I haven't learned at home."

"I hope I haven't been too harsh," said Edgar, as the ricksha turned into the gate of the mission compound.

"You are a gentle teacher," she assured him.

Thomasina boarded a houseboat the next morning for the trip Edgar arranged. Thomasina was excited. The family, Thomasina, a dog, a pig, and chickens lived with meticulous cleanliness on the crowded vessel. She would never have traveled into the countryside otherwise, nor seen the steep hills and the intensively farmed plots and the villages with the ubiquitous water buffalo. They sailed past the *Fei-lai ssu,* a Buddhist monastery clinging to the mountain above the Pearl River. She wondered if they took in travelers, like the Benedictines in Europe.

The countryside was calm this year, but floods and droughts and earthquakes could destroy the food supply and force families to sell their daughters, which she once thought unspeakably cruel. Now she knew that it was often done so that the daughter might survive.

When she returned to Canton, she was welcomed by the Wei family. She had helped their daughter, Shu Hui, leave the Immigration Shed when her intended husband died before she arrived in San Francisco. Reputable daughters, small-footed wives, and girls brought over to marry were treated as harshly as imported prostitutes. A request had come through the Chinatown branch of the family. Could the Jesus-woman help? Sidney Nussbaum checked into the case and got Wei Shu Hui released. Shu Hui looked like a disheveled angel when Thomasina found her. Her prestigious, Six Company–scholar's family rejoiced by giving a generous donation to the Mission.

"Must this woman have a degree?" asked Edgar.

"I don't think so," said Thomasina. "But she must be educated and if she has never taught young girls, she will probably not be happy."

Edgar smiled. "Are your girls such terrors?"

Thomasina and Edgar had driven into Canton, to the big Presbyterian church, where he had made appointments for Thomasina with half a dozen teachers.

Thomasina thought of her days with the mischievous Hsiang and replied, "Experience helps. Besides, these are American-Chinese girls, not as subdued as Cantonese girls. We give them freedom so they will know how to use it, but we pay the price. They can be boisterous, certainly noisy. Our teachers are not allowed to beat or humiliate them."

"So you need a woman who can manage a classroom, give instruction, and walk on water."

Thomasina laughed. "And change water into wine, when the budget is low."

Edgar's laugh boomed across the room. Thomasina enjoyed his presence. He reminded Thomasina of the muscular hatchet men who menaced Chinatown, but he was dressed in a seemly Western suit with a silk cravat and a waistcoat buttoned over a snowy shirt. Dimples appeared in cherub cheeks when he smiled, but Thomasina could see intelligence in his eyes that reminded her of Amos Cohn.

"Not quite what you were looking for, was she?" Edgar said after the last interview. His expression was rueful, but amused, as always. Nothing seemed to displace his good humor.

"No. We could never meet her requirements for accommodations. We live plainly at the Mission. Even I have only one room, and my office, of course."

"You Americans carry your democratic ideas to ridiculous extremes. You have a ready supply of household drudges—you could live like a queen."

"Perhaps that's why so many of the people in Chinatown have only minimal respect for me. I am female, Caucasian, and Christian. And I live modestly. I have little choice, but perhaps they think I should appear to have more prestige."

"Perhaps," Edgar admitted.

"Yes, but my Presbyterian conscience would bother me."

"Tell me about your Presbyterian conscience."

"It keeps me from making too many mistakes." Just for a flash, Thomasina thought of that day with Charlie, the picnic cloth on the grass, her dress up, her heart pumping, not wanting to stop.

"I wonder sometimes," said Edgar, "if we have pure Presbyterian teachings, this far from the source."

"Purer than mine, I have no doubt. You are probably more thoroughly versed in church doctrine and theology than I. I often wished, when I was younger, that I could attend seminary, but the work I was about always seemed to take up all my time and energy."

"And faith without works is empty," said Edgar.

"Oh, I *do* so passionately believe that!"

"And live it." Edgar had a soft expression for her.

Thomasina dropped her eyes, embarrassed that he had seen into her heart so easily. Then she cleared her throat and said, "I suppose we must keep looking. Do you have any more candidates?"

"Today, no. I must talk to my aunties and see what they have to say. They may have better ideas than I. They are always looking for a wife for me, so they know every young woman in Canton, I think."

"And will they find one?"

"Probably. To go unmarried in China is unthinkable."

"Thank heavens it's thinkable in America, or I'd be disgraced."

"Surely, you have had opportunities."

"Surely I did, but they never worked out." Thomasina thought of Charlie and tears brimmed. She blew her nose and pretended she had dust in her eyes, but Edgar wasn't fooled. He took her hand to comfort her and tears poured, released by his compassion. She had been so busy, she had forgotten to guard her emotions about Charlie. It was fun to be with Edgar, carrying on lively conversation, but he kept bringing to mind old buried memories, uncomfortable memories.

"We drove past a beautiful park when Mary picked me up at the train station," Thomasina said. "Could we walk there?"

"Chinese are not allowed."

"What? Not allowed in your own city!"

"The Westerners own the property." He shrugged.

"Then we will walk in the streets. What an outrage!"

"Proper ladies do not walk. They hire a ricksha, at the very least."

"But I need to move around. I'm not Chinese and I'm used to walking San Francisco hills. Besides, I've been cooped up all day and so have you."

"Let's drive to the Flowery Pagoda—you can see it in the distance—and you can walk up all the steps. Travelers go up because you can see for miles. Or we can go out into the country and walk beside the road."

"I sometimes forget I'm on vacation," she said.

The ricksha driver pulled them out of town at a leisurely pace; Thomasina relaxed and forgot her schedules and lists.

They got down from the ricksha when the road ahead was clear and walked toward a village between carefully tended paddies covered with water. Once there, Thomasina studied with great interest the farmhouses and outbuildings. An old woman preparing vegetables in a doorway asked something of Edgar. He explained: "She wants to tell your fortune."

"I don't believe in that kind of thing," said Thomasina.

"Of course, but it would be fun to hear what she says. What would a peasant woman know about an American missionary?"

Thomasina held out her left hand, but the woman wanted her right hand. The old woman squinted, squeezed her hand gently, turned it this way and that in the light, folded the fingers into the palm, then looked along the edge. She frowned, then said something to Edgar that Thomasina did not understand.

"What was that all about?" Thomasina asked when Edgar had paid the woman.

"She says you have an unfortunate destiny. For a Chinese woman. She said you would be no man's wife. She said your *chi*, your life energy, is strong and your life will be very long and that your heart is stronger than your head."

"I hope she's wrong about never marrying." Thomasina wanted to cry, "No! No! You must be wrong!" She turned away from Edgar so he wouldn't see her pain; she blotted tears. They ambled through the village with children following them, full of curiosity.

"I've told you about me," said Thomasina after a bit. "Tell me why you studied in America and what you liked or hated. Tell me about when you were in San Francisco. I feel I've made myself seem foolish and I want you to talk about yourself now."

"You are not foolish." He turned to study her profile. "You are the most interesting woman I've met. Too bad my aunties wouldn't approve."

Thomasina was shocked that he could so lightly speak of her in the context of a wife. Then a wave of affection for this charming man struck her, and it didn't seem such a foreign idea after all.

"I may not be Chinese, but I am Presbyterian. Tell them that in my favor." She could banter and tease, with a little encouragement.

Edgar asked for water and they drank out of a common cup, at another farmhouse, then they walked on. Edgar told her about his teachers at the mission school, the Americans with mustaches and tweed suits and the Chinese men in gowns. He sketched his family. He made light of the prejudice he met at college. They chatted, and she found herself wishing the afternoon didn't have to end. What would it take to make time stop? He returned her to the hospital compound at sunset and promised to find more candidates to interview.

"I'm looking forward to it," Thomasina said. And she realized she was looking forward to Edgar, not the candidates. The next day a messenger delivered a huge bunch of chrysanthemums with a note from Edgar. Mary found a huge porcelain vase, graceful and ornate, to receive them.

Another returned daughter who had dutifully married her arranged spouse and subjected herself to her mother-in-law invited Thomasina to her country home and explained that she had to remain firm for years in her efforts as a Bible woman who visited families in her village and read to them, but now her mother-in-law respected her. She proudly showed Thomasina her chubby baby whose face was almost perfectly round. He was just learning to walk, experimenting with balance and gravity.

"But you must tell me your secrets and we know Chinese gentlemen are terribly reticent and never reveal their inmost feelings." Thomasina could tease Edgar because he was used to American ways. "Otherwise, why are they considered inscrutable? I've scrutinized plenty of them and I know they are very human."

Edgar and Thomasina chatted in the ricksha as they drove into the city again.

"I don't know. Are you trustworthy?" he asked.

"I'll carry more secrets to the grave than most women are privileged to learn."

"If I tell you everything I object to about the Mission and our denomination, can you keep silent?"

"Yes, especially if you listen to my objections and complaints."

"You must remember that you are not a lone vigilante. The Chinese Six Companies have worked to stop the slave trade all along," he reminded her.

"Corrupt city officials in San Francisco keep it going, and scheme with the tong organizations. It's a Caucasian racket as well. 'The Municipal Crib,' we call one of the bordellos," Thomasina said. "City officials invested in it and skim the profits."

"It is easy to denigrate the Chinese as alien and heathen, but not always fair."

"I swim in a sea of anti-Chinese opinion," said Thomasina, "and sometimes I swallow some of it. I think of them as 'heathen' because I've heard it hundreds of times. I think of them as helpless children because so many of them come to the Mission needing help."

"You must forgive educated Chinese for their concealed contempt. We consider our culture older and more refined than yours. My family is an exception—we converted many years ago—but most Chinese see no need to change to another religion when Confucianism provides an ethical framework for their lives."

"Many women at the Mission choose not to convert."

"You are looking for a Chinese woman to broaden the curriculum. That speaks in your favor." Edgar's smile softened his criticism.

They pursued the current discussion on temperance, with Edgar stating that temperance should mean moderation, not abstinence. They talked about immigration, the status of women and Negroes, and other topics close to Thomasina's heart. She learned a new perspective on her work and where it fit into the larger schemes of the denomination.

For the few days they had together Edgar and Thomasina shared private and personal thoughts and ideas easily because the conversation was from the heart. They both knew they would never share more than words, but she felt he knew her better than her sisters. She had trouble believing she could become so fond of another man after the pain of losing Charlie.

Later that day, in Canton, she met Kang Wu, a California Chinese who had been a servant for her friends, the Unruhs.

"Missee," he said after the courtesies, "I beg to ask you to help my son."

Thomasina heard the effort it cost him to make this plea.

She looked around the room, decorated with wall hangings and carved wood furniture. The proportions of the room were graceful and the sounds of the city muted. Wu, who had worked as a docile servant in Los Angeles, was a man of means in Canton. His mother, a lady of great dignity and presence, had served formal tea. Thomasina felt greatly honored, and had been nervous about making gaffes. After the ancient lady had drawn up her silk robes and departed, Wu spoke to Thomasina.

"I want to send my son to San Francisco to learn about business there. No way for me to know my son is safe. Family in San Francisco all work and no one look after him. He could get with wild boys, or meet tong soldiers and admire them—lazy, violent hatchet men, not good hardworking Chinese."

"I know it is difficult to send a child off around the globe," said Thomasina.

"Not same with boys," Wu admitted, "but boys need guidance, too. Please, take first son back to Mission." Before she could say anything, he hurried on and she strained to understand his English. "If he lives in Mission, you guide him, teach him English, teach Bible. Other women living there are good, like you, and make him like their son. They would care about him. He is good boy, only twelve, and quick to learn. In just a year or two he could learn about America and come back to help his family."

Wu's eyes pleaded. She never understood why Americans thought Chinese "inscrutable." Perhaps their dignified public demeanor was misjudged. She had seen all human emotions in her girls and now she was seeing the depth of feeling of this man for his son. With great regret, she had to tell him: "The Mission is only for females. We have no provision for boys. Some of the women keep their boy babies, but we have no provision for older boys."

Wu looked down. She wished she could say something positive. He knew as well as she that Chinese boys were excluded from San Francisco public schools. "I will begin to work toward an orphanage for boys, where they all go to school. Perhaps it won't happen fast enough for your son, but if we don't have a vision of the future, how can it ever happen?"

Wu was not comforted. He thanked Thomasina for taking tea in his humble home and returned her to the mission compound.

The following day, Edgar fetched her from the mission compound for more interviews. The first candidate canceled.

"You work to change the law for taking the little girls, but you do not work to change the exclusion laws," Edgar pointed out.

"I should, but it is so complicated. My energy doesn't stretch far enough. I must choose my battles. In Chinatown, influential people do not support me."

"You must find a way to make prejudice costly. Business runs America and if they lose money, they'll find a way to accept Chinese as workers and consumers."

She asked him to explain and he spelled out the economic consequences of keeping Chinese down. They discussed how Chinese attitudes played into these fears and prejudices.

"I know that producing male offspring is important in Chinese culture, but the time will come when women must be given a voice, a vote," said Thomasina.

"Most of them know nothing beyond the kitchen and their children," said Edgar.

"Not if you don't teach them. If they are prepared, as boys are prepared, they can take their place as citizens. Sending Hsiang to college is the first step."

"I think this is possible in America, but not in China."

"I must believe it is possible, otherwise, why have I spent my life educating Chinese girls?"

Edgar took her hand. They were alone in the conference room. "I don't mean to criticize what you do. But it is difficult to accept change like this for Canton."

"You make me think about what I do. You bring out the best in me," she said softly. She squeezed his hand. "Debate with you sharpens my wits for other, less kindly people I must persuade."

"You make me feel as though I am the only man on earth when I am with you."

"Is that good?"

"No, alas," he said. "Our connection must remain impersonal and dispassionate. Anything more would be unsuitable."

"But I feel closer to you than I ever did to Charlie—" Thomasina pulled her hands away. The inconvenient tears began.

"Who is this Charlie, who can make you cry?" asked Edgar. He leaned back in the chair and Thomasina fumbled for her handkerchief.

"We were going to be married," she said, "but we couldn't work it out—family responsibilities, money, mundane reasons."

"But you still weep for him? He must have broken your heart."

Thomasina looked at Edgar, her guardian angel in Canton. She imagined him an angry Chinese dragon-angel, made of red and black lacquer, with a stylized grimace and stiff dragon wings. She owed him a bit more of her story.

"He did not break my heart." She hadn't talked about this to anyone since that day in Philadelphia. Perhaps she needed to. She thought for a moment, then sat straighter. This felt like confession.

"He was the anvil on which I hammered my heart until it broke apart." Like many outgoing people, she needed to speak her feelings before she could become aware of them. "I might have fallen in love with any suitable young man—with Charlie's brother Ben, with one of the young men who visited the Mission, or with a bachelor minister." She stopped to consider all the journal-writing realizations. Edgar sat quietly, listening.

"I wanted a family and Charlie was the man I put my hopes on—all my feelings and my passion. I did it to myself." Why was it so difficult to take responsibility for what had happened? "But I did love him."

"You will always," said Edgar softly.

"Will I always weep?"

Edgar shrugged. He opened his arms and although it was highly unsuitable, she rested her head on his shoulder.

"What a kind friend you are," she said at last.

"I envy Charlie."

"And I envy the woman your aunties find," said Thomasina.

After that day's round of interviews, Edgar suggested another ride into the countryside. The ricksha bumped over a dirt road, through the farms outside the city. It was quieter here, except for the rumble of the wheels and the pat of the driver's feet. Thomasina was grateful she didn't have to find her way around in such a strange place. She was grateful for Edgar as a guide.

"You make me think," she said, "I function best on intuition, or at least most easily. This trip has been one lesson after another. When I am in this country where Christianity isn't taken for granted, I am ashamed I've been so parochial, but at least now I can see the value of Confucianism and Buddhism."

"You are an easy pupil, and fast to grasp ideas."

"Don't patronize, Edgar. Even Americans can learn about China."

"Clever American, turning my words back on me." They drove in silence for a few moments, then Edgar said, "I can criticize you, and reproach you for your failings, but I cannot ignore your work. You have helped hundreds of girls and women. I salute you. And respect you. You already know I love you, however platonic that must be."

"You'll destroy me, Edgar, if you're nice to me. I'm used to being tough and thick-skinned. When someone treats me gently, I come apart."

"I think you should come apart."

"I have. I've trusted you and exposed all the emotions I usually hide. And you have patiently put up with all of it."

"I love you, and that makes it easy to listen to you. But very hard to be with you."

The words took her breath away, then she said, "I love you, Edgar. I could happily be your wife. I can imagine beautiful babies. I think I have discovered the last shred of prejudice in me. I would never have accepted a Chinese man as a husband, until I met you. Now, I know that I was narrow-minded and bigoted."

"You are a lover."

"We can never be lovers." Thomasina wanted to double over and scream. To sit properly took all her concentration.

"You misunderstand," he said. "You can love more than anyone I've ever met. You love your 'daughters,' your family, this unworthy Charlie. And the women at the compound here, and the people in San Francisco. God has given you the capacity to love and since it doesn't go to one person, it will light the world."

"I am weak and vulnerable, full of human failings, more shadow than light."

"God shines in you."

Thomasina dropped her head in humility at Edgar's pronouncement. They drove in silence for a long time. She wished she could put this moment in a lacquered box and keep it forever.

They had not found a suitable teacher when it was time for Thomasina to leave. She told Edgar, "If you find someone you think acceptable, let Mary, Lucy, and Evelyn Burlingame interview her and I will accept your decision."

She said her good-byes to Mary, Evelyn, and Lucy. Edgar took her to the train station and they clasped hands for the last time. He looked impassively after the train as it pulled out, but tears blurred her last image of him.

In Shanghai, she went back to work. She again stayed with Americans, and she spoke about the slave trade to Chinese businessmen at every opportunity. She tried to explain to the Chinese she met the nature of the traffic in young women and how American exclusion laws worked. She described in explicit detail what happened to the girls. Sometimes she feared she put people off, telling them things they preferred not to hear. She softened the terms because the reality was inexpressibly sordid. The merchants and Thomasina agreed to keep each other informed about girls traveling both ways across the Pacific.

The *China Mail* stopped at ports in Japan and in Hawaii. In between, she used her private journal to record impressions, lessons, people—to put on paper all that had happened in the last ten months. She realized that she stopped "talking" to Charlie in her head, but carried on imaginary dialogues with Edgar Cheng. Her recurring dream had stopped. She was ten pounds heavier and rosy from fresh air. She felt rested and slept long and deeply despite the movement of the ship.

She thought of the old sermon about the man who thought his cross was heavy and wanted a lighter one, so Jesus invited him to look over all the crosses; the man chose the one he wanted and it turned out to be his own. Thomasina chose her own again. She wanted to be Lo Mo again, to be Tamsen to her family, to be the ladylike but persuasive Miss McIntyre, a force for good in the life of the city.

Her boat steamed through the Golden Gate and a tug maneuvered it into its berth as the sun went down. She stood at the rail as the last light tinted the tops of buildings gold and amber, then deepened to pink and rose. Her city stretched up the hills in the softening light. Clouds bruised blue and mauve floated over the bay. The light was never the same, she thought. It must cast a spell on us so we always return.

Her sisters and niece and some daughters met her at the dock and as soon as she got through customs, hurried her back to 920 where a big celebration was in progress. The telephone rang endlessly and she answered questions and distributed gifts between bites of food prepared for the occasion. All the girls had grown and she exclaimed over each one and met two new girls who had come to the Mission while she was gone.

She embraced the girls, but most of all she embraced this life she was meant to live.

RECOMMITMENT

 1906

25

It took a while to get used to the girls' noisy shrieks, the melodrama of teenage friendships—the daily routine. Thomasina rescued girls and sheltered women. She talked to officials about legislation for playgrounds, public education for Chinese children, and changes in the immigration laws. She looked forward to the spring board meeting where she could put forth some of the new ideas she had evolved during her sabbatical.

The individual board members she had sounded out listened to her ideas about bringing a Chinese woman from Canton to teach her girls. She talked to her counterparts at the Episcopal and Methodist missions about a boy's orphanage. American businessmen's prejudice against the Chinese was by now so ingrained they scarcely realized they held the race in unthinking contempt. This unspoken assumption of moral inferiority somehow made it acceptable to ignore the real needs of the residents of Chinatown. She must break through this shell of indifference to bring any lasting change for her girls.

* * *

After her return, she wrote again to Charlie Ducik, telling him anecdotes from her tour and asking for his friendship. She was proud of herself for being able to write to Charlie as a friend, comrade to comrade. His response was friendly and she welcomed his comments. What she hadn't expected was the splitting recoil. She thought she had wept every tear she ever would for Charlie. She remembered that night in the hot cabin when she had been taken up by the fire of God's love. She had surrendered and become part of the universe, not a single languishing spark that didn't know it was one with a huge and glorious fire.

But now, as she settled into her destiny again, she made herself vulnerable to loneliness. She knew with hardheaded Scotch practicality that she was happy, productive, and enjoying her work. But opening herself to correspondence with Charlie reminded her she cherished a small hard core of longing for a husband, for sexuality, for children of her own body.

And the recoil snapped her apart, like a whip splitting skin. The night after she answered Charlie's letter, she lay in bed mentally reviewing the next day's agenda. She remembered Charlie's seriousness all that day in Philadelphia when she learned his light-hearted personality, which had attracted her, had matured.

And he was there in her mind's eye—his fair skin, the pale hair just beginning to thin into the family pattern, the gray circles under his eyes, the unfamiliar resolve in his mouth, the timbre and rhythm of his voice—more resonant, slower, more thoughtful.

Longing seized her, doubled her over, forced a cry of pain. Her belly cramped. She wept and grief shook her like a dead rat in a terrier's teeth. Charlie!

Her body swelled, forgotten juices ached for release. She thought she was starting her flow, but she was not. She huddled shaken with tears, the blanket stuffed in her mouth to mute the keening she couldn't stifle.

Help me, she begged. Where was the comfort of living a righteous life? Why was she punished this way? She had done everything she could to be sensible and straightforward. What treason was this? She didn't deserve to be tortured for her desires, for her years of waiting. Desires would dismember her. First they would rip off her feet, then her hands, then her head would snap from the torso.

Jesus help me!

She got out of bed and paced back and forth. She couldn't breathe past her throat, but she sucked in air until she drew regular breaths, then deep breaths, until sobbing died.

She muffled herself in a flannelette wrapper and got back in bed. Now that the seizure was past, she was wide awake, fiercely unhappy, and floating on a sea of sadness she hadn't known was there.

She knew now where suicides came from and immediately felt guilty for her harsh judgment of the Chinese women who escaped that way. Then she stopped herself.

This was foolish! She had brought it on herself. If she truly wanted to be in contact with Charlie, she'd have to be stronger than this. She had a hunch that he would prove a valuable friend, if she could get past her own feelings about him. But she wasn't as much in command as she thought.

Then the vision of Charlie returned, across the linen tablecloth at the seafood restaurant, and she wept. The quiet tears held so much pain, she thought they should scar her cheeks.

She turned and moaned into her pillow. This would never do. She had work to do tomorrow. She couldn't afford to waste her energy this way. Miss Culbertson had told her to channel her zeal into her work, but she could not see a way to use this heartache. She tried to exorcise Charlie with the memory of Edgar Cheng's smile, but it didn't work. She hadn't known Edgar long enough.

And she lay there, awake and bereft for a long time, waiting for the punishment to be over.

When Charlie's next letter came a week later, the same thing happened again. She was exhausted and didn't know if she could pay such a price. Then the punishment came without a letter and she knew she would have to live with emotions and memories that demanded expression, but had no outlet.

Most nights, she fell asleep as soon as she finished her prayers, but she never knew when the paroxysm of grief and longing would overtake her. She was always surprised that she had misjudged herself so completely. One night childhood fears of death and dark mingled with the grief of losing Charlie—she had to relive all the losses in her life. She remembered her big sister Annie taking her into bed when she was scared, holding her against her nightgown, and singing to her when she was six years old.

Thomasina never sang audibly. As Hsiang long ago discovered, she sang very softly or mouthed the words at services. But she was alone and nobody would hear if she sang softly.

"What a friend we have in Jesus," she began. At first the tears almost choked her, but she kept humming until she could whisper the words. "Just as I Am" went better. She changed keys in midnote and forgot the ends of stanzas, but she sang. She remembered when she learned the songs as a child. She blew her nose and hummed and pretty soon she quieted.

Judge Morrow and Thomasina's friend, attorney Henry Monroe, arranged for her to meet Andrew Carnegie when he visited San Francisco. She had ambiguous feelings about him. She knew this was an unequaled opportunity to ask for help for the Mission—after all, Carnegie had paid for hundreds of libraries across America. But she also knew he was a ruthless businessman and his steel company devoured workers, with men dying in accidents to produce his wealth. She couldn't pass up this chance.

She took Hsiang and Ching Leung who had been trained to teach English and two younger girls. They arrived at the door of the suite at the top of the St. Francis Hotel. Waiting photographers followed them inside. All four girls wore their best embroidered sams.

Ching Leung handed the bouquet of tulips and daffodils to Ah

Yoke, six years old, to present to Mrs. Carnegie. The baby, Ah Kui, looked at Mr. Carnegie, and with a child's sense of what was best, flew into the man's outstretched arms. Margaret Carnegie, their six-year-old daughter, was delighted and the photographer caught Margaret accepting flowers from the Chinese maidens. After that, the girls became instant best friends for the half hour of Thomasina's audience. Carnegie asked questions about her work, examined the goals, and made several good suggestions. It was a pleasure to converse for a few moments with someone else with a Scots burr. His features were large on a proportionately large head and he exuded quiet power. His wife seemed alert and interested although she said little. Thomasina was perspiring inside her shirtwaist. She did not ask for a contribution, even though that was the unwritten program of the meeting. She would wait and let the message of the girls sink in. She had been awed at President Roosevelt and she was awed at this awesomely wealthy and successful man, but never in her life had she been so awed she was struck silent. She explained her work briefly, trying not for poignance but information. She told him the larger implications of prejudice against Chinese for the workforce and the economics of the region. In her opinion, they couldn't *afford* to discriminate against the Chinese. Her work with the women and girls was part of a larger picture, to help make them good Americans, or if they chose to return, good Chinese.

Her girls left with gold pieces clutched in their hands. Everyone had enjoyed the meeting.

The next day Lo Mo and a small choir arrived at the train station headed for Riverside where they were to appear at the Mission Inn at a meeting. Carnegie saw them and invited them into his private car and they sang for him and his family.

Nothing had been arranged and the girls were delighted to see the fancy car and to sing; the Carnegies seemed to enjoy it all. Carnegie gave instructions to one of his secretaries and as Thomasina left, Carnegie handed her an envelope. "This is to do with as you please," he said. When she was back in the Pullman car and the girls were settled in their seats, hairbows were retied and trips to the rest room were accomplished, she opened the envelope. The figure took her breath away! Surely no one but Carnegie could so casually give so much. Now she could bring a teacher from Canton to San Francisco so that her girls would learn Chinese and all the aspects of Chinese life and culture that would be important for their future. The board would not have to find funds for this project and she was sure they would agree. She could write Edgar Cheng and tell him funding was assured.

She looked forward to the annual meeting. More than ever, she was comfortable in her role. She met each day full of fresh ideas, committed to the work at hand. Was it a Chinese proverb or something her father had said? Happiness is having work and being able to do it.

26

The Mission prepared for the annual board meeting. Minnie Ferree, who had replaced Wilhelmina Wheeler as matron, and the girls worked from attic to lowest basement sweeping, scrubbing, polishing until floors, woodwork, and windows shone. Curtains were washed and hung; a beautiful fishnet, the gift of a rescued girl, was draped in the chapel room. Thomasina's annual report was ready to deliver. Besides recording the Mission's activities for the board, it served as a printed piece to distribute to interested people who inquired about the Mission. She often took copies when she visited congregations for fund-raising. If she revised many times, she could get a lot of information into a small space.

Since cleaning went on continuously, it seemed, at the Mission, Thomasina was always surprised to find cobwebs in the corners and dirt under dressers that were moved. A troop of big girls attacked her room and left it shining, the items on her dresser meticulously returned to their original positions. Everything smelled of coal oil and vinegar and gleamed in the light. Even the dreary gray day couldn't disguise the polished floor, the soot-free windows. The sound of children singing in preparation for the program the next day followed her through the house.

This coming Sunday a young pastor from a country church would conduct the services. She assumed he wanted to familiarize himself with the Mission and the women's work. She wondered idly if he were married and if he weren't, what he would be like. But she was getting ahead of herself.

She would always know exactly when it began. Everyone in San Francisco would remember. In the last hours of the night, just before dawn, she heard her big dresser march across the floor. In the dim light from the streetlamp, she saw its huge shape lurch, then the mirror fell in tinkling bits. Her heaving bed tossed her on the floor. This was a dream. But no, the noise and the tremors were real enough. Another lurch and the dresser crashed against the wall, knocking plaster out.

A pause while she counted each breath, then a second tremor bounced her about and went on for an interminable moment.

Earthquake!

Panic gripped her. Would the building collapse with sixty women and girls inside? Her heart pounded, but she could not move. More tremors and thunder from the earth. The god mountain rumbled and all the earth shivered in fear. No, an earthquake was a geological event, and she must stay calm. She heard a baby's cry and knew she must get up and see to the little ones.

But she was paralyzed. She could do nothing about what was happening. She must ride the tremors and hope she was alive when they stopped.

She heard footsteps padding outside, then a knock.

"Lo Mo you come." Sun Lee's urgent voice broke through her fear.

Lo Mo got up, pushed her feet into slippers to avoid the broken glass, and hurried after the older woman. "Did the gas line break?" she asked.

Sun Lee, already pale, looked paler in the light of the lamp she carried. "Go see upstairs," she said and turned back to the kitchen on the first floor.

Lo Mo was afraid of what she would see. She heard girls crying. Another aftershock made the floor heave under her feet. The girls must be terrified.

Grinding noises. From underground, or was it bricks shifting in the walls? She heard the chimneys crash. Noises from outside penetrated, then a faraway explosion that made her cringe.

Girls were sobbing in their rooms.

Panic rose in her throat. She would begin screaming and she wouldn't stop. She couldn't think!

But she knew she had to stay calm. Panic would spread, if she carried the contagion.

What would Papa do? He had faced bandits with guns who came to the ranch. Pretend you are Papa. You must save your family.

Taking a deep breath, she began. She pulled her hands from the doorjamb that she had clutched since the last tremor. She tied her wrapper. She walked quickly but calmly from room to room and told each girl, "We are all right. Stay calm. Get dressed. Be ready to leave."

Almost before the bricks stopped tumbling, Miss Ferree was out looking for breakfast. With no chimneys, they couldn't make rice.

Someone pounded on the front door. Lo Mo sent Hsiang to find out who it was.

Women on the top floor wept. One clutched her newborn baby while silent tears rolled down her face and soaked into his blanket. He was just a few days old and the mother did not look strong. Thomasina tried to remember: did she have any pregnant women in the Mission? Another woman keened like a wounded animal, with her shawl over her head.

Lo Mo looked around at all the little touches the women had added to their spartan rooms—embroidered plaques, scrolls with stacked figures of calligraphy, scarves of bright silk. She kept repeating her instructions: stay calm.

Mrs. Brown and Miss Meyers, a field secretary, and several other board members had spent the night at the Mission. The older women comforted crying girls and helped them back to their rooms to dress. Mrs. Brown looked paler than Thomasina had ever seen her, but she stirred herself into action, directing traffic, comforting, organizing the older girls. They would find time to dress later. A few other board members walked to the Mission after the earthquake.

Thomasina went downstairs and while plaster was cracked and some furniture was topsy-turvy, the building seemed stable enough, except for broken windows. Sun Lee said the gas line was intact, but they agreed it was too dangerous to light fires.

Thomasina turned to find one little girl who clutched a worn stuffed doll following her. She reminded Thomasina of Mei Fa, who had held her skirts on that first picnic in the park. The girl looked terrified, but a harsh life had taught her silence. She held a corner of Lo Mo's wrapper with one hand. Lo Mo bent and hugged her, and the child wrapped panicked arms around her neck. Lo Mo was glad for some human contact to break her own fears for a moment.

"Where's your big sister?" asked Lo Mo.

The child shrugged. Lo Mo tried to remember who it was. Perhaps it was Hsiang, sent to answer the door, who now called up the steps.

"It's Mrs. Ng," Hsiang reported. "She has bread for breakfast. Miss Ferree already sent someone to the bakery." Behind Hsiang came Mrs. Ng Poon Chew with apples and a huge kettle of tea. God bless early risers!

One problem solved. Thomasina hugged the woman and sent Hsiang to find more girls to carry the baskets into the dining room. Thomasina dressed and whispered a prayer for San Francisco. The girls came at the bell and sat down to the last meal they would eat in the dining room at 920.

The girls, most of them dressed with hair combed, gathered

around the long tables. The peculiar smell of plaster dust filled the air and dried the back of her throat. The girls sang as usual and Thomasina led the Twenty-third Psalm with more fervor than she had ever felt. And she heard with sure clarity its unfailing promises.

Then Thomasina told them they must be ready to leave. "Roll up two of everything—underwear, sams, trousers, socks—in your blanket, but don't take more than you can carry. Put your strongest shoes and your heaviest coat on and find your little sister. Help her wrap her things. Make sure she has warm clothes. Then wait until it's time."

Just as they finished eating a severe shock startled everyone. Most of them hurried to an upper floor. Opening an eastern window, they looked across the city. Columns of ominous smoke rose from fires and hid the bay in places. How had the Mission, Thomasina marveled, a five-story brick building on the side of a steep sand hill, stood firm while other walls of brick and wood crumbled?

As she stood there, holding a small girl who cried to be lifted up, Thomasina heard a company of U.S. cavalry gallop by outside.

Everyone was sent to pack a bundle she could carry.

Thomasina consulted with Mrs. Brown. Three board members—Mrs. C. S. Wright, Mrs. F. G. Robbins, and Mrs. L. A. Kelley—walked several miles that morning. They talked over plans and decided the mission inmates must try to reach the First Presbyterian Church eight blocks up Sacramento on Van Ness Avenue. It was the only place they could go that was outside of Chinatown.

"We are facing a double danger," Thomasina said. "There may be slave owners among the refugees and people milling in the streets viewing the fires. We must be vigilant because they will take advantage of the confusion."

Andy Marrs, Dr. Marrs's oldest son, arrived at the Mission. "Papa wants to know if you can use me to help you."

"Is the First safe?" asked Mrs. Kelley. "Can we move these girls up there?"

"Yes, ma'am. Papa is getting water as best he can. You'll be farther away from the fires downtown. I've been down there already. It's awful. Skyscrapers collapsed and people are trying to salvage their stuff. Not enough wagons. People pushing trunks down the street. They're pitching tents in Union Square and setting up a kitchen."

"Where are the fires?" she asked him.

Andy said, "In the business district, and where hotels and restaurants were located." Nob Hill, with its wrecked mansions, lay between 920 and the business district. Fires were breaking out, he reported, and there was no water: the quake had broken the water lines. All the water in the reservoir had no way to get to San Francisco.

"Chinatown?" she asked.

"Not yet, but if they can't stop the fires, it'll move this way."

"Tell your father the pilgrims will begin as soon as I can get everyone organized."

Andy nodded and hurried out the door. Thomasina heard an explosion a few blocks away. It looked as though the Mission was doomed. If the fire reached Chinatown, it would sweep through the tinder-dry wooden buildings, jumping the narrow streets and alleys, and consume the intricate mazes she had braved in search of girls. All the banners and balconies and poor wooden buildings, all the basements and subbasements filled with people, would blaze.

It was almost noon when all the girls and women assembled in Culbertson Hall.

Big girls like Hsiang forgot their fears taking care of their little sisters. If she could do the same, Thomasina could keep working.

Lo Mo hoped Dr. Marrs knew what he was doing. She heard something grate, perhaps the concrete of the street, and the floor shifted with another aftershock. She heard a wall collapse nearby.

"I want you to go into the street and wait while we check the house," she told the assembled girls. The entry was littered with items too heavy to take and girls were crying. One was comforted with the promise she could keep a box of letters from her fiancé. Several girls had found every broomstick and mop handle in the place and rigged shoulder poles, like Chinese vegetable peddlers, so they could carry twice as much.

"We will walk up to the First Presbyterian together. Don't wander away. Big sisters keep track of little sisters." In the street Miss Ferree and the older women surrounded the defenseless ones like troopers and watched every stranger who passed near them.

The girls took one last look as they left. Most of them were crying. The older women looked after the infants. This was the last time they would see this building. Thomasina wouldn't think of that now. The board members and Sun Lee reported every room empty, but Thomasina had to see for herself. She had to say her own good-byes.

When she was sure the third floor, then the second floor was empty, she stopped in her room for her bundle. It held a few clothes, her smallest New Testament, her photos taken out of frames. She looked at her sabbatical journals and regretted leaving them. She looked at the familiar pictures on the wall and the spotless spread and curtains. She put on another pair of socks and her sturdiest boots. She added another sweater although she was warm already. She thought of the logs and the files in the office. She would have to find a way to get them later.

Out on the street Thomasina saw Sun Lee's tea caddy pulling the seams of her apron pocket.

Lo Mo counted heads. Everyone was out.

They looked like a huge traveling party, all clad in coats, ready to tour.

She would have to talk to Dr. Marrs about where to go from Van Ness Avenue. Where could she take all sixty? Where were all the other people in San Francisco going? The ferries would be running constantly, taking people across the bay and out of the crowded, dangerous city. She hoped Oakland and Berkeley and other outlying towns were undamaged and that her family was safe. Who would be in charge? How would people eat? She couldn't let herself think much now. Too many people depended on her. She raised her voice and Hsiang translated for the ones who didn't understand English. The mission population fell silent so they could hear.

"We must go to the big church. Our building might fall down, might burn." Some of the older women nodded. "We will stay there today. All girls must be good and little girls mind big sisters and not run around. I know you will make me proud of you."

A huge explosion a few blocks away made her flinch. Murmurs of fear rippled through the pilgrims. A few held each other and some cries escaped.

"We'll get organized soon," Thomasina continued. "Do not be afraid. Our heavenly Father loves us. He has saved us and He will keep watching over us. He did not bring you here from China to destroy you. We will pray for all the other people in San Francisco."

Already she wanted to cough from the smoke rising in the damp air, screening the thin sunlight. She looked up Nob Hill. The earthquake had not spared the homes of the wealthy.

"Are we ready? Everybody hold hands with somebody else."

Thomasina could not believe she was calmly giving orders. She didn't know what she was doing. She was as frightened as any three-year-old, but somebody had to give directions.

She asked an older peasant woman to show the other women how to tie their bundles on their backs; she watched and did the same. Thank heavens it was mild this morning and not raining. She got her burden on her back and shifted it until it was balanced. Then she waited till all the bundles were retied and in place. The little girls were quiet, whether from curiosity at what they were seeing or because they were so frightened, she didn't know.

"Let's begin," she said at last. She walked uphill and the girls and women fell in behind her. Some were crying, others were comforting. As they trudged up Sacramento she saw a woman in nightclothes sitting on her stoop staring into the distance. Rescuers dug in the rubble of the building behind her. A woman wearing a dressing gown walked barefoot through broken glass carrying a parrot in a cage. Thomasina heard the hoofbeats of a mounted trooper patrolling Mason. She saw a man dragging and pushing a huge trunk up the hill. If she could have, she'd push the Mission out of danger.

She didn't know if they could stay long in the First. The girls spread out through the pews and Miss Ferree went foraging again for something for dinner. Thomasina wanted to crawl under a pew and wait till it was over, but she found Dr. Marrs in his office, where every surface was white with plaster dust.

"Where do we go from here?" she asked.

27

Mrs. Brown, other board members who had been sleeping at the Mission because of the meeting scheduled for Wednesday, Dr. Marrs, and Thomasina met that night at the First for a strategy meeting.

The fires were spreading to Chinatown and up Nob Hill. The army was in charge, with tent cities and field hospitals going up in Golden Gate and Presidio parks. The girls were bedding down on pews in the church, cheerful and excited. Not even an earthquake could quench their spirits.

"The Mission can't stay here," Mrs. Brown declared. "Without water in the city, there's no sanitation. Disease will follow." For the first time the dynamic woman looked her age.

"We don't know what the food supply will be," said Dr. Marrs.

Thomasina listened to them, and to Mrs. Wright and Mrs. Robbins who had been at the Mission for the meeting and Mrs. Kelley, who had walked several miles to join them. Andy Marrs had reconnoitered again late that afternoon and reported that the fires were spreading. Rescue workers pulled living and dead from collapsed buildings and soldiers patrolled the streets enforcing martial law. Andy saw a man hopelessly trapped under a steel beam, seven stories of rubble crushing him. He begged the soldier to kill him. The soldier hesitated, then put his sidearm to the man's head and pulled the trigger. A quartet of college boys would form a phony line for water or bread and wait until twenty or so people lined up behind them, then they'd take off laughing. Andy came back with a tempered expression, as though he'd seen more than he could take in.

Later, when she saw photographs taken during those first days, the smells came back: plaster dust, brick dust, wood smoke, coal smoke, industrial smoke that stayed in their clothes for weeks. The smoke's greasy sheen marked every face.

"We couldn't believe what was happening this morning," said Thomasina. "When you said to come here, we did. I would have followed any suggestion at that moment."

"We received word from the seminary at San Anselmo," said Dr. Marrs. "You can lead your tribe there temporarily. Everyone who has a place to go is evacuating. The problems of the Mission are the same as any family, multiplied by sixty."

Thomasina felt as though she were carrying them all on her back. "Highbinders are out and eager to profit by the confusion. If they could, they would steal back girls they lost to us. We can't protect the girls in this chaotic situation."

Dr. Marrs wore a complete suit, with vest and watch chain, but without collar or tie. The other women had dressed hastily, but looked as they usually did, except that hairstyles were less elaborate. Thomasina hadn't looked in a mirror all day.

"In the morning, everyone must move again to the Sausalito ferry." Mrs. Brown had a smudge of white dust on her face.

"How will we get from Sausalito to San Anselmo?" asked Thomasina.

"In relays, as wagons are available. Take money to pay the drivers."

Thomasina nodded. She was having trouble getting from one

thought to another. Each new realization drained her of thinking power as she absorbed its meaning.

"I need to get records out of 920," Thomasina said.

"You can't carry them with you," Dr. Marrs protested.

"I can't let them burn."

Mrs. Robbins sighed at the word. All day they heard explosions as firefighters set off dynamite to clear a path the fire couldn't cross. But the fire spread just the same.

"If I bring the logs here, will you try to preserve them?" asked Thomasina.

"Of course. I moved some of ours to the basement. Unless this building burns, they will be safe. Or even if it does . . ." Dr. Marrs stopped to absorb that possibility. "Even if it does, we can probably find a safe place."

"Then I must go back and salvage what I can. I owe it to the girls."

"The patrols will keep you out of the building," predicted Mrs. Wright.

"I must try."

Thomasina and Miss Ferree left Van Ness Avenue at midnight and walked back to the Mission through a rain of ashes. Thomasina felt the specks on her face and imagined drifts of ash like snow of the damned. A handkerchief over her nose blocked some of the smoke. The wood-smoke smell of burning clapboard houses mixed with the brick dust and burning vegetation. They pulled a toy wagon that had served all the little Marrs children. They did not talk. They were beyond talking. The familiar streets were thronged with people carrying their possessions tied in bundles. A hugely pregnant woman sat on a stoop, then heaved herself to her feet and continued toward the park. Later Thomasina would learn that thirteen infants were born in field hospitals and all survived.

Some buildings seemed uninhabitable, with walls collapsed exposing floors of furnishings, like some grotesque showroom.

Floors had fallen in some; others looked perfectly normal. The people heading away from the fires looked calm, hopeless, and resigned.

The closer Thomasina and Miss Ferree got to 920, the fewer people she saw. Martial law had cleared everyone from the streets. She persuaded an officer to let them cross the lines to get to the Mission. There they found a soldier with a rifle standing outside 920. Acrid smoke blew up the hill. She heard the crash as another building fell. Chinatown was doomed. The wooden buildings had already begun to burn and 920 was in the path of the blaze. She could feel the heat and smell the smoke.

"You can't go in there, ma'am," said the soldier, a fresh-faced youngster with a still-pressed uniform.

"I must. I am the superintendent of this mission and we have come for our records."

"It might not be safe, ma'am," he said. "I have orders to shoot anyone who tries to enter a building."

Thomasina's Scotch determination steeled her. "Then you will have to shoot me, because I am going in."

"Please, ma'am. I can't let you."

"I am doing it in spite of you," she said, her chin in the air. Then she realized the boy was afraid to disobey orders and she said softly, "You did your best to stop us."

"Then hurry, please," he said.

Thomasina and Miss Ferree stepped through broken glass and fallen plaster. She heard Miss Ferree suck in her breath, in surprise. Thomasina went to the office. Her desk was covered with dust. The red glare of fires lit the familiar objects. She opened the cupboard and pulled out the logs. They dated back to the founding of the Mission, with entries written in Miss Culbertson's spidery hand. She thought of the bills and ledgers and all the letters in file drawers and knew they would be meaningless. She pulled a box of guardianship papers from a shelf and a folder of legal papers giving immigration status of some of the women and other official decisions.

Then she stopped. She could see her lithograph of Glasgow

hanging askew. She knew where her spare handkerchiefs were. She remembered the porcelain bowl in a presentation box she had received from a grateful family. She thought of all the books she must leave behind, and the collection of collars and cuffs she used to make her meager wardrobe look presentable, left upstairs in the dresser. Tears cleared dusty grit from her eyes.

She remembered hours spent in this office with Miss Culbertson and she thought of all the girls who had stood across the desk.

"O Father, please let us get through this. Guard the girls and keep them safe. Let me come back to this place and continue the work."

A terrific explosion rocked the area. The soldier stuck his head inside and shouted, "Hurry, the fire is moving fast." Thomasina tied a few silver bowls and cups and other gifts presented to the Mission in a pillowcase. She tied the files and box of papers together with heavy twine. How could she pick up eleven years of her life and carry it? Miss Ferree put a sheaf of papers in a burlap sack.

They took one last look around—at the shadows in the stairwell, at the hall strewn with belongings abandoned at the last minute, at the big room where so many earnest and inspiring meetings took place. She hurried out the door and they began walking uphill pulling the wagon behind them. At Mason she looked back at the sturdy brick building, at the soldier guarding the building. Flames wrapped around the Mission, she learned, and it had burned by dawn.

She was too tired to think. There were too many murmured conversations from girls stretched out on pews and on the floor. She heard sirens on Van Ness and voices from the street. A cool breeze blew in through broken windows. She wished for another blanket, and knew the others wished for one, too. They huddled together like kittens for warmth.

She remembered Papa and the ranch and the god mountain.

Why had God done this? Why now? Why San Francisco? The mountain was angry and shook the earth. Rocks fell and creeks shifted. The valley rippled. Frightened animals moved restlessly in their pens. Mama had held her and said soft things until she slept.

No one held her now.

"Take heart and call on the Lord," Miss Culbertson had said. He had to help her because this was more than she could do alone. The elders would help, the people in San Anselmo, her own family. She must get word to her family. If only the telephones worked! They would worry about her.

Her mind whirled with fear, worry, and fatigue and she couldn't sleep. She would have to pray to calm herself. But not her usual pleas and praises. What did she know by heart?

"The Lord is my Shepherd. I shall not want. I shall not want. I shall not want." She must believe that and never waver. She had always found a way, with God's help, and she would again. She didn't have to know the details of just how she'd manage.

The girls, still high-spirited, laughed and chattered as they breakfasted on cold bread and water. They would have to walk several miles to the ferry. Even five-year-old Hung Mooie carried two dozen eggs in hopes of having some to eat by and by. The girls had to abandon items laboriously carried from 920.

Old Sing Ho, just out of the hospital and blind, cheerfully staggered along with all her possessions tied in a huge bundle that she rolled down hills and dragged uphill. Two young mothers tied their babies on their backs while others divided their belongings.

Laughter stimulated the unwashed and uncombed procession that straggled through stifling, crowded streets. Thomasina saw people streaming downhill toward the ferry, carrying or wheeling in baby carriages what they had salvaged. Trunks pushed uphill yesterday had been abandoned. Andy Marrs scouted the fire and said it had consumed yesterday's encampment in Union Square.

The big hotel had been dynamited, but the fire jumped the line and burned its way up into Chinatown. Thomasina couldn't imagine all the people displaced from that warren. Women dressed in elaborate hats, wearing starched petticoats and fine boots, walked with those who wore bathrobes, dressing gowns, and slippers.

While the mission inhabitants headed to the ferry, others marched the other way, to the parks where the tent cities were going up. The mission tribe detoured around the fire, because it created an enormous updraft that sucked more air to fuel itself. The sun broke through the sickly light, bloodred and small. The smoky air seen from beneath pulsed rose and lavender, then mauve, yellow, and dun and the sun disappeared in the smoke. They walked to the ferry at the foot of Market Street. One wealthy woman carried nothing but her fur coats. One woman wept as she walked uphill carrying a dead infant. Thomasina wished her girls did not have to see these things, but everyone in San Francisco saw indelible scenes of horror and bravery.

Chinese with wheelbarrows and shoulder poles headed for the Oakland ferry. Thomasina and the adult women herded the girls closely so no opportunist highbinder could spirit one away. Once aboard the ferry, the girls and women sank to the floor on the lower deck of the steamer wherever they found space, too tired to find the saloon. They laid down bundles and babies, exhausted. They were hungry but knew there was no food for hours yet.

Thomasina looked at the faces and gave thanks. They didn't know when they would eat next or where they would lay their heads tonight but they were grateful for deliverance.

The long day continued. In Sausalito, they hired wagons to take them to San Anselmo. Negotiations were brief. The drivers knew the refugees had no choice, but did not charge as much as they might have. Once they reached San Anselmo, the only place available was a barn. They ate hastily prepared soup, biscuits, and fruit brought by the seminary students and faculty wives. They ate in relays since there were only a dozen tin plates and tea-spoons, but they would not go hungry since relief workers and supplies had arrived already. Girls who usually complained at the least change in routine silently accepted what came their way. The big sisters took charge of their little sisters; each girl found a space in the hay and wrapped up in her blankets to sleep. It was a warm spring night, but still chilly. Sometime after midnight it began raining.

Making the best of the situation became their highest aspiration. The last time Thomasina had slept in clean, fragrant hay, she was as young as Hung Mooie.

The next morning in the rain, again townspeople and seminary people came to their rescue. The girls stood in line patiently for oatmeal and bread. They huddled inside the barn. Tents, usually reserved for summer revivals and outdoor celebrations, went up nearby lessening the crush in the barn. Two girls began coughing and sneezing, and by evening two dozen children and several adults were ill. Bronchitis spread through the tribe. Thomasina had nothing to give them but hot unsweetened lemonade. There weren't enough handkerchiefs to go around.

The next day Dr. Frederick Seaton, a faculty member from the seminary, drove Thomasina in his rig to nearby towns. She had been given money, but she would have to persuade the landlord to accept Chinese tenants. She learned there were enough Chinese in the fishing village of San Rafael that she could find a place. It was greeted as though a fairy palace by her unkempt and rumpled horde. Roses and acacia bloomed and two blooming hawthorns almost hid the front door. Her heart rose. Gail Borden came from southern California laden like Santa Claus with necessary gifts. Bolts of cloth, a sewing machine, and boxes of bedding arrived. Borden supplied a big tent and desks, and classes resumed within days.

In those first weeks after the earthquake, she consulted with her board and other Presbyterian officials about rebuilding 920. They hired an architect and made arrangements to clear the site. The Mission would continue.

Invitations had been sent weeks before for a wedding at the

Mission on April 21. Yuen Kim, who had been at the Mission several years, a bright girl, was engaged to Henry Lai of Cleveland, Ohio. Yuen's fiancé spent a frantic two days before he found her in San Anselmo and Lo Mo quickly made arrangements. They were married on the stated day by Dr. Landon in the ivy-covered chapel at San Anselmo. The bedraggled audience celebrated and sent the couple on their way through a bower of service berry and wild crab from the hills, in a shower of early roses.

28

The place Thomasina found in San Rafael had served as a seamen's boardinghouse. Everyone would have to double up in rooms and classes would be held in the dining room. A bedraggled troop moved its few bundles of bedding and clothes to the new location.

Her prayers had reduced to one essential plea: "Please, Lord, get us through this." She repeated it over and over, like a mantra, until she slept. Letters from Charlie were heartening and the window of loneliness stayed closed through the crisis. She would never again assume she controlled her emotions completely. Ghosts hid, but they were there.

She knew her tribe couldn't stay in the house-and-tents compound in San Rafael, so she made the two-hour trip back and forth to Oakland many times in search of a suitable building. She thought about all the ideas she developed on her sabbatical on the long hours on the ferry. She loved to stand out of the spray and look over the beloved bay. The light on the water, that sun-dazzled light, soothed her, unless the water was choppy. The shimmer and flicker was hypnotic. Like a Catholic gazing at glimmering candles, she focused and prayed, or chewed over ideas and opinions Edgar had suggested. She loved to watch the fog as it pushed through the Golden Gate and spread across the water, filled the valleys and left the tops of hills like sentinels. The incessant movement of trolleys, horse carts, automobiles, wagons, and pedestrians disappeared. The fog muffled the warning blats from tugs. A silent lateen sail cut a triangular swath through the gray.

Six months after her bedraggled refugees arrived in San Anselmo, a sparkling group of clean, well-dressed girls boarded the ferry for the trip to Oakland. Older girls had sewed new outfits for their little sisters and Thomasina had one tailored suit.

"We don't have to worry about making decisions," she joked to Miss Ferree. "When we have no choices. Oh, but I do miss my collection of collars and cuffs and scarfs I used to dress up the same old suits." Miss Ferree dryly pointed out that her aprons had been easily replaced.

The older girls were disappointed in their new home, situated near the smokestacks and industrial manufacturing plants, but they soon adapted, as children do. It was the only place that would consent to rent when they discovered the tenants would be Chinese. Thomasina had used all her charm and persuasion on the owners. Gifts of food and money from friends in the Santa Clara Valley arrived in time for a Thanksgiving feast that year and preparations for Christmas began almost the same day.

Thomasina told the girls that the earthquake had opened cracks in people's hearts. The outpouring of food, clothing, and other necessities proved the goodness of God operated through other people. Privately, she wondered why the lessons of giving and receiving had to be so hard to learn.

The Chinese population of San Francisco stabilized in an area in Oakland soon after the earthquake. Every spare cot in a Chinese home in the Bay Area was occupied.

She loved the soft-edged panorama when she stood in the sun

on a hill in Berkeley and watched the fog cover Marin County, or watched rain curtain the city.

From the beginning, gifts poured in from all over the country as church mission groups and others sent money and survival goods. The Occidental Board could have decided not to continue the San Francisco Mission, a thought that worried Thomasina during those first chaotic days, but it apparently was never seriously considered. The board met on the ruins of the old building, then adjourned to Calvary Church. Many had lost their homes, the smoke still lingered over the city, and coffee for the meeting had to be prepared on a "curb stove" because gas could not be turned on in the church.

Thomasina was disappointed in the work of the architect. She wanted an inviting living room with a fireplace, something friendly and comfortable, something like a big country house, but the architect had more utilitarian ideas. He thought of her girls as "inmates" and the Mission as an institution, not home. The girls had narrow cells that stretched from the cramped hallway to a window. He ignored her pleas for a "homelike atmosphere." It was done as cheaply as possible, using clinker bricks from the old building. She wanted to cry out, "If it were your daughter, you'd want a little beauty, a little comfort!"

The huge arched design that graced the front of the old building was not replicated. The stair-step windows in front gave the new building its only distinction and over one hundred windows punctuated the new walls. Thomasina was grateful it existed at all. Besides the gifts of generous groups who supported the work of the Mission, she found donors so that each bedroom bore a plaque designating it the gift of a grateful Chinese or American family or group. This fund-raising idea had never occurred to Thomasina until she received a thick letter from Charlie. Princeton friends and faculty added their wishes to his for safety and good luck. He sent news of the Duciks, including one sister who recently married, to everyone's surprise. Charlie mentioned churches selling windows to families as memorials, told her she had one hundred opportunities although it would be a little harder since they were clear, not stained glass.

One problem she mulled over during this time was that the original purpose of the Mission was fading. She spent more time in lawyers' offices trying to get legal wives and daughters in the country than she had in the past and made more visits to the Immigration Shed where they were detained. She had several visitors from the First congregation who called regularly at the Immigration Shed with food, clothing, and encouragement for the incarcerated women. But she could not stop her rescues yet because she still received pleas from towns up and down the coast to help girls. Besides rescuing unfortunate *mooie jais* and women threatened or trapped in prostitution, she took in girls whose families tried to sell them as concubines to old men.

One strong-minded girl in Portland, Edna Chou, appealed to Thomasina because her father wanted her to return to China to marry according to his arrangement. The girl was born in America, knew she had rights, and found the courage to resist. The judge said that as an American citizen she could not be compelled and her father reluctantly agreed to allow her to live at the Mission and study. When people criticized the way the girls were treated— forced to help with the cooking and housekeeping, live plainly and do Bible study, Thomasina was reminded of Edna, who resided there by choice. The Mission was not her ideal, and probably Edna would have preferred a family who understood her aspirations, but she stayed three years, perfecting her English, then went to work for the telephone company in Chinatown, which employed women who could speak English and at least several Chinese dialects. Edna Chou was the beginning of the wave of independent women rising in Chinatown. Thomasina's predictions to Edgar were becoming manifest.

The Mission's goal was shifting from a refuge for prostitutes to an orphanage and school. She needed a separate place for infants and smaller children. That need would exist as long as new-comers arrived. Thomasina read John Dewey and absorbed some of the new ideas of educators. Wholesome recreation, kinder-gartens, and learning-by-doing—all of these ideas fit into the core purpose of the Mission, education.

In California the Chinese excelled in services and import trade. Their problems differed from the problems of European immigrants in other big cities. The Chinese were also farmers and fishermen and lived in the country, not just in the city. They had not cared to join the melting pot. Only gradually were the men de-ciding to stay in Gold Mountains and bring over their wives.

In the meantime, she knew that her rescues were necessary. Girls were still mistreated and this cruelty fueled her wrath. Her anger rumbled like a banked fire in the furnace of her genteel middle-class soul. She channeled her rage into action on behalf of the girls. Miss Culbertson had shown her the way.

Whenever she found herself thinking she was superior—with some education, with a kind of churchy sophistication, with ex-perience in the larger world of benevolence, politics, and immi-gration law, she remembered her yearning for Charlie, the way she accepted Carnegie's tainted money, the small compromises that kept the Mission going. She *was* the women she worked for. She was not different, in her heart. She had the same desires, the same hatreds, the same wish to live a peaceful life. She was merely the person in front who worked for them for her own salvation. And she could never explain that to her sisters, to Dr. Marrs, to Mrs. Brown, or to Evelyn. She might try to explain it to Edgar, be-cause he would understand better than any of the others.

Girls exploited the Mission as a place to detoxify themselves from opium. Thomasina knew this, but also knew that it was needed and allowed it to happen. Let the Mission be used by women who returned to prostitution—at least it had performed a merciful act. That grated on her Presbyterian conscience, but if the Mission withheld help from women considered undeserving, she set herself up as judge. She knew of women who had to get married in a hurry who became the best mothers and men who had behaved badly once, but subsequently redeemed themselves. There was a harsh strain of Puritanism underlying the efforts of the benevolence movement. While she would like every woman who entered the Mission to reform and become Christian, she knew that would not happen. Additionally, she had seen too many bad things done in God's name by righteous people. Let her save the women and leave judging to God.

If she couldn't help the opium-addicted girls, "the least of my sisters," it would be as though she were killing them. Occasionally one stayed and recovered and became a useful Christian, but she knew the statistics "looked bad." Above all, Thomasina could not turn away a dying girl. The girl might never embrace Christianity, never become productive, never be a shining example to anybody, but this was Thomasina's last chance to show the girl some kindness. All the Mission might do was ease her passage to death. But it would, God willing, do that.

The Chinese believed that when a person died evil spirits could affect anyone nearby at the time. What she once thought was extreme cruelty—dying people turned out into the streets— she now knew arose from profound fear and superstition. Then she remembered: "superstition" was what one called other people's religion. She hoped she had learned it was more than that.

When she thought back to things that stood out in her memory, she had to remind herself that nothing happened in isolation. While she was conferring on plans for the new building at 920, living in Oakland and begging or buying necessities for the Mission, she was also traveling up and down the coast in response to pleas for rescues. The earthquake disrupted the Chinese community and as people scattered to Portland, Seattle, and smaller towns in California, problems called her farther distances. The work of rebuilding the city put every available laborer to work, so the long-standing dislike of Chinese by labor unions who saw them as competition died. Court met in the Temple Israel building and Abe Reuf was getting all the blame for bribery of city officials over prize fights, gas rates, trolley franchises, telephone lines, and water rights, while the officials of the big corporations escaped. Amos Cohn was one of his attorneys.

She met with people who could get things done to change immigration laws. She could exert little pressure for change at the national level, but she could talk to lawyers and others locally who could influence legislation in Sacramento regarding bordellos, and see that it was enforced. The ambiguous stance toward ownership or indenture had to be changed before the legal status of the girls would improve. She had refused the strident activism of suffragettes because she felt she accomplished more with soft persuasion than noisy demands, but her frustration over these laws finally pushed her into their camp. A woman could pressure the men in her life to vote for her issues, but the results weren't certain. Women needed to cast their own votes.

Her sabbatical year subtly changed her other attitudes about laws for sanitation that affected the people who lived in tenements, especially those in Chinatown. She found herself distanced from the accepted American attitudes about Chinese culture. She had gotten beyond its exotic differentness and had learned to appreciate, and even love, its teachings, its attitudes about family, and the source of the "passive" attitude that had once bothered her so much. She had seen the paintings, the ceramics, the sculpture of its best artists. She had an inkling now of how the economic system worked for ordinary people, and why the men continued to come to Gold Mountains and leave their wives behind. She must find a way to let other people learn these things.

Thomasina still talked to groups about the work of the Mission. With every organization in San Francisco trying to raise money after the earthquake, she sometimes felt her voice was drowned out in the clamor.

Only Miss Culbertson might have predicted the next problem Thomasina faced because it was never acknowledged in public.

Most middle-class white women did not know it existed or even its name. Thomasina had learned every vice humans were capable of in the twelve years since she arrived wearing her best hat and chinchilla collar for an interview by the board.

When they moved back to 920, the girls paired off with their closest friends, putting in "dibs" for the best rooms.

29

Thomasina found Sooey Sim in a crib in Oakland when Captain Peterson of the Oakland police force led her on her first rescue trip after the Mission moved there. Later, she described the girl to her board as of "peculiar disposition, strong affections, and strong jealousies, and we pray for wisdom and patience to learn her nature." Sooey Sim's stormy temperament made problems with the other girls.

At first Sooey Sim did not trust the friendly treatment she received from the girls, Miss Ferree, and Lo Mo. Then she complained that they were always spying on her and she had no privacy. But Sooey Sim found the strength to go to court and testify against her owner. The girl knew that if she fell back into her master's hands, she could be killed as easily as a kitten. Whether it was bravery or hopelessness that motivated her, Lo Mo could not have said, but the girl steadfastly answered all questions about the story her family was told in her village, how she was treated well for a few days after arriving in San Francisco, then how she was taken to the house of prostitution in Oakland. She could remember dates in American time, which gave her credibility in the judge's eyes. She could speak a little English and the court ordered a translator. Thomasina guarded Sooey Sim closely because of the threats of reprisal. The girl never left the Oakland house alone, day or night. Thomasina did not think Sooey Sim trusted the mission people any more than she did her former owners, but only knew she was treated better. She was indifferent to their religious practices—the grace before meals, the morning hymns, the frequent Bible readings. Revenge against her former owner seemed her strongest motivator.

Then the new building was finished and they moved back to 920 Sacramento in San Francisco. Everything was fresh! Thomasina loved the raw wood, still being varnished, and the smell of paint—all pastels for the girls' rooms. Workmen came and went, and it seemed they would never get curtains on all one hundred windows. She wished they could have had balconies, as the buildings in Chinatown had, and a tile roof that curved up at the corners. This building was a box, without even a bay window to gather the light. She would ask generous friends in Chinatown about the best decorations to put up, so that the girls could see their rich heritage. Miss Ferree was overseeing the kitchen items as well as the furniture. Thomasina would have to get a new desk and file cabinets and begin again to fill them up.

With a hundred minor mishaps, forty girls moved in. It all seemed to be going smoothly. The difficult Sooey Sim requested a room with Susan, a girl who had grown up in the Mission. Susan's mother died a few months after Miss Culbertson. Susan Lee was thoroughly Christian and had never known another family. She and Sooey Sim planned the spreads and curtains they would sew. But Kim Yep, who had been Susan's best chum before Sooey Sim arrived, came to Lo Mo the day they moved into the new building, begging her to intercede.

"Lo Mo, you can't let Sooey take Susan."

"You don't own Susan," Thomasina said softly. It was always hard to learn this lesson for the first time. "She can decide for herself. Can't you think of some other chum you want to room with?"

"They're not chums, they're girlfriends."

"We're all girlfriends here," said Thomasina. "Everyone is your friend." Thomasina thought, maybe Kim Yep is misinterpreting. She said aloud, "Everything changes. Susan is older than you and maybe she wants an older friend who can teach her about life outside the Mission."

"Sooey Sim is teaching bad things, that's why Susan loves her. Like men-and-boys-making-love!"

Thomasina caught her breath. "They're lovers?"

"Yes, lovers." Kim Yep was crying by now.

"This can't be!"

"Yes, Lo Mo! I love Susan, but never bad way." Kim Yep took Thomasina by the hand and drew her to the top floor where the teenagers claimed their rooms.

Thomasina knew very well that the bagnios of Chinatown offered boys as well as girls. She found regular prostitution at least understandable, but men with men disgusted her. Then she tried to excuse Sooey Sim and Susan in her mind. Sooey Sim had lived in a bordello, seen everything sexual that could take place. Prostitutes helped each other and another prostitute might have been the only source of affection Sooey Sim knew. And Susan was still a child. She had begun her monthlies, but she had scarcely put away her dollies.

And most of all, Thomasina recalled when she was in love with Charlie how compelling the feelings were and what she had so urgently wanted in spite of prohibitions.

But she couldn't allow this in the Mission. "I can't believe it," she said to Kim Yep.

"I have been Susan's best friend since before the earthquake. This whore comes in and takes her away from me. This isn't fair! This isn't *fair!*" Kim Yep cried.

Lo Mo turned to see curious faces peering from other bedrooms. "Girls, go downstairs. Get your little sisters ready for dinner. This is a private matter." She waited until the other teenage girls left, then she walked the length of the hall and made sure all the bedrooms were empty.

Sooey Sim and Susan stood side by side in their room. Sooey

Sim, older and cynical, looked belligerent; Susan, younger and innocent, looked guilty, but you can't condemn a person on appearances.

"They are like man-and-boy-lovers!" repeated Kim Yep.

The two roommates moved closer together.

"We don't allow bad things here at the Mission," said Lo Mo. She saw Sooey Sim stiffen.

"They want the same room," Kim Yep asserted, "so they can do dirty things!"

Thomasina felt ready to vomit. "Oh, no!" she whispered. Sooey Sim put her arm around Susan's waist. Susan glared at Lo Mo defiantly and embraced Sooey Sim.

Thomasina remembered when she first came to the Mission. Sun Lee had told Thomasina about this kind of love long ago. The revulsion was stronger then, when she had been younger and more naive. She didn't think there was any kind of depravity she hadn't come across by now. But she had not found this under her own roof. And then she had a terrible thought: perhaps it had gone on all along and she hadn't seen it.

"This cannot be allowed," she said. She looked closely at the two girls. Kim Yep backed out of the room and leaned against the wall in the hallway, crying softly in misery now that she had vented her jealousy.

"You have been a strong and brave girl, Sooey Sim," said Lo Mo. Sooey was tall for a Chinese girl, very thin, her hair in a skinny queue. She wore a peculiar medallion carved from pale jade. She was not pretty, but her habitual undercurrent of anger gave her animation. "Only a few girls have been able to face the judge and speak the truth. But we cannot allow this to go on. Susan is the flower of our house. We did not raise her to have her sullied this way." She thought: if Susan could do this, then what have we accomplished? How sharper than a serpent's tooth!

Rage and empty hurt canceled each other out. Thomasina couldn't lose control. How could she handle this? She had a hundred things to see to. Furniture was arriving, the little girls were whooping and running in their playroom, getting used to everything new. Miss Ferree was busy and the cooks were trying to make their first dinner. The new telephone rang incessantly and Thomasina already regretted she had it installed.

"This kind of behavior will not go on under this roof," Thomasina said with great determination. "I need to think about this. Do not speak of this to any of the other girls. Now move your things into separate rooms. We have enough rooms for now," and she turned to include Kim Yep, "I'll talk to you after we eat."

She waited until Susan began to gather her clothes in her bedspread to be sure they obeyed. Kim Yep turned to her. "You favor Sooey Sim because she went to court. You make fuss over her and ignore all of us who have been here, trying to do what you say, for a long time. She is your star, the one the people talk about. You give her best room, best clothes, best everything! Your old daughters see this. Why love this whore? She hates us and only uses us."

Lo Mo couldn't breathe. Had she been guilty of favoritism? She knew she had favored Hsiang because she could translate. She favored Susan because she had known the child since birth. She tried so hard to be impartial that she even kept a record of which girls she took with her on errands so she wouldn't leave anyone out.

"Yep is just jealous," Susan lashed out. "She thinks she owns me. She wants me to do things her way." Susan threw her things on the bare mattress. "She can't stand for me to talk to another girl. Sooey Sim and I don't do anything bad. We talk. I teach her about the Mission and she teaches me about the rest of the world."

"What do you do when you are alone?" asked Lo Mo. "Do you touch each other in private places?"

Susan hung her head.

"This kind of friendship is bad," said Lo Mo. "That is why it isn't allowed." She looked at Sooey Sim who stared back levelly. "This is how you repay us for taking you out of that crib?"

Sooey Sim smiled. It seemed a sad smile to Lo Mo, then Sooey Sim shrugged and said something to Susan, who translated: "It happened as it was meant to happen. It is my fate to be unhappy." Tears rolled down Susan's flawless cheeks. Sooey Sim spoke again.

Susan shook her head. Lo Mo caught the word for the Mission and her name.

"What is it, Susan?"

"She will leave, go back to Oakland."

"No! It's too dangerous. They will kill her for testifying. Or if they didn't kill her, they would make her return to the life. If her master did not beat her to death, he would find more refined punishments." Lo Mo mulled the possibilities. "Move into separate rooms. I'll talk to you later. Kim Yep, go down and help with the little ones. They are wild. Don't talk to each other, or anybody else."

Lo Mo went down to her office. She had to thread her way between boxes of books and papers, then she sat turned toward the deepening twilight. She didn't light the lamp.

"God help me," she prayed. "What do I do about this? Lord, I can't do this alone." Then she lost focus and her mind circled over the problem. She was angry at Susan. This was how she was repaid for rearing her! What ingratitude! And then, if a girl reared in the Mission did not turn out to be a good person, what did that say about what they were doing? Susan grew up surrounded by the word of the Bible, taught with loving firmness, sung hymns, fed and clothed, taught right from wrong, and still this happened. All the doubts she had over the years rose again. Thomasina now knew how her brother Al felt when his oldest son was brought home by the sheriff. She felt as though she were at fault because she hadn't done better with Susan. But good sense said, of course, that she could not control every act that every girl committed. Susan was plump with a perfect complexion—a peach blush in her cheeks. Her brows were well shaped and her eyes large. She was pretty, but more, she looked—what was it?—untouched. And now Thomasina learned she had been touched in unspeakable ways.

She felt she was a failure. Not as Madam Director, that public role would remain intact. She was a failure as a mother. She had not prepared Susan for this possibility, trusting innocence to be its own defense. That ignorance had left Susan vulnerable. Lo Mo had naively assumed that Christian upbringing would protect Susan, but the ugly world outside the Mission intruded like a snake in the garden.

Sooey Sim was beyond fathoming. Hypercritical and demanding, refusing food, throwing her clothes out the window in Oakland, bruising her hand pounding on the wall—tempestuous and unpredictable. But like so many wild people, when she was affectionate, she was irresistibly, seductively charming. How attractive she must have seemed to innocent, inexperienced Susan. Sooey Sim's feral instincts made her canny and strong enough to go to court. Her rash outpourings made her dangerous and exciting.

Thomasina watched the color fade until the boxes and furniture were gray blocks and the streetlamps came on.

"O Lord, help me to find a way through this problem. Without pausing to thank you for our new home, I'm begging for help again.

"I am not wise enough to see the way out. And I know how compelling love and loneliness are.

"Help me now, today, and in all the days to come in this new, ugly building. You have set my foot on the path. Now, please guide my steps."

Thomasina went in to the first dinner in the new 920 without any answers to this problem. She knew rumors would spread quickly, had spread, so she told the girls that the Mission's problems stayed at the Mission and no one was to talk about things outside.

Two days later she got a call from a family in Fairfax who needed a girl to clean and cook. Thomasina asked Sooey Sim if she would go. The girl looked at Thomasina with contempt. "I will go. Problem will stay." She left the following weekend. Susan drooped around red-eyed for several weeks, then made up with Kim Yep.

Thomasina had struggled with her conscience about sending

girls out in service since her discussions with Edgar, but this time she was glad she could remove Sooey Sim from the Mission without completely abdicating responsibility for her.

She didn't want to think she was limiting the girls and she was pleased when Leen Wong returned to China to teach, the first non-Caucasian to represent the mission board.

Thomasina had thought she was doing a good thing, sending the girls out in service. Now she realized she had accepted the stereotype of Chinese as servants.

And worse, contributed to it.

NEW DIRECTIONS

1910

30

Augustus Booker had always been part of her life, it seemed. He had visited the Mission many times over the years and his daughters, Mary and Gertrude, were dear friends. Thomasina always looked forward to their visits to San Francisco.

Gus was a short man, who looked rotund because his pockets were always stuffed with something, bulging out his nicely tailored coats. One time when she was staying at their New Jersey house, he had pulled a newspaper-wrapped codfish out of his pocket, telling her, "Get it yourself. Then you know it's fresh."

She tried to imagine a codfish protruding from her handbag.

When he came to the Mission his pockets bulged with candy and the little girls soon learned that a shy hand outstretched would net them a piece.

Thomasina became friends with his daughters when they all attended the General Assembly in Los Angeles in 1903. Besides the two daughters, a few years younger than Thomasina, he had one son who was a businessman and a second who was a missionary in India, whom she had met when she was on her tour. Mary looked like Gus, a short, plump woman with dark, merry eyes and a bubbling infectious laugh. Gertrude must resemble her late mother in her slim, elegant figure and excellent carriage. She had beautiful strawberry blond hair that Thomasina envied, but Gertrude refused to do more than pull it back in a ribbon. She was more reserved, but when the three of them got together, they laughed a lot.

Thomasina had a long discussion with Gus on guardianship laws and the need to change the laws affecting disorderly houses. She was compelled to make people understand how important it was to enforce them against immoral traffic in women. What good did it do to protest, lobby, write letters, and persuade friends to talk to judges and legislators if the laws were not enforced? Gus listened closely. "My board has warned me that I'm tilting at windmills," she said and waited for him to say the same, but he did not tell her to stop. She outlined her plan and he agreed.

She began to put her beliefs into action that Sunday in October at the regional synod of California, Utah, and Nevada in Fresno. The Presbyterian church where the meeting was held was filled with synod members and interested people visiting from the area. Gus was there and planned to return to the Mission with her. If she told stories about her girls, people would be sympathetic. She didn't know how they would respond when she talked about enforcing vice laws, she only knew she must speak out.

She wore a blue-gray suit of British cut and a white blouse with an Eton collar. Her hair had been wild this morning, but she had gotten it up neatly. She looked out over the room and noticed more men than usual. She was a short, slight woman, shorter than many of her older girls, wearing the Sunday uniform of a church-going gentlewoman. She hoped she looked attractive because as much as she hated to admit it, how she looked and presented herself had a lot to do with how well her ideas were accepted.

She began as she usually did, talking about the work of the Mission.

"My dear friends, what is this home that you have so generously provided?" she asked the visiting church men. "A plain, substantial brick building that stands on the steep hillside overlooking Chinatown, where we listen to the mysterious sounds and sights that go to make up this miniature Oriental city. As one of our early missionaries said of work in Chinatown, 'We go to it as the pioneer Californian went into the mines, where with every stroke of his pick he expected to turn up a shovelful of gold sand.' To us it is a mine where we have struck gold."

Thomasina looked up from her notes. This metaphor for their work seemed to reach her hearers. All western states shared the gold rush history.

"That mine has proved an inexhaustible vein. It yields far richer and more enduring treasures than any bonanza of the Golden West. The treasures stored up are not all visible to human eyes, but are known to Him who seeth not as man sees. But let me tell you of some of our treasures, the endearing children and women who have come to us recently.

"Five little sisters from Portland, Oregon, none of whom has spent a day in school, are now at the Mission because of their dying mother's last wish. We recently celebrated the wedding of a girl who came to us four years ago. We searched three buildings for six hours before we pulled her from under a heap of rice bags, mats, and boxes where she had nearly smothered. She stood in radiant white at her wedding to a good Christian Chinese man. Our newcomers range from Woo Doon, a little boy whom we nursed after surgery for trachoma, to Kui Pou, an elderly lady who wanted to study Christianity and inquired if she might take a little wine occasionally and play dominoes, but not for money, she assured us. She is making progress in one of our English classes.

"We have a girl we call Chin Ah Ho. Only the dear Lord who watches over the uncertain destiny of such waifs as she knows her real name. The Honorable H. H. North, Commissioner of Immigration, was presented with this weird little domestic slave child. She was very small, very frightened, densely ignorant, and unbeautiful. Mr. North is loyal to the laws he enforces, but his tender heart pitied this girl. Would that pity touched more public officials. The child was originally denied entrance to this country, but Commissioner North appealed all the way to Washington to protect her and place her in our custody. She came to us with all her worldly possessions tied in a single handkerchief. Today, you could study every girl at the Mission and never recognize that dull, bewildered child who came to us. A bright little girl now joyously sings with her comrades. Oh, the blessedness of love and care for such waifs as she!

"Now these are stories with cheerful endings, but we know too many others that do not end on such a happy note. Christians! Today our country is ringing from shore to shore with a clarion call to men and women to unite in a determined effort to suppress the slave traffic! That great evil even now threatens to keep a foothold in this country.

"We are doing what we have been mandated to do since the 1870s when the Occidental Mission Board and Miss Culbertson began this work in San Francisco. We no longer have to fear highbinders' dynamite on our doorstep, but we have a challenge opening up for us. You have supported the Mission with alms but now I call upon you for something more: we need your commitment to enforce these laws.

"Until you accept Chinese people as equal—as workers, as consumers, as children of the Father—we do not follow the commandment to Love Thy Neighbor.

"The members of my board and I have importuned our representatives in Sacramento. Our efforts have gone on for years and we have used all our charm and persuasion and California has outlawed the 'sale' of human beings—forcing women into indentured subjugation. Laws to close disorderly houses are waiting the governor's signature. Congress has passed the Mann Act, which prohibits transportation of women across state lines for immoral purposes.

"The slave traffic came about because of the exclusion laws. With your weight behind this new legislation, long-standing injustice will begin to fade. It is not just a matter of putting faith into deeds, but something higher. As long as we prejudge Chinese, who are easily identified because of their appearance, we continue a civil injustice. Furthermore, we have put ourselves above another group of people simply because we were here, in America, before they arrived. When we limit these, the least of our brethren, we limit ourselves and we damage ourselves.

"If we don't lift our hands and raise our voices, we continue the cycle. For example, a Chinese cannot testify on his own behalf in American courts. A Chinese is barred by law from living outside his quarter except as a servant. Near Sacramento, where the Chinese population is ten percent, one half of the arrests are of Chinese suspects. And this from a notably law-abiding people. A qualified Chinese is barred from many schools and consequently from many professions.

"We have passed laws to address these impositions, and now I call upon you to press for their enforcement.

"Lend your strength to your Chinese brothers and sisters. We must set in motion a vast machine to abolish prejudice and enforce laws for the well-being of the Chinese. Sink the best of your intellect, your time and talent in this effort. It will repay you a hundredfold."

When Thomasina finished, her hands were shaking. She had not consulted her notes, but she thought she had spoken well. The applause was disappointing, merely polite. Had she miscalculated her audience? Were they not yet ready to respond?

People beyond her San Francisco circle of board members and mission supporters, men she most wanted to hear her message, seemed strangely silent. She took a seat beside Gus. She longed to slip out of her jacket and fan herself just long enough to cool down. She always worked herself up when she spoke, but so much depended on what happened today.

She knew in her heart that her effort had failed, but she couldn't let herself believe it. What did the stillness of the audience mean? They had been too attentive to be indifferent, but she had antagonized them.

Gus reached over and patted her hand, then in an effort to

cheer her up, offered her a mint from his pocket. She smiled and shook her head. Thank God for Gus. No matter what happened, she knew she could count on his friendship. They had often disagreed on the details of her work and how it was accomplished, but never on the fact that it must be done.

After the meeting broke up, she found herself surrounded by men.

"Is not the salvation of the girls your mission?" asked one pastor from Salt Lake City. "It is not your place to criticize men."

"Of course, but this is larger than just my mission," Thomasina replied. Before she could continue, another voice interrupted.

"Let lawyers take care of the law," said a synod board member from Nevada. "A Chinaman is not my equal before the law and that's the way it is."

"Don't you understand that church and state must remain separate? It is in the Constitution!" insisted one minister from Sacramento whom she had counted as a friend.

"Leave politics to the men," said another from Bacaville. "Competent professional men can handle these problems."

"This is about using the laws, already passed, for equal treatment. I'm not suggesting anything that isn't already in place. I ask only for the enforcement of those laws." Thomasina heard her voice rise and she felt herself pleading when she wanted to persuade. They hadn't understood at all.

"This is bigger than just my mission and our church," she persisted. "The Chinese are treated unfairly and this needs to change."

The men went away shaking their heads.

She felt utterly deflated when she went to lunch. She found Gus and sat beside him.

"The law was changed because women have pressured lawmakers. We understand the law very well. If we only had the vote, we could push it through, put some teeth into the laws!" She stopped then because she was close to tears. It had taken all her nerve to get up before this group and she had failed.

Gus said, "You'll feel better if you eat." Thomasina spooned soup and thought about what she had said. She had spoken well, as well as she ever did, but she had not moved her audience. She was not used to facing hostility when she stepped down from the podium. She ate half her food, then stopped. Failure closed up her throat. She wanted to go to her room and cry, but she had been staying with a local family and had no place to go. She had her grip stored in the back of the church where the meetings were held, and she would get on the train after the afternoon session.

She could not cry in front of these good people. She would not let herself.

Gus was his usual attentive, noncommittal self and later they shared his Pullman compartment on the late train.

"Your Scotch toughness got you through today, but you don't have to keep it up for me," he said lightly.

"I'm afraid if I try to talk about it, I'll cry and never stop."

"Go ahead," he said. And Thomasina knew that he would be there, no matter how she railed or wept, no matter how illogical or hurt or angry she might be.

"I think this is important and I'll continue to work for enforcement of these laws." The tears she predicted began, but she kept talking through them. "Today was the first time I've had to face the ignorance and superiority of otherwise good men. When they brought up their objections afterward, something happened to me. I have always resisted becoming a suffragette. I have too many other public issues to work on. I thought women who insisted on the vote were strident and demanding. Now I join them. If men cannot see what needs to be done, then women will have to do it. And we need our own political base, our votes, to make people listen to us." She wiped her face and sniffed.

"We can only do so much by example. I am an example of 'modest, gentle womanhood'; I stand up and talk about my girls and they sing songs for people and I have my hand out in supplication. But on this important issue, I am told I don't know what

I'm doing." Tears threatened again. " 'Let some man do it.' This is a wrong that demands righting. We won't be patronized and told, 'There, there, don't worry your pretty little head.' As though we hadn't the brains or the heart to do something important!"

"You must trust in the Lord's will," Gus consoled.

Thomasina had talked herself into tears and out again. Gus moved beside her and put his arm around her. Just this once, she would let herself be comforted. It had been a long time since a man had held her, even for so tame a reason as this.

"The Lord acts through people like you," Gus said. "You can trust Him, but you know you need to continue your work. Go ahead," Gus said. "I can listen for a long time."

"I will alienate you, too." Thomasina wiped her eyes and sat up.

"You can never do that." Gus said this with quiet assurance. Gus was giving her unquestioned support, a form of Christian love, for her work. He always paid her that great compliment: he took her seriously and listened.

She began again, recounting some of the steps in their campaign to get the laws passed. If bordellos weren't against the law, the police had no way to stop the slave trade. It was too lucrative. They could only close the cribs as "disorderly houses" and they reopened as soon as the wrist-slap fine was paid. Fine, moral Chinese wives, bewildered by the laws and knowing no English, were incarcerated at the new immigration holding place, Angel Island, while cunning masters taught girls destined for prostitution the right things to say.

She wept, blew her nose on Gus's big, no-nonsense handkerchief, and kept talking. After an hour, she felt emptied.

"What shall I do now?" she asked.

Gus had come over from Aberdeen and gone to work as a young laborer in a sugar factory. He had watched the sugar crystals separated for granulation and the molasses poured out as waste. As a good Scot, this waste intrigued him. He learned how the refinery worked, then he developed a process to extract the remaining sugar from the molasses. This process changed the refining industry and made him wealthy. One of his sons had joined him in the business.

Because she knew how bright he was, Thomasina listened to Gus when she might have ignored just another businessman. He looked a little like a banty rooster—thick chest and shoulders, softened a little with age, short legs. He was not very tall, but carried himself well. He exuded joie de vivre that was rare in a man his age—by the time a man reached his sixties, usually health or family worries had worn him down. He had lost his wife when his daughters were young and he had raised them lovingly. He embodied the Presbyterian ideal of stewardship and scholarship; he could quote Scripture when it suited him, but there was still something youthful and lively about him. Every now and then, Thomasina had a glimpse of what he must have been like as a boy joking and laughing. She liked this playful part of him, especially because he poked fun at her when she took herself too seriously.

But today he wasn't mocking or teasing. He had helped her, had listened to her, had held her in his esteem when others had shunned her. She was dumbly grateful. When she tried to articulate her gratitude, he shushed her. She murmured, "Thanks, Gus."

He opened his arms to her again and like one of her girls after an emotional outburst, she took refuge in his quiet endorsement. She allowed herself the warmth of his arms. Her rigid shoulders relaxed and her hands stopped shaking. She even dozed in this security.

He found a taxi and they arrived at 920 late that night. Thomasina didn't feel any of the wild, rash emotions that Charlie had once aroused in her, but later she would look back and know that was the day she began to love Gus.

A few weeks later she prepared for a trip to New York for an important mission meeting. She would stay at The Pines, the Bookers' home, at Gus's daughters' insistence.

31

When sister Annie visited, she and Thomasina went shopping for practical, long-wearing clothing. Thomasina stocked up on ready-made underthings for her trip to New York. Thomasina never cared much for sewing, although she had made stylish ensembles when she was in school. She remembered sewing a jacket with leg-o'-mutton sleeves so big she couldn't get them inside an overcoat. At the Mission she always had willing hands if she needed anything sewn. She had long ago given that job to the expert ladies in the sewing room. She was glad normal shoulders were in style, and simple skirts, without layers of taffeta petticoats. On this trip downtown she let Annie talk her into trying on a very expensive frock.

"A missionary doesn't need style," Thomasina replied dryly, "and I can't afford this."

If she pushed, Annie knew Thomasina would get stubborn, but every woman, even a missionary, needed a dress like this once in a while. "You'll be in New York with people from all over the country. Remember Paul, 'When in Rome, do as the Romans . . .' "

Thomasina hesitated. She didn't want to embarrass her host, but she hated to feel as though she were indulging herself.

"Besides," said Annie, "you'll be representing the Mission."

Thomasina nodded. "All right. But I'm not shopping with you again! Get thee behind me!"

The sisters laughed and the saleswoman went to fetch an alterations woman.

She worried about Annie and Helen, her single sisters. She was promised a pension by the board, but she didn't know if it would stretch to support three women. She would trust to the Lord and keep the spence, an old Scots expression that meant to be faithful to the work at hand.

To her that work meant using the law to improve the lot of Chinese immigrants, even if the western states' synod didn't agree. When she thought of how Gus had been so good after that terrible experience in Fresno, she felt warmly grateful. People she relied on, people who had always supported her work, betrayed her when she tried something out of her sanctioned arena. She looked at this crusade, if that is what it continued to be, as the natural extension of her work in Chinatown. She had one honest policeman she could call on—Gerard Finley, sergeant and head of the Chinatown squad. After a tong murder, Finley sent a message by finding enough evidence to put the killer in prison. Usually, Chinese crime was ignored to regulate itself. In a cynical moment, Thomasina wondered if they were only pushing the vices underground, but she could only deal with what she found and only deal with that openly. The law was her Carry Nation hatchet, opposed to the hatchets of the highbinders.

Otherwise, corruption was common in the city, beginning at the top. Abe Reuf was scapegoated, she thought, and convicted for influence peddling. Then Fremont Older, the editor who had pushed for his trial, befriended him, visited him at Alcatraz, and helped reestablish his career. Thomasina was glad Amos escaped being tarred with the same brush.

* * *

When she got to New Jersey, Gus's daughters greeted her. Mary and Gertrude said she was the only missionary who giggled. True, they always found things to talk and laugh about. They put her at ease and for a few days, it was as though she lived with her sisters again. Over the years, Thomasina had met other missionaries at the Bookers' home, a two-story frame house on a street in an old neighborhood. She loved the trees, turning colors now in the autumn coolness. She was so used to her good gray city on the bay that she forgot that most of the people in America still lived in some version of a small town, like this. It reminded her of her sisters' homes. Over the years she had met famous missionaries who were friends of Gus Booker: Wilfred Grenfell, a physician who worked with Eskimos of Labrador and Newfoundland and helped them set up community centers; John R. Mott, international Y.M.C.A. secretary; Dr. James C. R. Ewing, president of Forman College of India; Dr. Samuel Swemer, missionary to the Moslems; the socially gracious Dr. James Walter Lowrie, chairman of the China Council of Presbyterian Missions; and Sherwood Eddy, author and national secretary of the Y.M.C.A. in India.

This conversation was manna in the desert. Rarely was she able to meet and talk with other missionaries so these times when she could be with like-minded men and their wives were especially precious. Gus, with his bland good looks and prosperous demeanor, never tried to impress people with his intelligence, but Thomasina had learned to appreciate him.

"I haven't requested a place on the program this time," she told Gus.

"Why not? You gave a rousing talk in Fresno."

"Roused them to anger and negativity. Everyone here has heard about the Mission by now."

"That's not the reason. You never pass up a chance to tell people about your girls."

Thomasina looked at Gus. How did he know her so well? And knowing her, with her failings and pettiness, how could he still hold her in his esteem? "No. To be honest, I've lost heart. I know this needs to be done. It stands out like a dirty face. We need laws to do what won't get done without them—meat inspections, milk free of tuberculosis, clean water. We need to sacrifice some property in San Francisco hills for playgrounds so that children of the tenements can have exercise and fresh air. It takes laws to compel everyone to do it. And we need policemen and immigration workers who will enforce the law evenly."

"You believe this is the future?" Gus asked.

"Fervently. Maybe people are not ready to accept it today, but progressive social legislation is being passed all over the country."

"Then you must simply find a better way to present your message."

Thomasina laughed. "You make it sound easy. I tried being straightforward and you saw the reception it got."

"I love your stories about the mission girls."

"Those stories are easy—I live them. Putting ideas across must take a different kind of speechifying."

"It's hard to put complicated ideas in a few clear words," Gus agreed. "The best things are always the most succinct: 'What you have done for the least of my brethren . . .' "

"I have thought of what I said and how I could say it better and I don't think I could persuade a fly although I always have the imagination to see ahead."

"Someone has to be at the front."

"Yes, but my banner is muddy and my head bowed."

"Maybe just a short bit on the legislation, then an appeal to their hearts. When you stand behind a podium with your face flushed and emotion coloring your voice, you are nigh irresistible."

"Only to you, dear Gus."

Thomasina wanted to relax and enjoy this trip and not tie herself in knots over what she would say.

"I never thought you would run from a fight like this," Gus said.

Thomasina was stung! Gus was calling her a coward. She was

hurt that he, too, was turning on her. She wanted to run out of the room. She heard Mary and Gertrude moving around upstairs and she wanted to close the door to her room behind her.

"That's not fair!" she cried.

"I think you've got more spunk than this."

"I'll gather my forces for next time," she said.

"It'll be another seventy-six years before Halley's Comet appears."

"Not that long."

"Onward, Christian soldier," said Gus ironically. His words prickled and she wondered if they would quarrel over this issue.

She excused herself. Gus looked at her strangely. She saw his hard face, the one he had for business competition, for bankers and food brokers. She always felt lighthearted around Mary and Gertrude ever since the General Assembly in Los Angeles, when they had played hookey from the sessions to go touring. Gus had provided a carriage and driver and she remembered that as a sunny day in a lonesome time, when Charlie was at Princeton.

The next night Thomasina donned the famous blue dress in a lighthearted mood. She enjoyed the long trip to the city for the meeting in Gus's big Columbia touring car, a "wonderful machine man has made."

"I wish we could drive it to church on Sundays," Mary said.

"Wouldn't it be nice?" Gertrude added.

"By no means!" Augustus said. "Driving a car is labor and we do not labor on the Sabbath."

"Yes, Papa," his daughters said.

Thomasina smiled but said nothing. Didn't Gus think the streetcar conductor was laboring? Gus looked wonderful in a perfectly tailored Prince Albert with snowy linen and a cravat perfectly tied by Gertrude. Thomasina loved businessmen in their flawless gabardine. They might look alike as peas in a pod at meetings or in court, but there was something subtly sensuous about the good cotton of their shirts, the immaculate collars, the slight vanity of their watch chains. She liked the curve of a waistcoat with its close-set buttons, with its tiny pockets. She knew hand-sewn lapels by the slight pucker of the stitching. She liked the buttons to go unnoticed. Nothing looked more appealing, she thought, than a bathed, shaved, barbered businessman, sleek in his uniform suit. They were the successful ones, the best capitalism produced. Smugness sometimes marred the impression most businessmen made, but tonight Thomasina could compliment Gus and enjoy this special kind of attractiveness.

"This 1907 model of the Columbia can go forty-five miles an hour," Gus claimed. The motor purred under the hood.

"Please, not tonight. My hair will come down." Thomasina put on a duster provided and reset the pins in her hat.

From the ferry, the skyscrapers of the city loomed like granite mountains against the velvet sky. The lights on the Hudson shimmered and blurred in shifting patterns. As ugly as it could be in places, the majesty of the city always impressed her. Men's work, God's will. And all the people scurrying on their private, incomprehensible errands—thousands of people living and loving and having children, repeating the eternal stories a hundred hundred times. All to the glory of God.

Gus led them to their places in the huge church where the meeting took place. Thomasina listened to the program, putting new information where it belonged in the great Presbyterian scheme of things. Near the end of the program the moderator said, "We have an unusual honor tonight. Miss Thomasina McIntyre from the Occidental Mission in San Francisco is among us. Miss McIntyre, will you come to the platform and say a few words?"

Thomasina felt cold grip her vitals. She turned to Gus. "I didn't expect to speak. What shall I say?"

"You'll know," he assured her. "Your usual song and dance," he said with mock cynicism. She rose and made her way to the aisle, then looked back at Gus. He looked entirely too satisfied with this.

"My dear friends," she began. "Within my hometown of San Francisco is another city, a miniature Oriental country with people, language, and ways of doing things more foreign than you can imagine." She told the audience about the new mission building at 920 Sacramento with its substantial brick walls. She described the Mission's work and her girls and hoped the pictures she drew with her words would impress these important people. She put the new immigration laws into the context of the lives of the Chinese people she knew. And explained why the vice laws needed to be passed and enforced. Only a few sentences this time, and no scolding. Her words held their attention. The spirit was strong in her that night. Every sentence, although not rehearsed, fell into place. And yes, she could feel her face flushing and hear the tremor of feeling in her voice. Presbyterians valued common sense over charisma, but she must use this ability to reach each person tonight. She must use this power to fire their imaginations.

She left the podium to enthusiastic applause. Several people stopped her on her way up the aisle, but not to attack what she had said. Their warm acceptance cheered her. Perhaps she was on the right path, but had chosen the wrong approach before. If people knew the truth, they would make the right choice.

And just how much did Gus have to do with this?

32

Thomasina was used to people mouthing words of respect about her work while ignoring the underlying message. Tonight, she felt she had been heard: enforcing vice laws wasn't a legal ploy, it was salvation in new, modern dress.

Back in East Orange, Gertrude made tea for Thomasina and Gus, then the girls went upstairs leaving them in the chilly parlor. Gus offered to build a fire, but Thomasina liked the cool evening after the warm day. Gus put his teacup on the tray and picked up Thomasina's hand. She gave it a friendly squeeze. She liked this feeling of used-up-tired—that she had spent her energy in satisfying ways, that she had accomplished something that day.

Gus had stood arm in arm with her on the ferry, both of them exhilarated from the evening. She felt that he acknowledged her need for silence without having to know her mind.

She turned to Gus and saw his eyes dancing. She wondered what ideas were turning in his head. On an impulse, she stroked his smooth, ruddy cheek. He held that hand and kissed the palm.

"Miss Thomasina," he began, "would you do me the honor of marrying me?"

She did not expect this, but she wasn't surprised. She knew Gus was fond of her and she had done nothing to tell him she would rebuff him. Thomasina looked into his kind eyes. She hesitated, wanting to be certain before she spoke.

"Tonight, you stood before that audience in that blue dress," he said, "looking like an angel—beautiful and wrathful and loving. You must have guessed my feelings for you by now."

Thomasina nodded. She did not trust herself to speak.

"I love you, Miss Thomasina. I want you to be the mistress of my house as you are of my heart. I want to share the work of missions with you. I want you to bless my age, the best that's yet to be."

Tears ran down her cheeks now. What tender eloquence!

"I can offer you friends, security, and travel. I can offer you the comfort of my fortune. Forgive me if I say that is just money. I know when you have none it is important. But just now the love in my heart is stronger than circumstances, more persuasive than money."

Thomasina kissed his hand again. She brushed away tears.

"I thought, when my good wife died, that I would never want to join my life with a woman's again. I thought I could never love anyone as much as I love my children. In fact, when we first met, I loved you like my own child. If I could love everyone as I love them—completely and without stint—I would be a better person. Over time, that love has grown until tonight it flowers as the love of a man for a woman."

She must say something, but Thomasina, who could talk to highbinders and judges, could not produce a sound. As if fearing that void, Gus's voice continued.

"I do not know how it will be to break my celibacy—it has been years. I know you excite me as a man and that is compelling. I hope that if I don't excite you, at least I don't repulse you. I want this to be a union in every way: heart, body, soul."

At last he could find no more words.

Thomasina shivered a little and he put a friendly, warming arm around her shoulders. His whole relationship with her had been like this: friendly and comforting, helpful and thoughtful.

"I am very fond of you, Gus," she said after long thoughts. "Let me think about this."

"Is there any hope?" he asked, humble as a stable boy.

"I love you," she said. "I want to say yes with a clear heart."

"But you do want to say yes?"

She nodded.

Contrary to her expectation of tossing and turning as she mulled over this great decision, Thomasina fell asleep as soon as she pulled up the blankets. She felt safe and relaxed in this house. Her body took revenge for the tumult of the day, but her mind re-asserted itself and woke her at four in the morning. She drank some water and crawled back in bed, but she was too wide awake to sleep again.

She agreed with Gus, money that seems so important the rest of the time fell into better proportion now. She acknowledged the reality: she would not have to worry about taking care of her sisters. She would not have to wonder how she would survive if she lived a long time. She could travel, even visit China and India, where they would see Gus's missionary son. All the scrimping of a lifetime would melt away.

But the first emotion was a pang of loss: she would not be Madam Director. She would become the wife of a prominent layperson and continue to work from this vantage, but she would no longer be in the midst of the fray. She would no longer be sought for rescues. She would not go to court. She would not hobnob with immigration officials, or be recognized by judges and lawyers. She would not be asked to speak at churches about the work of the Mission and she would not hear the applause after the talk. On the other hand, she could drop responsibility for all the girls in the Mission but she would miss their loving warmth. She felt her horizons narrow and her world contract, but she tried to throw that feeling off.

She was amazed that sexuality, so long and successfully buried, should pop back into consciousness with such vivid persistence.

She couldn't help but think of Charlie—young, blond, physical. She had attended the wedding of Aggie Ducik a few years ago and saw him there. He was still single, still strikingly handsome, but the years had tempered him and he had become dignified where he once had been playful. He lived with his mother and remaining sister in the parsonage in Petaluma where he served his flock. Thomasina thought she detected a scornful twist of his mouth, a sardonic posture, but hesitated to judge him.

Gus would not be Charlie. The still-remembered length of leg wasn't there, the proportions of love—the slim torso, the tanned column of neck, the long sinewy arms. In fact, Gus was so short that he and she stood eye to eye, fitting partners. She didn't know if her body could still respond. She had kept herself reined in for so long, perhaps she couldn't react at all. That wasn't the point and she knew it.

The point was, did she want to make love with Gus? Middle-aged, short-legged, balding, pink-cheeked Gus with a heart as generous as the ocean? She mentally undressed him, studied his rounded belly, his no-doubt hairy chest and legs. She imagined his breath quick on her neck, his lips on her skin.

Then she felt herself click into place, like the lid of a watch case. The thought of his soft hands on her skin made goose bumps. She imagined his fingers manipulating her nipples, his tongue on her ear. She imagined all the things that happened inside of her, all the filling and emptying. Touching said what words could not. She needed to touch the blossoms of the flowers in the big wok in the mission entryway. She needed to touch the ironed linen before it went into her dresser. She liked to hold fruit as she ate it and feel the juice run down her wrist. She liked the soft San Francisco fog kissing her cheeks. She liked the crunchy leaves underfoot in Gus's backyard.

No mandarin, dressed in silk and eating delicacies, with ready concubines in golden beds was more sensual than she.

Now, all the erotic sensuality that had been missing from her life would be addressed. She imagined Gus's hands on her skin, stroking the starved flesh. She felt her belly stir. The skin inside her thighs prickled.

She would give Gus a great yes! for heart and body and soul.

"Mary, Gertrude, we have a surprise for you," called Gus from the breakfast room. "Miss Thomasina has honored me by accepting my proposal of marriage."

Gertrude embraced them together. "You were right, Mary. Oh, I'm so glad."

"I'd hoped for this." Mary kissed her father, then Thomasina.

"My dears, how did you know?" Thomasina said.

Mary beamed like a cat in the cream. "I can't think of anything more suitable."

"When will it be? Where will you go on your honeymoon?" asked Gertrude.

They hadn't quite gotten that far. Gus wanted a trip to the Orient, to missions in Japan and China, a visit to his son, a leisurely tour.

"You must stay longer now," Gertrude insisted. "You'll have so much planning to do."

But she had to begin putting her work at the Mission in order. She felt as though she were a different person, riding back across the country in the trains. The world had not changed much in the few weeks since she passed this way—the trees were beginning to shed their brilliant leaves, the crops were almost all in. She saw frost on the barns and fields in the morning.

But she was a different person—with different goals, different distractions. She made list after list, trying to order things in importance. She must tell her board, tell her assistant, and tell her family. She must decide what to do with all the things she had accumulated in the five years since the earthquake. She must train a successor as quickly as possible. Or perhaps the board would prefer someone who would come in with fresh ideas.

It gave her a pang of regret to think she could be replaced. She had worked for fifteen years to fill her role as Madam Director and she had given her most energetic years to the Mission. It was hard to let go.

She began weeping silently as she wrote, but she kept writing and started a new list of All the Things I'll Miss. Best get it out now and not snivel and sigh over it.

—Girls' hugs and laughter
—The smell of Chinese herbs as the cooks prepared dinner
—The company-is-coming excitement of board meetings
—The excitement (she had to admit) of raids
—The respect she received from the San Francisco community and the recognition she received from the Presbyterian community
—Being deferred to by people for her knowledge of the Chinese slave world and the American laws surrounding it
—Her sisters and brother looking up to her
—Leaving the fray, just as she had a bit of success in New York

After a while she stopped writing and the tears dried. How little was true Christian feeling and how much of it was her egotism! Was that all it meant to her? She was ashamed.

Sister Annie met her at the train station in Oakland to share the ride across the bay.

"Well, Tamsen, the East did you good. You look bonnie," she said, embracing her sister. Thomasina laughed and tucked her arm through Annie's and the two walked toward the depot.

"Does it show so clearly? Geography is not responsible for my looks."

Annie's eyebrows lifted. "And what is this?"

"After giving away so many of my girls, I am to be the bride after all."

Annie stopped short and turned Tamsen toward her. "What?" she repeated.

"Mr. Booker asked me to marry him and I have decided I will."

Once at the Mission, she saw that Nora Banks, her assistant, had kept everything running smoothly.

Thomasina set a date for late summer. She had so many threads of her life to tie up. After a wedding at the Mission, the newlyweds would tour China.

In the meantime, the rescues became more and more difficult. Thomasina and an Oakland minister, the Reverend Mr. Feather, and a friend of his tried three times before they could spirit away a pair of slave girls whom her informants told her had been cruelly used by their mistress.

She found her hands shaking and she quaked inside. She thought it was from overwork, or perhaps prenuptial jitters. A woman over forty was entitled to a few aches and pains. But even Nora commented. She told several members of her board of her plans and they rejoiced with her. Nora would be a suitable replacement.

"Dear Gus," she wrote. "You recognize my attempt to live in Him who is the calm in the midst of the world's turmoil. It pleases me that you see it."

Hsiang, who had finished school in the East, insisted she would return to 920 within a few months. Another daughter prepared to represent the mission board in Shanghai. This was the harvest she had sowed seed for all these years. Now her heart took wing for a new chapter in her life.

One July afternoon, Thomasina received a telegram. "Lean hard and take courage. Father died today." It was signed "Mary Booker."

Not dear Gus!? She got to her room somehow. Her trousseau hung in the closet. The itinerary lay on her table. Recent photographs sat beside it. Everything they represented was dead and she didn't think she had the courage to mourn again.

She lay on her bed, stunned beyond tears. She would stay here at the Mission. She would continue the work she had gladly prepared to leave.

Keep the spence, she reminded herself. Take heart. But the words held no comfort.

She had never agreed with her Chinese daughters' belief about fate or destiny, but perhaps she should. What had that fortune-teller outside Canton said?

She didn't think she had a heart left. No consolation could relieve this aching emptiness.

FRUITION

1920

33

The huge copper wok on the entry table overflowed with delicately shaded orchids the size of silver dollars. Greenery swagged the doorway. Sugary smells of pastry blended with roast beef and Chinese spices.

Thomasina looked around at the girls' bustling activity and their secretive smiles, and retreated to her office.

She opened the cupboard door to look in the mirror. She found her hair softly framing her face, the collar of her dress stylish, the color becoming. No more the restriction of stays, no more the exaggerated sleeves, multiple petticoats, the floor-length hems. She remembered the purple shirtwaist and her hair in a puffy pompadour the first day she came to this place—not this room, but Miss Culbertson's office in the old building, where the board interviewed her. Now it was hers, indisputably hers. Japanese wives and Chinese daughters, lesbians, prostitutes, and more abused girls than she wished existed in the world. She hoped she had responded. It was hard to conquer your prejudices when you breathed them constantly, but she tried.

Dozens of fluttery brides escorted down the stairs and given to proper Christian grooms. But never her. That was not her destiny.

Her hair had been white for so long, she couldn't use it as a mark to measure signs of aging. She wore rimless spectacles now. The damp climate was kind to old skin, but the wrinkles were there and a certain bony austerity that had come with age. She dated that from Gus's death—in the photographs taken before then she seemed timeless; now she looked like what she was: a healthy old woman, past the half-century mark.

And what a life, what a fortunate life!

She thought of all the people she loved and all the people who loved her, who helped her, taught her, contended with her, hurt her, pushed her, had faith in her—she imagined herself surrounded by all the people she had known, all smiling. Most of the faces were Chinese and female, and she was part of a scintillating Milky Way of people, each sparkling with God's radiance.

Today she wouldn't think of the girls reclaimed by masters, or too ill to survive or unable to adapt. She would think of the home in Oakland the Booker sisters had funded for the littlest orphans, and the boys' home that was coming along. She would think of Hsiang, who had returned to the Mission and was her assistant. They had grown together like vines, each supporting the other.

She would think of all the board members and their husbands, Dr. Marrs and all the other clergymen who had guided and helped her. She would think of Gerard Finley and Amos Cohn and Sidney Nussbaum. She would even think a kind thought for James R. Dunn, immigration inspector. (Praise God he had retired.)

A knock interrupted her roll call.

"Your sister is here," Hsiang said.

"Thanks," said Thomasina and gave her collar one last pat. She hugged Hsiang. "This is going to be an interesting day," she said.

"Let me know if you need to disappear," said Hsiang. Hsiang was a tall, elegant woman, today wearing a sam of apricot and amber silk embroidered with a dragon on one shoulder. Her eyes gave her a severe expression, but she had never lost her ability to mimic everyone and deflate the pompous.

"Hello, Annie," said Thomasina. "Stay beside me. I'm going to sit here like Queen Victoria and receive today. I'd never last standing in a reception line."

"The girls have done a beautiful job of decorating."

"Are Jessie and Clara and Terry here? And Al and his wife?"

"They'll be here in time for luncheon. Give me a kiss. I'm going to see what they're doing in the kitchen."

Thomasina greeted guests for an hour, then luncheon was announced, guests took their places at the long dining tables, and the big girls served.

She mentally withdrew from the hubbub. She sat at the head table, looked out over the room, and smiled and acknowledged friends who caught her eye. The meeting hall had been cleaned, windows washed, fresh curtains hung, floor waxed, woodwork polished. Generous sprays of spring flowers bloomed on each windowsill and low arrangements of poppies and pine trailed across each of the long tables. The fresh smell mixed with the food that arrived from the kitchen. She remembered another spring morning when the Mission had been cleaned and ready for a meeting—the day of the earthquake.

Beneath the draped chintz and flowers, it was a shabby, familiar, well-used place—scene of hundreds of Sunday meetings, scores of weddings, holiday celebrations, and honors banquets. The scarred and repainted wainscoting had absorbed the vibrations of a thousand thousand hymns sung by feminine voices. If she could pick up the room's waves of feeling, like a crystal set, they would be mostly good in this meeting room, with some anger at her failures. Years of girls' love, kindness, and hard work softened the institutional plainness. Industry and discipline supported the walls and hope held the ceiling up. Simple goodwill and generosity permeated the wood. Communion of thousands of meals shared and enjoyed polished the tables and laughter leavened everything.

She thought of all the fears she had lived with—how insignificant they seemed now. She thought of tears she had shed and others' tears she had dried. Daughters grew up and left and still the work went on.

She ate a little and talked to Annie and her brother, Al, on one side and Hsiang and Evelyn Brown on the other. Most of the women in the room wore Western dresses, but a few wore elaborate Chinese gowns and heirloom jewelry. A choir of middle girls marched out of the conference room and lined up to sing English and Chinese songs during the meal. They were dressed in sams, trousers, and curved slippers, but these were costumes now, not their best clothes. Thomasina caught Hsiang's eye. "Do you remember the first time?"

"Yes, and on the way home you told that woman on the ferry you were our mother. That statement was truer than you knew."

At last all the plates and bowls were cleared and Hsiang stood and tapped on a glass for attention. When the conversation died, Hsiang said, "All of us wanted to get Lo Mo something nice, something she would never buy for herself. She wouldn't hear of it, of course, so we had to do it very quietly. When I contacted all the old girls, money poured in from all over the States and from China. Tell them what you said." Hsiang turned to Thomasina, seated on her right.

"I told her I lacked nothing," said Thomasina, loudly enough to be heard by everyone. "Put it into your work. Ah Hsiang has learned that mission work means always having your hand out." Laughter rippled through the big room.

The huge windows were draped with evergreen that left a faint mountain scent now that the food was gone. Every light burned and candles flickered at midday.

"I wrote to the daughters who cannot attend that we redecorated Lo Mo's room," Hsiang continued. "We reglazed windows, repaired damaged woodwork. Lots of angry and unhappy little girls have taken their toll when Lo Mo brought them to her room for comfort or talk. We hung floral wallpaper, but painted everything blue, of course blue. Chu Wei from Canton sent a handwoven spread. And over Lo Mo's protests, I bought fabric for the dress she's wearing. Doesn't she look nice?"

And of course everyone applauded and Thomasina flushed with embarrassment. Hsiang was entitled to embarrass her after all these years.

"What she doesn't know is that before we did these personal presents, we did something more substantial. We have established a scholarship in her name at the Christian Hospital in Canton, administered by her friend Dr. Mary Niles. We received this message: 'Thomasina McIntyre has rescued hundreds of girls in the twenty-five years of her service. Now this scholarship for blind children will add to the list of those whose lives she has touched.' The note is signed 'Dr. Mary Niles and chairman of the hospital board, Edgar Cheng.' "

Another round of applause gave Thomasina a chance to catch her breath. Dear Edgar! She had never seen him after her trip to Canton, although they had corresponded. But the mention of his name could make her heart lurch.

"I would like to thank all the people who are here today," Hsiang continued, "and I think we should show the girls our thanks for all the work they did for this party." Hsiang led another round of applause.

"We would all like to spend the afternoon with Lo Mo reminiscing about old times. How can we do that? we wondered when we planned this day. We have asked some of the old girls and some of Miss McIntyre's friends to recall one incident to share. Would you begin, Sergeant Finley?"

The huge man got to his feet. A smile split his beaming Irish face. "I remember meeting this little woman and thinking she was too dainty to be any help. When I came to Chinatown I was told to enforce the laws—no gambling, no prostitution, and if one

Chinese killed another, he was to be prosecuted. I soon found out that Miss McIntyre was a fount of information. When she needed the law, I was with her." He recounted the raid when she crawled through the trapdoor. "By the time she and the girl got out, they both looked like coal miners, but one more girl was safe at the Mission when it was over."

Applause and a buzz of conversation covered Thomasina's embarrassment. She barely remembered that day, only that it was the last raid before her breakdown. She smiled and thanked Sergeant Finley.

Next, a middle-aged man recalled the rally in Palo Alto and the meeting in San Francisco when he was an undergraduate at Stanford.

Then an "old" girl, now an ample young matron from Fresno, stood. "Lo Mo has been criticized for exploiting the labor of Chinese girls. Yes, we had to keep the Mission clean and any of us would rather sew all day than scrub floors one hour." Knowing laughter rippled from Chinese women who had grown up in the Mission.

"During the Great War all the farm workers were gone, either to be soldiers or to work at better-paying jobs. Friends in the Santa Clara Valley, who had made it their habit to send boxes of apricots, plums, and other fruit to eke out the food budget, couldn't get their crop in. Prune plums were rotting on the ground. Lo Mo rounded up all but the littlest girls and we took the train to Sunnyvale. The farmers put us up in tents and we picked prunes all morning, rested, actually played in the afternoon, and picked again till dark. Lo Mo returned to the city, leaving us to slave and sweat and live in horrible conditions until we had picked all the prunes." Murmurs in the room confirmed.

"Well, I was fifteen and that was the best summer of my life. I had never known what it was like to have trees and birds and flowers around, dirt underfoot, stars at night. I had grown up on San Francisco pavement and thought flowers grew in the vendors' stalls. We ate American food, and I don't know how the farmers made a profit because working outdoors gave us all appetites. Boys from all around came by to 'help' and I met the man I eventually married. We were chaperoned, very closely chaperoned, but boys could visit and I got to meet American and Chinese kids my own age. After a long, carefully watched courtship, we married here in this room and I went to live in a small town where I always have trees and birds and flowers, stars at night, and my own plum trees."

Thomasina pressed her handkerchief to her mouth. She mustn't spoil this day. She smiled and shook her head. What an adventure that had been! She thought of Edgar and his story about the Jesuits and the Indian girls. It's an ill wind, after all.

Another woman described her relief on being released from the Immigration Shed.

Another described the rat traps when bubonic plague began to appear. "Lo Mo stood firm, she did not scream or become upset, but she turned white as a sheet when the inspector carried the dead rat out. Later, when she realized that one of us might have been bitten, she turned white all over again."

An elderly gentleman was helped to his feet. "I worked with Miss Culbertson, then with Miss McIntyre on guardianship cases," he said. Thomasina rose to her feet. It was Amos! Sidney Nussbaum stood at his side, supporting the fragile old man. "We had some adventures, let me tell you. Especially the time in San Diego when we rode the streetcar to the end of the line waiting for a girl to identify herself to us. We waited past the last trolley and would have spent the night there if a kind driver hadn't whoa'd his horses and given us a ride back to town. We hated to go home without the girl, so we began again, did our detective work, and with a little help from our friends, we found her in a drugstore when she was sent on an errand. We got her on the train back to San Francisco and the judge took pity on us and did not delay the proceedings."

Thomasina made her way through the crowded room to the old man.

"Most of you know Miss McIntyre as Lo Mo, rescuer of Chinese girls, or Miss McIntyre, Madam Director. I knew her as an adventure-loving woman, intrepid when necessary, feminine always."

Thomasina had held his hand during the last. It felt like a featherless bird of delicate bones and paper skin.

"My friend, how good to see you again!" she said softly under the noise of applause and conversation.

"Did you forgive me for going over to the other side?" he asked.

"Never! You were too charming, too much fun. I had to make do with Sid. He is only devilishly handsome and highly competent." Thomasina smiled at the younger man, whose face glowed with pride.

Amos searched her face and she met his eyes. She leaned forward and kissed him on the cheek. His beaky nose looked more prominent, the thick hair had thinned and turned white, he leaned heavily on his cane, but the spark was still in his eyes. He put his cane against the table and embraced Thomasina. She returned it wholeheartedly.

"I've wanted to do that for twenty-five years," he said in her ear.

"So have I," she confided.

Thomasina made her way back to the head table. She didn't know if she could survive this day.

An older woman described carrying her baby on her back when, as refugees after the earthquake, the girls and women streamed down the hill to ferries.

People must be getting restless, thought Thomasina, but no one left their places. Congratulations were read from absent board members, Susan Lee, and Mary and Gertrude Booker.

"Now we ask Lo Mo to say a few words," said Hsiang. "Even after twenty-five years, she doesn't speak Chinese. She understands it, she'll try a few words to be polite, but only I seem to know what she's saying." Laughter came from the audience. "Her Chinese, like her singing, is usually heard only by God."

Thomasina didn't think she could stand. The weight of love made her weak. However, a McIntyre doesn't shirk, so she took a deep breath, then another, then got to her feet.

"My dear friends," she began as always. "My dear friends," she repeated. "What good friends you have been! How lucky I am to be here today. I was a carefree and ignorant girl when I first came. Miss Culbertson taught me as much as I was willing to absorb. Mrs. Brown and the board continued her work. I had to learn lessons taught by the girls and women who came here, by my friends and helpers, by the Presbyterian community. I have a hard head, so some of the lessons were hard. But Miss Culbertson told me once, very early, 'Seek and ye shall find. Ask and it shall be given.' I don't think I believed her or even understood what she meant. But her faith was unmistakable.

"Seek doesn't mean you will get every wish that comes into your head. I think it means, in my life at this mission, that when I open myself in love, the people around me will help. I would not be standing here and the Mission would not exist without the help from all of you, from Sun Lee who gave me my first lessons, from Amos Cohn and Ah Hsiang and all my good friends, my helping friends.

"I want to say thank you, but thanks seems inadequate for what I feel and would like to convey, but it will have to do. Miss Culbertson always said, 'Take heart and call on the Lord.' I shall continue to do that, thanks to my good friends."

She paused a moment, then began a ringing tone, "Praise God from whom all blessings flow." The audience, person by person, raggedly took up the familiar song and sang it through a second time, their voices filling the room with joyful sound.

She sat and Hsiang held her while the tears flowed. These were not painful, wrenching tears, but the cup overflowing. Thunderous applause filled the room, and she wiped her face. Then chairs scraped and when she looked up, everyone in the room was standing, clapping and smiling. She put her palms together in front of her heart because she could not speak.

"Before we leave," Hsiang said after the tumult died, "I would like to say something to those who have asked us where the Mission will go from here. The trade in Chinese women has virtually died, thank God, but there are Chinese orphans and other immigrants who need help. Lo Mo is looking for an assistant. The work changes emphasis, but it will continue. Thank you all for coming."

Thomasina thought she might rise into the air, like some medieval saint, and float through the room on their good wishes. Whatever she might face, she had had this glorious day, this confirmation that her life had been well spent. And when dark days came, she would remember Miss Culbertson, whose voice still sounded in her mind, "Take heart and call on the Lord."

AMEN